ALSO BY JAMES BRADLEY

Wrack

The Deep Field

The Deep Field

A NOVEL

James Bradley

Henry Holt and Company   New York

Henry Holt and Company, LLC
Publishers since 1866
115 West 18th Street
New York, New York 10011

Henry Holt® is a registered trademark of
Henry Holt and Company, LLC.

Originally published in Australia in 1999
by Hodder Headline Australia Pty Limited

Library of Congress Cataloging-in-Publication Data
Bradley, James, 1967–
The deep field / James Bradley.—1st United States ed.
p.   cm.
ISBN 0-8050-6111-8
1. Women photographers—Australia—Fiction. 2. Paleontologists—
Australia—Fiction. 3. Missing persons—China—Fiction.
4. Blind—Australia—Fiction. I. Title.
PR9619.3.B655 D44 2000
823—dc21   99-055558

First American Edition 2000

DESIGNED BY KELLY S. TOO

Printed in the United States of America
1   3   5   7   9   10   8   6   4   2

*for Mardi
and my mother, Denise*

During the ten days between 18 and 28 December 1995, the Wide Field and Planetary Camera 2 was kept trained on a narrow patch of sky in the constellation of Ursa Major, the Great Bear. ('Narrow' here means smaller than the amount of sky blotted out by a single grain of sand held at arm's length.) These observations were analogous to the core of rock which geologists extract by drilling exploratory boreholes down into the interior of the Earth . . .

The [resulting] image of the Hubble Deep Field, as it was called, revealed a bewildering array of more than 1,500 galaxies at the uttermost edge of the observable universe. Of course, there was no way to measure the distance directly; that they were very distant galaxies was recognised, thanks to Edwin Hubble, from the extreme degree to which their light was redshifted. The faint light of the most distant of these galaxies was too feeble to show up against the background glow of the Earth's atmosphere and so was never going to be seen by ground-based telescopes, no matter how large they might be. Only the orbiting Hubble Space Telescope could return the haunting images of the distant universe to human eyes. It had seen to the outer limits of space—and also time.

The light from the galaxies pictured in the Hubble Deep Field has taken 10 to 12 billion years to reach us; it therefore carries information about those galaxies not as they are today, but as they were 10 to 12 billion years ago, soon after the universe was created.

TOM WILKIE AND MARK ROSSELLI, *Visions of Heaven*

For my part, following out Lyell's metaphor, I look at the natural geological record as a history of the world imperfectly kept, and written in a changing dialect; of this history we possess the last volume alone, relating only to two or three countries. Of this volume, only here and there a short chapter has been preserved; and of each page only here and there a few lines.

CHARLES DARWIN, *The Origin of Species*

Prologue

Photography is a kind of primitive theatre, a kind of *Tableau Vivant*, a figuration of the motionless and made-up face, beneath which we see the dead.

ROLAND BARTHES, *Camera Lucida*

This begins with the photos.

I doubt you would recognise them now, but in the years surrounding her death they were, if not quite famous, then at least respectable. Even now some odd ones still hang in galleries and private collections, but mostly they are gone: some packed away in atmospherically controlled storage facilities and warehouses, others sold off for a fraction of their original value, a few more in the hands of those who knew her. Most just vanished though, lost or destroyed, remnants of a past we seem to barely remember.

I have owned a book of them for many years, the catalogue from the retrospective the ICP in New York mounted the year after their death, and although the glue along the spine has perished so the pages tend to spill out, the paper is good and the printing has kept much of its colour despite the passage of the decades. And for all its frailty, there is a comfort in the book's weight and sense of age. I prefer my images like this these days: concrete, physical; I have grown wary of the virtual, the transitory. So little survives after all; we must hold on to what does.

The book has a solid cover, what was once called cloth binding, but the synthetic fabric that surrounds the boards at the front and back has frayed, and here and there the card protrudes, blunt and grey-brown. There is a dust jacket too, that nineteenth-century frippery of book design, on which is reproduced a portrait of the unfolding spiral of a fern's crosier, the colours moss green, slate grey, deep brown, the palette of the cold primeval rainforests that blanket the lonely valleys of Tasmania. Both serene and somehow forbidding, it is almost religious in tone, its limpid surface still, meditative, the subject an expression of an order at once simple and profound.

The flyleaf gives the date of publication as 2031, a time which seems so impossibly long ago: another age, another world. Sometimes my memories of those days seem more real than here and now, possessed of the terrible clarity of a dream. Yet whether I truly remember or whether all I am seeing are scrambled engrams bathed in the associative glow of the mnemonics I do not know. All appearances are deceptive, even memory. Especially memory.

The book was a gift from the ICP at the opening of the retrospective. I was nineteen, and they had been dead a year. I flew into New York on a shuttle out of Sydney, the snub-nosed ramjet punching its way spaceward, then falling back through the thin film of atmosphere half a world away. The flight was a long one, seven, maybe eight hours, but it seemed far longer to me. Despite the secession, the endless debilitating years of civil war, New York was still the centre of the world, and I fairly ached for the possibilities it seemed to offer.

Perhaps I was naïve, but I had not foreseen how the event would affect me. I suspect Sophie had though, for as I stood between her and Roland, listening to the Director give his opening address, I found myself choking back tears, thankful that Sophie had gently dissuaded me from speaking myself. I remember feeling Roland's arm around me, and letting myself subside into him. I remember also my sudden desire for him as I smelt his aftershave, the scent of his skin and shampoo, and the humiliating confusion of what I childishly thought of as grief's purity and this intense, inappropriate carnality. Looking back I find myself wondering what he would have done had I offered myself to him later that night, let a peck on the cheek become something more or arrived at his hotel door in the small hours of the morning. He was only fifty and still handsome, if a little beaten around the edges, and I was young, but no child. I would ask him if I could, but he has been dead more than a century, and he declined to leave a Sim.

I found the book a month ago, or, more accurately, Denzel found it. Denzel is my carer, and he was helping me clean the cramped space of the apartment. I came into the room to find him poring over it. This is old, he said, pointing to the date. Shall we throw it away?

Denzel likes to throw things away, which means he is probably the perfect person to be charged with the care of the Advanced. (When did we stop being old and become 'Advanced' instead?)

I stood next to him, looking down at it. No, I said, we will not throw it away. He looked at me, surprised I suppose by the note of steel in my voice. By way of explanation I opened the back cover, wincing to hear the ancient glue crack and splinter. On the inside dust jacket there is a picture of her when she was young, about the time I was born. Seeing the way I stared at it, Denzel leaned closer, following my gaze.

Did you know her? he asked.

She was my mother, I told him, and Denzel glanced up sharply, appraisingly.

Really?

I laughed, wondering whether it was the notion of someone as old as me having had a mother, the disparity in our appearances or the fact that my mother was in a book that made him so incredulous. Whichever it was, the truth is too complicated and Denzel's attention span is not long, so I just patted his beautiful hand.

Really, I said.

Since then I have spent many hours leafing through the book, turning each page carefully, wary lest I mark it with my fingers—after all, anything that survived the spasming passage of the new millennium's first century deserves to be treated with respect. And every time I find myself marvelling at the stillness of the images, their flatness. People tend to assume holographs and eidetics are just better versions of the photograph, three-dimensional, manipulable, but they are not. The two-dimensionality of the photograph, the stillness of its surface, these are not inferiorities, they are an integral part of the photograph's nature. It is not a captured space like a holo, nor can you reach into it and touch its contents as you can an eidetic's. Rather it is a moment caught forever in stasis: eternal, Platonic, perfect.

That day, the day Denzel found the book, I stood slowly turning its pages while he tidied around me. All of her photographs were beautiful, but it was the series she called 'Extinction' that caught and held my attention. I do not know what art is, but I do know there are things—objects, arrangements of words and space and colour and sound—which seem to move beyond the sum of their parts, creating something greater, something that transcends the pieces from which they are formed. The Germans have a word for it (the Germans always have a word for it); *Gestalt* they call it. Perhaps a melody is the purest example (music is usually the purest expression of human feeling in my experience). A melody is not just an arrangement of notes, it is an interaction between those notes. Remove one, change one, and it will vanish as quickly as it appeared. The melody is both of the notes and more than the notes. These photographs are like that, they transcend the sum of their parts, creating a space, a silence, into which we fall, and are transformed.

It might surprise you that I am writing a book about this; print, after all, has become rather passé these last few decades. Yet the book is a form I have grown to love more and more the older I have become. And I am, after all, very old indeed. But it is more than an Advanced's weird obsession with an outmoded medium that draws me to words. We both know I could have created this as a ractive, let you see the photographs, flick through them distractedly before scanning the text for passages you are likely to find interesting, but I want you to work. I want you to imagine them for yourselves, from my descriptions. From my memories. There is no coercion about this. If you want to see them you can. I have checked with the National Gallery in Canberra and the Art Gallery of New South Wales, and both have works hanging. And there are others too that should not be hard to find, in Paris and London to start with, but also in New York, San Francisco, Amsterdam, Shanghai. And if you do not need to see their physicality, the Lexica contains the archives and catalogues of countless minor galleries and private collections which have reproductions, bitmapped to a resolution finer than the human eye can accommodate. There is even a memory palace dedicated to her work somewhere amidst the data shoals of the merse, although it would be old now, slow and seldom visited. But if you can resist, do so, and use your imagination, listen to me. For I think she would have liked the irony of that, that her photos about time and memory might themselves have to be imagined back into being, conjured up through the poor filter of language.

I have chosen three to start with. They are found on pages 27, 34 and 38 of the catalogue. The first is the simplest. Like the entire series of which it is a part, it is a photo of an ammonite, those primeval cousins of the nautilus. The shell of this one has been divided down the centre, half of it cleaved away to reveal the fragile septa of its interior, preserved in stone that flakes like mica, glittering but fragile as glass. Somehow the inner chambers have not clogged with stone, leaving their spaces open to the light, and they fold, one upon another, like the chambers of some crystalline, spiral heart, the interior growing smaller as the spiral shrinks to a point.

The second is a photo of what at first blush appears to be an ammonite, but which upon closer examination can be seen to be not the ammonite itself, but its counterpart, the impression left in the stone when a fossil is removed. Like the photograph, the counterpart seems to mimic reality, but in truth it is something both less and more; a space, an absence, its very existence reminds us of what is missing, what has gone. This ammonite's shell was marked with toothed segments, each interlocking with its neighbours like the pieces of a child's jigsaw, the points facing inwards along the spiral, towards the centre. The impression becomes weaker the further it goes out from the centre until finally the mouth of it is barely visible, a ghost upon the stone.

This third is the most remarkable. It is a montage, the overlapping images recording the passage of a pair of hands through time and space. The hands, as silver-grey and translucent as one of Man Ray's experiments with primitive medical imaging, are exploring the surface of an unseen object, the soft light that lingers where they have passed revealing the furrowed coils of a third ammonite, just as a hand drawn across a clouded mirror reveals the reflection beneath. The exact outlines of the fossil are not clear; instead what we see are glimpses of its surface, or more properly the brevity of the body's exploration of that surface, the flickering passage of tactile memory. This effect made tangible by the overlay of the shots, the capture of the hands' motion around the object, exploring it, learning it.

There is a serenity about these photographs that is remarkable, given the tumult of her life and the times. To understand them we must go back, back to that terrible year when the world watched India and Pakistan go to war. We must imagine the ceaseless murmur of the feeds, the images of the escalating conflict bleeding into the planet's dreams as it waited for the inevitable news that things had gone nuclear. Endless grainy night vision images of tracer bullets skittering phosphorus pale across the Islamabad rooftops, the arcing trails of the missiles, the serried ranks of tanks moving inexorably across the dusty fields of the Indus. And when it finally came, the moment of the blast searing itself into the planet's collective memory, its enormity transcending the jerking video that recorded it, the broken sobs of the Fox correspondent as she waited for death. The screen bleaching white, then collapsing into static. Then nothing. New Delhi gone in the blink of an eye, wiped out in the space between the frames.

At least twenty million people died in New Delhi that day, fifteen million in Islamabad. And they were just the beginning; another fifty million were killed in the three blasts that were to follow before the madness ended. In the next few weeks almost a hundred million more were to perish from the secondary effects of the blasts. Even today the scale of these numbers defies comprehension, the very cleanness of them, the line of unblemished zeroes indicating the cheapness of a single life. For what, after all, is the weight of a single life in the face of millions? If we knew the true number would we weep all the more, accuracy piercing the numbness we feel in the face of such events? And how could a single mind, a single body, accommodate so much memory without breaking beneath the weight of it?

But they are remembered, not just in the white marble of the Five Monuments, but here, within us, within the bodies of those who lived through those terrible days. The waste from the blasts permeating our flesh, tainting our cells, gathering siltily in the honeycomb chambers of our bones. The lethal mist of the plutonium, its half-life longer than the whole of human history, entering us, marking us as it drifted earthwards, as surely as the thin, dark shadows of the dead marked the white walls of the ruins, making all of us witnesses to the frailty of life. Eons from now, we could be dug from the earth's embrace, that moment read from our bones, like meteorologists reading the history of climate from ancient wood, the rings of trees. Wherever time deposits the fragility of our bodies we will bear that moment with us, like the stones borne across the shifting continents within the melting glaciers of Gondwana.

Of course this is the way of the body, this remembering. We are vessels of time, our matter an archaeology of the lives we have lived, the bodies we have entered, the loves we have known. The caress of a lover's mouth against our nape, the motion of their breath as long as a heartbeat. The yellowing tenderness of a bruise, the fading corona of a bite, blood pooling beneath the skin. The furrowed trail of a scar, or the mothbeat of a pulse beneath our fingers. The silent adumbrations of healed fractures, their pale traceries disfiguring the blue-black translucence of the X-ray, bisecting bone, mute witness to the moment of impact through time; ineradicable. The peat-stained ache of the rope on the bogman's throat, his face composed as if for sleep. The phantom pain of a missing limb recorded in the aurora patterns of neural electricity. Our bodies inhabiting the porous space of memory, membranes in time.

My story began that year, the year of the bomb. I carry its memory within me as surely as she did. Maybe the radiation crossed the placenta. Or maybe it entered my body later, more softly. Whichever, that year is the bedrock on which my matter is built. The year the Turkish satellite fell to earth on the rocky shore of Daryacheh-ya-Damak, high in the windswept wastes of central Iran, trailing silent, colourless death across Afghanistan as it fell, its glassy wings twisting and collapsing in the searing clarity of the air. The year the student prince ascended the throne of the British Federation, his thin face uncannily like his mother's. The year *Prometheus* rode the lines of gravity outwards, into the void, to Mars. The year a lone swimmer surfaced into a cave beneath the blue waters of the Mediterranean to discover a lost world of painted animals and thin-limbed hunters etched across its stone walls. The ghostly shadows of hands beneath them, outlined in mouthfuls of ochre, their splayed shapes staining the stone down four hundred centuries. The athletic forms of bison and mastodon vaulting the high walls, picked out by the halogen beam of her torch, the reflected light of the water playing across them like the moving fabric of a dream, liquid, permeable. The silent space of the cavern a deep cathedral of memory, subterranean, a dreaming song of the stone.

The Luddites say the body is not supposed to live this long. I think this much is incontrovertible, but it does, regardless. It is the mind that bothers me, I do not believe it is equipped to handle a life as long as ours have become, this endless accretion of years. I am not the oldest, far from it, and already I have lived more than four times the biblical three score and ten. In this immensity of lived time, of decades and years and weeks and moments, with life constantly moving from one to the next, then the next, then the next, we begin to lose ourselves, to become confused and forget things. And so there are the mnemonics. They help us remember, make lifetimes ago seem like yesterday, although often yesterday itself eludes us. But the mnemonics also change us, we become suggestible, remember things that never happened, remember the smell and taste and vulgar detail of events and people that never were. The immensity of our memories becoming a sea in which we float. Or drown.

I am not confused, nor do I remember my mother's life, the things that went into the photographs. But as I stare at them day after day, I think I am beginning to understand, beginning to remember. It is not entirely the mnemonics. Deep in the infinite halls of the Lexica I found a monograph about her, a biography written just after her death by an American academic. I do not know how accurate it is, although I read in the foreword that I refused to be interviewed. I cannot remember refusing, but it was a long time ago, and I was very precious when I was younger. My Aunt Sophie talked to her, and so did Roland, so maybe it is not too bad, although I have no way of knowing. It helped me though, it helped me begin to find my way into her mind, to remember her. And I have my memories of her, of both of them, memories that grow keener, more tangible every day. I am telling you this so you will understand that this is reconstruction, this is imagining.

This is the truth.

APOCRYPHA

· 1 ·

When I was a child, my parents would rent a shack each summer on the southern coast of New South Wales. My memories of those times are fragmented and associative, but I remember the sound of the wind through the grasses of the sandhills, the murmuring of the waves reflected against the cliffs. I remember too the distant sound of the surf each night, the heat of the sun on my face and arms. I rarely swam, for the ocean always seemed a threatening presence, something uncontrollable and somehow malign, but on the hottest days my parents would accompany me into the waves, and I would feel the chill of the water move against my skin.

Left alone while they surfed and swam, I would explore the beach, sifting through the shells and pebbles and driftwood cast up by the Pacific. It was always shells that fascinated me, the sculpted smoothness of their shape, their enclosing form, the hard lustre of their openings.

As I grew older I began to collect the shells I found, classifying them by my own arcane systems, for there are no guides to shells written for the blind. And then, one day at fifteen, a museum educator placed a fossilised ammonite in my hands. As I grasped its stony weight and listened to her explain that it was almost 200 million years old, I found myself awed not just at the beauty of its spiral form and the secrets that lay within it, choked upon the stone that had gathered within its chambers, but by the sense that this thing had once lived and breathed, yet now had sunk through vast oceans of time, only to settle here in my hands.

SETH LaMARQUE, *The Language of Shells*

Drowning

Today everything exists to end in a photograph.

SUSAN SONTAG, *On Photography*

Caught in the thin sunlight where it surfaces from the earth's embrace, the broken face of the shale sweats oil like the flank of a beast. The oozing liquid staining the broken strata where they shear and slide, layer from layer, its leach marking lines of decay across the crumbling forms that swarm within. Like the etchings of some primeval Dürer, the finned shadows of fish linger amongst the fronds of ancient kelp and the tangled ribbons of sea grass, while here and there the biomorphic curves of shells—flat bivalves, conical snails, coiled ammonites—lie tumbled in banks like storm wrack. All of them silent, immobile: water, life, motion all transformed into leaking stone, heavy with the weight of memory.

Seen through the camera's viewfinder the face of the stone swims briefly, then resolves as the camera gauges the range and light and focuses itself, the memory button freezing the image in the camera's circuitry as it is depressed once, then again, each movement of the button slicing that moment free of time and space, a digital testament to its passing. The images captured, Anna lowers the camera, shrugging her hands deeper into her sleeves as she does, wishing, not for the first time, that she had remembered her gloves. Even through the swaddling Gore-Tex of her coat the wind has grown colder, and quickly, her nose running salt across her top lip, her ears aching. To the south and the west, across the vast basin of the ever-spreading Yangtze, the clouds are moving quickly against the wintry sky, their gathering weight rending and tearing in the wind. Beneath them their shadows chase in shifting patterns of light across the bare hills that fall towards the dam.

From behind her the wind carries the stink of cigarette smoke to her eyes and throat and, just for a moment, she allows herself the indulgence of swivelling to glare. Almost as if he had been waiting for her to give in and turn, Professor Zhou catches her eye from where he stands leaning against the battered chassis of the Landcruiser, and raises one hand in a languorous, mocking salute. The offending cigarette hanging loosely between the nicotine-stained fingers of his raised hand, its smoke straining outwards into the wind.

Next to Zhou, the driver, observing this unspoken exchange, says something in his harsh, heavily accented Mandarin, and the others laugh, turning as one to stare at her. Sensing this is another test of the indirect, taunting variety that Zhou seems to relish, she refuses to let their mocking attention intimidate her, staring back levelly. The steadiness of her gaze soon discomfits the others, and one by one they look away, turning back to their conversation, their voices lower, less certain. Not Zhou though. He holds her eyes, the seconds ticking by until finally he raises his cigarette to his mouth and, drawing back deeply, nods in one slow, shallow movement. The gesture provocative, challenging, an indication she has passed this most recent test, but conceding nothing more; no acceptance, no warmth. No friendship.

But this small victory does not help her temper; if anything it makes it worse, grist to the low, sullen anger that has been building within her since this job began four days before. Next to her she can feel Lo watching her, knows he will be wearing the bemused, oddly sympathetic expression she has seen on his face several times already. But she says nothing to reassure him, does nothing to acknowledge his presence. Instead she turns her attention back to the problem of the fossils, the uncertain, changeable light.

Confronted once more with the broken face of the hill, she twists and squints, trying to find some point that might suggest the unity she is looking for. But her mood has infected this too, and the images she seeks stubbornly refuse to resolve themselves out of the hillside's detail. Angrily she takes several shots regardless, willing them to find their own balance, although she knows even as she depresses the memory button that it is no use, these photos will be stillborn. Finally in frustration she places one of her booted feet on a lump of shale, kicks out hard to send it tumbling off its perch and away down the hillside where it lands with a thud and shatters. The noise and violence of its motion startling her, so she steps back, involuntarily, only to feel Lo's hand on her arm, restraining her.

Anna . . . he begins, but she shakes herself loose.

I'm going up there, she says, gesturing with her camera towards a broken patch of ground higher on the hillside, and without waiting for Lo's response begins to scramble upwards.

The climb is not a long one, but the scrubby grass and lichen that cover the hillside are slippery, and the wind eddies and gusts around her, constantly threatening to throw her off balance, so she moves unsteadily, one hand raised to catch herself if she slips. All around her the paraphernalia of the abandoned dig is covered by tarpaulins pegged tight against the thin soil. To the west one has twisted itself free and beats a staccato rhythm, the noise discordant against the keening of the wind, while beyond it, a flock of ducks moves quickly, a scattered V against the cloud. Earlier she photographed this same tarpaulin from almost this angle, the ragged shape of it where it had peeled back from the metal frame beneath silhouetted against a bruised and purple sky, but the memory of her pleasure in that single image, the purity of its wintry desolation, only serves to make her frustration more intense.

Looking back she can see Lo following her, moving crabwise up the steep slope, occasionally steadying himself with his hand. Embarrassed now by her petulance, she relents, slowing to allow him time to catch up, but even as she does, the light drops away so suddenly it might have been snuffed out. Surprised, she looks up to see a mass of storm cloud so low it seems almost within reach. To the north the hilltops are already obscured by rain and swirling cloud, and then the darkness of the stormfront is upon her, a solid wall of water that sweeps over her in a wave, each drop like a knife, so cold it burns. Below her, Lo motions for her to follow him down, then begins slipping and stumbling towards the cover of the Landcruiser, into which the others are already clambering, shouting and cursing. One arm raised to protect her face from the driving rain, she follows, but the few seconds it takes her to reach the bottom of the hill and cross the short distance to the Landcruiser are enough for the water to plaster her hair to her scalp and soak the surface of her coat. In her haste she slips on the runner, her shin cracking painfully on its edge, but Lo reaches out a hand and helps her in. When she pulls at the door to shut out the rain it does not catch at first, the dent in its side having buckled the body so it is difficult to close and she must pull again, harder this time, to close it.

Inside she is surprised to find laughter.

The weather changes fast today, says Lo, pressed in beside her.

Too fast, she says. I'm soaked.

A momentary confusion passes over Lo's face, and Anna realises she has spoken too quickly.

Wet, she explains, lifting her arms to display her sodden coat and hair. This time Lo nods comprehendingly.

Wet, he says, repeating the word as if to lock it down as a point of contact between them, and Anna smiles, liking him suddenly, strangely pleased by the realisation that he likes her, presumably finds her attractive. The moment broken by a harsh wave of smoke from Zhou in front of her.

We will come back tomorrow so you can finish then, he says without turning, eyes fixed on the hurrying rain and cloud visible through the windscreen.

She knows he has spoken English not as a courtesy to her, but as an insult, or more properly, a barbed condescension. From the far side of the cabin she feels eyes upon her, and turns to find the unnamed member of their entourage staring at her, while behind her the student assistant sits silently, seemingly determined to remain invisible. Lo glances from one to the other, clearly uneasy. Then, from the front seat, Zhou draws back heavily on his cigarette, the sound of his breath breaking the silence. With the lighted cigarette he gestures to the driver, the engine roars into life, and with a jerking movement forwards they begin the descent.

The journey back through the hills takes three and a half hours, the Landcruiser winding and slipping its way along a primitive corrugated track rendered almost invisible by the storm. Twice it sinks deep into the mud, and the driver, Lo and the student assistant are charged with digging it free, while Anna, Zhou and their unnamed companion stand to one side watching them struggle in the mud and rain, their faces contorted with effort as they slip and heave against the recalcitrant bulk of the vehicle. As the freezing water fills her shoes and runs in icy rivulets down her face and neck, under her collar and across her skin, plastering her coat to her thin frame, Anna finds herself cursing Nicholas, the journalist she is meant to be accompanying, who at this very moment is lying in his bed at the guesthouse, immobilised by the flu.

Inside the Landcruiser Zhou barely speaks, smoking cigarette after cigarette. He seems to have an inexhaustible supply of the cheap People's Republic brand favoured by the peasants of the region, which he shares with the driver, the two of them rendering the air in the cabin, already stuffy from the heating, almost unbreathable. The nicotine making Anna feel light-headed and nauseous.

Even Lo is silent, his good nature seemingly sapped by the rain and the oppressive mood that permeates the vehicle's smoke-filled interior. Once—and only once—he attempts to engage the unnamed man in conversation, but elicits nothing but what appear to be curt, dismissive replies, although Anna, who speaks little Mandarin, cannot be sure. In sullen fascination she watches the way the man keeps his eyes focused forwards, barely acknowledging Lo's presence.

It is almost dark when they reach the town, entering from the north, so that for a moment they glimpse the vast expanse of the rising river extending south and east to a horizon rendered indistinct by the sleeting rain. Its leaden surface choppy, capped here and there with white, rain moving in curtains across its surface. Then the hills rise around them, the winding road dropping fast towards the sprawling tangle of streets. On either side the hills are scarred and broken, quarried inwards until they form a jagged moonscape, the coal that lies in seams beneath their looming bulk excavated with picks and shovels by the townspeople, refuse and slag left where it falls, in piles and drifts. Two days before, when Anna first entered the town, some of the villagers were still working, despite the official directive that the town be evacuated, moving like ants across the cratered hills, baskets on their shoulders and heads brimming over with coal. Now they are gone, the quarries abandoned to the rain, the picks and shovels and baskets left in scattered piles, the rusting hulks of the trucks that carry the coal to the Yangtze stranded amongst the pooling mud. As the driver navigates the winding road Anna watches Zhou and Lo stare at this detritus, their faces silent, unreachable.

The town itself is like innumerable others in this region, the cracked concrete of the communist architecture stained with the grime of decades of coal fires. Rusting satellite dishes festoon the rooftops and walls, cables and wires strung between the buildings like the webbing of some vast, silicon spider. Passing a teahouse, Anna sees the PLA truck that had parked outside her window the night before, or one just like it. While soldiers chatted with the prostitutes working across the lane at the rear of the guesthouse, it broadcast martial music and what Nicholas translated as directives about relocation and evacuation. Today though it is silent, the speakers on its flatbed dripping in the downpour, while the soldiers shelter beneath the verandah, fading advertisements for Vietnamese ractoporn plastered to the wall behind them, the open mouths and pneumatic flesh of the ractors turned greenish with age, their fingered cunts peeling and jaundiced, faces by turn numb and hungry with simulated desire. Seated on upturned kerosene tins the soldiers cup cigarettes to their faces, talking and eating from steaming Styrofoam. As the Landcruiser edges past, Anna sees the flash of currency between two of them, a hand pulling back on a wad of New Yuan, then releasing it with a laugh, and briefly she wonders what they are selling—drugs, software, ractoporn, or whether it is something less tangible, but infinitely more expensive: business concessions, information, protection or some minor freedom.

Seeing her watching the soldiers Lo glances over at her, his head shaking almost imperceptibly. Anna looks away, trying not to think about the way her bladder strains and burns. At the door to the guest-house Anna and Lo make a desperate bid to avoid the streaming rain, crowding through the door into the noisy space within. Behind them Zhou and their unnamed companion walk steadily through the rain, unspeaking, faces grim. Her bladder clamouring, Anna hurries out the back to the outhouse and crouches in the reeking dark, the wind and rain screaming against the tin over her head. The animal heat of her urine rising between her legs, somehow reassuring after the atmosphere in the car.

Her bladder empty, she goes upstairs and knocks on Nicholas's door. He does not answer, so she knocks again, and eventually he appears, skin grey, a blanket wrapped around his shoulders.

Hi, he says, smiling weakly. How was it?

Anna bites back the wave of contempt that has been building since she discovered Nicholas had not bothered to have himself immunised against the swine flu before leaving Hong Kong.

Awful, she says. I got almost no shots worth speaking of and we spent three and a half hours getting back in the rain. Zhou smoked the whole way.

I can smell it, he says, his face wrinkling with distaste.

You feeling any better?

He shakes his head. I've decided to tell Zhou that we'll try to get some more shots when the rain ends, and then I'll do the interview by phone.

You think he'll go for that?

Nicholas shrugs. I don't care, really. This is just a filler piece—it's the photos that matter.

When will you tell him?

Probably in the morning. I want to call Derek to confirm and the links are down with the storm.

At the mention of Derek, the editor of the *Straits Times'* Sunday supplement who commissioned this piece, Anna winces. Good luck. She hesitates, about to turn to leave.

You need anything?

He shakes his head. I'm going to take some more painkillers and try to sleep.

When she returns to the communal area having washed and changed into dry clothes, Zhou and their unnamed companion have disappeared, and the driver has installed himself at a table in the corner with a man Anna does not recognise. As she enters, the two of them look up, unabashedly scrutinising her, speaking loudly to each other in words they know she does not, cannot, understand. The driver's companion is an older man, the left side of his face pinkly puckered burn tissue, the eye and brow gone, the remaining skin seemingly too tight on his skull, so the line of his mouth is distorted. Where the skin has been damaged his greying hair grows in wisps, lank above the half-formed nub of his ear. Seeing him, Anna starts and stares, before guiltily looking away.

When she looks back he is still watching her, although the driver has returned his attention to the glass of whisky he is nursing, presumably a salve for the rigours of the journey they have just completed. A cigarette clutched between the stumps of his first and second fingers, the one-eyed man smiles cruelly, and suddenly Anna knows she has seen him before in the narrow backstreets of the village, moving quickly despite his crutches, like a predator maimed but still dangerous, the empty leg of his old PLA fatigues pinned high, revealing the dramatic extent of his injury, his eyes as cold and black as a shark's.

Something about him chills her, fear rising like dark water from a well, leaking forth, staining the bright air of the guesthouse, and as her heart begins to accelerate she fights back an irrational impulse to flee. Then a hand on her arm makes her start.

Lo! she blurts, so that all around them the volume drops as people turn to locate the source of the disturbance.

Anna, he says, his hand still on her arm. Are you okay?

She nods. I'm fine, you just gave me a fright.

Releasing her arm he inclines his head in apology. I am very sorry, he says, and although Anna does not doubt him, she cannot shake the feeling that he is also, subtly, teasing her. Suddenly she wonders if there are hidden depths to the palaeontologist.

Have you eaten? she asks, and Lo shakes his head.

Not yet. I was coming to ask whether you would do me the honour of joining me. Again the private smile.

Zhou doesn't need you?

Professor Zhou is busy consulting the weather feed from the satellite station in Lanzhou. I am free for now, he says, and this time Anna is sure his tone is ironic. Your journalist friend?

Still sick.

Ahh, he says, I am sorry to hear it.

Enjoying his attention, Anna grins. Please, she says, sit down.

Seating himself, Lo gestures to the waitress. Will you have whisky? he asks. Glancing at the driver and his friend, she sees they are deep in conversation, the driver laughing his abrupt, barking laugh.

Yes, she says, suddenly certain, I'd like that.

They order wheat noodles and peppered lamb with Laotian whisky, which the waitress brings in plastic cups discoloured from too many washes. Wincing at the chemical edge to the dark, reeking spirit, Anna drinks deeply, three times, draining the glass but having to choke back on the gagging this induces. Her eyes watering with the burning, metallic aftertaste. Opposite, Lo regards her with raised eyebrows, but she does not offer any apology, simply places her glass on the table and waves to the waitress to bring her another, realising she wants to be drunk, wants the release the alcohol will bring. She knows that this is not a good place for her to be doing this, a European woman, alone, but whether it is the whisky or something deeper she does not care.

On the screen above the bar a space-suited figure turns slowly against a darkness in which a shroud of stars burn blue-white, cold and bright as ice, a lifeline floating like an umbilicus between it and the white hull of the command ship. Behind it another figure picks its way along a black mirrored wing. Chinese symbols stream past, right to left along the bottom of the screen, indecipherable, while in the upper right-hand corner sits the instantly recognisable red, white and blue of the Pepsi logo. Following her gaze, Lo swivels in his seat.

They're fixing the panel, he says.

I'm sorry?

The panel, it was hit by a meteor and damaged. They are repairing it.

On the screen one of the white-suited figures passes a buckled sheet of what looks like black glass to the other.

Who is it?

The American, Foster. And the other is Gromeko, Lo says with an indifference that is undercut by the very detail he is relating. As he speaks the waitress arrives with their food, wordlessly pushing their glasses aside and depositing the plates on the table with a clatter. Lo lifts some with his chopsticks, wrinkling his nose at it. Local speciality, he says with a sardonic grin, and Anna, loosened by the whisky, laughs, a signal for him to begin a long monologue about the region's culinary inadequacies, his voice a bit louder than seems wise to Anna, and more than once she catches people at nearby tables shooting them looks of annoyance. His manner so self-effacing though that she cannot help but laugh. But when she compliments him on his English, the satisfaction of his smile reveals an edge of vanity beneath the veneer of modesty.

I spent time in Canada as a student, he says, at the University of Toronto.

And? she prompts.

I was there for a long time, he says, I had a lot of time to practise.

When she presses him, he begins to talk, slowly at first, but gradually more easily, of the vast spaces of the Canadian north, of the ancient oceans and mountains submerged beneath the frozen soil and tonguing glaciers, their surfaces folded and buckled upon each other, the secrets embedded within them. He tells her of his time on field trips with an archaeologist friend, of drinking and drugs in tents high above the Arctic Circle through nights where the sun never set. His hands moving excitedly as he describes the wandering tracks of pre-historic trade and migration across the frozen sea, of bowls fired in China three thousand years before that have been found in Alaska, of Native American carvings found in Siberia. Of the walrus tusk carved in the shape of a long-muzzled bear, legs swept back against its body as if it were in flight, that he found one afternoon, just lying in the tundra, half covered in grass, and which, knowing it to be a remnant of one of the Dorset cultures, he prised loose and bore away to his tent without telling the team leader, his friend, and which he still has to this very day in his unit in Beijing. And then, his voice slower, more determined, he tells her of the years when he could not return home because of his involvement with dissidents in Canada, years he spent washing dishes and doing data entry in anonymous offices.

Then the conversation turns to her, Lo's mood seeming to recover as he probes her with questions that constantly teeter on the edge of impertinence, saved only by his self-deprecating manner, the unspoken suggestion that she need not answer if she prefers not. It is a long time since she has talked to anyone like this, and she feels herself responding to his interest, his easy flirtation. Her cheeks burning with the whisky. Some time after the food has gone, there is a moment when she realises she is drunk, that Lo must be as well, and she falls back in her seat, rubbing her face, the room spinning around her. At one point Lo stands, swaying with the unsteady dignity of someone who is very, very drunk, and weaves his way to the toilet. When he returns he fixes her with a look so serious that for a moment she thinks he is about to proposition her.

I know a little bit about you, he says, about your brother. How he is missing. As he finishes he sips his whisky, waiting for her answer.

How? she asks after a moment.

Nicholas told me. He said he went missing last August. He said he was your . . . Lo hesitates, shaking one hand as he searches for the word . . . *shuang bao tai*, your twin.

She nods. Yes.

Hard for you, not knowing.

Yes, she says again, but something in her voice must warn Lo off, for he pursues this line of questioning no further, beginning instead to talk about his and Zhou's work, their frantic quest to excavate and catalogue as much of the shale's memories as possible before the water swallows it; his regret that a resource so recently discovered will be lost almost immediately. Finally she asks him about Zhou, and the unnamed man who rides everywhere with them, and Lo looks around the room before replying in a low voice.

Professor Zhou is a good scientist, he tells her, but with his own life—he makes a dismissive gesture—he is not so smart. This man, the one whose name you do not know, he is, as you have no doubt guessed, from the authorities, come to keep an eye on Zhou, make sure he does not do anything . . . again Lo pauses, as if seeking the right word . . . foolish.

The blandness of the adjective somehow ominous, like so much in China.

Foolish? Anna asks. I don't understand.

Five years ago he was working on a shale deposit in Tibet. There was to be a refinery, a joint venture with an American company. But Professor Zhou made international scientists aware of it, organised a campaign with movie stars and politicians which embarrassed the government into preserving it for study. It was expensive for the people of China, which pisses off the government. Money for people is money for them.

So why didn't they just stop him working on this one?

Zhou found it two years ago. He is too public to get rid of, but he can be made to cooperate.

Hence our silent friend.

Lo nods.

But that's not going to happen here, is it?

Lo shakes his head. Not here. Three Gorges is too big a project to stop for fossils. He laughs suddenly, a sardonic bark of a laugh. They don't stop the dam for people, for villages, even for cities, why stop it for some old rocks?

I thought there was still some talk they might stop the project because of pressure from America and Europe.

Anna! he laughs, I thought you knew something of China. They don't care what the rest of the world thinks. The politicians and officials in Beijing only care for money, for power. This dam is big money, the biggest. And anyway, the West is too fearful of us now, they have too many problems of their own to deal with. Look at America! Or Germany. You think they're in a position to tell us what to do?

Anna does not reply immediately, suddenly understanding Zhou's attitude to her, his hostility.

How important are the fossils? she asks at last.

Important.

Anna clenches a fist, letting it strike the laminex surface of the table once, then twice, then three times, a sense of impotent anger rising in her chest.

Why . . . ? she begins, then cuts herself off. Will the fossils be destroyed when the region floods?

Some perhaps, but not all. They will just be inaccessible. That's why Professor Zhou and I are cataloguing as much as we can before the water rises too high.

But there's only two of you.

Lo looks at her, his gaze steady. Better two than none, he says.

Outside her room they pause, Anna slumping against the door so it bangs loudly, and she slips sideways into the frame, the two of them dissolving into hysterical, drunken laughter. It is a long time since she has drunk like this, she thinks, through the confusion of the alcohol. Not even in the strange, almost surreal weeks after the PLA came rolling in from the mainland, when it seemed her whole world was coming unravelled, or in those weeks a month later, when her body longed for the life that had been torn from it, its rhythms seesawing madly, had she turned to drink. Not like some of the others. Next to her Lo is leaning on the wall, his eyes fixed on her, even as his head sways and weaves, looking for some kind of equilibrium. His body close to hers. He reaches out a hand, brushing her fringe, her face, and she feels it on her skin, warm, alive. She has not been with anyone since Jared, and she has forgotten the warmth of skin. She wants to leave it there, but she knows, even like this, that she cannot, and carefully she removes it, places it back at his side. For a long time she does not release it though, and they stand, face to face, not speaking, until finally Lo slips free, turns and walks away. Once he has gone she closes the door, locking it behind her before crawling into the narrow bed fully clothed, trying to warm the sheets with the heat of her body. A draught blows under the casement of the window, which rattles in the wind. From somewhere nearby come the sounds of raised voices, a man and a woman, while from downstairs the amplified sound of the bar thumps through the floor. Gradually the trembling of her body subsides, warmth spreading outwards from her huddled form. One by one she eases off the layers she is wearing, until finally she lies naked between the sheets, their balled nylon rough against her skin. Extending a hand she flicks off the fluorescent glare of the overhead light, and in the darkness lies still. She is drunker than she had thought, and the room moves uneasily around her. From across the hall the voices of the man and the woman continue, lower now, but more insistent, while from outside the rain beats down like tides of sound across the tin roof. The wind rising to a shriek.

Alone in her bed she thinks of Daniel, remembers Lo that morning, crouched beside her in one of the trenches, out of the wind. The lump of shale, big as a bull's heart balanced on its end beneath his steadying hand, his raised mallet. Poised to strike, he turned abruptly towards her, smiled wickedly, looking for all the world like some vaudeville magician, then struck, not hard, but firmly enough to crack the soft surface of the stone. Putting down the mallet, he took the stone in both hands, and gently, as if opening an egg, let it part. And within, nested as if for sleep, the coiled form of an ammonite, its dark surface lustrous.

You knew it would be there, she said accusingly, and Lo grinned, clearly amused by his conjurer's trick. Extending a hand she had let her fingers play across its surface, the stone of its shell cold.

But Lo, eager to show her more, was already standing.

We should hurry, he said, I think there's a storm coming.

And that was when she had seen it, in the discarded face of the stone, the form of the ammonite printed so clearly it might have been a hand pressed into sand, the arrangement of whorls and wrinkles mirrored in the flattened grains. Almost involuntarily she had extended her hand, traced the spiralling image of the absent shell where it lay printed in the stone. One echoing the other, like her, like him.

Soon this room, this building, this entire town will vanish, swallowed by the flooding Yangtze, drowned. The people are going already, half of the streets are empty, but soon there will be none, this place once so full of life left to rot and crumble, left to the wind, the rain, and finally, the water that will rise slowly around it, lapping inwards until these streets disappear forever. Lying alone, the room turning slowly around her, Anna remembers the look on Lo's face when he tried to explain the importance of his desperate scramble to document this place before it is lost, recognises it as a kind of loss that she understands all too well. There is so little we can save, so little we can hold on to. Surprising herself she feels a lump in her throat, choking it back at first, then succumbing to it, surrendering, drunkenly weeping, slow sobs, infinitely sad, and when she has finished she knows she has passed a point, that she must leave China, leave Hong Kong; go home.

APOCRYPHA

· 2 ·

Five thousand years ago, the ancient Mesopotamians revered birds as sacred because their footprints on wet clay so resembled cuneiform writing that the Mesopotamians believed that if they could decipher the confusion of signs marked out by the birds' wanderings they would know the mind of the gods.

Fifty centuries later we too discern echoes of a hidden language woven through the fabric of our world, a language which whispers and hums in the myriad shapes and patterns of things living and unliving. Order is visible wherever we turn: from the spiral form of the nautilus, to the stripes upon a tiger; from the palpating rhythm of our hearts to the swirling eye of a tornado; from the Fibonacci sequences that occur again and again in the structure of plants to the flowing patterns formed by schools of fish and flocks of birds as they move, like one creature, through the ocean and air.

SETH LAMARQUE, *The Language of Shells*

Palimpsest

Great is the power of memory, a fearful thing, O my God, a deep and
boundless manifoldness; and this thing is the mind, and this am I
myself.

AUGUSTINE, *The Confessions of St Augustine*

When I was seventeen, I fell in love. He had a flat in Newtown
which he shared with several others, five dirty, chaotic rooms upstairs
from a pool hall. His bedroom window opened onto an alley in which
the pool hall's clientele used to fight and fuck and deal, their voices,
the sharp clatter of bottles, the low snarls and moans rising to the
window on the hot air. Someone nearby had a piano, and some nights,
at 3 or 4 A.M., after the dull thump of the pool hall's sound system had
died away, they would play Satie, the fractured melodies of the
Gymnopédies lilting out into the night. He was a medical student, and
he had a part-time job cleaning in a nursing home. His shifts finished
around nine, and every night he would ride his bike to the pool in
Victoria Park on his way home, swim laps until closing. I would wait
for him in his bedroom, and when he came in I would watch him
peel his clothes from his body by the light of his bedside lamp; he had
a third nipple, like a mole, above the hard line of his abdomen and an
Incan tattoo which looped his arm above the bicep.

Yet for all these details, I cannot remember his face, nor his name. I cannot remember how we met, cannot remember the first time we made love. I could not tell you the name of his street. Even the passion I felt for him, the desire so huge it filled every waking moment for weeks and months, seems hollow, faintly ridiculous. But I remember the warm nights, the rumble of the traffic, the sweet smell of benzene and LPG in the air.

By writing these things here I reduce them to assemblages of sensations—sounds, smells, the warmth of the air on my skin—and then to mere words; strings of sound, marks on a slate. But they are more than either of these, they are memories of being, which have lain submerged across my life, deeper than words, deeper than language, able to be raised in all their vividity by the scent of the chlorine he carried on his skin through those humid nights. That same scent that became first inseparable then eventually replaced him in the loam of my memory. This remembering somehow more vivid, more pungent, than the moments themselves, like the golden wine of grapes left to rot upon the vine, its flavour richer and more subtle than the words we might use to describe it.

Perhaps this sense of memory's fragmentary nature—the way the whole is lost, piece by piece, until only these scattered remnants are left, slivered deep into our bodies like glass intruding itself beneath the skin—is heightened by the mnemonics, or maybe the mnemonics are made necessary by this inherent tendency of memory. Either way we are left with a sense of incompleteness, a sadness, that no amount of documentation can prevent.

Nine months after I was born she took a photograph of herself, a self-portrait for the exhibition of the 'Extinction' sequence. Ordinarily she did not enjoy the interrogatory gaze of the camera, but in this shot she does not flinch from it, except that, paradoxically, her eyes are closed, as if by this gesture she denied the camera entry into herself, like some tribesman fearful for his soul. Behind her an immensity of sky, the sun's disc just below the horizon, its light spreading outwards from the ocean's lip, faded, dirty orange becoming dusty blue and finally, high above, something more like an absence of colour than a particular hue; the ebbing dark of night. Thin cloud ribbing the sky's periphery, lit from behind so it seems almost colourless, like streaks of silver nitrate. She wears a bikini top and a patterned sarong, her skin beaded, glistening; her feet bare on the runnelled sand. Her body is thin, leanly muscled, the subtle strength of her shoulders and abdomen clear beneath her tanned skin; her dark hair, thick with salt and water, is pushed back off her face to reveal the high bones of her cheeks, the delicacy of her throat. Her beauty is inescapable, yet somehow untouchable, separate. Behind her the wash of a wave is poised, and although there is no way of knowing, it is hard to escape the suggestion that it is retreating, uncovering the sand as it goes, leaving her in its wake.

I always loved this photo of her, not just for the enigmatic defiance of her stance, the way her simple refusal to open her eyes manages not only to register her ambivalence about her own work, but for the way it includes Seth within itself, within her. For many years after they died I kept it in the rooms and apartments I occupied, grateful for its capacity to remember on my behalf. Eventually though it became a reminder of how little I remembered, a talisman of my own forgetting. One day I tried to picture her face and could not, and when I took down the photograph and gazed at the stranger poised upon its flat surface, I found nothing I remembered, just an image, as false to my lived experience as these words are to that moment. And so I took the photograph and put it away, removed its admonishing gaze from my life.

My failure has not been excused by the passage of the years. But although I have forgotten my mother's face I remember other things, details, feelings: a perfume she wore, the tone of a voice, expressions I catch myself using, even now.

They say the shell carries its own history within it, a physical history of a life once lived and now past, frozen immovably into its spiral structure. And there are snails which pass memory in RNA from generation to generation. But just as the creature within fades and dies, so too does the essence of our memory leak away, leaving little but words, brittle shells that crack and crumble in our hands.

She finds it by accident, its shape hard beneath the outer cover of her camera bag.

Curious, she lifts the bag into her lap and yanks at the Velcro seals to open the pocket. Reaching in, her hands close around something solid and hard. Its weight surprising her as she draws it out, into the light, revealing a cloth-wrapped parcel. Baffled, she turns it over in her hands, trying to imagine what it might be, why she might have placed it there, before she unfolds the cloth. Inside lies the coiled form of an ammonite, its shape perfect and unbroken as if lifted from its grave cleanly, the grey stone parting sharply as obsidian. Wonderingly, she turns it over, examining the smooth curve of its outer edge, her hands tracing the hard outlines of its form, the inward motion of its spiral structure. It is not large—probably no wider than the palm of her hand, as thick as two fingers laid side by side—but its heaviness, its compact solidity, is surprising nonetheless.

Raising her eyes to the light that spills through the doors from the balcony, the dissolving glare of the UV, she lingers on the weight of it, gently hefting it in her hands, once, twice. Then in one quick movement she puts it down on the bed beside her, and digs into the pocket once more, looking for a note, a card, anything to explain its presence, although even as she does she knows it was Lo who placed it there, that morning three weeks before when she woke to the seeping, bilious misery of her hangover, the rain cold against her window. But there is nothing.

Cupping the shell in her hands she walks out onto the balcony. Outside the air is warm and humid, clouds hanging overhead as heavy as the sea, their dark weight broken and turbulent. Last night she could not sleep, her body electric with the approaching storm, the lightning arcing across the horizon, thunder moving beneath the air, subsonic, so the dogs barked and the lights flickered in the houses. The rain coming in solid sheets at three, gone again by five. Now it is quiet and grey, the air sometimes shivering sudden gusts of warm rain which catch in the leaves or dry upon hitting the bitumen, leaving a soft mark like a stain.

Three days ago, returning from her morning run, she stood by the balcony's edge, the sun on her skin. Eastwards lay the vast meniscus of the Pacific, while on either side the red roofs crowded the clifftops, the white sand of Bondi curving to the north, the long line of the swell breaking in ridging patterns beneath the cliffs of Ben Buckler. Overhead a gull rose into the blue, borne upwards in a slow spiral by the eddying thermals from the sandstone, and she watched it rise, letting her body lean out into the space of air beyond the balcony, the wind about her face, her neck. As a child she would cup the seashells she collected from the beaches to her ear, listen to the thooming rush of air that reverberated within their chambers. Her mother used to say it was the sea she could hear, that the shell remembered its home, but Anna heard something else too, a not-quite-vertigo where all was in motion but her. A temporal freefall, everything distant. This sense-memory rising unbidden, intense and associative as the wind and the air buoyed her outstretched body.

But today she turns her back to the ocean, letting her body lean against the balcony wall, the shell held before her. In her hands its weight is like a puzzle, a koan, its smooth surface perfect, yet somehow mute. Tracing its spiral once more, her thumb works in a circle, its line a constant motion outwards, each turn enfolding what has gone before, until her thumb skids off, into air, into ending, and she rolls the rounded weight of the fossil back into the cradle of her hands, lifting its weight to her nose and lips, the stone cool and dry, its scent the musty breath of new broken rock.

Finally, remembering the photos, she goes inside, unpacking her camera from its case, searching its memory for the photos she took that cold afternoon, then downloading the data into her slate. One by one, she sorts through them, noting with quiet satisfaction the richness of the colours, the clarity and strength of the composition. Looked at again, she sees them for what they are: commercial work; elegant, intelligent, professional, but even as she does she senses something else too, maybe not in the photos themselves but in their subjects, some resonance she cannot quite name. When she has made her way through them once she returns to the beginning, sorts through them again, more slowly this time, lingering over certain images. As she works she remembers the shape of the fossils beneath her hands as she explored the rockface, learning the angles of the protruding specimens, their textures as she prepared for the shoot, the minutiae of the day returning piece by piece. The cold of the wind, the smell of the smoke. Zhou's voice. Lo's smile. Closing her eyes she can almost summon them once more, their memory hovering just beyond the boundaries of recall.

It has been three weeks since China, three weeks since she woke in the guesthouse's narrow bed disoriented and alone, her head and throat and stomach clogged with the vileness of her hangover. A hugeness of sound filling the room, raw across her nerves like toothache, resolving slowly into an amplified voice bellowing incomprehensibly in Mandarin, distorted martial music booming and spitting. Dumbfounded by the assault on her psyche, she rolled over, dragging the thin pillow over her head, but it was nowhere near enough to block out the torrent of noise. Groggily she remembered seeing the PLA flatbed parked in the lane outside her window last night.

After several minutes of trying to convince herself that sleep was still possible, she gave in to the inevitable, and, pushing the pillow aside, pulled herself upright. Her gorge rising so she gulped back desperately on the acid that surged into her mouth, burning her throat and filling her nostrils with the stink of her churning innards. Behind her, freezing rain lashed the grimy panes of her window, the sky ominously dark. For what seemed like an age she sat slumped forward, trying to summon the energy for the next stage, until finally she rose, more than a trifle unsteadily, stumbled to the low washbasin in the room's corner. The sudden harshness of the fluorescent tube affixed to the wall illuminating her reflection in the mirror above the basin as she stooped low to make out her puffy eyes and grey skin. Although it was hard to tell through the distortion, the music from the truck's speakers seemed to change, one military band substituted for another. Miserably she pulled at her wetpack, looking for painkillers.

Nicholas was waiting outside her room when she returned from the showers. His dishevelled form hunched against the wall, face beaded with sweat.

I've had a call from Derek, he said. He's been watching the feeds from the weather stations; according to the simulations this rain's only going to get heavier. Since there's already flooding upstream, he thinks we should get out as soon as we can.

When do you think we'll be leaving?

Asap, he said, the two of them exchanging thin smiles, united for a moment in the awfulness of their situation.

Back in the cold space of her room she towelled her hair and dressed, rubbing moisturiser into the battered skin around her eyes to relieve the thump of her head. The PLA truck had moved away, and the room was quieter, but rain still lashed the panes of the window, a drumming noise that rose intermittently to a roar. The alkaline stink of the tap water clinging to her skin. Activating the ancient screenset which balanced on a table beside the window she surfed through the channels—home shopping, game shows, dubbed American comedy— until she found a newsfeed. Images of flooding and muddy water coursing down narrow streets, of buildings collapsing and teams of men and women desperately sandbagging walls and doorways against the rising water ghosting across the dirty screen, the frame scrolling slowly from top to bottom, reception distorted by the storm. The audio untranslated.

In the end it took two and a half days to make the trip back to the Autonomous Zone, a day and a night in a hired car on the flooding roads, followed by a night on the hard benches of the airport, then two shuttle flights on old Soviet Tupolevs, the fabric of their seats sour with smoke and sweat and four decades of fear and boredom. The rain began to lessen by midday on the second day, but by then the damage was done, the poorly constructed surfaces of the road heaving and buckling as the foundations washed away from beneath them, leaving treacherous subsidences obscured by muddy water of uncertain depth. As the car made its way through the streaming water, Anna gazed through the windows at the struggling lines of the displaced outside. Their meagre belongings hoisted on shoulders, balanced in barrows, piled on the trays of ancient trucks. Faces lined with despair as they watched the car pass, eyes dull and exhausted. Cages of chickens piled one on top of the other, red-combed heads bobbing and weaving, lizard eyes wide; cows and pigs led by children. Dogs running barking around it all, worrying, tormenting, giddy with the excitement of migration. The smell of wood fire and kerosene thick in the air. Two and a half days of bad coffee, too much sugar to disguise the taste, of airports and forced conversation with Nicholas, who smelt of fever and stale sweat.

Back in her tiny apartment in Western she rang Sophie in New York, telling her what she had decided. It was late there, after midnight, and in the background Anna could hear talking, a sudden burst of laughter. I can't do it anymore, Anna told her, willing her voice to be steady, not to break. I'm like a ghost, a shadow, I can't even remember who I was.

Do you want to come here, stay with me? Sophie asked her. I can lend you the fare if—

I've got money, Anna said, I just want—

To go home, Sophie said. I know, I understand.

I need a place to stay.

You have friends, you could—

Anna cut her off. No, no friends, no-one I know. Sophie's face flat and pixellated on the screen.

He was my brother as well, Sophie said, her voice taut with rebuke. The words hanging between them, unanswered, unanswerable.

I have to go, Anna said at last. Call me if you think you can help.

Two days later, Sophie called back, telling her she had found an apartment near Bondi that friends of friends needed someone to mind for two months, beginning in a fortnight, an earlier arrangement having suddenly, fortuitously fallen through. Anna chafed at the delay, needing to be gone, away from here, the two weeks seeming like months. At Hong Kong airport she thought of Daniel, the mystery of his absence, listening to the PA call the flights. Later, the engines of the plane whining, the banking neon of the city's blocks stretched beneath her like the canyons of a reef, bright against the predawn light the scabbed perspex of the window cold against her cheek.

A week later Anna climbs the sandstone stairs to the Museum, passing through the doors in search of something she has no name for. After the din of the streets the Museum is quiet, and cool, the air tinged with a faint, fusty smell that seems to belong to another time. Taking a guide from a dispenser near the door, she begins to explore the galleries. At first she is struck by the changes; the backlit datanodes with their coloured touchscreens and murmuring soundscapes, the plexiglass tubes where gloved and goggled children jerk and twist spookily in immersive environments visible to them alone, the voice-activated holograms as clear and sharp and three-dimensional as reality itself, yet translucent, immaterial. But amongst them are other displays which seem little altered since the days of Queen Victoria. Long wood and glass cabinets filled with lacquered and desiccated specimens, labels printed decades before yellowing beneath them. Glass jars filled with the coiled forms of snakes and rats and foetuses, slick, blind and bloated with formaldehyde.

When he was a child Daniel loved the Museum, and their parents spent many afternoons in here with the two of them, looking on as they lingered amongst the displays. It was the physical objects that fascinated Daniel, the stuffed bears and antelope, the immense skeleton of the T-Rex. But Anna found herself returning to the remnants of human life, the flaked arrow heads and tools, the bones carved into the semblance of bodies, the reproductions of paintings from Lascaux and

Kakadu, their inscrutability fascinating her. Confronted with the evidence of life lived and lost so long ago, she could not help but feel touched, like reading a letter written a lifetime before and never delivered. Once, in the War Memorial in Canberra, she was reduced to tears by a letter written by a soldier about to die in the trenches of the Western Front, its simple language and directness unhinging her so she wept and wept.

Eventually she finds the gallery devoted to the ancient oceans. The reconstructed skeletons of ichthyosaurs and primeval crocodilians hang overhead, suspended from the chambered ceiling by dark cords. Slabs of stone on stands reveal knuckled fins and blunt skulls, sharp teeth and eyesockets. In one corner an ammonite occupies an entire platform, its diameter the height of a grown man, the curved nick of the opening thirty centimetres across. And between them, glass-topped cases filled with the litter of the past, detritus that has become precious by virtue of its chance survival. Shells, skulls, the finned forms of fishes and urchins and kelp and weed.

For a long time she moves slowly through the room, hands pressed open against the glass cases, wishing she could reach in and handle the specimens. She is not sure what it is she is looking for, but it is as if Lo's mysterious gift has struck a chord within her, and for a brief moment she has felt the echo of something deep inside, some connection, some clarity, which these objects that have travelled like driftwood across great oceans of time are part of. At one end of the gallery stands a rough-hewn hunk of stone, fenced in by ropes. Pausing before it she stares down at the ridged bones of the plesiosaur fin embedded within it, the bony fingers like one of the Giger creatures that inhabited the nightmares of her childhood. Then, glancing over her shoulder to check that she is alone, she steps past the ropes, runs her palm across it. The stone's surface as cold and shiny as glass.

Two days before she had lain upon her bed, donned datagoggles and gloves, let herself sink into the merse. With a photo of Lo's gift to guide her, her console's searchware sought out information that might interest her, articles and drawings, not just about the extinct ammonites, but about their cousins, the nautili, and other cephalopods, octopi and squid and cuttlefish. Fascinated, she watched holos of the mating rituals of the squid, the elaborate, writhing dances of their courtship, then old video of octopi navigating mazes and solving colour puzzles, startled to learn of their high intelligence and complex behaviour. As holos of octopi and squid surrounded her she watched patterns of colour chase across their skin, surprised to learn these rippling colours are not just camouflage, but a system of communication as sophisticated as those of dolphins or primates, of which humans understand nothing. From there her searchware led her to a Sri Lankan artist's memory palace, a place of thalassic light and rippling, oceanic soundscapes, where she floated through a holo of magnified nautilus shell, the curving architecture of the chamber walls like sheets of mother of pearl. In a children's education centre she handled an eidetic of a nautilus shell, tracing its brown stripes with the tip of a finger, then releasing it as the system instructed, the shell not falling but floating away to arm's length, then growing a head and tentacles, colours playing across them like liquid shadows, before the now living creature darted away, quick as thought.

Elsewhere she read about the strange eternal geometry of the ammonite's shell, about its rapid, iterative evolution, about morphospaces and adaptive landscapes. And finally, in the Ashmolean, she came across a library of eidetic replicas of ammonite species. One by one she examined them, whispering their names to herself—*Echioceras, Pleuroceras, Dactylioceras, Siemiradzkia, Psiloceras*—so delighting in their mysterious beauty that when the Museum offered her translations and explanations she refused, wanting to remember them as if they were cabbala, invocations of the creatures they described. Last of all she picked up a *Spiroceras*, its coils unwound like a ram's horn or a spiral traced in sand, and marvelled at its seeming fragility.

The room had grown dark when she ungoggled, her eyes aching and stomach queasy from too long in the virtual space of the merse. Morning turning to afternoon and finally dusk, the low cloud feeding slowly inland, the light across the horizonless ocean grey-blue.

. . .

By the time she emerges from the Museum it is raining, the drops hot but scattered, the humid air broody with their plummeting weight, their heavy plop against the asphalt. Across the road, beneath the canopy in Hyde Park, the leaves whisper with them, the fecund smell of the earth rich in her nostrils. An ibis stalks across the path before her, its carriage regal despite its filthy plumage, feathers ruffled against the dampness. She is grateful for the grey quiet, the sense of drift, reluctant to lose the momentary connection she felt in the Museum, but as she clatters down the cracked steps into the railway station, the warm stink rising around her, she can already feel it slipping away, the billscreens that plaster the walls whispering and cajoling, video and text dancing across them. Beneath her feet the mosaic floor has been worn almost blank by the passage of countless feet, overhead the questing tendrils of tree roots crawl from the fissures in the ceiling, their intrusion subtly threatening.

Through the turnstiles the smell that rose around her as she came down the stairs grows stronger; hot rubber, diesel, and beneath these two something closer, more human, an acrid smell of urine and sweat, the caseous reek of unwashed bodies that rises from the huddled forms that cluster along the walls, faces turned away in sleep or resignation, their meagre belongings gathered to them.

As she passes she recalls a story told to her by an expat one night over dinner in Hong Kong, about the tunnels and basements of the city having become a haven for these people, the dispossessed, the lonely, the mad, the lost. Troglodytes, he called them, and Anna shook her head. Morlocks, more like, she said softly. This man, an Australian colleague of Jared's, had spoken of a maze of abandoned train tunnels, access passages, bomb shelters, drains and cellars stretching from the Quay to Pyrmont and Central and beyond. Of lost rivers covered over and piped down crumbling tunnels, of forgotten caves and creeks, even a lake, as long as a football field, its water as still and clear and fresh as a mountain stream, which lay somewhere beneath the roar of George Street. He told her of a mining executive who swam laps there every day, a torch strapped to his goggles. Then he had laughed, saying there were fish down there as well, native perch and catfish, carp too, all gone pale in the darkness, eyes grown huge and dishlike. And Anna, not believing him, had smiled and asked, What? No crocodiles? And then he had stared at her, his coarse, conceited face ruddy with drink, before laughing, his tale discarded in favour of something else, something new.

At the time the story had seemed ludicrous, a myth from another age reborn in modern guise, but now it seems more plausible. As she winds her way along the platform, a man, his face black with grime, murmurs and yips, hands snapping at unseen flies, another sits a metre from him, mutely staring. A woman nurses a child on a bench, a paper cup beside her for coins. A man in a suit, his torso bare beneath the jacket, sits weeping in the dark space beneath a staircase. Turning aside from them Anna sees her reflection caught in the glass face of a billscreen on the far side of the tracks, colours moving beneath it. Her face, his face, both caught in ghostly superimposition upon the advertisement. The station seeming to recede, voices echoing along the vaulted chamber growing fainter. A stirring in the air around her, the motion of a body against hers. Five metres away a blood cell twists and mutates in the womb of a woman, leukemia beginning to burn in her blood. Then the warm exhalation of the tunnel as the train approaches, a shear of air and shrieking metal, dividing them as it thunders by, an immensity of light and sound.

In the half light of ocean moon she wakes with sudden clarity. That afternoon, in the station, her reflection, she had seen it before. Not her face, not his, but that look, that ghostly gaze. Naked in the moonlight she pulls at her slate, flicking through its memory. The blue light of the screen drawing her into being. Eventually she finds it, one image, one of those ones that made up her second exhibition. She and Daniel side by side, their thin bodies and uncannily similar faces, wide mouths and almond eyes staring impassively at the camera, their beauty made freakish, almost eerie, in its strange, stylised distance from the viewer. Her arm crooked across her chest, her hand covering one of her small, dark-nippled breasts, leaving the other exposed. Looking at it she remembers the opening night, the narrow space of the gallery. She had retreated to the back room, where Jadwiga, the gallery's owner, had an office, separated from the main area of the converted warehouse by a partition. The small space crowded with canvases and prints, unpaid for, unsold, awaiting collection. From here she could hear the crowd talking, voices raised against each other's echoing din. A woman's whinnying laugh. The sententious tones of the young television presenter who had interviewed her earlier that day, seated alone on a tall stool in the midst of the gallery's white space, the camera operator allowing her beauty room to move amongst the silence of the photos. She had flicked idly through a magazine until Jadwiga appeared around the corner and grabbed her by the arm, telling her she had to get back out there, everybody was here; asking her did she realise she was going to be a star, she was going to be so big everyone—here she stopped and said it again, as if the idea was too much to grasp—everyone was going to know who she was. Jadwiga's hand on her arm propelling her back into the crowded space. Outside Jadwiga drew her towards a man whose name she would never hear, but as she went she saw Daniel standing in front of one of the photos, this photo, enlarged so their faces and bodies loomed, twice life size, from the wall. As if feeling her eyes upon him Daniel turned, his face unconsciously mirroring the image he stood before. A chill of premonition running through her body like electricity as she looked around the room at the other pictures, all of her or Daniel, all dark, distant, almost clinical, then back to see Daniel grinning, his eyes mocking the man Jadwiga was introducing, oblivious to her sudden vision of loss.

At 10:20 P.M. Tokyo Standard Time, on a freeway outside Yokohama, a lorry carrying plastic piping to a building site in Tokyo loses steering control and slews sideways, crushing a smaller vehicle driven by Saori Murakami, wife of Yasuhiro Murakami, the Japanese physicist aboard *Prometheus*. Saori Murakami is killed instantly, as are two of her daughters, the third dying on an operating table three hours later from massive internal haemorrhaging. The truck driver escapes without serious injury.

A tag on the medical records of the youngest daughter alerts the paramedics to her identity, an alert that is repeated on the systems wired into the rescue team when the car's registration is entered. Within the hour the news has begun to leak, spreading through the feeds and the nets. Two hours later, Mission Control at Kennedy calls a press conference, at which the waiting media are told that Murakami has been informed and that the crew have made a request that their privacy be respected for the time being. Official condolences and assurances of support are made.

By the time Anna arrives back from her run at seven, the feeds are alive with it. Overnight, Svenson, the mission commander, has made a statement on Murakami's behalf, thanking the public for their messages of support, and as Anna brews coffee, the pot gurgling and spitting, she sees it replayed, sees Svenson's space-tan pallor, her drawn expression.

It is more than two months since *Prometheus* had anything like a two-way conversation with Earth, the communication time lag having stretched beyond anything workable after only a month. Since then crew members have been reduced to these set pieces, often pre-scripted, as they struggle with the problems that have beset the mission almost since it left earth's orbit and swung outwards into space, towards Mars. Despite being the creation of a dozen nations' exper-tise, the craft has been plagued with technical difficulties. There have been oxygen filtration malfunctions on at least three occasions; guid-ance systems have twice failed to fire, necessitating a series of frantic EVAs to repair the faults before course correction became impossible; and the computer systems have developed peculiar and seemingly intractable glitches. Six weeks after launch, intense solar flare activity stranded the astronauts in the tiny radiation shelter for almost a fort-night, a space barely larger than their eight bodies. And most recently, part of the power array has been damaged by a meteorite.

Watching Svenson's image, flattened and staticky from the com-pression protocols, Anna is struck once more by the magnitude of the risk these eight men and women have agreed to take. A six-month journey to a dead planet in a craft little larger than a bus, endless dark-ness and cold on every side. Eighteen months in a habitat on the planet's surface, unable to breathe the atmosphere, drinking recycled urine and sweat. Then six months back to Earth. Like many others, Anna is unsure what sense to make of such courage. For while she sees the mission is an act of faith in a future that seems increasingly uncertain, even its crew—four men, four women; two Americans, two Russians, one German, one Japanese, a Brazilian and an Indian—an expression of international solidarity in a time when the world seems to be dissolving into a ragged patchwork of atrocities and police actions, border skirmishes and tense, angry stand-offs, she also sees it as something far vainer, an astronomically expensive act of hubris. Yet they are there, further from Earth than any human has ever been.

Once she has finished her coffee she flicks off the feeds. The night before's memory of Daniel's image, of the exhibition, has stirred up a tangle of guilt and regret. Unable to sleep, she had spent the hours after she woke rehearsing not just her shame, her sense of failure at returning alone and empty-handed, but also her guilt about her behaviour four years earlier, when she left without warning. In the quiet of the moonlit bedroom the solutions had seemed easy, a matter of forgiveness sought and given. But now, in the light of day, it seems less simple, a process fraught with danger.

As she washes and dresses she cannot shake her apprehension. Twice she stops what she is doing, half decided to give the task she is about to undertake away, but each time she manages to pick up and continue.

In the street outside the sun is already high, the patches of low cloud that shrouded the sea just after dawn burnt away by the heat, while out over the ocean another pressure front can be seen approaching, great banks of blue-white cumulus that pile one upon the other, billowing plumes rising into the blue of the morning sky. As she walks down the hill towards the train station on Campbell Parade, Anna stares out at the distant cloud, its contours clearer in the filtered light of her glasses, this reminder of the constant cycle of the weather, of the moving cycles of fronts and calms, cloud and wind, calming her.

But at Bondi Junction the train is cleared, commuters herded out of it into waiting buses to complete the trip to the city because of problems on the line ahead. Together with the other passengers Anna troops into an already crowded bus, fighting her way towards one unoccupied seat. As more passengers clamber on behind her, angry shouts about overcrowding begin at the rear of the bus, and Anna, aware of the eyes directed covetously towards her seat, looks away, out the smeared window at the passing cars, the tree-filled gardens.

When the bus stops outside Town Hall Station she does not descend to the trains, deciding instead to walk the half kilometre to Jadwiga's gallery. On Elizabeth Street the traffic is stationary, backed up around a roadblock, where a dozen police officers, all combat boots and body armour and electronics, are checking IDs and scanning cars with sniffer devices. As she passes, Anna stares at the bubble-headed riot helmets that shield their faces from scrutiny and wonders why they have allowed themselves to be made so inhuman, whether it is for safety, to intimidate, or both.

When she reaches it, Jadwiga's gallery is almost as she remembers. The café on the corner has new chairs, and the patrons scattered amongst the streetside tables are perhaps a little better dressed, but the tiny street is still shaded by the scruffy wattles, their dirty bark fragrant in the hot air, the narrow terraces that rise three storeys on either side still as unkempt as ever. Anna barely notices though, her stomach queasy with the prospect of what lies ahead. On one of the balconies a bird sings, a long trilling cry that rings out over the rooftops; somewhere else the shriek of a drill rises and falls. At the door she lifts her hand to the buzzer, not looking up for the watching eye of the camera.

The first time she exhibited here, the door was always open, but soon after there was what Jadwiga would only ever describe as 'a scene'. An exhibition of paintings destroyed, the canvases ripped, gashed with razors and screwdrivers and daubed with paint, graffiti sprayed across the inviting emptiness of the walls. Jadwiga herself assaulted, seriously enough to warrant almost a week in a hospital bed. Anna remembers visiting her, Jadwiga holding court amongst her tribe of well-wishers, refusing gifts of fruit and chocolate as 'beneath them'—'Can't you try harder?' she had shrieked to delighted laughter. Her face puffy with bruises, one eye swaddled in bloodstained padding, clotted and black. Anna gave her flowers, opulent tropical blooms that flared orange and yellow against their green wrapping, and Jadwiga had drawn her close, so Anna could feel the thinness of the older woman's body, the gesture uncharacteristic for its sincerity. Be careful of yourself, she had whispered, you're too precious to lose.

It is four years since she has seen or spoken to Jadwiga, four years since her sudden cancellation of the exhibition she and Jadwiga had planned. Even at the time it had felt cowardly, calling Jadwiga out of the blue to announce her decision to leave. Jadwiga who had supported her, been her friend, Jadwiga whose insights and intuitions she valued. Jadwiga who had lent her money when she needed it. Anna, consumed by the raging fever of her love had forgotten all that, dropping her with a phone call. And now she is back, walking in unannounced (although she knows she could do it no other way), expecting—hoping—that Jadwiga will be here, that she will open her arms once again.

Frightened she will give up and walk away if she doesn't do it immediately, Anna jabs at the intercom buzzer, releasing an electronic chime. Hearing the click of the lock, she pushes the door, but before she can enter a tall man pulls it away from her, his spare frame filling the doorway. Beneath a stained vinyl jacket he wears ill-fitting trousers and a filthy shirt several sizes too small. A coat of grime across his neck and face, their bones prominent beneath sallow skin and a grizzled beard. As he pushes past her she recoils involuntarily and he stops for a moment, so close she can smell the foulness of his breath, see the sarcoma that bubble in the cleft of his throat. His eyes sliding down from her eyes to her mouth, her breasts, then up again, his gaze meeting hers so she can be in no doubt as to what he is thinking. Then before she can speak he steps past her, down the stairs into the street and away.

Inside it is cooler, the long space lined with huge canvases, washes of colour through which muted marshscapes emerge. Several other people are littered around the gallery, silent before the canvases or whispering in hushed tones to one another. Anna notices she is trembling, folds her arms tight to try to contain the motion of her body. But Jadwiga does not appear. Wanting a moment to collect herself, Anna begins to walk slowly around the gallery, looking at the paintings. At first she is disappointed to discover she does not much like them, finding them unimpressive, too quiet, too wan, but as she moves from one to another that initial reaction is replaced by a growing admiration for the sense of depth the artist has managed to catch, the way patterns and potentials seem to eddy beneath their simple surfaces. Glancing discreetly at the other patrons, she tries to gauge their reactions, but they are professional viewers, their opinions hidden beneath a veneer of dispassionately engaged attention.

As she circles the gallery, Anna knows she is only delaying the inevitable. Jadwiga is here; Saturday afternoons are her busiest time, even if her practice was always to remain out of sight, letting her patrons peruse the work without interference. So Anna is surprised when she sees Jadwiga emerge from behind the partition that leads to the office, stiff and straight, and hurry towards the door. But before she reaches it, a woman detaches herself from the two friends with whom she is standing, and in a low voice asks Jadwiga something. Arrested in mid-flight, Jadwiga turns, poised, friendly, points at one of the canvases and nods. The woman says something to her friends in a low voice, and Jadwiga begins to move towards the door, but noticing Anna staring at her, looks back inquisitively. This time she stops where she is. Neither speaking. Then Jadwiga begins to walk towards her, slowly, deliberately. Anna realises she does not know what she wants to say, and stands mutely as Jadwiga stops in front of her, her face impassive. When Anna does not speak, Jadwiga folds her arms.

You look well, she says.

Thank you, Anna replies lamely.

I didn't know you were back in Sydney.

I haven't been here long.

Is Jared with you?

Anna shakes her head. Jadwiga does not reply, just narrows her eyes.

How is Jean-Paul?

At the mention of her husband's name something passes across Jadwiga's face. Not quite a flinch, more a moment of hesitation, but it is enough to make Anna freeze.

What? she asks. Has something happened?

Jadwiga stares at her coldly.

You haven't heard?

No, why?

Follow me, Jadwiga says. This business is not for my clients. Turning, she walks back towards the office.

In the narrow space behind the partition, a younger woman is standing by the desk, her attention focused on the console in front of her. As they enter she looks up.

Mathilde, Jadwiga says, this is Anna Frasier.

Mathilde stands, extending a hand to Anna. The photographer? she asks.

That's right, Anna says. As she speaks she keeps turning to look at Jadwiga, who stands beside her in silence.

I've seen the pieces in Jadwiga's flat, they're very impressive.

Anna releases Mathilde's hand. Thank you. It's kind of you to say so. Glancing at Jadwiga, Mathilde closes the console.

I'll be outside, she says, excusing herself.

Sit, Jadwiga says, gesturing at a chair.

As Anna seats herself her feeling of dread increases, exacerbated by the way Jadwiga props her thin body against the bench, arms folded, eyes trained on her crossed feet.

What is it? Anna asks. What's happened?

Jean-Paul is dead, Anna, Jadwiga says, her voice flat.

Oh God, Anna sighs, I didn't know.

Jadwiga looks up at her sharply. No, I suppose you didn't.

When?

Seven months ago.

. . . How?

Leukemia.

Anna does not need to ask to know. Like a silent fire, leukemia has started to spread, its vectors unidentifiable, striking a suburb, a school, even a building, one person falling sick after another, then as suddenly as it arrived, vanishing again, leaving some dying, others untouched. At first the rate of increase was slow, within statistical norms, but as the numbers have begun to grow it has become clear something else is at work. Some say it is viral, an unidentified retrovirus carried in the blood and spread across the air. Others say it is environmental, a reaction to the biosphere's increasing toxicity, or a hitherto unobserved genetic resonance triggered by microwave density in urban areas, where its spread is the fastest. But for all the theories, the truth is nobody knows. All that is certain is its inexorable spread, the rapidity of its victims' decline.

I . . . I'm so sorry, Anna says, but even as she speaks she is assailed by the memory of the last time she saw Jean-Paul, late on a Friday night in a restaurant in Chinatown, the place crowded and smoky, fish and crabs moving in tanks on every side, the air tumultuous. It was the night after she had rung Jadwiga and told her she was leaving, the exhibition was off. He was there with clients, had spotted her across the crowded dining area, crossing deliberately to her table, his long hair falling into his eyes.

You are leaving, he had said, his accent sliding around the words, stronger now he was a little drunk.

She had nodded convulsively, sure he would be angry, fearful of this side of him she had never before seen, the knowledge of her betrayal of Jadwiga making her cowardly.

Is he a good man? Jean-Paul had asked, one hand braced against her shoulder.

Yes, she had said, he is. Is Jadwiga angry?

He shrugged. A little. It is a bad thing you have done to her, but she will get over it. She loves you, you know. You are her protégé.

Anna had blushed, not knowing how to reply.

I have clients, he had said then, I must get back to them. But little Anna, you be careful in Hong Kong—she still remembered the way he said it, as if it were one word: 'Hongkong'. It is a dangerous place. Then he had made as if to turn away, but stopped, the move half completed, and knelt beside her.

Anna, he had said, his voice urgent, almost a whisper, you make sure this man, he love you too. Remember that if you are so mad for this thing that you will destroy anything to have it, it can destroy you too. Love is dangerous, my sweet, love is dangerous. And then he had taken her head in both hands and kissed her brow. Be careful.

For what seems a long time the two of them sit in silence, Jadwiga studying her shoes intently, Anna trying to accommodate this turn of events. Jadwiga and Jean-Paul were such a part of her life, ever since college. United in their very public marriage, they had seemed inseparable. Both had been married before, Jadwiga to a defrocked Jesuit many years older than herself, and Jean-Paul to an actress in his native France, and this second marriage had come late for both of them, the two of them treating it as a gift, a surprise they were somehow awed by.

You should have called me, Anna says, I would have come.

You left me, Jadwiga retorts. It was not my job to come looking for you. An edge of her native Hungarian slipping out from beneath the flattened Australian vowels in her anger.

I'm sorry, Anna says again. For everything. She rubs at her face, trying to hold back tears.

Saying sorry changes nothing, Anna.

No.

Besides, I hear you have lost someone too.

Startled, Anna looks up, only to see Jadwiga hesitate, as if the malice that motivated the remark has shocked even her.

Yes, Anna replies, her voice level. I have.

Do they know anything yet? Jadwiga asks, her voice less bitter, and Anna shakes her head.

Nothing.

It is a terrible thing, says Jadwiga. To lose a brother.

Anna nods. When she does not speak Jadwiga clears her throat, her tone pointedly conciliatory.

Why did you come if it was not about Jean-Paul? she asks.

To see you, Anna says, sniffing. To apologise.

Jadwiga touches one of her eyebrows, pressing it upwards with one fingertip in an oddly delicate motion.

Good, she says. Do you have anything to show me?

Startled, Anna looks up. No, she says quietly, but seeing Jadwiga smile she laughs, her tears making her snort and gurgle.

Nothing at all?

Anna wipes her nose. I'm about to start work on something, I think.

Oh?

Ammonites.

Jadwiga looks perplexed. I do not know these . . . ammonites.

Here, Anna says, reaching into her bag and producing Lo's gift. This is one.

As she watches, Jadwiga unwraps it and turns it over in her hands.

I see, she says, though she does not sound convinced. Where will you get them?

I'm not sure yet. I thought the Museum might let me use their collections.

I have a client whose son works at the Museum, Jadwiga says. I could call her, see whether she could arrange for him to talk to you.

Anna hesitates. Not because the offer is unattractive, but because she knows it is more than an offer of assistance, it is an attempt to repair the relationship that she, Anna, so damaged.

Yes, she says at last. I'd like that.

2:14, and still she cannot sleep, her body restless, her mind racing like the nights of the full moon where the tidal motion of the water in her brain keeps her awake for two, three days at a time, until exhaustion pulls her back into uneasy dreams. Not sure what else to do, she dresses and goes out into the moonlit streets, her body slipping into the motion quickly, intuitively, the beat of her feet against the asphalt steady. Out here, amongst the gardens and silent streets, it is like another world, a secret world, and as she runs she feels the desperation of her insomnia begin to fall away, replaced by the rhythmic calm of the endorphins.

In Hong Kong she did this often, the cold air of the apartment, the computer-regulated light, interfering with her already fragile biorhythms. Like her, Jared was a light sleeper, his metabolism almost birdlike, and when the markets were moving fast he would go a week at a time on two or three hours sleep a night. But he did not suffer this restless, fitful insomnia that has kept her within the shadow world of the sleepless for so much of her adult life. So, deep in the tropical nights she would dress, take the lift the sixty floors to the gleaming lobby where the guards sat bored and drowsy before the panels of video screens and smart systems, and run through the humid air. The city quiet, the normally crowded streets empty save for the slow-moving hulks of the sanitation trucks and lorries bearing plastic-wrapped goods or other, less savoury, cargoes better transported under cover of darkness, the ever-present taxis swishing by, the occasional sputtering motorbike, sometimes loaded high with market goods; sides of meat, bound leaves, dirty roots. Overhead the shadowy shapes of the trees, their leaves clasping and rustling in the darkness, the neon-tubed glass and concrete walls of the towers rising through the soft air. Here and there the sweet smell of Chinese baking, the coloured lights of shopfront brothels, the girls leaning from the balconies half-dressed. One street she often took held a line of sweatshops, always busy, even in the depths of night, open-sided buildings in which rows of women hunched over tables piled high with the gusseted innards of cheap sandshoes, cotton shirts and designer suits. Faces sometimes lifted to watch her pass, like characters in a play noticing an audience for the first time. And here and there, where the hillside dropped precipitously, framed between an escalator and a wall or rickety tin, lighted rooms picked out against the darkness like video screens, windows open for the night air, giving unexpected glimpses of unclad bodies lounging in chairs or across unmade beds. Bedside fans whirring audibly. Everywhere the choking sweet smell of rot and flowers and drains. And afterwards, she would sit in the half light of their bedroom, her bare knees drawn up to her chin, watch Jared's sleeping form, the play of dreams across his face.

Her sweat cold against her skin in the refrigerated air.

Monday morning she calls the number Jadwiga gave her. She is directed to vidmail, a brisk message that identifies the speaker as the man she is looking for. He is younger than she had expected, and better looking, in an unstudied way, surfer blond hair above a tanned, intelligent face, but his message is brisk to the point of curtness. She leaves her contact details as directed, but she has barely disconnected when the phone rings back, his face appearing on the screen as she reconnects.

Anna? he asks.

That's right.

How can I help you? As he speaks he gestures to someone off screen, apologising immediately. It's a bit crazy in here this morning, and as he says it Anna sees for the first time a flash of humour, which makes his earlier impatience less off-putting. Explaining her relationship with Jadwiga, Anna is relieved when he interrupts to say he knows Jadwiga. But when she explains the purpose of her call he loses interest.

We have someone who handles these sorts of things, he tells her. I could put you on to her if you like.

No, Anna says, realising he has probably mistaken her for some green art student, I actually wanted to come in, have a look around first.

There is a momentary pause. When were you thinking of coming in?

I didn't have a specific time in mind, whenever's easiest for you.

• • •

At Dylan's suggestion she arrives late that afternoon, just before closing, which he says will give her a few hours to look around in relative peace, as well as a chance to examine the Museum's collection without having to pay licence fees. At the staff entrance she asks for him, and a few minutes later he appears through a security door. As he shakes her hand, Anna is aware of the spark of interest in his eyes.

He leads her down several flights of stairs and through a series of doors into a long room filled with metal cabinets, their painted doors scratched and bent. As they walk he keeps up a lively stream of chatter, explaining the sorts of specimens kept down here, pointing towards various objects as they pass them. Then, one finger raised, he stops, opens one of the cabinets to reveal shelves laden with chunks of stone, out of which the coiled forms of shells can be seen bulging.

Maybe you should start here, he says, pulling over a trolley and lifting several specimens onto it for her to examine.

These are *Beudanticeras*, he says, as he sets the first two down. They're from a limestone escarpment in central Queensland. Grabbing another one he heaves it onto the trolley. If you're after more unusual looking species, there's this sort of thing, with the heavily crenellated shell ridges, or maybe this, which is a *Hyphantoceras*, where there's variation in the coiling.

Glancing up from the array of ammonites he has spread before her, Dylan hesitates, then grins, a mite sheepishly.

I'm going on, aren't I? You'd probably rather be left here on your own, just poke about a bit.

That might be best, Anna concedes. Are there things I can and can't touch?

Keep track of where you get them from, and if you're not sure where something came from leave it out and someone who knows where it goes will put it back tomorrow. And don't drop anything.

I'll try, she says.

How long will you need?

I don't know. Is an hour too long?

That's fine, says Dylan. I can go and catch up on a few things, you buzz me when you're done. There's an examining table with a light behind those cupboards there. Feel free to use it if you want.

Once he has gone she wheels the trolley towards the examining table and unloads the specimens Dylan has placed upon it. Once they are unloaded she flicks the switch on the overhead lamp, pooling the bench in a powerful white light. The air-conditioning hums in the background, but otherwise the room is quiet. On a shelf to one side a series of specimens lie waiting to be returned to their places. Two fish; a collection of strange marine creatures—sea urchins and other less recognisable forms; a delicate fanned creature spread over two flat pieces of stone which once were part of one larger piece; strange, not quite spherical lumps of rock, seams stitched into their surface like scars. Glancing over her shoulder, to check she is still alone, she reaches out to the first of these specimens, a fish, wide and flat like a flounder. The scales glitter like mother-of-pearl as she runs her hand over them, marvelling at the way their shifting light has been preserved across a hundred million years. After a moment her hand strays to the form of the other fish. Longer, uglier, more primeval than the first, its teeth protrude from its massive lower jaw like jagged glass, irregular, rapacious, its sinuous body giving the dual impression of speed and cruelty. Stroking its armoured head, she wonders how much is preserved within, whether there are stone veins, a crystalline brain beneath the bony exterior. Lower, the squared scales press against her fingers like a code, undulating unevenly where the rotting fish has been crushed by sinking mud before hardening into stone, eons before.

Finally she turns back to her gathered ammonites. Most of them are unremarkable, but there is one at least that draws her attention, perhaps not as striking as some of the others, but cleaner, more insistent in its geometry. She is noting its reference number into her codex when she hears the door at the other end of the specimen room open. Assuming it is Dylan she looks up expectantly, but the footsteps seem to turn aside before they reach her. There is another sound too, an irregular tapping, light and quick, which seems to move with the footsteps. After a moment both stop, and there is the noise of a cabinet being opened, then a drawer being pulled forward. Then footsteps, the gentle tap-tap beginning again. Curious, Anna moves towards the source of the sound, and between two of the banks of shelves she sees him walking towards her. His left hand is held away from his body, feeling the face of the shelves as he moves along them, while his right holds a long white cane which he sweeps before himself, connecting occasionally with the shelves with a quick click. He is dressed formally in a suit, his dark hair swept back off a long, aquiline face. Mirrored glasses obscure his eyes, and for a moment Anna thinks they must be goggles, that the cane is some kind of wand and he is deep in some hidden, machine-generated reality. But his movements—quick, confident, graceful—are not the movements of someone who is mersed. He approaches Anna faster than she had expected, then, only metres from her, he veers away down the passage that bisects the rows of shelves. As quietly as possible she follows, but as she rounds the corner she discovers he has stopped and is standing, waiting for her.

Who's there? he demands, and Anna, thrown off balance by his sudden proximity, takes a step back. He is tall, she realises now, considerably taller than she is, and there is something about the way he stands poised before her which reminds her of a predator caught off guard. But even though she is barely a metre from him he seems not to have seen her, his head moving in sudden jerks from left to right.

Who's there? he demands again. Is it you, Dylan?

Taking another step back Anna realises with a start that he can't see her, that he is blind. It's not Dylan, she says as evenly as she can. My name's Anna, I'm a photographer.

As soon as she has spoken the rapid movements of his head cease, his attention fixing on her.

What are you doing here?

Excuse me? she says, incredulous at his tone of interrogation.

Visitors aren't supposed to use the collections after five o'clock.

I organised this through Dylan Boyd. I'm considering using the collection for a project I'm working on.

He hesitates, as if digesting this piece of information.

Is Dylan with you?

No, he went back upstairs.

I see, he says, the displeasure in his voice palpable. Perhaps you could remind him about the opening hours for visitors when you see him. Now if you'll excuse me.

Before she can respond he has turned and is moving away again, his hand playing along the cabinets as he goes. Two rows from her he stops, turns once more into one of the aisles and vanishes from sight.

Left alone, Anna stands motionless, listening to the tapping pattern of his cane as it moves through the shelves. Eventually the tapping ceases, replaced by the sound of a drawer sliding open, specimens being moved around. As quietly as she can, Anna moves towards the sounds, pausing at the corner of the aisle the blind man vanished down. Halfway along he is standing by an open drawer, head tilted up, his hands moving across a specimen. His lips slightly parted, as if he is murmuring to himself. In profile she sees the lines of his face are stranger than she had thought, long, almost equine, the cheekbones and mouth too prominent. His dark hair streaked with grey, falling almost to his collar. Not certain whether she thinks him handsome or ugly, she watches him lift the specimen he is working on, his long hands running over its surface.

As if sensing her presence he hesitates, swivelling his head towards her. She catches her breath, not moving, not making a sound. For what seems a long time they stand like this, until he relaxes, turns back to his specimen, and Anna, her heart beating fast, backs away around the corner.

That night, as she reviews her day's work, she finds herself returning again and again to her encounter with the blind man. Even now, alone in the apartment, she feels on edge, jumpy. It is not just his abruptness, his dismissive manner that has unnerved her so profoundly. Instead, she cannot shake the feeling that his blindness had made her less than real, invisible. Closing her eyes, she can still see the cruel line of his mouth, the velvet movement of his hands upon the stone, soft, caressing, almost sexual.

In the specimen room she opens the bag, draws her camera forth. The curved plastic of the casing smooth beneath her hands, not slippery, but silky, its weight reassuringly solid. Dormant it is featureless, the ergonomic surface of its body moulded to sit in the hands with a naturalness that makes it seem an extension of the arm. Turning it she checks for external damage, then disarms the security protocols and activates the internal systems, the covers retracting, lenses and viewfinders emerging as the device comes to life in her hands. Flicking through the menus she directs the software to run an internal diagnostic, checking the moving parts and the read-outs as the systems chirrup and whisper within.

The camera is old now, a model famous amongst photographers for the idiosyncratic design of its interface and a litany of system quirks, but over the years Anna has grown used to its oddities, the process of mastering them having created a kind of bond between the two of them. As she works she lets her hands guide themselves, until the movements come more easily, almost unconsciously, just as a swimmer remembers the rhythms of their stroke through the motion of the body. And like that hypnotic patterning of muscle and water, the stroke, breath; stroke, breath of swimming, she feels her body and mind become one as she runs through the physical mantra of her equipment checks, her imagination coming loose from the bonds of her conscious.

It is not easy to enter this state, but at its best the connections she seeks seem to slip into place like gears, as if she were discerning something already there for the first time; simple, obvious, irresistible. Most days though she just works, jobbing it, waiting for the moments of flow she knows are there, just out of reach. Nor does it last, always brief, always partial, the connections uncovered wont to slip between her fingers like water, the captured image seldom matching the glimpsed understanding within.

This is her third day here. Even on that first afternoon she knew she had found what she needed. At first Dylan was reticent, but when she told him she was happy to pay for access at the set rates he relaxed, speaking to the collections supervisor on her behalf. Now she has the run of the place for four weeks, time enough, she hopes, to complete the task that is beginning to form in her mind. But although she has access she is finding she cannot apply herself to the work. Every time the door to the specimen room opens she jumps, the skin on the back of her neck rising as she listens to the click-clack of the feet on the linoleum. In the halls of the Museum she finds herself constantly plagued by a sense of being observed, of eyes upon her, but when she turns she is always alone. The tips of her fingers alive as she traces the grooves in the examining table. And all the time it is him she is thinking of, the coiled danger she sensed in him, his separateness. The line of his mouth, its disdain.

Earlier, he passed the glass wall of the library. Anna looked up from the volume open before her to see him side by side with a man she did not recognise. The two of them deep in conversation. Reaching a staircase the other man ushered him towards the stairs, and the blind man turned, not losing the beat of the conversation, his free hand raised to emphasise some point obscured by the muffling glass. From the foot of the stairs his companion glanced back towards Anna, their eyes meeting for a brief second. Acknowledging her with a conspiratorial motion of his eyebrows, this other man smirked slightly, the gesture sickening in the casualness of its cruelty. The blind man starting up the stairs behind him, unaware.

And yesterday she saw him climb the stairs towards the staff door, his cane sweeping the steps before him. Below them the roar of the traffic, horns blaring. Each step taken deliberately, but with a certainty that seemed to attest to long familiarity. At the top he slowed, seeming to anticipate the low tap of his cane colliding with the glass of the door before it happened, extending a hand to find the metal handle, his fingers closing around it. Pressed into the doorway Anna was so close she could have reached out and touched him, but she did not. As he opened the door he paused, head dipping as if he were listening, then he was gone. Exhaling, she realised she had been holding her breath.

Afterwards, alone in the specimen room, she lifted a hand to her eyes, trying to blot out the light that leaked between her fingers. In that close-pressed, fleshy dark she tried to imagine his world, its strange disjunction of public and private, always seen, never seeing, but raising a hand in front of herself she found nothing but air.

As she finishes priming the camera she hears the door to the specimen room open, her body tensing at the remembered sound of the cane on the linoleum, the sharp report of his shoes. Following the sound of his feet she slips in beside the row of cabinets, angling her body so she can observe him. The hand still holding the primed camera pressed against her breast. He has opened a tray and is examining an ammonite, his brow knotted in concentration. As she watches he runs his hands across it, then pauses and taps his finger twice against the stone form of the shell. His obliviousness to her observation of this private moment exciting her, making her reckless, she raises the camera, framing him between the shelves, depresses the memory button. His face freezing at the tiny whirr of the motor, he spins towards her, one hand groping for his cane. As if his motion has broken a spell, Anna lets her hand fall and turns, fleeing for the door.

For every creature that lives, countless billions have died; for every species that walks or crawls or flies or swims, a million more have vanished. The bodies of the lost returning to the peaty darkness from which they were whelped, slipping downwards into the earth's embrace. Bone into stone, flesh into earth. The genetic memory of countless generations petering out to nothingness as a species vanishes, its extinction irrevocable.

Yet here and there fragments remain. The fossilised tracery of a fern in cool stone. A scaled and segmented insect, its chitinous wings unfurled, caught in the amber of an ancient tree. The ochre red of a toothed bird's feathers sunk deep in the shale. The enigmatic mark of a clawed foot pressed into river mud a hundred million years ago. The frozen forms of mammoth and bison entombed in the blue-white ice of the glaciers.

The crannied space of the earth a fabric woven upon the layered sediment of memory and forgetting, a tapestry, a palimpsest.

APOCRYPHA

· 3 ·

The distinction between the animate and the inanimate, the living and the non-living is an ontological fiction embedded at an almost primal level in human culture. But it is a fiction nonetheless: matter has an innate tendency to organise, to form patterns which move towards a state of criticality, a point between the rigidity of excessive order and the turbulence of randomness. Once in this state patterns will persist almost indefinitely, riding the edge of chaos like a surfer borne effortlessly upon the transition between the sameness of the unbreaking swell behind them and the potential disaster of the roil before them.

There are deep rules governing the behaviour of matter in such a state, and these rules are the same whether the system is a living cell or the spinning eye of a tornado.

SETH LaMARQUE, *The Language of Shells*

Curved Time

Discoveries made about the structure of space and time always react on the structure of the mind. Other kinds of discovery enrich human knowledge without affecting its basis. However, anything to do with conceptions of space will suggest very different ways of constructing knowledge. The discovery of America brought only a few names of rivers and hills, and a small number of geographical rarities like the Niagara Falls; it was not, in the end, an event for the human mind. But with it came the inference that the Earth is round, and heaven and thought, heart and reason, were thrown into disarray.

GASTON BACHELARD, *L'Expérience de l'espace*
dans la physique contemporaine

If I try to imagine him now, he slips away like water. Yet he has always been a part of me, his genes tangled within my own, our beings connected deep within by the spiralling poetry of our DNA. I have his hair—or had, it is biosynthetic now, like most of me, but once it was dark and thick—and although I cursed it for its unruliness, in truth I knew it was a gift. I have his forehead too, high, proud, and beneath it his bladed cheekbones. I was never a beauty, not like my mother, it was always him I took after. In my thirties I had some minor changes made, hoping they would bring my body closer to the image I held within my mind, and the harsher edges were shaved away, my face softened, the lips made fuller. But I left my eyes, perversely perhaps, because they were his. The eyes of a blind man.

My first memory is of his eyes. Sometimes it is hard to know what we remember, what we have imagined, but I remember this, I have always remembered this (although it occurs to me that this memory of always having remembered could itself be a phantom of the mnemonics, but I will not pursue this thought, for I fear that way lies madness). We were on Principe, in the Gulf of Guinea, so Anna could photograph the island where Eddington conducted his famous experiments. Sometimes I think I remember the island, the dark green rows of the cocoa palms whispering in the breathing wind as they dropped towards the blue glass of the bays, the aching white of the sand, although in truth I cannot be sure: in the porous space of memory images and sensations shift and run, one washing into another until nothing can be trusted. Perhaps this is why I occasionally wonder at the clarity of this particular memory; surely in the almost three centuries that have passed since that day it should have faded as so many other, more significant memories have, the raw stuff of it leaching away like a fading photograph. But memory obeys no rules: like the ocean it casts up its flotsam without sense or reason, so that sometimes the strangest things rise out of time's wash, cut free and floating to the surface as we fossick amongst and around. Two days ago I found myself humming a song the island women sang all those years ago, the Portuguese tripping off my tongue as if it were yesterday.

I do not know why I remember this day in particular, although it is certainly the first time I remember mersing. Hard as it may be for us to imagine now, the merse was still in its embryonic stages. Although its arterial networks enfolded the planet, they had hardly begun the outwards journey. Images ticked in from tiny probes that moved, antlike, across the silent Moon; from a relay orbiting the ice mountains of Europa; from the frozen deserts of Mars and the International Space Platform and from the high dome of the comets, far above the plane of the solar system; information pulsing and flowing through the satellite networks, permeating the air as the datapackets rode microwaves to mobile receptors, whispering along the twisting, glassy capillaries of fibre-optic cable as they branched and spread like the runners of a vine across the continents, beneath the ocean. Life had taken root there too, the digital equivalent of the first prokaryotes moving restlessly down the lines, feeding, changing, growing. Elsewhere the first wild Thinkers had awoken and begun feeling their way through the strata of their worlds. But despite these protozoic flickerings of the digital ecology, the endless complexity and variety that now permeates our world was yet to appear. Even the immersive technologies were in their infancy, many people still connecting manually, interfacing with the nets through the two dimensions of a screen, but it was spreading, not only as a technology, but as a concept, wreaking its effects on the culture and consciousness as surely as a virus does upon the genome. The human mind was being transformed, just as language had transformed it a million years earlier, accelerating its cognitive evolution, altering the species beyond recognition in little more than a flicker in the planet's history.

I cannot have been more than two, so my immersion was carefully chaperoned. Seth held me in his lap, and I remember Anna beside me, so tall, her avatar thinner, more formal than her corporeal body. I do not remember how we got there, just the goggles on my face, the momentary dislocation of slipping into the merse, a heartbeat of falling, then, almost instantaneously, it was around me, buoying me, lighter than water, but liquid; warm, like the womb I had barely forgotten enfolding me once more. I was aware of Seth's body beneath me still, but far away, like a voice calling from the other side of sleep. Then we were in a gallery, a circular space suffused with a deep blue shadow, its proportions possessed of the eerie perfection of geometry: transcendent, eternal. At its centre was a simple stand, made of what seemed to be the most flawless crystal, a font which was bathed in a light so soft, so beautiful that it made me ache to look at it. The topology was conventional, corporeal, but the matter of the place was like nothing I had ever seen before, fluid, each particle of its liquid oneness a node of meaning, able to be entered and explored, like a world constructed of mirrors, where each mirror is an idea, and within each mirror lie more mirrors, each opening into other possibilities, other places. Possibility refracted within possibility, outwards and inwards and upwards towards infinity's bounding in every direction. Around us a whispering, not a sound but a presence, the deep shadows of the space somehow shifting, as if ghosts moved unseen through its fabric. I doubt I understood the significance of what I was seeing, an object so immense in its implications that it had been re-created in countless virtual chambers just like this one; all I saw was the eidetic of the fossilised shell the Prometheans had excavated from that broken cliff face near the Martian equator, the one that was to become known as the First Relic. It stood on its crystal altar at the room's centre, the geometry of the room pulling the eye to it inexorably, barely fifty centimetres in diameter, although to my child's eyes it seemed much larger. At first I was frightened, something about its ali-enness viscerally abhorrent, my mind rebelling at some primal level just as we do when we are presented with the microscopic images of the visages of ticks and tapeworms expanded hundreds of thousands of times; disquieting imaginings of a diseased unconscious. Nervous, I drew closer to Anna. She did not let go of my hand, but she did not let me back away either. Instead she knelt beside me, lifted me towards it slowly. It's only a fossil, she said reassuringly, it can't hurt you, and taking my hand she placed it on the cool stone of its side. Touch it, she said, letting her hand rest there with mine until I was no longer afraid, and slowly, tentatively, I let myself begin to explore its contours, my tiny hands playing across the crenellated ridges of its spiralling curves, the armoured bumps upon the outer shell, the strange flanged maw of its opening and the six holes ranged around it, large enough for three of my child's fingers to enter, through which, five hundred million years ago, a tentacle had slithered and stabbed, as this alien hunter stalked its prey through the vanished Martian oceans. Gradually, as my hands explored it, I found myself no longer afraid, the relic's alienness not vanishing but being incorporated into a new understanding of its nature. The stillness of Anna's unbreathing avatar behind me. And then, finally, her hand on mine so that I turned, saw her smile tenderly.

It's beautiful, she said, isn't it?

Once we had ungoggled, I felt for the first time the strangeness of returning to the corporeal world from the virtual, its solidity and lack of association having been transformed in those few minutes from normality to something staler, flatter. Like coming down off acid or the gengineered *ayahuasca* we took in the 2030s, the world seemed so quiet, so two-dimensional after the sense of shifting possibility and webs of association that I sensed lay beneath the surface of the gallery's layered virtualities. Beneath me, Seth still felt solid, ungiving, not like the surfaces . . . inside? through there? Even at two I sensed at some primitive level that the words I knew could not accommodate what I had just experienced—it had been elastic, but permeable, like the skin of water, a surface tension that resists, then yields, then suddenly and without breaking, gives. I turned on his lap, reached up to touch his face. I remember the need to feel his skin, to explore the texture of it, suddenly strange to me even then. I needed to know whether my hands could slide through the surface of him, to know whether he was as solid as he had been before. Whether the world had been altered or only me. His face as grave as ever. And for the first time I pulled at his glasses, trying to dislodge them.

I saw him flinch, as if he wanted to pull away, but she touched his shoulder from behind me and, reaching over, carefully removed them, exposing the sightlessness beneath. I do not know what I expected, whether I expected anything at all; certainly I remember Anna telling me I never really understood what it was for Seth to be blind until much later, but I was surprised by the paleness of his skin beneath the glasses, the blankness of his gaze. Some of the blind had eyes that were repulsive to the sighted, staring, damaged, half opened, but Seth's were simply blank, dark like mine, but unfocused. When he was a child, Rachel, his sister, had coached him to keep them still, helping him learn the ways of the sighted, and like the good student he was he had remembered her lessons. His eyes did not dart around, his head did not bob. Wonderingly I ran my fingers around them, across the pulsing thinness of his lids, as wonderingly as I had explored the relic a few minutes earlier. This experience cannot have been a comfortable one, but he endured it without complaint, even, I like to believe, enjoying it. I have no doubt he loved me, in his own way, but his love was a private thing, rarely expressed overtly, as stern and proud as he was himself.

I do not know what thoughts passed through my mind as my hands wandered across his eyes and brow, the white line of his scars. I have no memory of whether his sightlessness seemed strange to me. All I remember is the gallery, the relic, his eyes.

The same eyes I see here in my mirror, all that remains.

November heat, the air as hot and still as glass. No wind. Even the gulls riding thermals above the cliffs seem to have fallen silent. At water's edge, the motion of the surf deep and slow as a sleeper's breath, the light chasing along the waves as they roll inwards, outwards. The nights clear and cool, the heat of the day bleeding upwards to space.

For four days she does not return to the Museum. The daylight hours spent on the beach, anonymous amidst the crowds, sometimes reading, sometimes sleeping, but mostly swimming or riding the waves as they roll ceaselessly in from the Pacific. Behind the laundry door in the apartment she finds a battered handski, dried sand still crusting its curved base. Brushing it clean, she clips it on, the way its angled shape extends her arm making her feel sleek and dangerous, sharklike. But in the confusion of the inner break it soon proves a liability, too easy to strike unsuspecting swimmers, so, fearful of accidental injury, she strikes outwards towards the farthest break, where the surfers pace each other back and forth over the hulking weight of the swell, the water darker, colder. Out here the waves are larger, more threatening, but it is quiet, the shrieks and laughter of the beach carried over the backs of the waves as if from far away, the surfers rarely speaking, watchful and silent as hunters. It is a long time since she has surfed, but she soon feels her confidence returning, remembering when to catch a wave and when to let it pass shorewards, the spume rising from its back as it recedes. Nor has she forgotten the way to surrender herself to the water, her body relaxing into its rhythms: the swift striking of the first strokes as the wave builds behind her, speed gathering as she unfurls into it, its momentum catching her and lifting her into a moment of gliding flight. The sculpted blade of the ski slicing the wave's glassy surface as she slips across it, the water seeming to rise against her as she shoots downwards. The sudden thoom as the wave closes over her, its face a curving dome of water she skids along, as it contracts inwards, quickly, always too quickly, as if time itself were hastening, its closure casting her down so the roil envelops her, pummelling her as it sluices around her, before she cannons out again, the wall of white bearing her forwards, elated and spluttering. Her skin deepening in the glare of the ultra-violet.

The evenings spent mersed, riding the ebb and flow of the data, enjoying the sense of dissolution, of possibility; or reading, sprawled on the bed, the balcony doors open to the night air. The sound of cars and jetliners mingling with the sound of the waves. Salt water drizzling in sudden floods from the cavities of her nose and ears, warmed to the temperature of blood.

But she cannot ride away the unease she feels coiling in her belly. Like a hidden shame the photos she took that afternoon in the specimen room lie unretrieved in the memory of her camera. She cannot forget the intensity of his face as he stroked the green surface of the stone, its inwardness. And try as she might, she cannot forget the sense that she was an intruder, that her act of raising the camera and capturing that private moment was a violation.

This is not a new sensation, this creeping shame about the trespass of photography. Even by the end of her student years she was unprepared to work with human subjects who were not models, and reticent even with those who gave themselves willingly, knowingly. After all, she did not enjoy the camera's intrusion, so how could she turn it on another? The only exception Daniel. This time though is different, worse, his blindness making her actions somehow more reprehensible, and not even the cool wash of the surf can cleanse her of this feeling of dirtiness, of besmirchment.

On Saturday she calls Jadwiga, needing someone to talk to, but Mathilde tells her Jadwiga is in Melbourne for a week. Fearful

Mathilde can see her unease, Anna rings off quickly, leaving no message. Alone again, she reviews her research so far, reading the notes she has made, trying to concentrate on the literature she has managed to find about shells and their symbolism, but she cannot concentrate and gives it away.

Still, she does not delete the shots.

Late on Sunday evening there is a rumble in the distance, more felt than heard, like a train passing beneath city streets. For several seconds she lies listening, a book open on the bed inside the crook of her arm. When it does not come again she walks to the balcony and looks out over the rooftops. But there is nothing there; only the lights of Bondi reflected across the sea's smooth surface, the half circle of moon pale above ribbed cirrus. And later the wail of sirens in the distance, rising and falling.

But Monday morning the feeds are alive with reports of a bombing in a Coogee minimart. Over video of firemen dragging hoses, and billowing smoke, a photo of the attendant killed in the blast is superimposed. An Indonesian student working nights, he grins behind glasses, his skin made almost black by the photo's overexposure. The Minister for Public Order, smiling and shirtsleeved on the doorstep of his suburban home, urges the Upper House to pass the government's new Suspected Offender Detention legislation, designed to bring New South Wales into line with the other states, as soon as possible, allowing police the discretion they need to deal with this sort of situation.

An hour later she is waiting at the Museum's staff entrance for Dylan, who arrives looking harried. Apologetically he explains he has to give a presentation to the media in an hour and a half as part of a PR exercise for a new bequest, the colleague who was to have done so having come down with the flu. When he asks her whether she minds if they postpone their talk to another day she shakes her head.

That's fine, she says, I understand.

If it's any help I can organise for you to have access to the library and the specimen room for the day instead.

If it's not too much trouble.

And so by mid-morning she is alone in the specimen room once more. From her codex she retrieves the reference numbers of the specimens she examined the week before, and one by one she gathers them from their shelves. It is a slow process, not hastened by her tendency to be distracted by other specimens sharing the shelves with the ones she seeks. Eventually though she has them all, along with several of the new finds.

One by one she places them on the examining table, taking several low-res shots of each. Then she shifts them about, examining different angles, waiting for something to catch her attention, for the colours, the textures, the play of light to resolve into something. What she is seeking is the moment of clarity where she feels the physical actuality of the object and the ideas her research has given her run together and, for a brief time, coalesce. The moment where, like the swirling rainbows of oil on water, these disparate threads knot together into an image that expresses, more eloquently than words ever could, this sensed understanding, this prearticulate, primitive meaning she feels moving within herself. A visual poetry that will capture this meaning, contain it, and, like the hum of a tuning fork, resonate with it.

Daniel once called this the click; that sense of sudden understanding, when the unformed, always just inaccessible stuff of the imagination suddenly intrudes into the world of the conscious. That moment when something new comes into being. Maybe rough, maybe only half-formed, but powerfully and undeniably there. Daniel had been talking about maths, and they were both drunk and a little high, but as he described the feeling of seeing a theorem or a proof bring an idea into focus Anna knew it was the same feeling her own work sometimes gave her.

She is closer today, she can feel it, but there is something missing still, something crucial. But she will not let go, wanting to try to force herself into this elusive understanding, so she does not back off, does not retreat, swapping one specimen for another, scrawling notes, drumming her fingers on the scarred wood of the table in frustration. Finally, dispirited and angry, she lays down her camera. There is a tightness behind her eyes, the beginnings of a headache, and distractedly she massages the bridge of her nose, but to no effect. Looking down at the mess in front of her she considers packing up for the day and heading home, but the thought of it is more than she can face.

Outside the mid-afternoon heat is almost liquid, the sun glancing off car windscreens and windows so she has to squint, even behind sunglasses. Each shard making her head throb. Across the road in Hyde Park it is cooler though, dappled light falling brokenly across the flagstones where they buckle and heave, pushed up by the questing roots of the dark-trunked figs. At an outdoor café in one corner of the park she finds a table in the shade, orders a sandwich she does not want. At a nearby table a loose group of men and women are talking and laughing, noisy despite the heat. Looking over, Anna recognises several of them from the Museum. One gives her a grin, waves, and Anna, hoping he will not cross and force her into conversation, waves back. She eats half her sandwich slowly, stolidly, barely tasting it, leaving the other half untouched, then sits in silence, not wanting to return to the Museum but stubbornly unprepared to give the day away.

Flicking through her codex she sees a note she made to herself about an exhibition by an artist she once knew which is being held not far away. Grateful for the excuse, she decides to take advantage of her proximity, hoping a couple of hours away from the fossils will help her headache.

The gallery is down an alley, a staircase descending suddenly between two buildings, before opening out into a wider space, from which heavy fire doors give onto an old goods elevator. In the stark whiteness of the interior the works are hung far apart, each print containing curving manifolds of pale flesh. Sunken deep in the curtaining folds of some sylvan gloom, their soft, almost erotic surfaces reveal themselves on closer examination to be the bodies of the victims of violent death, the delving architecture of the post-mortem—folded skin, cold, dark-blooded meat, a staring eye or the deep concavity of a blow—

seeming to resolve out of the blue-green light. The effect is unsettling, all the more so in the antiseptic cool of the gallery, and Anna leaves feeling dirty, jumpy, as if the paintings and their violence have seeped into her like a stain, leaving her cold despite the heat. The clamour of the street somehow unreal. Glancing from face to face as she hurries, pushing her way through the crush of people, she sees only grotes-querie, the loud, crowding, hectoring faces swinish, like the milling damned of Breugel's imagination, their lewdness a prefiguring of death. Looking around she is suddenly aware of watchful eyes and bodies, their secret language of signals and motions, of the beggars and the smacked-out, head-loose junkies lolling in the doorways, against walls or posts.

These streets have changed over the years. Once a grid of aban-doned office buildings, overhead wires and decaying second-hand shops, traffic choked in the space between them, over the last decade they have been transformed into the hub of inner city life, a place where upmarket eateries and designer shops jostle for attention along-side Chinese cinemas and merse galleries, market stalls and street ven-dors, brothels and strip bars and sex shops. As the hill drops westward, towards Chinatown and Darling Harbour, the tattoo parlours and bars give way briefly to crowded Chinese supermarkets and restaurants, vegetables and fish and meat displayed streetside on footpaths slick with the wash from hoses, the air thick with the stink of refuse.

As the area has developed it has become more expensive, more fashionable, high-rise apartments with private security climbing sky-wards, the upper floors of office buildings and warehouses converted to living space, ensuring a population that stays after dark, descending from homes far above to eat and drink in the restaurants and bars, a population that is mostly young, prosperous and successful.

But the area has another population too, an amorphous, shadow populace barely glimpsed by neighbours skilled at not noticing, not seeing. They are the ones huddled on street corners and doorways, sprawled on benches by bus stops and under trees in parks, drinking or sleeping or singing to themselves. They are the ones who sit in ragged lines along the sandstone base of the overpass the train rumbles along from Central to Museum Station. The ones who gather each night in the parks and empty lots to wait for the mission kitchens, faces turned to the exhortations of the preachers.

They are the people who fall through the census, who slip free of the interlocking databases of the banks and government, their mail returned to sender, address unknown, their phones disconnected, credit cards cancelled and bank accounts closed, the evidence of their lives disappearing piece by piece until one could think they had never existed at all, their fading traces no more than a chimera, a glitch in the webs of data. They are the ones who don't come back for second term, who walk out of prison and never look back, who wander away from the asylums and hospitals without thinking to say they are going. The ones who take lifts from strangers, bound for anywhere but where they are. Sometimes they flare back into life, made real again as their profiles pass through the police computers; sometimes they appear in the systems of the clinics, sometimes in the records of those few hospitals that admit the uninsured. But more often it is their DNA or dental records which identify them as they lie cold and still on a steel-topped table. Otherwise they are nameless, stateless, roaming through the streets and alleys, scavenging spoiled fruit and half-eaten takeaway from bins, hustling or begging or stealing for the rest, anxious for the next score, the next chance, wary lest they become someone else's. No-one marking their passage, so they pass unseen.

They are everywhere, of course, in every suburb of every city. Dislocated, unemployed, hungry, but it is places like this to which they are drawn. Some, like the hollow-eyed, scabrous junkies and the pale, fading crackheads come for the drugs, desperate to satisfy their numbing, all-consuming craving. Others come looking for a place to hide, where no-one knows them. Some just ride the trains to Central and never go back. The lucky ones find shelter in grimy squats and derelict buildings, others sleep in alleys or dumpsters, under cardboard in parks or railway stations.

But the winter before last a cardboard city began to grow in the broken shadow of the Brewery. Covering an entire city block, the site was to have become what the graffitied placard still describes as 'a new landmark in inner city living'. But in the aftermath of the crash the finance melted away like water, and the project ground to a halt. The jackhammers falling silent, the cranes dismantled, the site offices borne away to other, newer projects, until all that was left was the shell of the once sprawling building, tumbled masonry and girders, the rusting skeletons of the vats and pipes that wound through the complex. And when even the security companies abandoned their contracts for non-payment the homeless moved in, grateful for the shelter from the rain and the freezing south-westerlies that blew down from the mountains.

At first it was only a few of them sleeping rough on the broken ground, rain pooling around them as they huddled in, away from the winds. But gradually they multiplied, and come summer the shelters began to grow more permanent, tents and lean-tos constructed out of sheets of tin and plastic stolen from building sites; sofas and armchairs scavenged from the roadside; posters tacked to the broken brickwork. Of course local residents complained, so did businesses. But the Hong Kong developer who owned the site had collapsed into a bewildering maze of finance and leverage agreements, a tangled mess the courts are still, even now, trying to unravel. And the receivers have had little taste for throwing good money after bad simply to keep the site unoccupied. All in good time, they say, all in good time. But as the months have passed that time has come no closer, and the Brewery, as it has become known, has developed a strange, semi-official legitimacy. Left alone by the police and the council it goes its own way, largely unmolested.

The sun has fallen below the level of the city buildings by the time she reaches Hyde Park. The warm air rich with the scent of grass and blossom, a golden light soft on the walls of the buildings that climb the rise towards the Cross. On the stairs to the Museum the sandstone radiates heat across her face and body. But the staff entrance doors do not open automatically, and glancing at her watch she realises to her surprise it is after five. Peering through the doors she sees the guard is still inside, and raising a hand she knocks on the glass. The guard looks up, his momentary hesitation a silent rebuke, then presses a button, the doors unlocking with an audible click.

At Anna's request, the guard buzzes Dylan, but he is not in his office. Luckily the guard remembers her, and with a slight shake of his head agrees to let her go back in unsupervised. Thankful, Anna hurries past him and down the stairs, worried she will be too late. But when she reaches the door it is unlocked. Moving quickly, she begins shifting her specimens back onto the trolley.

She is only half done when a noise makes her start. A specimen clutched in her hand, she straightens, listening. For a moment nothing, then she hears it again, this time more clearly, the sound of a drawer being closed at the far end of the room.

Who's there? she calls, suddenly nervous. When there is no reply she feels her heart begin to stammer. She knows she could just leave, close the door and walk away, but she does not.

Then he is there, beside her, his thin form so close she could touch him.

Anna, he says, and it is not a question, more a greeting.

She swivels to face him, her heart pounding. Jesus! she exclaims. Do you always sneak up on people?

I'm sorry, he says, although he doesn't sound it. I didn't realise you hadn't seen me.

She stares at him, not sure how to respond and angry, as much at herself for having been so rattled as at him.

Were you working?

She hesitates, wary. Earlier, yes.

Photographs.

Research, she says, preparatory work. I'm not ready to shoot yet.

Dylan said you were interested in ammonites.

They're what I've been researching.

Why?

I'm sorry? she asks, her annoyance returning at his interrogative tone.

Why are you interested in ammonites in particular?

For a long time she stares at him. Do you have a name? she asks at last.

He lifts his arm towards her, hand outstretched. Seth LaMarque.

She looks down at his hand, its gracile fingers. When he does not withdraw it she reaches out and takes it, noticing as she does a network of white scars that run beneath it, around the palm and into his sleeve. As she releases it she suddenly wonders whether she should take the hand, guide it to the contours of her face, but does not. In that moment she has a sudden sense of the immensity of the gulf between them, of how little she understands of this strange, stiff man's world.

And what is it you do? she asks.

I'm a palaeontologist. I'm officially employed by the University, but I work here part of the time on attachment.

But you're . . .

Blind? I know.

How do you see the fossils?

He smiles gently. My research isn't primarily focused on fossils, although I can see them well enough with my hands, I'm interested in biological systems.

I see, she says, although she is not sure that she does.

And yours?

She shrugs. I think I'm still coming to grips with it at the moment. But there's something about the shells I'm trying to get at; they're more than just relics, or perhaps less; it's a muteness, like a letter or a . . . a poem, but written in a language we've forgotten. Does that make sense to you?

A great deal, he says. They're like ciphers, or closed systems of meaning. You can contain them, but you can't get inside, can't enter that system. It's not just a physical thing, it's something to do with the perfection of their form, their geometry, as well.

Despite herself Anna grins. That's right. I suppose you're going to tell me I've made the most banal observation imaginable.

No, he says. Not at all.

For several seconds they stand like this, unsure what to do next, as if some defence has been breached but neither is quite prepared to move past it. Eventually it is Seth who speaks.

Will you let me show you something? he asks.

Of course.

He steps past her towards the examining table she has been clearing. With his left hand he reaches across it, quickly exploring the remaining fossils in deft, fluid movements of wrist and finger.

These are the specimens you've been working with? he asks.

Some of them, she says.

As she answers he fixes upon one of them, a medium-sized shell, maybe twenty centimetres in diameter. It has been carefully cleaned, the surrounding stone pared away until only the shell itself remains. Anna knows it well, having spent some time examining it, delighted by the complex layers of ochre, brown and pale white crystal that comprise its various chambers. Drawing it towards him he turns it on its edge, quickly exploring it with his hands, face raised away from it, intent.

You see here, how the coils sit one upon the other? he says, playing his fingers along the spiral between the coils; and here—his finger tracing the lines where the chambers meet—the sutures, how their edges are divided into these U-shaped saddles? These are some of the signs we use to identify and classify the species. For a moment or two he turns the shell in his hands, examining it, cupping its weight, caressing it, as if it were a breast: warm, soft, liquid. Finally, he lays the shell back on its side.

Give me your hand, he says, his voice low.

Questioningly she looks at him, but his face is still raised, almost expressionless now. Tentatively she extends one hand, placing it by his, her index finger spanning the air between them. At the moment of contact he takes it in his, his palm covering the back of it. Her breath catching. She feels the pulse of his blood. Gently he lifts her hand towards him, places it on the folded spiral of the fossil. A slight pressure indicating this is where she should stay, he slips his hand back, his fingers sliding across her own, parting them one by one, opening her hand beneath his like a fan. Their bodies turning inwards towards each other, his breath against her brow.

Close your eyes, he murmurs.

Why? she asks.

Trust me, and to her surprise she does as he asks.

For a long moment nothing, then slowly he begins to move her hand across the shell's cool surface, guiding her around its spiral form, running her fingers along the circling marks of the sutures, coaxing them into the fissures that crease its form.

Tell me what you feel, he says.

I . . . she begins, then hesitates, words failing her. I don't know how.

Concentrate, he says, his voice lower, more insistent. As he speaks his hand turn hers along the spiral once more. Try to remember what you feel, the texture, the number of ridges. Remember what connects to what. Don't let your eyes dictate what you feel, let your hands see in their own way, with their own logic. Imprint what they see in your memory, then use your imagination to give that memory shape. Remember it like that and the shell will become part of you, something complete in your mind.

I've seen the way you walk through this room, as if you have a map of it in your head. Is that what you mean?

Yes, he says, his voice urging. Make the shell part of you now and it will never leave you, never.

As he speaks she realises she does not know where her body ends and his begins, as if they had flowed together, like mercury, like water.

These shells are a thread, he is murmuring, not through space, but through time; a warp running through the changeable matter of the earth. Once they breathed and swam, now their breath stains the stone, wets our hands across oceans of time. They are the earth's remembering of what was, and will not be again.

And then, without warning, his hand is no longer there, and Anna, startled by its sudden absence, gasps.

You've opened your eyes, haven't you? he asks, and Anna shakes her head, blinking in the glare of the overhead lights.

I'm not even going to ask how you knew.

He smiles, as if enjoying this small triumph.

Have you always been blind? she asks.

Always, he answers. Always. She does not reply, does not know how to. In the silence Seth touches his fingers to the glassless face of his watch.

I have to go, he says, but as he turns she steps after him, placing a hand on his arm.

How did you know it was me? Before, I mean.

He smiles. You wear the same perfume as my sister, he says, then slowly continues to walk away from her.

After he has gone Anna leans over the table once more, tracing the fossil's form with her fingers, slowly, gently. She has the sense that she has experienced something profound, a glimpse into another world she had never imagined. She is still there when the security guard enters the room, his steps ringing as he advances down the rows of shelves towards her.

We're locking up now, he says.

Pushing the shell away, she stands.

I'll be right there.

That night, although she has promised herself she will not, she opens her codex, accesses the scanner agent she has paid to search for Daniel, the scanner agent that has monitored the nets ceaselessly for the last year, alert for the digital equivalent of his footprint—bank transactions, identity checks, credit applications, passport controls or border crossings, airline tickets, police reports, parking tickets, pizza orders, net access, DNA matches from hospital patients or blood tests or morgues—anything that links to him. As the agent processes her encryption sequences she feels her heart beat faster, her finger drumming the side of the codex in a rapid tattoo, nervous despite her knowledge there will be nothing there, that the scanner would have contacted her immediately had there been a trace of any kind.

It was not always like this. In the days and weeks after the morning the PLA came rolling in from the mainland, the rumbling of the tanks breaking the still, humid air of the dawn, she chased his ghost through the streets and across the nets, searching frantically for some sign of him, some evidence that he was alive. Heedless of the danger, she criss-crossed the city time and again, never able to grow used to the shifting patterns of the violence, the surreal way one street could be awash with bodies, the low roar of the riot vehicles advancing through the broken glass and burning petrol, the hiss of the water cannons, the clamour of rioters as they collided with the shields and batons of the soldiers; while only metres away almost preternatural quiet reigned. The way the PLA could be jeered, pelted with food and broken masonry, yet only hours later be treated as heroes as they dispatched looters from shops and homes with live ammunition. The boutiques and department stores holding fire sales swamped by bargain hunters, while outside their Mercedes and BMWs were being overturned and torched by angry mobs. In the babble of the merse rumours spread like wildfire, as agitators and observers and businesspeople tried to keep track of events, or searched for loved ones, no-one ever sure what was true, what was not, who could be trusted and who was InfoSec. And as the markets began to collapse and capital poured outwards, taking banks and businesses with it, the merse hummed with the frantic passing of information, some reliable, some not; everyone trying to stay one step ahead of the maelstrom that was enveloping them.

Her only clue a ticket on a KLM flight to Ho Chi Minh. Booked the morning the tanks came, it was paid for in cash and then left empty when the plane departed only half an hour before the airport was closed. After that, silence.

The mystery of the ticket still haunts her, but in those first weeks it tormented her. It had soon become clear that no-one would talk to her; the Embassy staff deluged with other, more immediate problems, his friends either missing or fled, the University closed until further notice.

And so, alone in the tiny room in Western she had rented with the little money left accessible after her accounts were frozen, she became the prey of wild fantasies about his intentions, his fate, elaborate structures based on supposition and guesswork and liable to collapse without warning, leaving her alone once again with the cold fact of his absence.

Inwardly she knows that after this length of time silence can only mean one of two things—either Daniel does not want to be found, or he is dead, but part of her refuses to accept what even she knows to be true. Certainly her family; her mother, her father, Sophie, have tried to mourn, to move on, but unlike them, Anna will not let herself yield to the inevitability of his absence. There are lists of the dead his name is not on, she tells them; he was a foreign national, even Internal Security would not have killed him; he is hiding somewhere for reasons he cannot or will not share. But as the months have wound on without any word, the fight to hold this in, to contain the grief that she will not let herself feel has grown more consuming, until now she cannot let herself imagine that he might be gone for fear it will all fall apart, that she will come unravelled.

But most of all she cannot believe he is dead because she cannot accept that it could have happened without her knowing at some visceral level. She would feel it, she is sure of that, even now. There is something between them deeper than language, as ineffable, as undeniable as consciousness itself. He is half of her and she is half of him, that is clearer now than when he disappeared. Losing him would be like losing her reflection. Like losing herself.

We come from darkness: borne nine months in the deep space of the body, we float, suspended in the amniosis, dreaming sightless dreams, waiting.

Waiting.

The steady metronome of our mother's heart, the flickering echo of our own tracing the passage of the days and months. No space; just the inwardness of this liquid dark, a universe measured in the hot motion of blood, this palpating rhythm of twice-thumping hearts.

Then the womb ripped open, our soft, writhing form spilled squalling into the light. They say we cannot remember, that our body is designed to forget this moment, but in the depths of the mnemonics I have encountered it: first the lengthening incision of light coming like a hole torn in the shape of the world; then the harsh, booming, screeching clatter of sound. Then the icy chill of the operating theatre, the freezing air burning in my lungs, choking me. The clawed hands of the surgeon, their latex reek. A terror so huge words cannot give it shape: primal, utter.

In the beginning everything was one: time, space, matter; a singularity without dimension or age. Its symmetry perfect, complete. But then this singularity cracked, a flaw appearing in its oneness, then again, and again, time and space rushing outwards, multiplying, dividing, like the embryo bubbling forth from the egg's mad divisions, like God on the deep waters dividing light from dark. Like the disjoinment of birth.

They have a name for those of us born untwinned, who ride those months alone. Singleton. But in truth we are all singletons, cast out from the womb, torn free of that place where all is one, thrust into a world where we live alone, trapped in the prison of our flesh, imprisoned by words when all we seek is dissolution.

Perhaps this is why we forget, the oneness of the dark seared from our minds by the white fire of birth, perhaps we could not bear the knowledge of its loss. But we sense it, always, a lost knowledge that moves somewhere beneath, within. An absence touched only in the wash of dreams, in the red dark of sex. A longing we cannot articulate, cannot encompass.

But the blind remember. They are not born to light, to space. Their worlds assembled from the evidence of the skin, the hands, from sound and smell and taste, a manifold of sensation cast upon the darkness, enfolding, accretive, given shape by memory, by the endless beat of time. For the blind there is no space, only time: each place an arrangement of moments, a catalogue of remembered points measured out in the body's passage from one to the next, depthless, breadthless, colourless. The bodies of others an assemblage of the detail the sighted overlook too easily—the timbre of a voice, the rustle of cloth or the brush of wool, the gentle pressure of a hand around an arm. A lover's body a litany of taste, smell, touch, the rehearsal of its schema in memory like drowning.

And there is beauty in their darkness, shapes and patterns in time. The rhythm of the seasons, the rustling veil of the rain. The steady breath of the surf. This is the world that Anna glimpsed in the quiet of the specimen room, a world she cannot understand, but which, like the sun, she can only see out of the corners of her eyes.

Much later, alone in the apartment by the sea, she walks through the dark space of the living area. Moonlight, dappled and glassy, falls across the table's surface. Her outstretched hand moving through it like a body's passage through a phosphorescent ocean. Silence filling the rooms.

She cannot sleep tonight. The memory of Seth's hand moving like static across the back of her hand, her neck and face alive where his breath brushed her skin. This wakefulness almost sexual. Over the ocean filaments of cirrus thread the deeper blue of the night, the gibbous moon's pale light permeating them until they glow. The murmuring of a comedy show floats between the buildings, tinned laughter rising and falling on the edge of hearing. The scent of salt and frangipani heavy on the night air. Like something caged, she circles the room once more, her body hungry, urgent.

Outside the sound of the ocean moves through the streets like rain. Slipping under the railing at the end of the street she drops to the path below, its pale line picked out from the surrounding rock by the moonlight, ghostly. The shrubs on either side caught in luminous negative, leaves pale. Ahead of her the path drops into the cove, the darkness like a well, but as she descends it retreats, gradually resolving into a narrow band of sand, the broken surface of the rocks. Two boulders, the height of a grown man, cleaved open, their interiors honeycombed, like fossils of some ancient hive. The sandstone walls of the cove still warm with the sun's heat, even now, hours after dark.

On the beach the sand slips and squeaks beneath her feet as she walks towards the water's edge.

The memory of the ammonite's curve almost tangible beneath her hand, she closes her eyes, feels the darkness, touches it. For a long time nothing, then slowly, surely, she feels the world around her recede. Extending a hand, she laughs delightedly at the way her body seems to be dissolving, breaking apart, like beading water or quicksilver, its physical boundaries replaced by a web of sensation, a world unto itself, liquid, diffuse as light.

Taking an experimental step forward, she feels the water wash around her ankles, the sensation so intense she gasps. Something licks against her, weed or plastic, and she draws her foot back, steps away from the water. And then, her fingers fumbling blindly for the buttons of her shorts, she strips them away from her body. Her shirt next, sloughed off like a skin. She feels the breeze move across her, the down on her skin lifting against it, then, tentatively, she takes another step forward, alert to the way the sand seems to shift and grind beneath her feet, to the sound of the breaking waves, the shifting patterns of sensation unfurling all around her. The sand damp now, the ocean's water warm between her toes as they dig in, seeking purchase. Another wave, around her thighs this time, the water seeming to flow down her as it passes. Her crotch and nipples tightening as she moves deeper, the water rising about her with every step. And then she is in, sliding beneath the surface in a long, shallow dive, her swift, powerful strokes propelling her onwards, deeper. Her skin an immensity of sensation, panoptic, its surface the limits of the universe, curving to infinity in every direction, time expanding as space recedes. The water surrounding her, supporting her, no up, no down, as she pulls herself onwards, the suck of the surf dropping away as she goes deeper, the water growing chill. She remembers the images of Foster and Gromeko turning slowly against the backdrop of stars, their white-suited bodies and mirrored helmets floating, worlds unto themselves, wonders if this is what freefall is like.

But eventually her lungs begin to ache, and blindly she turns what she hopes is upwards. But her head does not crest the surface. Fear flicks her eyes open, instinctive, but the darkness is still there, surrounding her, no longer gentle, but threatening, water in her mouth, against her eyes. She feels herself kick convulsively, frantically, and even as she does she tries to clamp down her rising panic, years of swimming in treacherous surf having taught her the ocean will never forgive those who are afraid. Willing herself to be calm she strokes onwards, looking for some glimmer of light, trying to gauge which way is up, but she is too disoriented, and every way looks the same, her thin body too bony to float, her lungs burning, aching. And then suddenly she is lifted sideways by a motion in the water, pulled deeper, released momentarily, then thrown onwards in a great surge and down again, the remaining breath knocked out of her, so she gulps back on water, the ocean entering her in a rush, invading her, overwhelming her. Then the rip sucking her down again, something sharp against her skin. Cold now too. Things disconnecting, slipping away from her, and although she can feel the brine in her throat and lungs, it is as if it is no longer her body, as if time itself has slowed, her movements a ballet as ancient, as eternal as the motion of the stars, the wheeling planets. With sudden clarity, she realises she is drowning, the notion so ridiculous she wants to laugh.

How long this moment lasts she does not know, although somehow she is aware she is no longer fighting, that she has relaxed into the ocean's push and pull. A calmness pervading her as her consciousness seems to collapse inwards towards some kind of vanishing point, a singularity, time streaming after it from all directions. Suddenly, she feels the air, her head breaking the surface, dark water moving around her. Hungrily she gasps it in, great, gulping breaths which make her cough and retch, hot fluid streaming out of her as she flounders on the shifting surface. A wave breaks behind her, the foam preternaturally white in the moonlight, its force dragging her under once more, but this time she struggles to the surface.

Gradually orienting herself, she realises the rip has pulled her out past the first break into the channel, then thrown her back here, into the roil where the sea floor rises to the base of the cliffs. With long, unsteady strokes she begins to swim towards the rocks, her body aching and weak, the looming dark of the cliff face rising above her, the surface of the rocks revealing itself in retreating sheets of light as the moonlit water washes across it. With frightening ease, the swell lifts her onto a shelf of stone, weed slipping beneath her feet as the water drains away. Heedless of the way the rock slices and tears at her flesh, she claws her way upwards, towards the dry rock and sanctuary, her body racked by choking, sobbing laughter, water coming in gouts from her mouth and nose.

The next morning she wakes in a swelter, breath juddering, bolt upright in the bed. Something foul lingering on the edge of consciousness, a dream she cannot remember. The room baking hot, a long panel of sunlight lying crosswise on the bed. Her body awash with sweat. Kneading her temples, she stumbles to her feet, tripping on the sheet as she lurches into the bathroom, sipping greedily at the tap-warmed water.

Back in the bedroom she slumps down on the side of the bed, head cradled in her hands, fingers lost in her tangled hair. By her side the clock reads 10:47. She does not remember when sleep claimed her, only knows she has slept the too-deep sleep of summer mornings, waking groggy and enervated. With one hand she explores her throat, which aches as though sprained, then the grazes that sting her knees and along her forearm from the heel of her hand, her fingers recoiling from their tenderness. The night before returning in pieces, shaming her. Here in daylight, her behaviour seems little better than that of a child; irresponsible and absurd. She is old enough to know the danger of these waters, of any water, particularly at night, and with a rip. And then, when she limped back to the apartment, blood seeping from her hands and back and thighs, the phone ringing, the noise loud in the silence. Sophie's face filling the screen.

Anna? Why are you whispering? You weren't asleep?

No, she said. Not yet. As she spoke she shifted her weight, wincing.

Are you alright? You're wet.

I was in the shower, she lied.

There was a pause, then Sophie asked her how things were. The apartment?

Hearing the edge of reprimand in her elder sister's voice, Anna hesitated, not wanting this conversation to end in confrontation. It's fine, she said. No, better than that, it's beautiful.

And you?

I'm fine too, Anna said wearily.

Again there was a pause, longer this time. Anna, already feeling the inexorable slide of this conversation towards conflict and recrimination, decided to end it.

Was there something in particular you wanted to talk to me about?

I just wanted to know you were alright. You haven't called.

Sorry.

Have you been working, what have you been doing?

. . . I'm tired, Soph, it's late here.

From half a world away she heard Sophie's daughter's voice, demanding something from the next room.

I'm on the phone, Gwynny, ask your father, Sophie called. Gwynneth's voice coming back, sulky.

Please, Mummy.

No! Sophie snapped, her voice tense.

Then Sophie was back with her.

Look Anna, I'm worried about you. You can't keep wallowing in this, you have to let go. We all think so.

All?

Us, Mum, Dad. And you should call them. They say you never return their calls either.

Anna felt her jaw set, anger rising. I have to go, she said again.

Anna? You—

But Anna never heard what Sophie had to say, her finger pressing down on the end button. A moment later the phone pealed out in the darkened room, but Anna had already switched it over to vidmail.

Irritably, she begins to dress for her morning run, knowing even as she does that it is too late, it will be too hot, but determined to try nonetheless. But as she paces herself along the cliffs her breath comes raggedly, her body tired from lack of sleep, the sapping heat. On the cliffs past Bronte she can go no further and, gasping for air, stops, turns back. To the north the first fires of the season are burning, flames chasing from tree to tree, across gullies, down hillsides, the gusting wind turning the fires unpredictable, capricious; but on the cliffs it is quiet except for the squawking of the gulls, the lapping water. Overhead, ash drifts against the empty sky, flakes falling to dapple the glassy sea.

Something about the studied way they avoid each other's space, the way Dana's eyes follow Dylan's hands and mouth, tells Anna they were once lovers. In normal settings it might not have been so noticeable, but here, in the cramped space of the espresso bar behind the Museum, the fastidious way they hold themselves apart is made apparent by their forced proximity.

When this realisation first dawned on Anna a few minutes before, she wondered why Dylan had brought his colleague along. But as he finishes an anecdote about his disastrous holiday in Syria the year before last, she catches his eyes on her, probing, and realises she has misunderstood; this lunch is not about him and Dana but about her. She is not helping Dylan make an uncomfortable situation easier, he is presenting Dana to her as a sort of trophy. Although surprised by the look in his eyes, she does not let herself show it, laughing politely at his anecdote then, in the silence that follows, asking about Seth, enjoying the flicker of disquiet that passes across Dylan's face.

What about him? Dylan asks.

I don't know, what's he like?

When Dylan does not reply, Anna turns to Dana, who looks away.

What? Anna asks. You two don't like him?

It's not that, Dylan says. He's . . . difficult—

Intolerant, Dana interjects, her voice cold. Rude, vindictive—

Dylan places a hand on Dana's, his eyes warning. He made a complaint about Dana when she was an intern.

It doesn't matter now, Dana says, her voice tight. But watch out for him, he's got a vicious streak.

Surprised at the venom in the younger woman's voice, Anna decides not to pursue the question. Angrily Dana drinks the last of her coffee and declares she has to get back. Standing abruptly, she says goodbye to Anna, her voice curt, and leaves.

Once she is out of earshot Anna looks at Dylan questioningly.

I've never got the full story, he says, but I suspect there was something between them. He pauses meaningfully. Whatever it was, though, she's not the biggest fan of the guy.

I can see that, Anna says. And you?

He shrugs. I don't actually have a lot to do with him. Occasionally he asks me for help with the odd specimen he can't identify by hand, or to find old paper records his codex can't read out to him or transfer to Braille, but it's amazing how much he can do without me—often he can identify a specimen faster than I can.

You said he was difficult.

That's not quite the right word. He's . . . contained, I guess: professionally and personally. I sometimes think that's one of the reasons he gets people's backs up—he doesn't need their help and he's got a bit of a tendency to let that show. And his being blind somehow makes that worse. Why do you ask? Have you been reading one of his books?

Anna shakes her head. I met him in the specimen room. He seemed interesting.

Dylan snorts, not altogether kindly. I suppose 'interesting' is one word. When he continues his tone is meditative. He's quite brilliant in his own way, although I'm not sure that what he does actually qualifies as science. It's weird, almost hermetic stuff about the inner structures of nature.

And shells?

Dylan looks up at her. That's right.

Where could I get his books?

I've got one of them in my room. Drop past and pick it up before you go. Reaching out he takes her hand, turns it to examine the scratches inflicted by the rocks two nights before.

Where did you get this?

She pulls her hand away. In the surf, she says, her voice flat and expressionless.

Declining his invitation to walk back to the Museum with him, she stays at the table, preferring the lunchtime jostle of the espresso bar to the silence of the specimen room. But as she swigs at the long neck of her mineral water, she can feel the eyes of others upon her. She knows this sensation well, just as she knew the look in Dylan's eyes earlier, the nakedness of his desire. All her life her lithe body, the strange angles of her face and throat, have drawn men, sometimes women, to her. As a teenager the men were usually older, their heavy, hairy bodies finding excuses to press themselves against her in lifts and queues, their cars slowing to idle beside her as she walked the leafy streets between her parents' Woollahra home and her school in Darlinghurst, the too-close attentions of her friends' fathers. And always the pressure of eyes upon her, the unwelcome slither and grab of roving hands, the whispered obscenities and shouted lewdnesses.

For Daniel it was the same, his androgynous beauty even more luminous than her own, the almond-shaped eyes deeper, his knowing mouth more affecting amid the spare planes of his face. But Daniel learnt sooner than she how to use his beauty. There were always girls, although he hardly seemed to notice them, but he knew other things too, things that frightened Anna at fifteen. How to look at the men without his parents or friends noticing, how to return their gazes with enough ambiguity to keep them watching. Often he would come home with small gifts—ice creams and chocolates, then later CDs, even money—until one afternoon, not long after their fifteenth birthday, he arrived home late after school, clattering into the house and upstairs without stopping. Perturbed, Anna followed him, only to find him sitting on the corner of his bed, his body huddled over his legs. On the floor was a new Discman, still in its box. When she asked him where it had come from he looked at her, eyes dark with fury, told her he had found it in one of the alleys behind William Street, abandoned by some junkie. And although he did not look away, did not flinch, she knew he had lied to her.

That day was an ending of sorts. Outwardly little had changed: they were still bound together by their uncanny sameness, their shared beauty, the exclusivity of their coded gestures and intermingled lives, but beneath the facade things were changing. They spent less time together and, when they did, Daniel was often sullen and withdrawn. Once they had spent their evenings working together on their homework; now Daniel spent the time alone in his room, listening to music and reading manga comics over and over. For a long time he skated by nonetheless, cribbing Anna's homework in the mornings before school or relying on his natural ability in tests, but eventually his marks began to falter. Their parents, worried about him, asked her many times if she knew what was wrong, but Anna, loyal to him, parried their inquiries, pleading ignorance or lying. In their finals Daniel scraped bare passes in every subject except mathematics, in which he topped his year, and although his marks overall were insufficient to get him into university, a dispensation to study maths was eventually organised three weeks into the academic year.

Anna, meanwhile, took a place at the School of Arts, specialising in photography. She had become fascinated with the camera and its power in her second to last year at school, enjoying it at first for the distraction it offered from her more academic subjects, the way her photography course allowed her to leave the school grounds and roam the streets looking for subjects. And perhaps also for the sense it gave her of a world unconnected with Daniel, an activity he did not share with her, his increasing alienation from her frightening her more than she cared to admit. But it quickly became something more than a schoolgirl's distraction, the subtle predatoriness of the process touching upon some deep-seated need, so that by her final year she knew she had found something that made her feel adult, complete. And safe. For with the camera in her hand she was released from the gaze of those around her, a watcher at last, not the watched.

At nineteen this alone would have been enough. As she grew older she had found the constant attention her beauty attracted oppressive. But beyond the desire for anonymity she found something else, a pleasure in the coolness of the photograph, its impassivity. She found calm in her work, retreat, the noise and unpredictability of the world she inhabited somehow distanced by it. And slowly this coolness began to become part of her, an imperturbability as deep as it was still.

Over the years she has learnt the irony of this protective distance; the way this separateness, this unattainability, is itself alluring, a challenge many men find irresistible. Sometimes it is nothing worse than an attraction to women who are independent, but other times it is something more primal, less gentle; an urge to mark, to defile. But it remains nonetheless, a barrier as purchaseless as glass. Or water.

The book is slim, little more than a monograph, its dust jacket bearing the image of a counterpart, the curved teeth of the sutures raised like weals upon the soft grey of the stone. In the corridor outside Dylan's office Anna traces its spiral with two fingers, the matte finish of the photo pulling gently at her skin as they circle inwards.

She reads it twice that day. The first time quickly, and then, that night, more slowly, the bedside lamp's light warm against her nape and shoulders. She is not sure what it was she was expecting, but not this. Not this strange, almost marmoreal prose, the beautiful parsing and rhythm of the words. The first time through, particular sentences keep arresting her, the images resonating with something far below the verbal, but the second time they seem to come alive, a lived understanding threaded through them. As she reads she can see what Dylan meant; this is not quite science, at least not science as she has always understood it. Just as individual words, hard little things of light and dark or sound against silence, can combine to create the prism of a poem's space, so this seems to be using science to build an understanding of the universe's patterns, a poetry of life, something rich enough to encompass its flux and ebb through time and space, an understanding of it as a totality, not a collection of parts. And like a poem the book seems to refract within itself, implications moving like cloudshadow through the words, hinted at, almost tangible, but elusive. At its centre lies the sibylline beauty of the shell, and like the shell's spiral, the text seems to move constantly around itself, never closing, living on in her mind.

When she has finished reading it for a second time she closes the book, raises it to her mouth, drinking in the smell of the paper. The rough-cut pages like a feather against her lips. The book is a beautiful artefact in its own right, a designer's fantasy of an eighteenth-century essay, the elegant lines of the antique font, their elongated ascenders and descenders pressed deep into the creamy paper with technology designed to emulate the almost lost art of hot metal setting. As she read she felt the depressions beneath her fingers, tactile, and marvelled at the appropriateness of this conceit. On the inside of the dust jacket there is a photograph of Seth, half in shadow, eyes masked by his glasses. His cavernous face like one of Caravaggio's soldiers or saints, a violence lurking beneath the almost erotic beauty of its bony lines, the scar across his lip hinting at a cruel sensuality held in check. Looking at it now, she feels something that troubled her about the book begin to slide into place. There is something in its pages, not quite a coldness, but a distance, an indifference, a sense that its beauty, its obvious passion is somehow unconnected to the individual objects of his contemplation. And the more she turns this thought in her mind the more it troubles her.

This disquiet has not left her two days later when she rounds a corner in the Museum's basement and finds him waiting by the closed doors of the service lift. At the sight of him she stops, shrinks back into the corridor, one hand raised to the wall. He stands turned away from her, the gauntness of his tall frame visible beneath the tailored lines of his jacket. His left hand grips his cane, held parallel with his leg, his right rests upon the satchel he wears across one shoulder. As if aware of her presence he turns slightly, and she glimpses his face in profile, the long nose, the angularity of his cheeks and brow. His dark hair pushed back behind his ears. Anna remembers Dana, the sudden flare of her anger in the espresso bar, Dylan's suggestion that the two of them were lovers. Could they have been? she wonders, trying to imagine this strange aloof man and the straightforward Dana together. The thought seems incongruous, but Dana's anger was so sudden, so irrational. And there, within this thought, another, a desire that walks across her skin, along her spine. Anna wants to know what it would be like to have his hands upon her body, his mouth against hers. Her breath coming shallow, quavering.

Then the lift chimes, the doors swinging open. He hesitates for a moment, listening, then steps forward, the doors closing on him with a clatter. Her heart loud in the shallow cage of her ribs.

. . .

Back in the silence of the specimen room she cannot concentrate.
Although she has begun to select the specimens that are to be her subjects, she feels no articulacy, the grammar of this project coming to her
crude and misshapen, her preliminary shots mute and clumsy. Her
frustration only made the keener by the knowledge that there is
something here, something powerful and unrealised, the memory of
her hand exploring the shell's shape, that fleeting glimpse of another
way of seeing moving just out of reach. And so she pushes the specimens back and forth, adjusts lighting, constructs shots, but it is artificial and mechanical and she knows it. Each time the door opens she
jumps, wondering if it is Seth; and each time it is not she is unsure
whether she is relieved or disappointed.

At five o'clock she packs her things, walks out into the smothering
heat. The sky overhead is grey and flat, the sound of the rush-hour
traffic almost overwhelming. She has always enjoyed the feel of these
summer Fridays, their sense of the week ending; people spilling into
the streets from offices and shops, music rising in the dusky light,
schoolkids with bags on their shoulders hurrying here and there.

Away from William Street it is quieter, the roar of the traffic dying
away, replaced by the burble of talk, the pulse of music from the open
doors, jacaranda blossom falling across the street in pools of colour.
The fetid stink of rotting garbage mingles with woodsmoke from a
pizzeria, cat piss with the smell of cut flowers crowded into buckets
on the kerbside. On Stanley Street she wanders alongside the open-
fronted cafés, eventually spotting an empty table at a place she used to
frequent and, moving quickly, claims it as her own. But as she does she
hears a voice that is suddenly, unmistakably familiar. Turning, she sees
him standing just behind her, his arm hooked through that of a
younger woman who meets Anna's eyes, her gaze frank and direct.
Thrown, Anna glances from her to him and back again. There is a
moment when she knows she could sit, pretend she had only stared

from the surprise of seeing a blind man, but she hesitates too long, and it is gone. Next to her Seth tilts his head to one side.

What is it? he asks his companion. But before she can answer, Anna steps towards him.

Seth, she says, it's me, Anna. When he does not respond, she adds lamely, From the museum.

He smiles. Yes, I remember. This is my sister, Rachel, he says, indicating the woman by his side, who holds out a hand.

Keenly aware of the intentness of the other woman's gaze, Anna takes the proferred hand. I'm alone, she says, gesturing to the table behind her. Would you like to sit down?

Rachel touches Seth's arm. Seth?

Thank you, he says, that is if you don't mind?

Not at all.

Rachel places his hand on the back of a chair and he seats himself. Side by side their physical resemblance, although more suggestive than overt, is unmistakable. Like her brother, Rachel is thin, although as she lowers herself into her seat Anna cannot help but notice the thickness in the other woman's waist, the pregnant press of her belly against the tailored front of her trousers. And where Seth's looks are oddly angular, hers are softer: the high cheekbones less prominent, the mouth kinder, set in a half smile that suggests a wry humour. Her dark hair falling sleekly around her shoulders. But it is her eyes that Anna is most struck by, deep, liquid, the pupils almost black.

Do you work at the Museum? Rachel asks, glancing between the two of them.

No, Anna says, I'm a photographer. I'm using the Museum's collections for a project I'm working on.

Would I have heard of you?

Anna inclines her head slightly. Probably not.

And the project is . . . ?

Fossils, sort of *memento mori* stuff.

Sounds fascinating.

If it works it might be, Anna says, demurring. She has never enjoyed discussing her work, particularly not with strangers. Rachel is about to ask something else, when to Anna's relief a waiter appears, Seth stiffening when Rachel orders a macchiato. As soon as the waiter is gone he leans towards her.

You shouldn't be drinking coffee, he says, his voice low.

I really don't think a coffee's going to do either of us any harm. It's the booze I've got to stay away from.

And the cigarettes.

Rachel glances towards Anna. You see what I have to put up with? she asks with a grin.

How far in are you?

Just past five months.

Boy or girl?

She shrugs. I asked them not to tell me. I wanted it to be a surprise. And anyway, it gives Seth something else to complain about.

Next to her Seth snorts affectionately.

As they talk, Anna watches the two of them, their physical likeness becoming more pronounced the longer she is with them. But it is not just the physical similarity that unites them, it is a certain intensity of attention, a tendency to pause momentarily before responding to a joke or a question, an odd directness in their questions, and in Rachel's case, her gaze. A physical closeness too, Rachel's hand moving constantly to Seth's, touching it: to emphasise a point, to direct a question, to guide it towards something. Watching them, Anna cannot help but think of Daniel, his fading reflection of her.

Then suddenly Rachel is standing, excusing herself.

What is it? Seth asks.

Nothing, she says, just a bit of nausea.

Do you want me to come with you? Anna asks, realising Rachel has turned pale benath her tan, but Rachel waves her down.

I'm fine, she says. Just give me a minute.

Once she has gone Anna stares at Seth in silence, suddenly uncomfortable alone with him.

Did she look sick? he asks.

A bit, she admits.

Seth does not reply.

Has she been sick much?

Probably more than she admits. She keeps things from me.

Anna does not reply. She senses her earlier answer has not satisfied him, that he suspects her of keeping things from him. And indeed, his blindness seems to provoke a protectiveness in her, a desire to disguise unpleasant truths, to tell the same smothering lies one might tell a child. Yet he is not a child, a fact the edge of anger beneath his last remark demonstrates, and she senses that to treat him thus would be an act of foolishness. His warmth has gone, the edge of menace she felt the first time she encountered him apparent once more. His rigidity has returned too, and he sits stiffly upright and immobile in his chair. A slight tic plays across the scarred ridge of his lip, a tremor that twitches once or twice, then stops.

What is it? he asks irritably.

Nothing, why?

You've gone very quiet.

She hesitates, not wanting to admit she has been watching him, fascinated by the shifting weather of his moods. His changeability frightening her. Where, she wonders, is the man who took her hand only days ago, initiated her into the silent space of the stone?

Then Rachel is back. She looks pale, and her eyes are red as if she has been sneezing. Or retching, Anna thinks to herself.

I'm sorry, she says, I think I'm going to have to go.

What about the recital? Seth asks, his voice hard.

I'm sorry, Seth, Rachel says, I just don't think I'm up to it. Maybe Anna could take my ticket. She looks inquiringly at Anna.

Anna hesitates. Seth and Rachel have tickets for a program of sixteenth-century religious music by a Russian ensemble later in the evening.

If you don't use the ticket it'll only be wasted, Rachel says, looking as if the conversation is wearying her.

Anna glances from one to the other. At least let me pay you for it, she says, reaching for her bag.

Don't be ridiculous, Rachel says, I'd rather it were used.

Anna returns from walking Rachel to a taxi to find Seth has opened his codex, one hand resting lightly on the table in front of him, enclosed in a glove. He gives no sign that he has noticed her approach, but as she reaches for her chair he asks, Was she alright?

Startled, Anna jumps. I think so, she says. She said it was just morning sickness. Sitting down she watches his gloved hand moving slightly, the fingers sliding right, then left, then back again.

What's that?

It's a Braille interface, he says, unpeeling the glove. Same principle as any of the tactile interfaces, except it produces Braille across the fingertips.

I see. Can't you just use speech software?

I do, he says, folding the codex and glove away into their case, his fingers finding the catches and stays with quick, practised movements. But speech is slow; I read much faster than my codex can talk. So I use this for most things. Computers have been a huge boon for people like me, although that may be changing—it's practically impossible for me to access a lot of these new immersive virtual environments.

I suppose it must be, Anna says, as he slips his codex back into his bag. She finds it jarring, the way he can seem so helpless, so dependent on others, yet a moment later reveal a glimpse into a world where he is independent and in control.

The codex gone, the two of them are left alone. Although Seth's face betrays nothing, Anna has the sense that he, too, is nervous, unsure what to say or where to start. They know so little about each other. She picks up a sugar sachet and begins folding it, the sugar within straining against the paper as it is compressed until finally the sachet ruptures, sugar spilling onto the tabletop.

What do you think of Rachel? Seth asks as Anna sweeps the sugar grains together, arranging them.

Something in his voice makes her cautious. Why?

Instead of answering immediately, Seth raises his glass to his lips. He drinks, several shallow sips, the gesture calculated, theatrical.

I sometimes think people find her a little off-putting, he says at last, replacing the glass on the table. Her personality can be a bit . . . forceful.

Not at all. What does she do?

Seth smiles thinly. She's a solicitor at a drop-in centre near Central. Junkies, street kids, homeless people. His lip curls back as if he has tasted something unpleasant.

You don't approve?

She was top of her year at law school, she has a doctorate from Cambridge, but she's worked in a succession of refuges and drop-in centres. Legal Aid was the most salubrious job she's had, at least until the government closed it down.

Is it the job or the people she works with you don't like?

I'm not sure I see the distinction, he says coolly.

For several seconds Anna does not reply, something curdling within. This tone of disdain is one she has heard many times amongst Jared's friends, but to hear it in Seth's voice is a shock.

These people can't help what life makes of them, she says, voice low.

I did.

Oh come on, she says, it's not that simple: no-one chooses to be on the streets.

She was held up, just last week. There were four of them, it was after hours, and she was alone. She let them in because they said they needed help, and once they were in one of them grabbed her from behind while another held a syringe of blood at her throat.

Oh God, Anna says. They didn't inject it though? She wasn't hurt?

She was lucky. But next time, who knows?

She must have been terrified.

These people don't care who they hurt.

Anna is about to object, but thinks better of it. Is she married? she asks instead. Or—

No. Neither.

Then who is the baby's father?

Seth does not reply, but in his lip the tic she saw earlier flickers once more.

Seth?

I don't know, he says, his voice flat. She decided to keep the father a secret. I think the father deserves to be informed.

You mean she hasn't told him?

No.

Is that fair?

If it were me I'd want to know. But she says she's the one who carries the thing, and he could just as easily have been a turkey baster.

To her surprise Anna sees the ghost of a smile on his face.

I suppose that's true, she says, chuckling.

Indeed, says Seth, chuckling now too, I suppose it is.

In the Concert Hall the singers file in towards the pool of light that falls in a widening shaft from above. All of them, men and women alike, are dressed in black, the austere lines of their suits expressing the asceticism of another time through an androgyny which is thoroughly contemporary. Their thin faces masklike beneath their brutally cropped hair. Without speaking they assemble, and at a gesture from their conductor, begin.

Ten minutes earlier, reading the program notes' claim that the singers see their music as the creation of something transcendent, a lived connection to the divine, Anna had wondered how any Russian could believe in a God who has visited such misery and turmoil upon their homeland. But as they sing, the music rising upwards through the shaft of light, she understands the allure of such purity, its capacity to offer faith, even in the face of death, its simultaneous yearning for transcendence and knowledge of its impossibility. The music is like a layering of light upon light, a complex prism through which a litany of human pain and exultation is refracted. After a time she turns to watch Seth, his ugly-handsome face still, as if the music has entered his body, inhabited it. With a flicker of guilt she takes advantage of his blindness, allowing herself time to study the strange cast of his features. With her eyes she follows the line of the scar that runs through his top lip upwards, realising for the first time that it is part of a longer scar that passes over the bridge of his nose before vanishing under the right lens of his glasses. Another bisects his left eyebrow, a third slicing sideways across his chin. All of them so pale they must be very old. Earlier, he asked her to read the program notes to him, his brow knotted in concentration. Partway through he placed his hand on her arm, and she stopped, looked up, and somehow grasping what it was he wanted, repeated the sentence she had just read.

Once the recital has finished, they climb to the Opera House restaurant, the internal structure of the chambered space rising above them, its joists like immense ribs or bones. Seated by the windows they eat rock oysters, the slippery gobbets of taste cold against their mouths. Outside, across the dark space of the Quay, the Passenger Terminal is filled with golden light, the green-lit span of the Harbour Bridge behind it. As they eat they talk quietly, of the music, of Seth's work and, briefly, of hers. Not long after they sit down several of the singers enter: dressed casually they look less monastic. Anna watches them take a table, smiling and laughing.

The singers are here, she tells Seth, leaning close so her voice does not carry, but he barely acknowledges the remark. Feeling rebuffed she withdraws. He sips at his beer. It occurs to her that his lack of interest might be more than just self-obsession, that his experience of the music might be somehow independent of them, like a recording, but still his dismissal rankles.

Then, when they are finished, and the restaurant has almost emptied, they stand to leave. Several tables away Anna sees the singers have also risen, and as they move slowly towards the exit their paths converge. At the door one of them, a small woman with dark hair and a tiny, birdlike head, notices them approaching and with a gesture moves her companions aside, allowing Anna and Seth to pass. Beside her, Anna stops.

The performance was wonderful, she says. This close the woman is older than Anna had initially thought, furrowed lines crinkling the corners of her mouth and eyes. The prominent structure of her cheekbones made more fragile by the ageing skin.

Thank you, she says, then looks at Seth.

And you, she asks in her heavily accented English, what did you think?

Anna feels him stiffen.

One of you has a burr on the lower registers, he says.

Anatole, she says with a chuckle. He has a throat infection. It is good you notice, you are the hardest kind of audience. She raises a hand to his face and moves it in front of his eyes. No distractions.

Watching the woman's hand, Anna feels a flicker of distaste, a sense that this action is somehow a violation of his privacy, whatever its intent. When Seth does not respond she pulls on his arm, eager to be away from this woman and her unsolicited intimacies.

Thank you, she says again, less warmly this time.

No, says the woman, smiling beatifically, thank you.

Outside the hot air is almost liquid, heavy with the salt smell of the harbour. Somewhere eastwards thunder rumbles, and Anna suggests a taxi, but Seth says he would rather walk for a while; he likes the pregnant fullness of the air, the scent and sound of the approaching storm. Turning away from the city they walk out along the promenade beside the Opera House, towards the point. Above them the sails are phosphor pale, luminous and fragile against the dark cloud, the lights of the city spread across the water to their left, the neon of the signs and the halogen immensity of the towers pooling upon its surface, rupturing like the liquid fabric of a dream each time a ferry or a Jetcat passes. Out on the point the crowds are thinner, and they walk more slowly, their bodies close. The sound of Jamaican timpani drifts across the water from the nearby quay. Overhead, galvanic veins of lightning dance within the clouds, each flash illuminating the distant coves of the harbour in shifting patterns of glaring white, ghostly.

On the outer edge of the promenade a Javanese shadow theatre has been erected, a lamp behind the fragile fabric of its surface outlining the elaborate shapes of the puppets. A small crowd has gathered, and Anna watches the puppets, sinister and beautiful, dance and sway, the stylised movements unfolding with the irresistible, hypnotic logic of a nightmare. The gusting wind shaking the screen intermittently, so the figures twist and distort, darkling reflections caught in a sideshow mirror.

Do you ever feel as if you're not quite real? she asks, watching the puppets dart and parry. As if you're watching your life from outside?

For a long time he does not answer, his face still, impassive.

I know some blind people who spend most of their time on the nets, he says, because there it doesn't matter that they can't see. Some of them say it's no different from real life, they can talk and travel and even have sex if they've got access to a skinsuit.

And you?

I envy them. But I don't want it. It seems like defeat to me, like retreat.

But? she asks when he does not continue.

But I still don't have what they have there. I'm not sure I can even imagine it.

As he speaks a brief scattering of heavy raindrops spill across the cobbled ground. Feeling them on her cheek and arm, Anna looks up, where the cloud's dark bulk hangs so low it seems it might catch on the sails of the Opera House. Beside her Seth wipes at his face, a drop beaded down the lens of his glasses. The rain melting back into the hot air almost as soon as it strikes the ground.

Taking his arm she draws him away, back towards shelter. Although they barely speak she can feel his body beside her, its closeness. She has the sense she has just been offered a glimpse of something few see, one that has surprised him as much as her. Finding a taxi, they slide into the back seat, their bodies parting, then touching, then parting once more. In front of them the driver hangs a cigarette out his window, the smoke snatched away into the air as he drives. But while Seth gives him directions, his heavily lidded eyes watch Anna in the mirror, unblinking.

Seth's apartment is in a backstreet of Surry Hills, only a few blocks from Jadwiga's gallery. The taxi pulls up, and Anna gets out to help Seth into the street, but he slips free of her arm, unfolding his cane and walking towards the building, leaving her to follow. Somewhere down the street music can be heard, and behind it, not far off, the rumble of traffic. In the darkness of his doorway Anna watches him produce a key, insert it in the lock. She is aware of the taxi driver watching them, but she does not turn to him, not wanting to give him the satisfaction of knowing he is bothering her.

Thank you, she says, I had a wonderful evening. And thank Rachel for me.

I will, he says. Their bodies so close now they are almost touching, but they do not. She wants to reach out, to touch him, but something in his manner warns her not to.

I have to go, she says, the taxi's waiting.

From the shadow of the gateway Anna watches the taxi turn, its lights shearing across the cream frontage of the flats opposite her block, relieved to be out of it. All the way back the driver staring at her in silence, his eyes in the mirror like something dirty, his anger palpable. Once she had paid him she opened the gate and stepped inside, into the darkness of the garden, watching the driver sitting in the lighted space of the cab, attention concentrated on the screen beside the wheel. At first she was worried he would not leave, but eventually he swung the cab around and away. Slipping back out into the street she watches the red glow of the taillights vanish around the corner. For a long time she stares after it, then, arms folded across her chest, she walks slowly away down the narrow street towards the cliffs. The streetlamps and houses dark, whether from the lightning or some other cause she does not know, but when she reaches the bottom of the street she sees it is dark in Bondi too, and southwards for as far as she can see. At the cliff's edge she finds a ledge of stone and sits, the wind pulling at her like unseen hands. Halfway back from the city rain fell, torrential, but here it is dry. Out over the ocean the storm walks on skeletal limbs of lightning, the restless sea illuminated in great swathes of blue-white light. Closing her eyes the lightning remains, now red-black against her eyelids, the crackle and spit of the electrified air crawling across her skin. A memory rising unbidden of that summer, seven or eight years before, when the weather began to change; that weird, too-hot season of rainless night, rolling thunder and aerial electricity. The air delicious with ions. One night on the feeds she watched a scientist explain the phenomenon, describing how the lightning arcs were symmetrical, leaping outwards towards space as well as downwards to earth, and she remembered a lesson in her school laboratory half a lifetime before, heavy curtains blocking out the sunlight, a whirring globe sparking blue for the delighted school-girls. Hair rising in the charged air.

It was the summer she lived in a studio above Darlinghurst, high up where the ridge falls away sheer to the basin of East Sydney and Woolloomooloo, the crowded roofs and banked walls of apartments spilling down to the harbour. The flat was expensive, beyond her means, one long room bent around a roof garden, hot in the daytime, when the searing sun beat through the flawed glass of the walls, the UV so strong her eyes could barely open against it. But it was not the days she was paying for, it was the nights, when the roof became an enchanted place, a platform above the city, poised on the drop, the city and harbour spread beneath it. The smell of citrus from potted kumquats, the sweet stink of jasmine and frangipani from the garden. Everything blooming out of season, driven to distraction by the elec-trified air.

In the nights Anna stayed up there, listening to the sounds of the streets below, the cars and rumbling trucks, the creaking roar of the garbage trucks on their illegal midnight runs, midway between the restaurants and wherever it was they dumped the refuse now the landfills were full. The laughter, the voices, the careless harmonising of the Samoan garbos all rising as if from far away.

No-one slept that summer—like the plants they were mad with the electricity—and Anna spent the long nights reading Ondaatje and Allende and Marquez and dreaming of love, while the lightning shifted and played across the night sky, illuminating the blue-black geography of the clouds' massing firmament.

It was the summer she turned twenty-five, celebrating her birthday in her magic garden, her friends dancing to 'Moon River' over and over again, half eating, half drinking a melting vodka sorbet, sugary and lethal, until the police arrived at four, Anna greeting them at the door with her hair tied up like Audrey Hepburn, a cigarette holder hanging drunkenly from her lips. Her pupils like saucers from half a tab of ecstasy. One of the policemen had let her kiss him on the cheek, her breath sweet with alcohol, lips chilled from the sorbet. And after everyone had gone, she and Daniel had sat smoking resinous dope and laughing, while the lightning danced around the dome of predawn sky, both of them feeling the intuition of a strange, hidden web of significance from the ecstasy and the dope and the booze, until the sun rose slowly past the massed bulk of the Heads, far to the east, and Daniel had let her rest her head in his lap, the close smell of his leathers rich in her nose, comforting, some lost memory of childhood perhaps, and she had fallen into a shallow, dreaming sleep in the quiet of the dawn. Before she slept he had said he was going to apply for a lectureship at Hong Kong University, and she had laughed, asked him why. It's a good position he'd said, they've got funding for research in my field. And besides, it's all happening in Asia, it's where it's all coming together. It's all happening everywhere, she'd said, like we're accelerating into the future, and the remark had seemed both profound and hilarious. I'm going to take it if they offer it to me, he'd said, his voice quiet, and she had kissed his hand where it brushed the hair from her eyes.

It was the summer of her third exhibition, the exhibition that sold out within minutes of opening, where the *Herald* called her a star, clearly and unambiguously, where dealers rang from New York and Shanghai and Hong Kong and Paris, where Anna found herself the focus of an attention she had once sought and now found uncomfortable. Where she allowed colour to seep back into her work, a muted marine palette of blue, green and mother-of-pearl. Colour rising through the dark patterns of the photos like water through stone, geological. The exhibition that Daniel never came to see, and where Anna, almost hysterical from stress and happiness and relief and fear at the opening, didn't notice his absence until afterwards, when Jadwiga asked after him, and a strange emptiness seemed to ring through her, the tension of the last few weeks draining away, leaving her empty and tired.

• • •

Reaching down she opens her hand against the ledge, experimentally closing her eyes, trying to imagine once more what it might feel like to be blind: the rough, scratching warmth of the stone pulling at her skin, sand rasping, the heat of the long-gone day still within it. There is something here, she knows it, a pattern that lies beneath the surface of these objects, of what she feels, something as insubstantial, as tangible as the lines of force that guide birds across the empty sea, the secret language of magnetism written through the matter of stone. But each time she tries to capture it with her camera it slips out of her grasp, the hinted pattern vanishing as the image freezes, leaving only empty shape and colour, mute as the moving clouds, shape without meaning.

Space, surfaces, time. The ideas flowing through her, coalescing then slipping apart, like water, like a name on the tip of her tongue. There, almost tangible, but unreachable.

Not yet.

APOCRYPHA

· 4 ·

For more than a century the scientific paradigm has been reductive, declaring the proper way to understand the world is to break it down into smaller and smaller units, then study the properties of those units in isolation. The most remarkable success of this reductive program is undoubtedly the discovery of the DNA molecule, and the myriad discoveries about the genetic foundations of life that have flowed from that discovery.

But this program of scientific reductionism implicitly assumes that individual units considered in isolation are the source of all the properties of any particular phenomenon, or more simply, that the whole is nothing more than the sum of its parts. In the case of biology, this has resulted in the pervasive assumption that the study of life and the study of the genome are identical, rather than complementary, that is to say, that life can be understood from DNA, or even that life is DNA.

But just as the whirlpool that appears when a plug is pulled from a basin of water cannot be explained by looking at the individual water molecules, the sorts of phenomena we regard as life cannot be properly understood by looking at their DNA. Instead these patterns, these self-sustaining systems of organised matter which we call organisms, are complex and ongoing processes of interaction between their myriad parts and the environment they inhabit. And just as the whirlpool is an emergent property of a multitude of water molecules collectively engaged in the transfer of matter and energy from the basin to the drain, so too life is an emergent property of an organism, of which DNA is neither the defining nor even a necessary part.

SETH LaMARQUE, *The Language of Shells*

Love

Only fools, charlatans and liars predict earthquakes.

CHARLES RICHTER

At first she thought it was a door slamming. A storm had blown up while she slept, and outside a wet wind gusted amongst the trees. A dog began to bark, then another. Then it was there again, not a door, but thunder, or something like it. The window clacked against the frame; once, twice. In the valley outside a flock of herons took flight, their cries echoing forlornly.

In the soft light she could see his face, half turned away, deep in the private world of sleep. Her face to his back, the smell of his hair on the pillow. This close she could feel the warmth of him, radiant, but when she raised her hand to touch his skin where it protruded from the rucked sheet, it was cool, goosepimpling in the damp air.

Experimentally she moved her body, feeling the slide of the cotton sheet across her breast, belly, thigh, the rawness between her legs throbbing dully. Overhead, through the veil of the mosquito net, the fan moved slowly, its shadow veering across the carved teak of the roof. Her skin electric, every sensation amplified. Ever since they'd disembarked at Phuket airport that morning, she had been like this, her body jittery as if its rhythms had fallen out of synchrony with the motion of the earth. Then the window smacked once more against its frame; beside her she felt its report echo through his body, a ripple across the surface of his sleep. He murmured something indistinct, a frown marring the placidity of his features. Shivering at the cool wash of air from the window, she swung her legs free, standing to latch it.

The floor wet beneath her feet where the rain had blown in.

From the window the valley below was visible. The beach of the bay a crescent of silver broken by the inky lines of the painted fishing boats pulled high above the tidemark. Moonlight drawing her into being as she stood by the open casement. The smell of rain rich in the air.

Shivering in the cool wind she took the window in one hand and tried to close it, but it refused to fit. Once more she tried, pushing harder, but still it would not close. With her fingers she traced the line of the frame, saw it no longer followed the shape of the window, as if it had been pushed out of alignment by some unseen force. Not knowing what else to do she shoved it hard, jamming the latch to hold it in place.

On the bed he still slept. Folding her arms she leant back against the window frame, the motion of the wind pressing upon it. The frown had gone, but his brow was still knitted, as if in perplexity, the shadows of the trees outside moving across his features like water, a shifting pattern of soft light, blue shadow.

With his touch he unmade her. He could place a hand upon her back, draw his palm across her face or leg, and she would be unable to speak, unable to move, her senses gorged. When they were apart he was like a drug, his absence as immediate, as inarticulate as the craving of addiction, shaming, horrible. With each hour she felt herself unravel into the need for him, until she was the need, until there was room for nothing else. But when she was near him it was like a madness, a lunacy of the flesh, mad for him, hungry drunk like an animal in heat.

Love does this, it destroys us. A motion within the matter of our bodies, tidal, as relentless as the collision of the continents beneath our feet, the pressure builds, until it gives in a moment of fury, cataclysmic, stone moving like water, destroying everything that was certain, without warning, without reprieve.

He stepped out of a doorway in front of her, walking backwards down the stairs and shouting something back the way he had come, sent her sprawling.

Still laughing, he turned, his smile dying as he saw Daniel helping her to her feet.

Oh fuck, he said, his accent making the profanity sound almost quaint, I didn't see you there. Are you alright?

I'm fine, she said, the crowd around her jostling, but he had already reached out, taken her arm. Looking up she saw he was drunk, his breath sweet with wine, his face and hair muzzy. But not even the rosiness of his flushed skin could disguise the delicate lines of his face, the dirty gold fall of his hair. His mouth. She could still feel Daniel's hand on her arm. She shook herself free, and for the first time the stranger seemed to notice Daniel, his eyes narrowing as he looked from one to the other. Behind him two of his friends were beginning a slow clap.

Taking her arm he turned her body slightly, saying something that was drowned in the wail of an airhorn.

What? she shouted back.

Your dress is torn, he said. Looking down she saw he was right: the fabric had torn up from the hem and now flapped like a rag.

Let me pay for it.

She shook her head. She was finding it hard to concentrate, the adrenalin, the alcohol, his scent making her giddy, thick-tongued and stammering with desire.

No, I couldn't . . .

Please; if I'd been looking where I was going it wouldn't have happened, he said, but before she could answer a woman appeared beside him, Chinese or possibly Eurasian, her body lithe beneath some shimmering synthetic and fake fur, holographic make-up dancing along her cheekbones.

Come on! she said, pulling on his arm. Looking at Anna she smiled insincerely. Sorry, she tinkled, he has to come now!

Let me call you, he suggested. What's your number?

I haven't got a pen, she said weakly, and fighting against the determined efforts of his companion he waved her excuse away.

Don't worry, he said, I remember numbers.

Helplessly she looked at Daniel, silent beside her.

So do I, he said sourly, then rattled off the eight digits. The stranger seemed about to say something more, but just then a string of firecrackers detonated percussively beside them. Anna jumped, and he was already gone, the crowd closing around him. She stared after him, suddenly aware her cheeks and neck were hot with blood.

Months later she was to wonder at this meeting, at the unlikeliness of it. Had either of them been more attentive they might have stepped past each other in the crowd, never met. So much would be different.

She was in Hong Kong to visit Daniel. She had arrived two days before Chinese New Year, the city already bursting at the seams; the streets and malls crowded with people and flowers and noise. In the parks peach blossoms clung to branches, the windows of the shops and apartments festooned with hothouse narcissi bought from the stalls that seemed to have sprung up on every corner. Firecracker skins littering the footpaths in drifts, red as rose petals.

On New Year's Eve, Daniel and Briar took her to a restaurant on the slopes to watch the fireworks, and with the other diners they clustered on the balconies to watch the sky above the harbour explode, the falling curtains of coloured fire and dancing lasers reflecting across the sleek surface of the water and the glass-sided towers.

And afterwards, pushing half pissed and laughing through the melee in the streets, shouting to be heard over the din of the firecrackers and motorbikes, the beating drums and the thumping techno, she watched Briar and Daniel stop to kiss, their arms and bodies entwined, oblivious to the noise around them, and walked into a man coming backwards out a door.

Both of them knew it would happen.

Even that first day together they knew, the only question was when. Two nights after he knocked her down, they rode the elevator to his apartment. They had eaten at a noodle bar down by the ferry terminal, drinking Tsing Tao out of bottles, and afterwards walked by the water watching the boats and neighbouring islands floating, suspended on the dark water. A dourly middle-aged Chinese couple had stood facing them until the fortieth floor, the four of them staring past one another, determined not to meet each other's eyes. As they passed the thirty-sixth he winked at the woman, a grin cracking his face before it flicked back into impassivity. Anna watched the startled look on the woman's face, biting back on a giggle as the lift chimed and she hurried out after her companion. His glance reducing her to helpless mirth as the lift doors closed, and then, in one convulsive move, the two of them falling sideways against the lift wall, her mouth on his, his hands pulling her upwards against him, hot, urgent. When they reached his floor he jammed his hand in the lift doors to wedge them open as they struggled into each other, shirts and jackets opening as skin sought skin.

In the bedroom they pulled their clothes from their bodies, kicking and scrabbling, the hilarity of a moment before becoming something else, something darker. She tasted blood in her mouth, heard his breath fast and ragged in her ear. The heat of his entry. Neither speaking.

The second time it was slower, their mouths, hands, tongues exploring each other, each learning the smell and the taste of the other. It frightened her, the way she lost herself in the motion of their bodies. And at the end, nuzzling his raised hand with her cheek, lips, teeth like a cat, the shuddering mainlining wave of her climax. Afterwards, lying next to him, his face disassembled this close, she began to shake, her body trembling so violently he drew her to him, cupped her head to his neck, pressed the length of her against his body. She felt so small in his arms, so frail. The smell of his skin and cologne clinging to her like a stain, her musk lingering on his fingers and face.

Later, both almost spent in the grey light of the dawn, his body's weight against her thighs, knotted deep into her outstretched hands as he held himself above her, their bodies not quite touching as they moved against each other, their breath coming ragged and hot, needing this, needing him, her final spasm a brutal, battering thing, more like pain than pleasure.

I don't know your name, she told him when he rang, and he laughed. Jared, he said, Jared Steerforth.

. . .

The photos were above the phone, four black-and-white photo-booth images of Daniel and Briar. She saw them the night she arrived, glancing at them with the quick, semi-interested attention of a professional. In two they mugged, pulling faces, in the third Briar was pushing playfully at Daniel, her hair mussed and upright, and in the fourth they were kissing, Daniel's hand cupping the back of her neck, pressing her hair. Her chin tilted up, mouth open, as if she were listening to some secret Daniel was whispering, breathing it into her, his drawing mouth pulling hotly at her lower lip, while her upper protruded just slightly. Her hand open, pressed against his shoulder, bracing herself against the river of feeling that seemed to flow through her. Her hair still awry.

It was not until later that Anna saw the candour of this final image. There was an intimacy to it that made the observation of the moment seem intrusive, an edge of voyeurism that was only made worse by their apparent heedlessness of the camera's watching eye, the intense privacy that was bound up in that captured moment, in the dissolution of their bodies' melt. Secured with two pins, one top, one bottom, the photographic paper had curled inwards in the humidity, and with one finger Anna brushed at Daniel's face, flattening it against the board, feeling the emptiness that had been haunting her since her arrival, keener than ever.

She had been eager to come: Daniel had told her so much about Briar, and Sophie, who had met her on her way back to the States with Gwynny, had remarked how happy he seemed to be. But then, at the airport, Briar had kissed her quickly, her manner polite but cool, her glance establishing immediately that they would never be friends. But Daniel was the same as always, and within minutes they were laughing, chattering at each other in their own language of private jokes and shared references, incomprehensible to the outsider. Briar looking on, face closed. Back in the apartment she watched the two of them organising dinner, the way Briar opened up at his touch, at his attentions, watching also Daniel's manifest pleasure in her presence, the way he would let a hand rest on her shoulder, the private kiss in the alcove by the door when they thought she was unpacking.

At first she was alert for signs that he had changed, that the intimacy they shared had died back or been somehow circumscribed. Gradually she came to see that he was just happy, happy in a way she had never seen him. But instead of leaving her relieved, this discovery cast her adrift. For watching him with Briar she began to wonder if this thing she shared with him, the madness that would infect them when they were together, the wild, almost hysterical laughter and childish games were as real, as complete as she had always imagined. The first night Briar went to bed straight after dinner, leaving the two of them alone together, and, his hand on her hair, he told her he loved Briar, said it amazed him, devoured him. Twisting to look at him she saw the way he receded as he said this, drawing back into the private world he now shared with Briar, a world she could never enter, never share.

She met him in the park opposite the Cenotaph. Daniel gave her directions, but she raced ahead of them the whole way, eager to be there. As she wound her way down through the streets and laneways, the sun fell clear and pale between the buildings. Since her arrival the wind had been blowing from the north, low, roiling cloud spreading from horizon to horizon, dank chilly rain drifting into the streets in long skeins of moisture. But overnight the sullen mists had dispersed, leaving only the biting wind which whistled up the streets, blowing the debris of the previous evening before it.

He was already waiting when she arrived, lounging on a bench by a fountain. He did not see her approach, and for several seconds she hung back, watching him. He looked different in daylight, paler, slightly smaller, but his face was as beautiful as it had been the night before, his hair tousling in the wind. Then he turned, a smile opening out his face as he stood to meet her. Both of them laughed as they stood awkwardly, not sure how to greet each other.

You're here, she said.

You didn't think I'd come?

She laughed, careless and exultant. No.

All afternoon they wandered through the streets and laneways, their bodies respectfully distant, each small collision like a tremor, heart-catching. Finally, as the sun began to drop, they sat on dirty benches amongst the foliage on the Peak. The city spread beneath them, hawks circling above the rooftops, cloudshadow speeding across the water, racing up the sides of the towers. Each huddled close against the wind, Anna thankful for the leather jacket she had worn.

I thought Hong Kong was meant to be tropical, she complained.

Not in winter, he said. And besides, the seasons are fucked. Last year it snowed in January, and the trees didn't blossom for New Year. People said it was a bad omen. But then last summer was the hottest on record. Falling silent, he stared at her, and Anna felt a tenderness so intense she had to fight not to tremble. We've only barely met, he said at last, yet I feel as if I've known you forever. It's stupid, I don't even know what you do.

I'm a photographer, she said. And you?

I work in the markets.

You're a trader? So you wear one of those dreadful jackets?

He grinned. No, thankfully, I work with currencies. AIs do most of it, I'm sort of a nerve centre.

Do you like it?

Yes, he said, I suppose I do. The world economy is so complex these days it's like some vast organism, an ecosystem, with tides and storms and famines and fires. I'm not sure whether we ever controlled it, but these days it's about as controllable as the weather.

But you try to control it all the same?

Not control: harness. If you're in a clipper, you can't shout down a storm, but you can try to run before it, ride it out. What's in there isn't just dollars and yen and meaningless strings of commodity prices, it's a huge, constantly evolving world of its own. It's dangerous and it's complicated, but it's beautiful too, if you know how to look at it. Does that sound strange?

She shakes her head. I don't think I've ever heard anyone talk about the economy as beautiful, but no, if you put it like that, it doesn't sound strange. In fact it sounds like the sort of work my brother does.

That was your brother you were with last night?

Daniel, yes. We're twins.

And he lives here?

He's a mathematician at the University. It's a contract position, in a research group that's working with modelling complex systems.

Has he been here long?

Since May.

Jared nodded, as if digesting this piece of information. How does he find it?

Hong Kong?

No, the University.

He likes it, I think. Why?

It's a pretty volatile place. Lots of demos, strikes, that sort of thing. The authorities tend to turn a blind eye, but I often worry when I see the stuff some of the student groups do to provoke the government.

You're not pro-democracy?

Jared shook his head. Of course I am. Pro-secession too, at least in principle. But I'm a realist, and I've lived here for a long time. Any change of the sort people want is going to be slow and painful, and the last thing anyone wants is another tragedy like Tiananmen.

You don't think that's likely to happen in Hong Kong, do you?

He shook his head. Not at the moment.

She leant back, regarding him appraisingly. After a moment he looked up, meeting her eye and smiling.

I'm sure your brother's too sensible to be mixed up in any of that, he said, but somehow the remark sounded insincere.

For a long moment she stared at him. The night before last Daniel and Briar had taken her out with a group of their colleagues. One, Chiu, a mathematician like Daniel, had talked at length about the democracy movement, about the day-to-day problems of organising, about arrests and rumours of surveillance. Briar too, as if this was a subject she understood well. Daniel had sat and listened, smiling his easy smile, an expression that combined bemusement and vague indifference. But afterwards, as they were leaving, she saw Daniel and Chiu arguing in lowered voices, Daniel's finger jabbing at the other man's chest.

Daniel's never been political, she said. With a start she glanced down at her watch. Oh shit! she exclaimed, Daniel!

Jared rose to his feet. What?

I'm meant to be going to dinner with him. I forgot.

His faithless heart.

The first time she learnt of it was three months after they met, at a party to which Daniel and Briar had invited them. A loud, reckless affair, spilling across a whole floor of an apartment block filled with a melange of students and publishers and television producers and academics, friends of the four people holding it—two lecturers, a writer and a journalist. In a quiet room Daniel produced a bag of coke, shook out a line for himself, Briar and Anna. Anna kept looking over her shoulder, not sure where Jared was but aware he felt out of place, worried for him. Then he opened the door, looking in to see Briar wiping her nose.

Jared, old chap, Daniel said, aping his accent, fancy a line?

Jared shook his head.

No, he said. Thanks. His voice chilly.

You're sure? Briar asked. It's good.

Jared glanced from one of them to the other, but not at Anna, who sidled up next to him.

Go on, she said, elbowing him softly. He looked at her, his face unreadable.

Alright, he said, hesitating a moment too long before he spoke, then taking the thousand-dollar bill from Daniel, rolling it tighter as he bent towards the tabletop.

She did not see the way Daniel had looked at him, the challenge in her brother's eyes.

Ten minutes later on a balcony off the bedroom she helped him to the ground, dizzy, pale.

What is it? she asked, and he looked at her, eyes dark with anger.

The coke, I have a heart condition.

What? Why didn't you say? Feeling him turn to stone in her arms, his matter unyielding, closed, even as she felt her own heart start to race.

I didn't think it mattered.

Of course it matters. Do you want me to get someone?

No, I'll be fine, he said, his voice expressionless. She stroked his hair but he did not look at her, just gazed out over the lights spread beneath them, the boats upon the harbour beyond. From inside came a sound of breaking glass, hoots and cries of glee.

Later, their bodies negotiating forgiveness in the silence of their bed, leaving each of them gentle and sad.

I'm sorry about tonight, she said as they lay in the darkness. He kissed her fingertips.

It wasn't your fault.

It was, she said, I should have known it wasn't your . . . our scene.

I shouldn't have let him goad me.

And then, her betrayal unthinking, she said it. It was wrong of him to goad you. I don't know why he's so jealous.

It's not your problem, it's his.

You're right, she said, I know.

They had four more days before she left. A photographic assignment back in Sydney she could not postpone beginning on the morning of the fifth. As it was, she changed her flight, arrived an hour before the shoot was due to begin, stepping off the plane into the wet benzene stink of Sydney summer. Everything distant, hallucinogenic from lack of sleep. His absence like a dislocation in her being, nothing quite real.

On her last day she awoke early to find the bed beside her empty. Jared had risen before dawn, dressing in the light that spilled in through the bathroom door. As he bent over her, his skin fresh with shaving cream and soap, she had kissed him, her body wakening as she tasted his mouth, playfully tried to pull him back into the bed, but he had only laughed, untangling himself from her grip. I have to go, he said, I've got a meeting.

Later she woke a second time to the sound of rain against the glass, the room winter dark. Rising, she walked to the wall of windows, gazed out at the coiling wisps of cloud that broke around the building, feeding in from the north. Through the rain the shapes of the towers rising silently, their lighted windows seeming to float in the half light. Slowly she walked through the apartment, so quiet without him. The clock by the bed told her she had overslept, but when she called Daniel, whom she was meant to be spending the day with, he did not answer, no hint on his vidmail of where he might be.

By the time she had dressed the rain had eased into a steady drizzle, the streets outside dirty grey with it, the passing taxis and cars whirring across the wet asphalt. It took her half an hour to find her way back to Daniel's apartment, all the while hoping he might have returned, but when she opened the door she knew he was gone. A note by the phone telling her he was at lunch with Briar. It did not suggest she call.

With one hand she crumpled the note, as if destroying it might excuse her lapse. Since New Year's Day, when Jared had called, she had hardly seen him. Two nights before, the four of them—Anna, Daniel, Jared and Briar—had eaten in a restaurant over the water. From the moment they arrived Anna had seen it was a mistake, Briar's silent animosity making all of them edgy. She fought to connect with Daniel but could not, as if he had retreated, and as she grew more nervous she felt Jared next to her growing tense in turn. All she wanted was for Daniel to share this exhilaration she felt, to see that maybe, just maybe, this was the love that others found so easy, but the harder she tried the worse it seemed to become. And afterwards, Jared sullen and silent as they walked through the darkened streets, his body cold beneath her touch.

In the days since the dinner her and Daniel's dealings had been confined to a few phone calls, every moment spent with Jared instead, the two of them inhabiting the strange timeless world of new love, eating barbecue meat in brightly lit restaurants at 4:00 A.M., walking through the markets at dawn, sleeping here and there for an hour or two. And while Jared was there she had been able to let that be enough, to skate over everything else, reckless. But alone in Daniel's apartment, she found herself aware of her impending departure as she had not been before, the real world intruding into the fantasy of the last week.

For a long time she stood, suddenly adrift, a sadness settling, like the emptiness that used to take her as a child when Daniel went somewhere without her. Needing motion, Daniel's note still balled in her hand, she shouldered her bag, walked back out into the streets. She had no plan, no itinerary, all she wanted was some space. When she felt like this at home she would swim or ride the ferries, back and forth to Manly or Cremorne or Balmain, letting the motion of the water, the slowly moving folds of the harbour calm her, enjoying the sense of being away from land, the demands of family or friends. And so, not knowing what else to do, she found her way to the Star Ferry terminal, boarded a ferry out to the island. Cold rain falling in drifting sheets across the sea's expanse, making the islands indistinct, sheathed in low mist and the seascraping cloud. Beneath the baffled roar of the engines she could hear the hydrocat skip the broken surface of the water, the white-peaked swell striking the hull like a drum. The heat of her tears coming unexpected.

All day on the shoot she was distracted, cranky, wanting to call him, frightened by her inability to control this tumult of feeling. That night the way his features crowded the flat screen, the lagging distance of his digitised voice making her feel crazed with his absence. She could not bear it, she said, she needed to be near him, to smell him, to touch him. The night outside wretched with heat and bats and the stink of the garbage trucks.

Even then she knew she had to go back, to be with him, but when she rang Daniel a week later to tell him he seemed truculent and distant.

Are you sure about this? he asked. You hardly know him.

I thought you'd be happy for me.

Please, Anna, he said, listen to yourself, and perhaps he would have said more, but she flicked the screen off, refusing to hear him.

It is in the darkest hours we come closest to the truth; that sleepless time of doubt and certainty just before the dawn. It is then we see that love has gone, or maybe never was; see the slow fade of all we once held true. It is then that we are most alone.

How long she stayed there she never knew, the darkness of the valley at her back, adrift in the nowhere space of the hotel room. The soft rattle of his breath annihilating her, the space between them uncrossable. How does it happen, this loss of one's self, how do we never notice until it is too late? The earth shifts beneath us, spasming, until nothing is as it was.

Five hours before she clawed and bit at him, her body frenzied with desire, her loss of control frightening her, repulsing her. And afterwards, her skin slick with sweat, she reached out to him, needing his touch, his understanding. But he only turned away, silent in the netted cage of the bed. The memory of his rejection searing itself into her matter like a scar, disfiguring, an ache that will not pass.

Perhaps it was a madness, she tried to tell herself, perhaps her body felt the coming of the earth's disquiet, like the rats that swarm from their burrows and nests in the hours before an earthquake, like the suiciding fish or the shrieking of pigs driven wild by something unseen, their cries inhuman and horrible. But for all she tried she knew it was simpler than that.

Love is not completeness, it is a perpetual incompleteness, a movement towards a boundary that is always in view but never attainable. It is the desire for immersion, for the oneness we can never have, a reaction against the very nature of what we are, our aloneness.

APOCRYPHA

· 5 ·

It is in this process of suspension between opposites that we truly encounter the heart of these photographs: inside/outside; life/non-life; geometric/organic; lost/found; enclosed/enclosing, paradoxes all.

MICHAELA RUTHVEN, *Anna Frasier: A Retrospective*

Blindsight

A crystal, a flower or a shell stands out from the usual disorder that characterises most perceptible things. They are privileged forms that are more intelligible for the eye, even more mysterious for the mind, than all the others we see indistinctly.

PAUL VALERY, *Les merveilles de la mer: Les coquillages*

I am confused today. I teeter on the shifting shoals of the past like an animal lost on the drifting ice. With each step the ice fractures, splintering cracks haring outwards with a noise like fire, until they resemble the filigree patterns of a leaf. Or veins. The black water welling about my feet, chill as death. No stars, no sun, no perspective, just ice stretching to the horizon in every direction, without bearing or scale. But I know there is a centre to it, something dreadful and hidden, for all the while I can feel the ice moving beneath my feet, twisting inwards, its treacherous loneliness slowly orbiting some hidden pole. Is this what the world's end looks like? This place where the only sound is the creaking of the ice as it tears, the lonely call of the birds. This terrible, forsaken place.

Outside it is cold too. I can hear the wind, see the grey ocean. I know it is only the mnemonics falling out of balance, but I need the doctor, and without Adeleine I do not remember how to find her. No, not Adeleine, she was the one before, I need the boy, the beautiful one.

I see his hands but I cannot remember his name.

How old am I? Two hundred? Three? I do not even know that. This is not a life, this creeping death, my body primped and prodded, filtered and scrubbed, my organs sliced out, replaced with vat-grown meat, tiny machines let loose to claw their way through my capillaries. Synthetic skin, blood, hair. The nucleotides of my body rewritten so my cells can replicate for eternity. Cancer harnessed for the good of the species, until we seethe with its ghastly fecundity.

The nights are the worst, terror rearing out of the dark like the whorled, scalloped cliffs of some monstrous berg. The dark ocean beneath. The tinkling of the ice in the frozen air like a choir.

How long is it since I started this? It is so hard to know, the seasons wheel by so fast I barely notice them.

One year joining the next, time out of joint.

Anna's dreams that night are uneasy, troubled. Twice she wakes, jolted from sleep, unsure of her location. The first time the front has moved in from the ocean, the hastening wind sending a vase spiralling to the floor in the next room, the sound of its shattering echoing through the empty house, tearing the membrane of her sleep. In the half light of the storm she stumbles to the windows, where the blind rattles and thumps, bolts them closed. The room singing with ghosts.

The second time the room is quieter, rain falling steadily outside; heavy, rhythmic waves of sound washing across the sloping roof. This time her dream remains with her, her body humming with it: Jared, his face hidden, the cool movement of his skin against hers, electric, the uncertain beat of his heart in the cradle of his chest. In the darkness the red LED of the alarm reads 3:57, deep night. She had forgotten his fickle heart, its weird arrhythmia. She remembers a night spent with Daniel, not long after the party where Jared had slipped and fallen, his heart beating crazily, where Daniel, cocaine-high and jitteringly lucid, had tried to explain to Jared the mathematics that drove the ectopic beat of his heart, the sequence of its irregularity counting 2, 5, 8, 11. Jared's eyes glassy, his mouth hard as he watched Daniel talk too fast, moving almost without pausing to a discussion of feedback loops and fractal geometries, her heart aching as she wished he would stop, be silent. Be still.

The rain moving against the low roof, sleep washing through her.

When she wakes again it is a sullen, dirty day. A cold wind disturbs the clammy air, which clings to her skin in the heat of the sun, like sweat from a foreign body. The sand at the beach is littered with the detritus of the storm, paper, rubber, bags, weed. A child's doll, one arm raised above its head, its hair tangled in the wrack, one blue eye staring blindly. The reeking body of a pelican, neck and bill twisted back in death, the feathers matted and filthy. The water grey and choppy, moving treacherously, unpredictably. An ominous yellowy brown tinge to it in the grubby light. Anna strips down to her bathers, wades out into the dirty water, which pushes against her, seething. When she is thigh deep she stops, the faecal smell of it enough to warn her away. Hurriedly she wades free, climbing the stairs with her towel in search of a tap to wash it from her skin.

Angry, thwarted, she winds her way slowly up the path to the clifftops. Her eyes ache, a high whine of a headache singing inside her skull from lack of sleep. Back in the apartment it is quiet. Running the shower she washes herself carefully under the warm water.

In the living area she finds the shattered remnants of the vase and, crouching, begins collecting the largest pieces, intending to vacuum up the residue. One of the shards, a curving claw of green glass, slices into her, cutting a long line along her palm. She looks down at it and swears, surprised that there is no pain. Then, almost immediately, blood begins dripping onto the floor, and she hurries to the bathroom, looking for something to staunch its flow. Wrapping toilet paper around it, pain comes, sudden, intense, and she presses the paper harder, trying to damp its edge.

The blood takes a long time to slow, and Anna is forced to stay still, her hands pressed together. When it finally stops she unwinds the sodden paper to expose the puffy white line of the cut, extending from the second knuckle of the first finger of her left hand, three centimetres across her palm. A dull ache throbs along her arm. Gingerly she pulls at the edge of the cut, wincing as it sends a stabbing pain through her hand, blood trickling from it once more. Looking at it she is reminded of the scar on Seth's face and, wondering if this too will scar, she lifts her right hand, her fingers tracing out the lines of his wound. The hair on her neck rising as she strokes her lip where the scar bisects his.

It has been a week since Denzel found me. Seven days and seven nights that passed in the flicker of an eye; seven rotations of the earth beneath my feet I would not remember had the house's systems not kept track of them for me.

I was naked when he found me, chilled to the bone. It has become winter once more, and somehow I had levered the window open, wanting to breathe the ocean air. I cannot imagine how I looked to him, a ludicrous old crone slumped in a pool of piss by a window she cannot remember how to close. Half starved and babbling about people centuries dead.

In the week since then I have barely written, my body and mind so shocked by the sudden imbalance in the mnemonics that I have been almost mute. But gradually the numbness has begun to fade, my cognition beginning to reintegrate once more.

Twelve hours ago I rode the merse, telepresenced a glider as she soared out on the edge of space. She was beautiful, the gengineered structure of her bones making her body feel almost weightless, intelligencers in the clinging nanofibre of her skinsuit letting the wind play against her skin as if it were a summer breeze, not the freezing gale of the stratosphere. Feedback systems in the suit's wings meshed with her nervous system, and through the telepresence I could feel them too, their expanse like trembling water, the wind beneath them like an unseen hand, lifting us as we turned and soared.

I do not know how long I flew with her, nor how many others

were there with us. As we crept northwards the aurora danced around us in shifting sheets of light, while far below, beneath a ribbing of blue-pink cloud, dawn stole westwards across the Canadian north.

That high the Earth no longer seemed flat, the planet's curve visible against the horizon. The soft blue of the atmosphere fading to a pale line, then nothing, then the upwards fall of space. For a time we surfed the racing line of dawn, riding crosswise, north-westwards, and as we went the land beneath began to change, the green of forests and farms giving way to tundra, then the bare slopes of mountains, snow-capped, the tonguing white of the glaciers.

As we flew I remembered Seth talking about the ice, long, long ago. The way the fickle, flickering progress of the planet's seasons are recorded in it, not just in pollen or dust, but in the ancient cold of the glaciers themselves, an imprisoned presence as palpable as the ice. The way this memory attests to the constant ebb and flow of the seasons; the sudden convulsions that reave the Earth's deceptive placidity.

It is in the ice and the stone that we are rebuked, he told me, for in their memory lies time deeper than we can imagine. Their very existence a reminder that our time here is limited, and that we too shall pass.

Perhaps it is the way Jadwiga looks from side to side before she emerges from the laneway that makes Anna stop at the corner. How Jadwiga does not notice her she is not sure, but Anna recognises her immediately, the contained physical energy that hums through her body unmistakable. Slightly unsettled by Jadwiga's behaviour she does not call out as she watches the older woman hurry across the footpath to the far side of the street, around the corner and away.

It is only chance that Anna should have been here on this corner at this precise moment. Several days before she had admired a walrus skull in Dylan's office, bought from a curio shop on Glebe Point Road. Her hand still too sore for work, Anna had decided to visit it, and as a result spent the early part of her afternoon wandering amongst the market stalls, galleries and second-hand bookshops of Glebe. The smell of patchouli mingling with the wet scent of the warm asphalt and the sharp, animal aroma of the ferals' unwashed bodies; the beat of dance and the crackle of degrading vinyl blending with ankle bells and drums; kelims and second-hand clothes jostling for space next to stalls selling crystals, cut-price skingear and pirated ractives. The curio shop was nestled between a bookshop and an alternative therapy co-op, its high windows filled with an eclectic mix of objects, from animal skulls to greening copper instruments to books and medical charts. Inside, the shelves were stacked with object upon object, arranged in no apparent system: scientific drawings in racks, shrunken heads, nineteenth-century collections of seashells and fossils and butterflies in wooden cases, callipers and scalpels and all the various implements of human dissection of the natural world. The owner of the shop, a tallish man with shoulder-length grey hair, had walked her through the objects for a full half-hour, and Anna, as much out of politeness as anything, had eventually bought a nautilus shell divided in two in a wooden display frame, one half set behind the glass to reveal the delicate brown stripes against the pale shell, the other turned to reveal the gleaming mother-of-pearl of the interior, the folded geometry of the chambers.

With the framed shell in a bag, she had wandered back towards Parramatta Road, intending to walk back through Chippendale to Central and visit Jadwiga at the gallery. Enjoying the quiet, she meandered slowly, her route taking her through shaded streets, pleased by the huge pale trunks of the gum trees, the litter of leaves and nuts that stippled the broken asphalt beneath them. Here and there the walls were covered with fading murals painted in the 1970s and 1980s, idealised images from a long lost dream of social cohesion and change. But as she drew closer to Central the area began to change, the warehouse conversions and redevelopments standing empty and unfinished, the tattered plastic of the hoardings and defaced signs stark between the carefully maintained and restored terraces and older developments.

Unsettled by the manner of Jadwiga's exit from the laneway, Anna walks towards it. It is unremarkable, an old dunny lane no more than two metres wide and bordered on each side by the blank walls of two terraces, peeling patchworks of damp and graffiti. Looking over her shoulder she stares after Jadwiga, perturbed, then begins slowly down the lane. After thirty metres it turns right along the back fences of the terraces that front the street. The bitumen beneath her feet potted and cracked, other, older surfaces visible through it; gravel, concrete, and finally reddish clay. Bamboo and weeds lining the sagging fences. Once more she hesitates, knowing she is intruding, but again it is only a moment before she continues, following the lane until it ends in a broken wooden fence, its palings bowed around a huge Moreton Bay fig, the musty smell of the dark leaves and dirty wood strong. Beside the tree the fence has collapsed, the cyclone wire pegged in to cover the gap pulled aside to form a sort of makeshift gate.

Stopping beneath the tree, she wonders again what Jadwiga was doing here. The only way she could have entered the laneway is through the gate, but peering through it into the space beyond, all Anna can see is the back wall of some kind of factory or warehouse. Long abandoned, its faded concrete is nearly obscured by a thick growth of creeper which crawls under the eaves and onto the sloping roof, fat, budded flowers wound amongst the tangled foliage. Here and there the high square windows that are set into it have been broken, the glass jagged within the rusting frames. Between the fence and the wall a narrow yard is visible, weeds and nettles growing high, some as tall as small trees. Somewhere nearby a bird caws, its shrieking call giving this vision of decay a loneliness that belies its location, the clatter of a train passing Mortuary Station three streets away.

Anna pushes on the wire. It gives easily, so with a nervous, surreptitious glance over her shoulder she steps past it. Inside, the grass and weeds move with the breeze. Something about this place, its sense of silent abandonment, making her heart beat faster. The dark soil beneath the fig slippery with rotting fruit, their bright-coloured flesh and seeds livid. Other, more human remnants lying here and there; a rusting paint can, discarded fits, plastic spoons, burger wrappers and plastic bags.

Beyond the tree's ring of darkness, an old goods door stands open in the wall, and Anna picks her way towards it, placing her feet carefully to avoid the needles that protrude like spines from the soil.

At the other end of the yard, almost obscured by the weeds and creeper, she notices a rusting corrugated iron roof, some kind of building beneath it. Avoiding the stinging burrs of the weeds, she follows the side of the warehouse towards it, emerging into a cleared space in front of an old transportable. Positioned on bricks, its plywood walls are swollen and cracked. A sofa, stuffing sprouting from its split covering, sits in front of it; needles and refuse scattered all around it. Anna walks nervously towards the door, surprised to see a sizeable padlock attached to a bolt. With one hand she shakes the door in its frame, but the padlock does not give and she releases it, poking idly with one foot at the empty tubes of oil paint that litter the ground outside the transportable. Wondering if this place is some kind of squat inhabited by artists, she wanders back along the side of the warehouse towards the goods door she spotted from the laneway.

The goods door is a metre or so off the ground, but Anna lifts herself in without difficulty, careful of her injured hand. Inside it is dim, light falling from far above in long shafts. At some point part of the first floor has collapsed, and rubble, beams, boards and plaster lie in jumbled heaps all around. The floor creaking ominously beneath her feet. Although it is hard to tell in the poor light, the place seems empty, left to the rats and possums and pigeons, the air thick with the stink of mildew. Nervous and uncomfortable, she is about to go back the way she came when she hears a movement. Turning reflexively, she is startled to see a figure standing close behind her. Her body tensing, she takes a step back involuntarily.

Who are you? the figure demands.

Nobody, she says. I was just looking.

Are you a cop?

No, I . . . she hesitates, frightened of triggering some kind of outburst, not sure what to say.

Bullshit! the figure declares, stepping forward. Now he is closer, Anna sees he is only a kid, fifteen or sixteen, thin but poised, like a dancer on the balls of his feet. His grimy face, which in another life might have been handsome, is sallow, his dark hair shaved back to a concentration camp fuzz.

I'm not a cop, Anna says, willing her voice to stay level. I promise. As she speaks she glances quickly from the kid to the open space of the door and back.

Then why are you snooping around here? he sneers, stepping forward threateningly, his right eye moving crazily in his skull.

I'm not, I mean—

As she speaks someone shouts a name outside, and the boy turns towards the cry. Seeing her chance, Anna springs past him, hoping to make the door before he catches her, but he is too quick, jumping to intercept her. Swinging wildly, she hits the side of his head with her injured hand, yelping as pain shoots along her arm, but the blow is enough to knock his grip loose, and she stumbles away, trying in vain to regain her balance as she makes for the door. As she reaches it a man's figure leaps past her, muscles moving beneath tattooed skin, and with a thump he collides with the boy, knocking him backwards. Glancing back she sees the two of them sprawling across the floor behind her, but as she does she collides with another figure. Looking around in surprise, she stops dead.

Rachel? she blurts, but Rachel does not reply, just pushes past her, one hand raised to silence Anna as she hurries towards the boy's assailant, who has managed to restrain Anna's attacker; one of the boy's arms twisted high behind him, struggling even as the man tightens his grip. The older man towering over the boy.

Jesus, Blaze, she is shouting, go easy! and as she says it the man lets his attention stray from the boy, who in one fluid motion twists free, his foot swinging upwards to connect audibly with the man's groin. With a muffled yelp the man slumps forward, the blood draining from his face, and as he does the boy kicks him once more, knocking the larger man to his knees. Kicking him again he bounces from foot to foot, ready to strike. Anton! Rachel shouts, advancing upon him, and, noticing her for the first time, he pauses in his bouncing motions.

Anton, Rachel says again, lifting a hand towards him, her voice firm, warning, but he breaks away. Hugging her wounded hand to herself, Anna shrinks away from his as he flies past her and jumps out the open door. Anton! Rachel shouts after him. Anton! But he is gone before she reaches the doorway, across the yard, through the wire and away, vanishing around the bend in the laneway.

Turning to Anna, Rachel gives her a look that is half concern, half suspicion. Are you alright? she asks, and Anna stammers out a yes. That settled, Rachel hurries over to where her companion has pulled himself to his knees. Tall and powerful, his close-cropped hair's gingery colour and his sun-damaged redhead's skin make him look as if he is in his forties, when in fact he is probably no older than she is. His legs are bound in tightly strapped bike leathers above massive workman's boots, his singlet exposing looping Samoan tattoos that wind around his right shoulder and arm as far as his sizeable bicep. His craggy face adorned with rings protruding from ears and eyebrow.

You're okay? Rachel asks, crouching beside him, her hand on his shoulder. He looks up at her disparagingly.

Oh yeah, he groans, just dandy.

Rachel squeezes his shoulder, then turns back to Anna. If you don't mind me asking, what the hell was going on just now?

Surprised by the edge of steel in the other woman's voice, Anna shrugs her shoulders.

I don't know, he came out of nowhere.

You didn't do anything or say anything?

He thought I was a cop.

And why on earth were you in here in the first place?

I saw someone I know come out of the lane, I was curious, she says, aware how weak it sounds.

Rachel still looks at her suspiciously. You're bleeding, she says, and Anna, looking down, sees blood is spattering onto the dirty floor from her injured hand.

It wasn't him, she says, I cut it earlier.

We'll still need to get it looked at.

And I'll just lie here and die, shall I? suggests her companion.

I think that little love tap's going to be the least of your worries once word gets out that Anton whipped your butt, Rachel says, helping him to his feet, and the man laughs sardonically, the noise subsiding almost immediately into a wince.

Not if I get the squinty-eyed little fucker first. At this Rachel looks at him, her face thoughtful.

Who was he? Anna asks.

He's called Anton, Rachel says, he's a client of mine. He sleeps at the Brewery most of the time, but lately he's been hanging out down here with Lewin.

Lewin?

The guy who lives out the back. He's supposed to be some kind of painter. Was he the person you saw?

Anna slowly shakes her head. No. But something about the name is familiar. You said his name was Lewin? she asks.

Michael Lewin, Rachel says. Do you know him?

I know of a Michael Lewin who was a painter, but he's supposed to be dead.

Well this Michael Lewin is very much alive, Rachel says, putting a hand under her companion's arm to support him. Vinh should be back at the Centre, she says to Anna, he'll look at that hand for you.

The Centre is half a kilometre towards the city, several shabby rooms on the third floor of an office building, its street frontage occupied by Chinese grocers and bakeries. Ushering Anna before her, Rachel moves through a reception area lined with battered chairs and couches. In one room a loose collection of kids sits slumped before a screen, absorbed by the feeds, while in the next another couple sit goggled at ageing consoles. In the third room a plexiglass screen protects a counter, beside it a security door which Rachel opens with her palm.

Inside is a long space broken up by dividers, two glass-walled offices opening off it at the far end.

Can you get Vinh to have a look at her? Rachel asks the tattooed man, and he nods.

I'll talk to you once you're done, Rachel tells Anna.

As he leads her across the room, Rachel's companion looks down at her.

I'm Blaze, by the way, he says. I don't think we were introduced.

She smiles. Anna.

At the end of the room Blaze raps twice on one of the doors, glancing through the glass partition before pushing it open. Inside is a well-lit space, more a cubicle than a room, containing a desk, three chairs and a bed. Doctor's instruments are set out along a shelf, and against one wall a metal cupboard is protected with a padlock. Behind the desk a man is seated, looking up at them from behind a console. His head and neck thin and birdlike, eyes huge behind steel-rimmed glasses.

Vinh, Blaze says, this is Anna. Anton had a go at her.

Vinh swivels to face the two of them. Motioning her to sit down, he extracts two latex gloves from a dispenser and pulls them on, his movements fastidious and precise. It's just the hand? he asks.

She nods. I grazed my knee too, but otherwise I'm fine.

May I? he asks, and she nods, gritting her teeth as he pulls off the blood-soaked dressing. Underneath it the gash is clotted and swollen with blood, the edges puckered and wet. She looks away as he examines it.

Ouch, he says. How did you say you did this?

I didn't. It was with a broken vase.

Well you'll be pleased to know that it probably looks a lot worse than it is, but it's still going to need stitches.

Anna shrugs, and he looks at her impassively.

The bad news is I'm going to have to finish what Anton started and pull the sides of it apart, break the scab, so it can heal neatly.

Which will hurt, Anna says dryly.

Quite a bit, he replies. Are you ready?

Once her hand is stitched, Anna wanders back into the office area. Rachel is nowhere to be seen, but Blaze is sitting on one of the desks, talking on his earpiece. Seeing her he finishes his conversation.

How's the hand?

Six stitches, she says, looking at it ruefully.

Could have been worse.

If you hadn't turned up it probably would have been. Thank you.

Blaze grins. I doubt Anton would have done much more than scare you. But in future I wouldn't go poking about in derelict buildings, particularly not round here.

As he speaks Rachel emerges from the office next to Vinh's.

Anything? she asks Blaze.

He shakes his head. Not yet.

Fuck, she exclaims, loud enough to attract the attention of the girl at reception.

What's wrong? Anna asks.

It's Anton, we need to find him. She pauses. You said you saw a friend come out of there. Who was it?

Anna hesitates, not sure whether she should involve Jadwiga in whatever is going on here.

She's an art dealer.

Rachel and Blaze exchange glances.

Would she have been there to see Lewin?

Even if it is the same Michael Lewin I'm thinking of, I don't know what she'd be doing there. As I said, he's supposed to be dead.

Rachel taps her front teeth with her thumbnail. He's got a past, I know that.

The Michael Lewin I'm talking about was around when I was starting out about ten years ago. Something happened, I don't know the details, but there was a scandal, child sex or something, and he just vanished. No-one knew what had happened to him, although some people thought he'd skipped bail and fled the country. Others thought he'd been murdered or committed suicide. I think as time went on and his work dried up people just assumed he must have died somehow.

That's all you know?

He was a junkie, big time. Do you think we're talking about the same man?

It seems too much of a coincidence for it not to be, says Blaze, but as he speaks the receptionist calls to him from the counter to tell him he is wanted on the phone.

I know how this must look, Anna says, once they are alone.

Rachel eyes her cautiously. It does seem to be a day for coincidences.

I'm just glad you came along when you did. Were you following . . . what's his name? Anton? Or was it just a fluke, you being there?

A bit of both, I suppose. Anton's not a bad kid, but he's been in therapy with a court-appointed counsellor for the last few months. The therapy's part of a suspended sentence for some trouble he was in a while back. But he didn't turn up this week, so the matter's been referred for mention on Monday. If he doesn't turn up to court then, the chances are the magistrate will issue a warrant for his arrest and the cops'll sling him inside. We were trying to find him before that happens.

And now?

I don't know, Rachel says. He probably thinks he's in deep shit with us too for attacking Blaze like that. The stupid thing is Blaze has a real soft spot for Anton; I thought Anton trusted him, and now that's fucked.

I'm sorry. I didn't mean—

It's not your fault.

Is Blaze a lawyer as well?

Rachel shakes her head. No, he's a social worker.

Anna raises her eyebrows at his corded forearms and biceps. Pretty impressive for a social worker.

He's an asset, believe me, says Rachel, and smiles ruefully.

So this is what you do?

Mostly.

Seth said you were at Cambridge.

Rachel laughs, a short, sharp laugh and not kind. Anna is reminded irresistibly of Seth. He hates this job.

What will you do now?

I'm not sure. We should probably go back and wait for Lewin to turn up—Anton spends quite a lot of time with him.

Could I come? Anna asks impulsively.

Rachel looks at her sharply. I can't stop you if you want to, but this isn't a game.

I know that. I want to see if it's really Michael Lewin.

I'm not sure he'd appreciate that.

He doesn't know me.

Rachel glances over at Blaze, who is still absorbed in his phone conversation.

Alright, she says at last. Wait until Blaze is done.

As they walk the last hundred metres of the laneway, Anna feels herself growing nervous, her heart beating faster. She tries to breathe slowly in an attempt to calm herself, not wanting to admit to her discomfort at returning to the scene of the afternoon's events, but when she feels a hand on her arm she jumps nonetheless.

You okay? Rachel asks. You look a bit edgy.

I'm fine, Anna tells her, although she is not at all sure that she is.

In the yard there is no sign of Anton, so Blaze, motioning to Anna and Rachel to remain where they are, jogs quickly to the goods door and scans the interior of the warehouse. When he indicates he has seen nothing, Rachel leads Anna along the path through the undergrowth, Blaze coming up behind them as they reach the small open space in front of the transportable.

He's around, says Rachel, pointing to the padlock, which has been released. She knocks sharply on the door, and when it is not answered immediately she knocks again, louder this time. When there is no reply to the second knock Blaze places a hand on the door, pushes it open.

Lewin, he calls, it's Blaze and Rachel, from the Belmore Centre, as Rachel steps past him through the open door, Blaze and Anna close behind her.

It is the smell that strikes her first, the reek of fever sweat and unwashed body mingled with oil paint and turpentine, a combination so strong that Anna has to cover her mouth to choke back on the bile that rises convulsively in her throat. The smell made intense by the suffocating heat. The interior is dim, the only light coming from the grimy windows and a kerosene heater that is burning in one corner, and it takes Anna's eyes a moment or two to adjust, but when they do she gasps, the cluttered space of the room resolving itself into a sea of colour and shape. On every side they are piled one on top of the other, miniatures to two-metre canvases, jostling for her attention. Body after body sculpted out of paint in rich, amber hues, their elongated, almost naïve contours and angular faces reminiscent of Modigliani's women. There is no roughness to the composition though, no dissolving lines or hesitancy; just the length of the curves, colour so deep one could drown in it. Buttock, hip, breast, armpit, leg, all stretched and flowing, hands and feet extended. And in every painting the women seem to look back, watchful and aware, their almond-eyed gaze neither kind nor cruel, just inscrutable as a cat's. This effect heightened by the shadows that cloak them, the richness of the tapestries and the sudden, irresistible pools of colour that surround them: swathes of Klein blue in a falling curtain; an extraordinary green glimpsed through a half-open window; dark crimson on a curved chaise beneath them, their immediacy, their sheer lushness deepening the field, drawing the viewer in to the women's private worlds. And behind the paintings, where the walls of the transportable are visible, a collage of tattered pictures, all of women, not just bodies but faces, parts of faces, torn from art books, porno mags, fashion catalogues, yellowing and curling beneath discoloured sellotape.

Is it him? Rachel murmurs.

Certainly looks like his work. Have you seen these before?

No. They're incredible.

As they speak Blaze emerges from the next room, hand pressed to his face against the smell.

He's not there either.

Rachel looks around the room, shaking her head in amazement.

We'd better get out of here then; the last thing we want is him thinking we were mucking around with his stuff while he was out.

Next to her Anna is still moving slowly from canvas to canvas, overwhelmed by the wealth of paintings.

These are extraordinary, she says, but Rachel is at her side, ushering her out.

In the yard a figure is standing where the path emerges from the weeds.

Lewin? Rachel asks, shading her eyes against the glare of the afternoon sun, bright after the dim interior of the transportable.

Maybe, the figure says, taking a step back. Who wants to know?

I'm Rachel LaMarque, from the Belmore Centre. Anton's solicitor.

Anton who? the figure asks, but before Rachel can reply, Blaze appears behind them.

What the fuck is he doing here? the figure demands, stepping back.

Lewin, Blaze says softly, it's been a while. Surprised by the animosity in his voice, Anna turns to look at him, but Blaze's face is impassive.

Relax, Rachel says, we don't want any trouble. We're just trying to find Anton. We know he comes here to see you.

Lewin does not answer straightaway. Now her eyes have adjusted to the light, Rachel sees he is tall, his wasted body swaddled in jumpers and jeans despite the heat.

You say you're Anton's solicitor?

That's right. We met one night the winter before last at the mission truck by the viaduct. You'd just gotten sick.

Lewin stares at her. I remember, he says. You were there with that doctor.

Vinh.

Yeah, Vinh.

So have you seen Anton? Rachel asks.

Lewin looks from her to Blaze and back again. Nah, he says, his tone derisive.

Bullshit, Blaze says, stepping forward. He was here before.

Rachel lays a hand on his arm, restraining him.

I was out, Lewin says. Why are you looking for him, anyway?

He didn't turn up for counselling, Rachel says.

So? His therapist's a fuckwit.

That's as may be, she says. What matters is that if he doesn't appear on Monday when it gets called over they'll issue a warrant for him and he'll go inside.

Lewin shakes his head once or twice, then ambles towards them, limping heavily on his right leg. His aggression of a moment before seems to have evaporated.

Who's your friend? he asks, walking up to Anna, coming so close she can see the broken stumps of his teeth, smell his feculent breath. Fighting the urge to back away, she holds her ground.

I'm Anna, she says.

Anton attacked her, Rachel says.

Lewin looks at her with a renewed interest. Really? he asks. That's not like Anton.

Staring back at him she can see the ruin of his once handsome face visible beneath the all too obvious signs of leukemia; the hollowed craters of his cheeks, the black lumps of the sarcoma that swarm across his neck beneath the thinning hair. Suddenly he raises one hand, touches her cheek, running his fingers across it.

I know you, don't I?

Anna shakes her head, her teeth gritted, refusing to flinch. No. But I remember you from before you disappeared, she says. He nods slowly, then reaches down and takes her injured hand, turns it over so the dressing is visible.

Did Anton do this to you?

No, I did it to myself.

Throwing his head back he laughs. Things aren't that bad, are they?

Next to her Rachel steps between them, breaking Lewin's grasp.

So, have you seen Anton?

Lewin shrugs. He's probably back on the trains.

If he turns up will you tell him we were looking for him? And tell him not to worry, Blaze is cool.

Lewin looks up at this, his rheumy eyes bright with interest. Been hassling the kids again, hey Blaze?

Fuck you, Blaze says softly. Then he turns to Rachel. I've had about as much of this fucker as I can take. I'll wait outside.

Sure, Rachel says, and Blaze walks away. The older man watches him go with contempt in his eyes.

How are you feeling? Rachel asks, once Blaze is out of sight.

Sick, he says.

But you're still painting?

For now.

You could come in and see Vinh. Or go to St Vincent's.

He looks at her disparagingly. I might as well get a Band-Aid. As he says this he begins to cough, a terrible, wet cough which seems to take hold of his body, wringing it until blood-flecked gobbets of mucus are dribbling from his scabby lips. Finally, bent over, hands on his knees, the cough subsides, and he wipes at his mouth. Rachel kneels beside him.

Why don't you come in? It can't make things any worse.

Yeah, yeah, he says weakly. Maybe sometime.

Lewin does not move aside to let them leave, so they must step past him, Rachel first, then Anna. As Anna passes him he puts a hand on her arm.

I know you, he says, his breath hot in her ear.

Shrinking back she shakes her head.

No.

Yes. You were at the Cross Street Gallery three weeks ago. I saw you going in.

She twists free of his grip, staring at him angrily. I don't remember you.

He laughs bitterly. Why would you? His words taunting her to respond, but she does not, just hurries after Rachel.

Blaze is seated on a car bonnet when they emerge from the laneway, tossing stones at a streetlamp. Rachel watches him throw one upwards so it strikes the plastic cover with a loud *tock*.

Jesus, Blaze, she says, you're as bad as they are.

Blaze shakes his head. He's a vicious fucker. I wish we could get Anton to stay away from him.

I understand how you feel, Rachel says, but he looks out for Anton. Better him than some pimp.

Blaze tosses another stone, striking the lamp once more. You recognised the paintings? he asks Anna.

It's the same Lewin alright, Anna tells him.

So it was him your friend was there to see?

I suppose. Looking back down the laneway, Anna hesitates. He's dying, isn't he?

Rachel nods. Leukemia.

How many of the people you work with have got leukemia?

Rachel sighs. A third maybe. There's nothing we can do for most of them.

Anna nods, digesting this information. What are you going to do about Anton?

He'll turn up. Like Lewin said, he's probably on the trains.

Where does he go?

Nowhere, he just rides around. All day sometimes.

There is something in Rachel's voice as she says this, a regret that pulls Anna's eyes to her.

Don't look at me like that. He's just a kid, we can't get involved.

Listening to her, Anna wonders whether she is lying for Anna's benefit or her own.

Later that evening, in a sushi bar in Chinatown, Anna watches Rachel eat, barely touching the sashimi she has chosen for herself. Noticing Anna watching her, Rachel grins, expertly flicking a piece of sashimi onto her plate.

Is this too crass? she asks.

In front of them the food moves by on a silent track, borne from the kitchen out around the counter and back in a long loop, while on a holoprojector in the middle of the restaurant a leather-clad go-go girl dances in a virtual cage to beat-heavy nippopop.

Anna smiles. No, she says, there are a lot of places like this in Hong Kong. I had a friend who liked them. The thought of Roland making her smile.

Oh? Rachel asks lewdly, her mouth full of rice and fish.

Anna laughs. It's not like that, he was just a friend. But as she says it she remembers Jared too, and looks away. Through the kitchen window the chefs can be seen, one working, face down and intent, two laughing at some private joke. Sensing her watching, one looks up, still laughing, their eyes meeting for a moment before he looks away.

I totally forgot, Rachel says beside her. How was the concert?

Wonderful, Anna says, turning back to see Rachel regarding her with an amused interest over the top of her glass. Why, has Seth said something?

Rachel sips. Should he have?

Anna laughs, blushing. No. For a moment she traces the lip of her glass with her finger.

Tell me about him, she says, feeling the danger in the question, the way it imposes on this somehow unreal acquaintance that seems to have developed between the two of them. Rachel watches her, unreadable, her expression suddenly, inescapably reminiscent of Seth.

What do you want to know? Rachel asks at last, although her voice is not as friendly as it was, more guarded.

He seems so aloof, so . . .

Cold? Distant?

Maybe.

He's certainly the second.

And the first?

I don't think so. Though he doesn't suffer fools gladly. And he's very solitary, quite driven, so he doesn't have a lot of friends. I'm not sure he really wants them though.

Anna considers this last remark, wondering how much of it is truth, how much assumption. He's older than you, isn't he?

He's forty next year, so there's almost eight years between us.

Big gap.

Rachel smiles slightly. I think I was . . . unintentional.

Without meaning to, Anna glances down at Rachel's belly.

Mine's no accident.

Embarrassed, Anna feels her cheeks flush.

Seth told me about the father.

Or lack thereof. Arching her back, she studies Anna. He's really pissed off about it.

Why?

I don't know. Sometimes he can be surprisingly conservative.

You're very close, aren't you?

Rachel nods. Our parents died when I was quite young.

I'm sorry.

To be honest I barely remember them. What about yours?

They're in London. My father works in theatre. My mother was an actress back in the eighties, but now she teaches.

Would I know her?

Anna shakes her head.

Brothers, sisters?

I have a sister, she says, in New York. She's a musician. And I had . . . have . . . a twin brother. He's . . . missing.

Rachel looks at her quizzically.

It's a long story, Anna says. To her relief Rachel is tactful enough not to pursue the question, but as a result neither speaks for several seconds.

Seth told me he's always been blind, Anna says at last, and Rachel nods, swallowing a mouthful before speaking.

Our mother was prescribed an anti-nausea drug which affected his optic nerves. He was lucky—a lot of the other kids were deaf as well, and some were brain-damaged.

As Rachel speaks Anna cannot help but think of the almost three months when life was growing inside her, of the pain of its loss. Not just the pain of the procedure, but the absence it left within her, dull and deadening. Her memory of those months filtered through their aftermath, the lonely room in Western, the nights watching the feeds numbed and miserable, as if some part of her had died too. The absence more than just a memory, something deeper, more visceral, something torn from the very matter of her cells. Next to her Rachel taps the stainless steel of the counter, her reflection distorted in its burnished surface. Watching her, Anna wonders whether she could have borne the child. It would be nearly six months old, it might be beginning to sleep through the night. And it would be hers. When Rachel eventually speaks again her voice is softer, less certain. It frightens me, you know. We're so fragile, and a child . . . she opens her hands in a gesture of helplessness.

You've had genescans done, haven't you? Anna asks, her voice harder than she meant it to be.

Of course. But it's more than that. She looks at Anna for a long moment. Would you do it?

What?

Bring a child into this.

I thought you'd done it on purpose.

I did, Rachel says, her eyes haunted, but sometimes I look around me and I wonder about my right to do it.

You can't think like that.

I know.

For several seconds they sit in silence. Do you think there was ever a time when it wasn't like this, when it looked like things were going to get better instead of worse?

Anna shrugs. Maybe.

It's just we have all these things, all this technology which was meant to make things better, to make us free, yet we're still fighting the same old fights. Rich against poor, those who have against those who don't. All it ever seems to do is get worse.

Do you really think that?

Rachel nods. It's gradual, but every year we seem to slip back a bit further, more rights are eroded, there are more people on the streets. It's little steps, so people don't notice, like the cops starting to carry semi-automatics and wearing body armour. At first it was just a few of them, some of the time. Now it's all of them all of the time. We just get used to the changes, forget how it was. How it could be.

In the street outside Rachel hails a taxi, her hand clasping Anna's as she stands by its open door.

After we met last night it occurred to me I should get some pictures taken of this, she says, her free hand indicating the heavy curve of her belly. If I were to ask you to do it, would you?

Anna smiles. If you want me to. I'd have to hire studio space, and we'd need to talk about exactly what it is you want, but it shouldn't be too complicated.

I'll call you then, Rachel says, as the taxi door closes behind her.

I dream only one dream. There may be others I have dreamt, unknowing, ones that have not come with me into waking, but this is the only one I have ever remembered, and it has never changed across the immense span of my life, never altered or blurred.

It is a dream of a time before words, my thoughts the unformed stuff of sensation. I float, suspended, the pulsing umbilicus spiralling about my body. The closeness of the womb surrounding me, enclosing me. My eyes are open, and oddly there is light, a dim, reddish glow. I see/hear/feel my hand—marvellous, strange—see/hear/feel the motion of my mother's blood through the womb wall, see/hear/feel the thump of my heart. The amniosis in my lungs like warm frazil. This is all there is, nothing happens, just this moment, my hand, the blunt nails on the fingers, the crabbed crosswise of my palmprint, this moment without beginning, without end, directionless now.

We dream ourselves, we know this. Each night born backwards in sleep, slipping inwards through the warm suspension of our dreams, our senses bleeding into one, until we cannot distinguish what we see, what we hear, what we feel. No inside, no outside, just the pulse of being, as primitive, as ineffable as pain or orgasm's release. And there, in the depths of that synaesthesia, form murmurs, a stirring in the fabric of being. Like a word or a name forgotten and then remembered, hours or days later, its lucidity comes suddenly, inexplicably, its geometry revealing it, separating it from its newly other.

It was once believed that the fossilised remains of shells lived, if not the quick hot life of flesh and blood, then a slow, silent life, an inwards life as ancient and unknowable as the creeping motion of the glaciers or the continents. Just as the embryo in the womb unfolds from the matter of its mother, taking on a form and life of its own, so too the stone was believed to give birth to the sculpted lines of the stone shells and fossil teeth. Pliny called them tonguestones and Ammon's horns, solid dreams drawing substance from the mothering fabric of the earth, their emergence no more mysterious than the teeming forms of the outer world, the geometric language of shells, the Fibonacci sequence of pinecones and sunflowers or the schools of fish and flocks of birds that shift and turn as one. But no less either.

Perhaps we do this too, our inner worlds resolving from the raw stuff of dreams and sensation like signal from noise, or the fossil shell condensing from the stone, like the pooling patterns of the butterfly's wings or the fearful symmetry of the tiger's stripes. Like the perfect logarithm of the ammonite's spiral, the infinite arc of its curve.

On Friday night, two weeks after Daniel vanished, there was a knock at her door. A young man dressed in jeans and a dirty T-shirt stood outside. His thick hair, so black it was almost blue, worn long.

Chiu? she asked, incredulous. I thought . . . I mean I'd heard you were arrested.

Chiu smiled thinly. Not yet. As he spoke he glanced nervously over his shoulder, staring back down the narrow corridor. From two floors up came the sound of a man shouting, then a muffled thumping that seemed to go on and on before falling suddenly, ominously, silent.

What are you doing here?

I heard you were looking for Daniel.

She felt herself beginning to shake, suddenly afraid of what he had come to say, of Chiu himself.

Yes, she said, willing her voice to stay steady. Do you . . . do you know something?

He shook his head. Only that I told him to get out while he could.

He bought a ticket to Ho Chi Minh.

Then he is there somewhere.

She shook her head. He never got on the plane.

Something flickered behind Chiu's eyes. Have you talked to Briar?

Briar was gone too, seemingly without trace, the apartment she and Daniel had shared closed by the police, the door nailed shut. One night she had managed to find Briar's parents at their home in Surrey, but when she told them her name the father had hung up without a word.

She's gone, Anna said. I looked for her.

No, Chiu said, she's still here. At her brother's.

Several floors away the sound of the street door opening echoed up the stairwell, the noise making Chiu jump.

I don't know where exactly, but somewhere on the Peak. From below come the sound of heavy feet, the chime of the lift. Chiu stepped back, his voice low. I have to go, he said, twisting away as she reached to stop him.

Why are you doing this? she asked, and he looked back at her, his face closed, unreadable.

Daniel is my friend, he said.

Standing in the hallway Anna watched him slip away down the staircase, vanish back into the confusion of the city.

An hour later she was standing at a white gate, pressing an intercom button. When there was no response she pressed it again, holding it down without release. A moment later a voice barked from the console.

Mut-ye?

I'm looking for Edward Hallard, Anna said, guessing that if Briar was indeed hiding here the chances of convincing her brother to let her speak to her were better than those of convincing the butler or a guard.

Do you know what time it is?

Glancing at her watch she saw it was almost midnight.

I need to see him.

There was a long pause. And your name is?

Anna, she said, Anna Frasier.

The intercom disconnected with a click, and for several minutes Anna waited by the gate in the dark. A breeze was blowing off the harbor, not cold, but cool enough to make her uncomfortable in her thin shirt. Sleek cars slipped by now and again, expensive engines almost silent, their headlights moving across her, their halogen glare blinding. Finally a uniformed figure, two large dogs straining at leashes

in front of him. When he reached the gate he stared at her appraisingly, then spoke quickly and quietly into the headset he wore over
one ear. Almost immediately the gate began to open.

Briar was waiting on the verandah at the top of the drive, one arm
folded across her chest, a lighted cigarette in her hand.

Anna, she said. What a surprise.

Despite the even tone Anna could hear a quiver of something she
took to be anger beneath the modulated English tones.

I'm looking for Daniel.

I can't help you there, I'm afraid. He's probably in hiding with the
rest of them.

Like you?

Perhaps.

Anna looked up at the mansion in front of her. Pretty ostentatious
for a hideaway.

Briar didn't reply. Although it was hard to tell with the light
behind her, Anna thought she looked thinner. Drawing back on her
cigarette, she exhaled the blue smoke into the night air.

Was there something else?

Whether the question was calculated to enrage or not, Briar's glass-
cutting English vowels and patrician disdain combined to do exactly
that. But Anna's need kept her calm.

He had a ticket booked, to Ho Chi Minh.

The airport was closed.

Anna shook her head. No, this plane left before they closed Chep
Lak Kok.

Maybe he couldn't get there. They closed the roads and the trains,
after all. Or maybe the plane was overbooked and he couldn't get on.
Or he might have been caught in a firefight, pinned down. I don't
know why you'd think I know.

Incredulous, Anna stared at her just long enough to see Briar
flinch. You know why, she said, her voice cold.

As if this final jibe had cracked her armour, Briar nodded to the
guard who stood behind Anna, his dogs panting.

I think it's time for Ms. Frasier to leave, she said, her voice trembling. As the guard's hand closed around her arm, Anna stared at Briar, the anger in her gaze transfixing the other woman.

What kind of person are you? she demanded softly, but Briar did not reply. At the gate Anna looked back, saw her still standing there, immobile, the smoke from her cigarette coiling around her in the verandah light.

Only later did she realise Briar had not needed to be told Daniel had missed the plane.

She never saw Chiu again, but she did see Briar, if only once, weeks later. Anna stood upon an escalator, rising through the gallery of some Wan Chai mall. Not three metres from her the curved glass wall of a bar protruded into the atrium of the mall, and there, at a table by the window, sat Briar. She was smoking again, her hand shaking as she raised the cigarette to her mouth in a quick, jerking movement. Her hair was longer than Anna remembered, pulled back harshly from a face that looked haggard and drawn, its dark skin lustreless. A gold fury gripping her Anna stared, willing Briar to look up, to notice her, feel the hatred she bore her for her callous disavowal of Daniel, who had loved her so easily, so well. As they drew level, Briar looked up from the glass she held in one hand, perhaps sensing Anna's eyes upon her. Anna did not know what it was she was expecting, but certainly not the way Briar stared back at her, her eyes not angry, but afraid, ashamed. Then in one sudden, convulsive movement Briar stood, stubbing out the cigarette in an ashtray, and turned, pushing her way back through the crowded bar.

5.13 A.M. and Anna wakes with a start, the taint of her dreams racing with her into waking. Like an animal she scratches and claws at herself, convulsive, the nocturnal horrors crawling across her skin like insects, alien, violating. Her heart pounding like a train. Ignoring the dull throb of her hand, she rises, yanking her bathers and running shoes on, desperate to be free of the enclosed space of the apartment. But once she is outside the pain returns, and she finds she must run with her hand cradled to her chest, each step jarring. To her left the sun nudges over the discoloured water of the ocean, the vapour trails of jetliners marking the dome of sky. Needing to expel the poison of her dreams, Anna runs faster, willing herself to ignore the pain in her hand. When she reaches the pool the attendant blinks at her sleepily, still setting up the register's systems for the day ahead, but Anna slaps her coins on the counter, pushing her way through to the poolside to shed her clothes and seek the water.

In the light of the dawn the pool's surface licks like oil, the face of the cliff above reflected in it. From the block she dives, the chill of the water knocking the breath out of her, driving her to swim the first two laps too quickly in a flurry of movement to warm her limbs. But then the blood begins to move, and she allows herself to relax into the buoyancy of the water, the salt of it against her skin, in her mouth. Her injured hand against the water like a slap, thirty times a lap.

After two kilometres she drags herself from the pool, her muscles flooded and stiff with blood, skin chilled, and seats herself out of the breeze on the leeward side of the wall. Carefully lifting her dressing to examine her hand, she sees the wound has puckered, and bloated with water strains at the stitches, the soft skin already tearing around them.

Others have arrived now, but not many, moving quietly around the edge of the pool, adjusting goggles and caps, surveying the lanes for space. Surreptitiously Anna watches an elderly woman, her pale flesh loose and speckled across massive shoulders, unstrap her artificial leg, the stump flexing at the knee as she carefully wraps the prosthesis in her towel and lowers herself into the water. As she strikes out with a steady, deliberate stroke, another woman, younger and tall, pauses close by, her back to Anna, and Anna watches as she pulls the elasticised lip of her bathers down around the curve of her buttock. Glancing over her shoulder the younger woman catches Anna watching her and smiles a knowing, complicit smile. Hi, she says, and Anna, suddenly envious of the woman's ease within herself, scarcely manages to stammer a reply. The woman's gaze lingering just long enough to let Anna know that she has been assessed and passed, before she takes two quick steps and knifes her thin form into the clear pane of the water, her passage barely ruffling the surface.

For five minutes, maybe more, Anna watches the younger woman pace herself up and down the inside lane, but eventually she slips back into her shorts and singlet, retying her shoes in preparation for the return trip. Out on the cliffs her breath comes hot, ragged, her pace broken and distorted by the necessity of holding her hand against her chest. The breeze has dropped, the air growing warmer, while overhead the gulls wheel across the choppy water, white against dirty blue. She remembers Daniel, his only half-joking refusal to own a mobile, claiming he could feel the microwaves through the bony wall of his skull, boiling his brain in its pan. Here by the enormous space of the ocean she almost believes him, the silent murmur of invisible radiation, the endless leak of the feeds out into space, almost audible.

Later, beneath the shower, she lets the warm water run over her scalp and face, losing herself in its wash. Opening her eyes she sees her reflection in the steam-clouded pane of the mirror opposite, her hair slicked flat against her head, the thinness of her frame somehow stark in the misty glass. Her reflected face the face of a stranger.

Thursday morning she visits Jadwiga, and they drink thick, bitter Turkish coffee in a café two blocks from the gallery. High-pitched Turkish music echoing through the room as they talk. Anna agreed to the meeting a week before, knowing Jadwiga uses these informal sessions as a way of structuring her artists' delivery schedules, although she would never be so tactless as to ask a direct question about the progress of their work. All the same, Anna agreed without pleasure, Jadwiga's suggestion reminding her how little headway she had made since they first spoke almost a month before. And while Dylan's manner remains friendly, she cannot shake the suspicion that he is beginning to feel she is imposing upon his offer of ongoing access. But the events of the weekend have added another layer of trepidation, Anna not certain how she should approach the question of Lewin and Jadwiga's relationship with him. Silence seems not just dishonest, but fraught with danger. Lewin's claim to recognise her from the gallery raising the real possibility he will mention meeting her to Jadwiga, in which case her silence will no doubt be construed in an uncharitable light. Nonetheless, unable to forget the way the older woman crossed the street as she left the laneway, she is certain Jadwiga will not be pleased to have the subject raised, unsure that their friendship has sufficiently recovered to survive an unwanted intrusion.

To her credit Jadwiga does not flinch when Anna finally raises the matter by telling her simply that she has met Michael Lewin. Jadwiga holds her coffee in front of her face, her blue eyes so pale as to be almost transparent, but bright.

Where? she asks.

At his squat near Mortuary.

What were you doing there?

Anna does not answer immediately, this being a question she had hoped to avoid, known she could not.

I'd been in Glebe, she says at last, looking down, but uncomfortably aware of Jadwiga's gaze. I was walking back and I saw you. It was just a coincidence.

Jadwiga says nothing.

You seemed so . . . purposeful. I wondered where you'd been and I went to look.

You were spying on me?

No, Anna says, I was just curious, and I know how this must look.

Again Jadwiga does not reply.

I thought he was dead.

Sometimes I think it would be better if he was.

But what happened, why were you there?

Jadwiga looks up, inquisitive. You don't know the story? Pursing her lips, she thinks for a moment. No, I suppose you were only a student, you wouldn't have known.

I met him when he was still at art school, it must be almost twenty years ago now. He was a real *enfant terrible*, frighteningly talented, arrogant, magnetically handsome in an almost Byronic way, right down to the limp he'd picked up in a motorbike accident. I don't really understand what he was doing at the school, there was nothing that bunch of plodders could have taught him, and I think he knew it. Certainly he treated them with contempt. I was working for Rosanna then, so it was her he came to see, not me, but I was there the first day he came, and I still remember the way he parked his bike on the footpath out the front, strode in as if he owned the place. He told us who he was and Rosanna almost refused to see him—he'd had an appointment the week before and he'd not turned up. She'd been furious, but—luckily, I suppose—she relented, and he threw a pile of drawings and some slides onto the table. You think you can sell these? he asked.

Even that first day he wasn't nervous, not even with someone as powerful and despotic as Rosanna. He was too arrogant for that, but his arrogance wasn't conceit, just a certainty about his talent. He didn't care what others thought about him, and you could tell. And just when you thought he was too intolerable, he'd do what he did that day, turn and smile this private smile, as if to admit you to the ongoing joke of his life.

I thought he was the sexiest man I'd ever seen.

Anyway, Rosanna took the stuff he'd shown her, and she scheduled an exhibition in her smaller gallery. It was early work, not quite there, and his influences were a little too obvious, but the energy, the sense of depth and colour, were already there, and so was the power of his composition, the understanding of the female body. They sold out in half an hour, which was a minor sensation in itself.

By then I'd come to know a little more about him, some from friends, some from what he told me himself, and I was young enough, stupid enough, to find what I'd learnt exciting. Binges, drugs, booze, the endless women, all the stuff you've probably heard. And the smack. I'm not sure whether it was common knowledge, but even then he was a junkie, had been for years, but he'd kept it under control, and although sometimes it got a little out of hand, he treated his habit with a casualness that seemed convincing enough. It was just part of him.

After the show ended we all went to a restaurant around the corner from the gallery. Michael was electric, like a lightning rod, and I couldn't take my eyes off him. He filled the room with his presence. And after the others left, and it was just us left there, well I . . .

I was still with Pyotr then, although we were near the end. It was Michael who gave me the courage to finally leave him. We lasted two years, on and off, until I couldn't take it any more and broke it off. We stayed friends though, and eventually I represented him after Rosanna retired. Jean-Paul never knew what there had been between us . . . what there still was . . . I never wanted him to.

As he became successful he got more and more out of control. He spent a year in Paris on a fellowship, which a lot of us thought would calm him down, but he came back worse than ever. It wasn't just the heroin, it was the booze too, the way he lived. It was terrifying. Anyway, after Paris he met Susan. She had money, and she took him in, paid his debts off, cleaned him up when he was a mess. But by then he was too far gone for any of that to really help, and pretty soon he was stealing money from her, hocking her things, typical junkie crap. And although I don't think anyone realised at the time, he was beating her too. It was horrible really, it was as if the drugs and the booze had hollowed him out. All that seemed to be left of him were these monstrous rages and suicidal depressions. And the lies.

Then one night he set to work on her, broke her nose, fractured her skull, punctured one of her lungs. It was ghastly, and it may have been the cause of what happened next. Susan had a daughter called Naomi. She was about twelve, beautiful looking, smart. Still is. She lives somewhere near the gallery these days I think; certainly I see her around from time to time, although I don't think she remembers me. Susan was in the hospital for weeks, and Michael had been formally charged with her assault. Jean-Paul and I had taken him in, because although the judge had given him bail he'd had to provide a surety and agree not to return to Susan's house. I put up the bail because nobody else would, and I took him in because I thought it was the only way I could make sure he wouldn't run off or kill himself. But when Susan came out of hospital, Naomi apparently told her some story about how Michael had been touching her. I don't know the details and to be honest I don't want to. Maybe it was true; after all, Michael was so out of his brain by that point I don't think there was much he wouldn't have done. But I knew him, or thought I did, and it seemed so out of character. So maybe he didn't do it, maybe Susan put Naomi up to it, maybe Naomi made it up to get back at him for hurting Susan, which he did, horribly. I don't know whether it really matters now.

I put up money for his bail a second time, and then again as other charges came leaking in: possession, theft. Did I tell you he'd been stealing from her? You name it, he'd done it. It was horrible, and it cost me a lot of friends when I wouldn't turn him out, but how could I? He had no-one else. I held a show of his work in an attempt to raise some money for his legal bills. I sold one painting. So Jean-Paul and I covered those costs as well. All the while Michael continued to act as if it was some enormous joke, sacking his lawyers, missing court dates, behaving like a maniac, which I guess he was by then. And then the committal began, and everything changed. I didn't see Naomi's evidence—they closed the court—but his lawyers thought she was very convincing. I suppose I thought he'd done it as well by then, but he needed a friend. The committal was scheduled to run for three days, but on the lunchtime of the second he just vanished. Took nothing, left no note. Most of us thought he'd drowned himself or been murdered—he had owed a lot of money to some bad people— but there was never any body. Of course the police thought I was involved, so Jean-Paul and I were questioned over and over again. And we had to pay the bail money, which cleaned us out. Jean-Paul almost left me, but he stayed. I wouldn't have blamed him if he'd gone.

Then about eighteen months ago he turned up at the gallery, wanting money. Jean-Paul had just been diagnosed, and although I was still angry with Michael I took him out to eat somewhere, and he listened to me talk. He said he'd been living on the streets, moving from city to city, staying clear of trouble. He'd changed, but there was still something there that I knew, and I responded to that, despite myself. I asked him about his work, and he said there was nothing, but he wanted to start again. That was what he wanted the money for. I said I wouldn't give him money, but I set up an account in my name so he could get materials. I thought about telling the police, but he was so sick, so ruined, that I didn't. I don't know who else knows he's back, I haven't told anyone, but maybe there are other people he's seen. But he is working, and the stuff he's doing, it's extraordinary. And I think that only makes it sadder; he could have been so much more.

. . .

Jadwiga's story comes back to her two nights later as her taxi glides across the expressway towards the city, Lewin disappeared, from police, from everyone, then reappeared, walking back in when all had given up on him. But Lewin had reasons for vanishing, and nowhere to go. Daniel could always have run to her or to Sophie or their parents if he was in trouble. But something about Jadwiga's story has heartened her, made her think, however briefly, that there may still be hope.

Rachel's apartment is the top two floors of a grand terrace, the ageing intercom making her voice harsh as she answers Anna's buzz. Inside, Anna climbs the stairs slowly, the bottle of wine she chose at the cellar in Bondi cold in her hand. At the top, Rachel is waiting, the door open. When they spoke on Tuesday morning Anna thought Rachel sounded edgy, as if their closeness in the sushi bar had been soured by the sense that each had revealed too much, but she smiles welcomingly when she sees Anna, kissing her cheek like an old friend. Tonight's invitation came Tuesday morning, catching Anna unawares. Her blood moving faster as Rachel told her Seth would be there.

Once they are inside, Rachel pulls the cork on her bottle, and the two of them walk slowly out onto the deck, where a table has been set. It is a blue night, and Rachel has lit oil lamps around the edge of the deck, so the light is warm and soft.

The others are late, Rachel tells her; Blaze called to say he and Paul fell asleep after gym, but they're on their way.

And Seth?

He'll be here soon.

Did you find Anton?

Rachel sips at the glass of water she has poured herself. Eventually, she says.

What about the hearing?

It was okay.

And Lewin?

I haven't seen him.

For a while then neither speaks. Sipping her wine, Anna notices an object on a pedestal which is visible through the doors.

Rachel follows her glance. It's a sculpture Seth gave me, she says, starting towards it. Anna follows her.

The object is stone, about a metre long, irregular, like the pelvis of some ancient monster folded over on itself again and again. Its surface as smooth as that of a pebble rounded by the motion of the water, and beneath the surface the stone swirls and eddies in shades of green. It is not aerodynamic, yet it has an appearance of movement, like the body of a woman swimming, long hair flattened and moulding around her as she pushes her way through the water. Rachel watches Anna examine it, trying to make sense of it. Finally Anna looks up in exasperation.

I'm not sure I understand, she says.

The sculptor is blind, Rachel says. Touch it.

Putting down her glass, Anna closes her eyes, much as she did with Seth in the specimen room, running her hands along the breaking curves of the sculpture's length, her hands pushed apart by the folded gaps within it, the surface cool and slippery. As she does she feels the down on the back of her neck begin to rise, her breath catching in her chest, as if an erotic charge has been transmitted from the object to her.

Then, harsh and abrupt, the intercom sounds. Anna opens her eyes, stepping away from the sculpture, suddenly awkward and exposed.

Seated opposite them, Anna cannot help but notice the way Rachel anticipates his needs, her constant, almost unconscious attention. Even when deep in conversation with another, she has one eye on him, like a mother with a wandering child, alert for danger. It is not quite fussing, nothing so overt, so smothering, more like the familiarity of old lovers, the rhythm of their bodies second nature. To a stranger this might seem like closeness, something to be admired, but as the evening progresses Anna becomes aware of the way he strains against her attentions, insisting on finding plates for himself, the way he tenses beneath her touch as she tries to draw him into conversations, the flicker of resentment as she serves him. But if he is genuinely annoyed he hides it well, conversing politely with Blaze and Paul and Anna in his strange, slightly formal tones. Halfway through the main course Anna realises it is a tutor he reminds her of, the ritualised exchange of information designed to distance the teacher from the student. And if he seems slightly disengaged, it is hardly surprising, most of the conversation turning upon Blaze and Rachel's work, the Centre. Paul, Blaze's partner, is a lawyer, and shares many of Blaze and Rachel's concerns. For some time the three of them argue over a paper Rachel has been drafting, and while the conversation turns between them, Anna watches Seth, his face giving no clue to his thoughts. Eventually she realises they are talking about the Detention of Suspected Offenders Bill she heard mentioned on the feeds the morning after the bombing and, waiting for a break in the conversation, leans into their circle, asking about its intent. Paul looks at Rachel incredulously, as if to register disbelief that anyone could be so naïve.

She's been out of the country for several years, Rachel tells him, and Paul nods, excusing her, the gesture generating a sudden flash of dislike in Anna.

There was a lot of debate in the feeds about it last year, Rachel explains, but basically it's a drastic assault upon civil liberties.

It gives the cops carte blanche to arrest and detain people without having to demonstrate due cause, interrupts Blaze. All that's needed is a perceived threat to the public's safety or amenity.

I thought the cops already had pretty unfettered powers, Anna says, looking from Blaze to Rachel.

Rachel nods. They do, but this legislation is designed to take away most of the controls that are still there.

It also creates a series of technical hurdles for anyone alleging police brutality, which will serve to make evidence obtained under duress far more easily admissible, Paul says grimly, but before he can go on Blaze breaks in again, his voice tight with barely controlled anger.

When it comes into effect it will create a situation where the police can arrest you without having to show reasonable cause, or detain you without charging you or giving you access to a lawyer for a period of up to three months and there'll be nothing you can do about it.

Surely the government wouldn't dare—

They're up twenty-seven per cent in the polls as a result of it. People think crime is out of control.

Is it?

That depends how you look at it, Rachel says. But the fact is that these laws aren't about crime, they're about homelessness. The government and the cops want to be able to take action without interference from people like us.

The pipes hiss as the water floods the glass. From outside, Anna can hear Paul lecturing the table; he has grown more belligerent with each glass of wine. From behind her she hears the movement of a body, turns to find Seth standing in the doorway.

Anna, he says, moving closer to her. She does not answer. He seems taller tonight, more angular.

I wanted to talk to you, alone.

Why?

You asked about not feeling real, about seeing your life from the outside.

She wants to touch him, put her hands on him.

I do know what you mean, he says. I know what disconnection is like, his body coming closer, his hand raised to her face.

No, don't do this, she says, suddenly frightened.

Please.

For four days it rains, the unstable offspill of a cyclone that turns somewhere off Brisbane. The air so wet it condenses on the skin, cool and clammy. In the silence of the specimen room Anna works methodically, finding as she often does that the grey quiet of the rain concentrates her thoughts, releasing a lucidity that other, brighter days lack, images forming in her mind, then appearing once more in the camera's eye. On the Monday and Tuesday she conceives and captures the first image with which she is happy. It is of a counterpart, the elegant intricacies of the hollowed impression so perfect, so unlikely, that it seems impossible to believe they are the work of blind nature, the composition of the shot such that the viewer's eye is drawn irresistibly inwards along the curve of the spiral to where its winding eye disappears into nothingness. The effect is powerful, a sudden contraction of vision, a turning vortex which speeds up as it rushes towards sudden collapse, like the hastening suck of water exiting a sink or the inward fall of light into a singularity, faster and faster and then . . . Nothing? Or maybe sudden calm, the quiet space of another world beyond the looking glass. The memory of his hand against her cheek, her sudden recoil crawling across her skin; the unexpected press of a stranger's body on the train or dripping rain upon her neck as disabling as hot breath in her ear, fingertips on a lip.

On Wednesday afternoon Dylan appears by her work table, knocking gently on an adjacent cabinet as he approaches. She turns, startled.

We've a new exhibition opening tonight, he says. If you'd like to come, I can leave your name at the door.

And so, three hours later, Anna wanders slowly through the exhibits. Beyond the partitions the sound of speeches rises and falls, but here in the galleries it is quiet, the light soft and dim. Anna has wandered past the preparations several times a week, but she has never thought to enter. Now she is here, though, she finds herself lingering over the displays, intended to represent the breadth of human funerary rituals, from the foetal skeletons of neolithic Spain, their spindled ribs and flattened skulls surrounded with rounded stones and seashells and dusted with petals, to the swaddled mummies of Egypt and Peru, and the seated burials of the Aboriginal tribes. In other cabinets the tools of the embalmers' revenance are arrayed, and elsewhere reproductions of century-old photographs of the Native Americans' tree burials. Many of the exhibits are on loan from European museums; shards of skull and tooth, Celtic burial stones carved with spirals and angular runes; while from Beijing has come a company of jade soldiers from some imperial necropolis. The sombre design of the cases and displays subtly incorporating countless datanodes, from which images, text and simulations can be accessed. But it is the body of a bogman dragged from an Irish swamp that Anna finds herself drawn to, throttled and cast in to sink beneath the peat. His wizened lips pulled tight across jutting teeth, the rope left about his shoulders like a necklace, its fibres matching the impression in his peat-stained flesh, one hand raised, clawing at the air above him. There is something unspeakably macabre about it, not just the means and nature of his death, its brutality, but other, lingering questions. What did this man do to deserve such a fate? Was he victim or criminal? Did his death come quickly, unexpectedly, or did he wait for it through fear-drenched nights and days? And why was he denied the rites that might otherwise have guided him into the next world? As Anna stands gazing through the perspex lid of his newfound coffin, she feels someone behind her, knows it is him.

Vanitas, she says in a soft voice.

What?

Vanitas, the exhibition's title. Do you know what it means?

It's Latin for 'emptiness', he says. *Vanitas vanitatum*: 'Vanity of vanities, saith the preacher, vanity of vanities; all is vanity.' Ecclesiastes, I think.

She turns to face him. It's a motif used in painting which acts as a reminder of the inevitability of death, of the transience of existence and the futility and emptiness of ambition.

I'm afraid my art theory is a bit lacking, he says, a smile playing across his mouth.

There's a whole school of Flemish painting devoted to it, she says. Guttering candles, clocks, skulls and wilting flowers. Seventeenth century.

And your work? The ammonites? You told Rachel they were *memento mori*.

I did, but I don't think they're quite the same. There's an emptiness to the Flemish paintings, a kind of cold, northern bleakness. Everything is irrelevant because one day the saviour will return. It's too monastic, too sweeping for me. Anyway, the very existence of the fossil is testimony to some sort of continuance, don't you think?

'One generation passeth away, and another generation cometh, but the earth abideth forever.'

She smiles. I suppose. Ecclesiastes again?

Yes.

Do you believe in an afterlife? she asks him.

No. Do you?

She turns to look at the twisted body of the bogman beside her, only centimetres from her fingertips. His eyes hooded, half closed.

No, she says after a moment. I sometimes wish I did, that I could, but I can't. We make our own way.

From outside comes the sound of applause, its intrusion breaking the spell of a moment before. What are you doing here anyway? It's not as if . . . she falters . . . as if—

As if I can see it? No, I'm here in an official capacity.

Near the entrance the guests have started to move amongst the exhibits, talking and laughing as they wander from one to the next. Some hold glasses of wine, and waiters move between them with trays of finger food. Anna looks around, feeling their presence to be an intrusion. As if sensing her disquiet, Seth extends an arm.

Shall we go somewhere else, he suggests, somewhere quieter?

As they leave she sees Dylan watching them, the look in his eye as he nods across the room making her turn aside, somehow ashamed. Their bodies close, arm linked through arm, they wander up through the galleries, the lights dim now, the sound of their footsteps and their voices echoing in the empty space. Describing no particular path, they move from room to room, talking. In some, deactivated wallscreens and holosuites stand bereft, while elsewhere the bones of lost behemoths rear upwards or float overhead, suspended. For a time they pause before a cast of the skull of a carnivorous dinosaur, Seth exploring its curved teeth, each one longer than his hand is wide, and she watches the peculiar intensity of the action, the concentration on his face. Eventually, with a hand on hers, he draws her towards a small passageway set off to one side.

Where are we going? she asks, but he does not answer, only instructs her to take a narrow staircase that is visible through a low arch. At the top he unlocks a door with his security pass. Outside rain falls steadily across the rooftop, making the lights of the city and Woolloomooloo blur and diffuse.

It's pouring, she says, resisting his grip, we'll be soaked.

We're only going to the greenhouses, he says. You should be able to see them, they're not far, and she does, a trio of greenhouses set on the far side of the roof. After a moment's hesitation she lets him draw her out into the rain, the two of them jogging side by side, half following, half leading each other towards the dark shapes. At the door to the first she grasps the handle, hustling him inside, pulling it shut behind her, gasping at the rain that trickles down her neck.

Inside it is hot, the air still and wet with the scent of earth and flowers. The city's light barely penetrating the glass, so the confusion of greenery looms in every direction, the bright motes of flowers dancing against the darkness. The sound of the rain drumming upon the glass enclosing them.

What is this place? she asks, pushing slowly through the leaves and blooms.

The botanists run it. They breed orchids in here. Dope too, I suspect.

Do you come here a lot?

Occasionally. I love the smell, the fecundity of it.

I wonder whether the flowers seem to smell stronger because I can't see them?

Perhaps. There are blind squid that see through smell, their tentacles guiding them through the water by touching scent molecules. Some of the ammonites too, we think, particularly the hunters.

As he speaks he comes close behind her, his breath audible beneath the drumming of the rain.

What is it that you're hiding? he asks now, his voice low.

Hiding? she says, not turning. I'm not hiding anything. Quite the opposite: it's as if when I'm with you everything comes pouring out.

Maybe hiding isn't the right word. But there's something about you, a separateness, a privacy—

A disconnection? A tremor in her voice as she says it.

No, not that. We all feel that.

Then what?

You guard yourself so fiercely, it's almost as if you're afraid of something. Is it me?

For a long time she does not answer, then, finally, she turns, taking his hand and lifting it to her face. Never that, she whispers, never that. Her voice hoarse.

Opening his fingers, he lets their bony architecture slip slowly downwards. The sound of her blood hot in her ears, the filigree patterns of her capillaries dilating beneath her skin as his fingers pass over her forehead, across her eyes, closing their lids, around the ridge of her cheekbone, the line of her jaw and throat. His thumb on her lip like a fever blister.

. . .

Alone in his bedroom, they shed their sodden clothes, piece by piece, bright flashes of pollen staining their skin where the flowers touched it. Her lips curling back in a snarl as he takes her hand, caresses each finger in turn in the hot suck of his mouth, the aching contusion of his pressing teeth, then down, across the heel of her hand, his lips and tongue moving against the network of veins on the underside of her wrist. The heaviness of blood. Her breath catching as she draws his hand free, places it upon her breast. His hand cupping the liquid weight of it, drawing her close so his mouth nuzzles her skin. The pale vulnerability of his chest, hairless as a child's.

Is it dark? he asks, and she feels herself slipping forward.

Yes, she says, there's just the sky.

She cradles his head in the crook of her body, his sleeping face quiet, gnarled in the darkness. His eyes flicker, dreams moving beneath them like clouds.

With one finger she traces the line of his scar, across the nose and downwards, until her finger reaches the point where it creases his lip, and his head jerks and recoils. Still sleeping.

On the edge of sleep he murmured, Do you hear the rain?

When I was a child my room was in the attic. I would sit by the window and listen to the rustling of the rain, the sound of the dripping beneath the eaves, the frogs in the garden. Nothing else mattered, not when it rained, I could imagine I was adrift some place where my parents and school and all the rest of it was irrelevant.

She feels it too, this contraction. All night this winding in, until there is only this moment, this room, the closeness of their bodies. This is the gravity of the flesh, this pulling in of the world; the weight of our bodies' dark cavities, the deathwatch tock of our hearts. She remembers the movement of his hands upon her body, the way they sculpted her form, like wind on sand, on water, moulding the rise of her hip, her breast, the hollow of her waist, throat, armpit.

As if he were making her anew, tracing her shape out of air, translating it from darkness into being.

Sun floods the bedroom when she wakes, motes of dust dancing in the long shafts of light. Its excess of clarity making the events of the night before remote. The bed beside her empty. Her clothes have been removed, and through the bathroom door she can see them hanging.

Wrapped in a towel she walks slowly down the shallow stairs from the loft into the living space. When they arrived last night the lights were off, the only illumination the reflected glow from the low-hanging clouds. In daylight she sees the apartment is larger than she had expected, a long, narrow space, rising a full two storeys to the raftered roof above, lit by skylights. She calls his name but he does not answer. Down on the ground level it is as neat and minimal as it was in the bedroom—a table by a kitchen, two sofas with a simple rug, a grand piano near the door. A flatscreen pushed to one side, input for a sound system beside it. Other than this it is empty: no books, no clutter or sharp surfaces. Just echoing space.

She walks slowly to the far end, pausing beside the piano, its lid and cover down. Reaching out she runs her hand along the varnished wood, then carefully, quietly, pushes the cover back to expose the keys. Letting her fingers fall, she trails them lightly over their surface, first one way, then the other, not striking them, before letting them come to rest. She presses one down and a note rings out, the sound muffled by the lowered lid, but resonant and powerful nonetheless, echoing through the empty space of the apartment.

Behind the piano another staircase rises to a mezzanine and she begins to climb. She says his name again, quietly this time, almost certain he is not here, and again there is no answer. On one side of the space at the top of the stairs a console sits on a long desk, while floor to ceiling shelves run the length of the wall opposite, filled with bulging volumes. On a low table in one corner stands an object Anna does not recognise, something like a printer, but bulkier, older looking. There are two low display cabinets, glass-fronted.

Walking past the desk she pauses long enough to glance at the neatly piled books, the handheld scanner beside them. In a tray sit pieces of paper marked with Braille, and as Anna runs her fingers over them, marvelling that this seemingly indistinguishable rash of dots can be interpreted at all, she realises the object in the corner is a Braille printer. In the centre of the wall beside it is a goods door, the original retained and varnished to reveal the rough cut of the ageing wood, a heavy bolt holding it closed. Anna draws the bolt, opens the door to reveal a view of a tree and sky, the sandstone wall of the house behind. The rain has dispersed somewhere in the night and the heat is already rising.

Pulling the door and bolting it, she continues to the shelves, noting all the spines are spotted with the raised bumps of Braille titles. In the far corner a block of stone sits on a stand, the fossilised face of an ammonite protruding from it. Maybe seventy centimetres in diameter, the shell's surface is marked with a complex web of bumps and ridges, preserved with remarkable clarity. Extending a hand, she caresses it, carefully tracing its contours, the black stone cold and glassy beneath her fingers.

Then she hears a footfall on the stairs. Spinning round, she sees Seth behind her.

I was looking for you, she stammers.

Hearing her voice, he begins to walk towards her. I went out for milk, he says, coming closer. I didn't want to wake you.

She nods, then remembering the futility of the gesture, swallows, twice and hard.

Seth steps past her, raising his hand to the ammonite on the pedestal.

Did you see this? he asks, his hand sliding along its outer edge. Realising he is attempting to find something neutral they can talk about, Anna turns with him.

It's beautiful, she says.

A thoughtful expression on his face, he smiles, although not kindly.

Don't let its beauty fool you, he says. This creature was a hunter, as swift and unfeeling as a shark. It preyed on its own kind, smaller species.

Why tell me that? she asks sharply.

I don't think its beauty can be admired without acknowledging the paradox of the inner creature's viciousness, he says. You see these? he asks, indicating the raised markings on the shell. They were designed to alleviate friction in the water as it swam, creating a sort of boundary layer of turbulence that let it move more quickly. So the very things we respond to as beautiful in it are the things that helped make it a killer. One is inseparable from the other.

Do you think all beauty is cruel?

No, he says. Cruelty is a human notion, just like the beauty of this individual object is a human notion. Neither has meaning in the larger scheme of things. And in the end it's the whole that counts, its continuance and diversity; the meaning of any single part is infinitesimal.

She caresses the shell, thinking. You don't really believe that, she says. I've seen the way you handle the shells. It's almost sexual.

He grins, seemingly genuinely amused. I think that's a good word for it. But you're wrong, it's not the aesthetic qualities of the individual object I'm responding to, it's the way they let me glimpse the patterns of the whole, the way order is written into the fabric of the world. Sex is like that too, at least sometimes, the way you touch something beneath language, beneath all the noise of the world and your self. Something so deep and immediate that just for a moment it's like you're part of the whole, as if a wave has caught you, lifted you up so you're part of the ocean.

I sometimes think that sex is when I feel most alone, she says. That moment only ever reminds me of how far away we really are from each other.

He extends a hand, draws her face to his, his mouth gentle and hot. Anna, he says. She feels the wash of their bodies, the illusion of melt, and then the heat of tears in her eyes, and pushing at him she tears herself away, separating them, his body yielding to her desire to be free.

I have to go, she whispers, her voice hoarse, but he does not reply, just straightens and withdraws, cold and distant once more.

A week passes, days of white heat, nights wretched with humidity and the whine of mosquitoes. Too hot to read, Anna spends the timeless hours between midnight and dawn surfing the merse or scanning the feeds for content, growing high and jittery on the hypnotic flicker of the screen and the glutting images. Thursday night an unemployed academic releases plutonium in a Yokohama subway train, exposing hundreds of commuters to its silent, creeping poison, the train's internal sensors stopping it in a tunnel to prevent the contamination spreading. Twelve hours later a jetliner loses power just after take-off from a Russian industrial town Anna has never heard of, crashing earthwards through a Soviet-era housing estate, the impact igniting the gas mains and sending fires and explosions ripping through whole suburbs. For nearly two days the fires rage, and when they are spent, the victims lie tangled in the smoking carcasses of the buildings, their blackened faces seared and twisted beneath the hoaring frost of the water, ice crusted on hands clawed by the heat. In Sydney, fires still burn through the National Park and the tracts of bushland north and west, the smoke and floating ash dirty against the sky, their glow visible from Anna's balcony at night.

On the Sunday it is Gromeko's birthday, and in honour of the event the astronauts hold an impromptu celebration, pouring champagne in the zero-G so it fizzes and spits like a living thing. Their faces ash-pale from months without natural light, grimy from water rationing, they laugh and sport, almost as if they are purposely trying to contradict the rumours of friction and discord that have begun to circulate through the newsgroups. Murakami is there too, despite the rumours he has suffered some kind of breakdown in the weeks since the death of his family, although he stays at the back, his face never visible to the camera wielded by Foster, until near the end when he turns to face it, and just for a moment the rings of exhaustion around his eyes, the grey pallor of his skin are visible. The mechanical motion of the plastic cup as it rises to his lips, the hunted look in his dark eyes.

And once, amongst the game shows and product promotions and reruns of shows that were barely watchable the first or second or third time, there is a segment on the mopping up in Islamabad, the UN crews in their white contamination suits demolishing a mosque while a crowd of the dying watch and jeer.

On the Monday she has a session at the Museum. Seth is nowhere to be seen, so she accepts an invitation to eat with Dylan at lunchtime.

Where did you disappear to the other night? he asks, and Anna, a fork poised in front of her mouth, stares back at him without flinching.

Nowhere really, she says, chewing steadily. The flicker of a smile around Dylan's mouth annoying her, although he is too canny to push the point.

Rachel calls twice, leaving messages, but uncomfortable about the conjunction of her and Seth, Anna does not reply. Then, on the Thursday, Rachel calls when Anna is at home. When she realises Rachel wants to discuss the photos she has asked her to take, Anna feels a sense of relief, but coupled with it a disappointment. Rachel is brisk, almost as if embarrassed about this decision to be photographed, but Anna agrees to call Jadwiga and see if she can swing studio space sometime soon.

When she calls, Jadwiga is friendly but distant. All the same, she phones Anna back within minutes, telling her she has someone who will let her use their studio as soon as the next day.

. . .

The air in the Centre is uncomfortably warm when she arrives just before five. A pair of kids, fourteen, maybe fifteen, are engaged in an endless, circular argument about their behaviour earlier in the week, while beside them an older woman murmurs to herself. Anna shifts in her seat, uncomfortable with their proximity, fearful their attention might turn to her. Twice the receptionist looks past them at Anna, but before she can break off her phone call, Blaze appears through the heavy security door, holding it open to allow a young woman to exit before him. She cradles a baby which lies silently in her arms, not asleep, but staring. Its silence somehow more disturbing than red-faced cries would have been. Seeing Anna he raises an eyebrow, then finishes farewelling the woman and her child without missing a beat. As they leave Rachel appears at the door, interrupting. Seeing Anna she smiles thinly.

I've got a message from Community Services saying Anton's gone AWOL again.

Oh fuck, he says, glancing at his watch.

So you haven't heard anything?

What's happened? asks Anna, interrupting.

Anton's missed another session with his counsellor, Rachel says.

Blaze glances around at the inquisitive eyes of the waiting room. Let's do this inside, he says.

In the light from the windows, Anna sees the exhaustion in Rachel's face, the bruised skin beneath her eyes.

We can't keep chasing after him like this. He's got to learn to take responsibility for his own actions, Blaze says, once the door has closed behind them.

Jesus, Blaze, listen to yourself.

No, you listen to yourself. You're losing your objectivity about this one. You're overtired and you're letting your emotions get in the way of your judgement.

I'm always tired, Rachel snaps. Next to her Anna shifts uncomfortably, feeling like an intruder.

Blaze looks at his watch again. It's after five, he says. I've got Paul's parents arriving for the weekend at six. I'm already late, and the last thing I need is to be chasing off after Anton. Besides, the odds are the magistrate'll can him Monday whatever happens. This is the third time he's done this.

Rachel stares at him angrily. Right, whatever. I'll handle this on my own. As she walks away towards her office, Anna looks up at Blaze, who waves a hand in exasperation.

She sometimes forgets we can't save all of them.

Should I wait?

Blaze looks towards Rachel's office where they see her through the glass partition, standing behind her desk, one hand jabbing at her console.

I know this mood. She'll spend the whole night looking for the little shit if she has to.

Across the room Rachel has emerged from her office and is walking towards them.

Is the air-conditioning off again? she asks Blaze.

Maria went to see about it hours ago. She should have been back by now.

Well make sure it's on before we leave tonight, or else by Monday morning this place will be like a sauna. The weather feeds are saying it's going to be in the forties by Sunday.

Turning to Anna she runs her hand through her hair, pushing it back off her face. I don't know how long this is going to take.

I can call the guy whose studio we're borrowing. I don't think he needs us out of there by any particular time.

Would it be a problem for you to do that?

Not at all.

Why don't you go and have a drink somewhere? It's filthy in here.

I could come with you, Anna offers weakly.

Rachel glances at Blaze, who looks back without speaking, his mouth still set in irritation. After a moment she turns back to Anna.

Sure, she says. Why not?

Are we going back to Lewin's? Anna asks as they push their way through the crowds milling around the Chinese grocery beneath the Centre.

Not if I can help it. We'll try the Brewery first.

The mention of the Brewery makes Anna hesitate.

You mean the place up past Central? The tent city?

Rachel looks at her coolly. Yes. Why?

Is it safe? I thought even the cops wouldn't go there.

Rachel snorts derisively. The cops know better. And I wouldn't go there at night or alone. But they're people who live there, Anna. They're not monsters or wild animals.

Anna nods, chastened but not quite convinced.

It is almost six by the time they get there. Near the main gateway a number of older men and women, some Aboriginal, are passing around a brown-bagged bottle. In their midst a grizzled man has fallen asleep across a crumpled wine flask, yellow piss darkening the broken asphalt beneath him. One or two of them recognise Rachel, looking up and slurring greetings as she approaches, their eyes bleary with drink. She acknowledges their welcome, kneeling down beside one of them, a battered looking Islander, his black hair turning grey, face cracked by the sun and the drink. He raises the bottle to her in friendly salute.

Hey, pretty lady, he says, his good-natured face creasing into a smile.

Hey, Vinnie, Rachel replies, brushing something from his shirtfront with the back of her hand. How's it going?

He laughs, exposing a line of teeth which gape brokenly. Pretty fine, pretty fine. When's the little one coming?

Not long now, Rachel says.

You still going to call him Vinnie?

It might not be a he.

Vinnie's a good name. Strong name. As he says this he puffs his barrel of a chest outwards.

Yeah, Vinnie, it is a good name. But look, I'm trying to find Anton. Have you seen him?

Vinnie rubs his head with the swollen knuckles of his hand.

He was here before.

So he's around?

Oh yeah, I think so.

Rachel turns to the woman beside Vinnie.

Is that right, Susie?

Reckon.

As Rachel questions Vinnie and his friends, Anna finds herself admiring her straightforward manner, the way she talks to them directly and honestly. She is sympathetic and friendly, without sounding pitying, firm without sounding superior. Remembering the embarrassment and discomfort she felt in the waiting room not half an hour before, Anna finds herself envying Rachel's ease. As Rachel seeks assurances that the man slumped over the cask is okay, a voice comes echoing across the broken walls of the Brewery, clear and sweet, rising above the sound of the traffic, the passing crowds. Anna looks around, startled.

That'll be him, Vinnie says, and Anna looks at Rachel in surprise.

Didn't I tell you he could sing? Rachel asks, smiling.

Anna shakes her head. You know you didn't.

They follow the voice through the gates, the broken shell of the building looming above them on three sides. Suddenly nervous, Anna glances around, keenly aware of the many eyes upon her, the huddled figures crouched in their cardboard beds and makeshift tents and, higher up, the watchful faces of the groups that sit upon the exposed floors of the ruined structure. With the air of someone who knows her way around, Rachel leads Anna towards a slip of rubble, rusting reinforcements jutting twisted from slabs of concrete, then clambers upwards to the first floor.

At the top she glances from side to side, trying to ascertain the source of the voice. The song is an old one from before Anna was born, plangent and sad, a lover longing to throw his arms around his beloved, sung slowly and unaccompanied.

Rachel gestures towards a flight of stairs. This way, she says.

They climb slowly, picking their way over the drifts of rubbish.

Be careful where you step, Rachel says, looking back at Anna who has a hand across her nose to ward off the stink of human waste.

I was, she says grimly.

At the top of the stairs the singing can still be heard, but Rachel, drawing Anna closer to her, says: Be careful, okay?

Anna nods, glancing around as Rachel leads her through to a huge room, where tumbled machinery and rusting vats and drums are piled. On the opposite wall windows give onto another building and in one, his back to the frame, knees raised to his chin, Anton gazes out into the alley below, his voice lingering on the last words of the song. Hearing them he looks over, a jumble of emotions playing across his face.

Stepping forward, Rachel motions to Anna to remain where she is. On the sill Anton seems to tense, as if for flight.

We need to talk, Rachel says, but Anton doesn't answer. Moving closer, she smiles. I liked the song.

It's old, he says, his voice once again the ugly, flat voice of the street, its harshness so unlike the sound that had echoed through the building only moments before.

I know. I used to love it when I was your age. At this Anton breaks into a mawkish grin, his lean face suddenly boyish, wall eye skidding from side to side in his narrow face.

Was it about someone in particular? Rachel asks.

Anton stares at Rachel with a look of panic. No, he says, a flush spreading up his neck, making his protruding ears glow. Nodding past Rachel at Anna, he slips down off the sill, keeping his back to the wall.

Lewin said she was cool.

Rachel turns to look at her.

I am, Anna says.

You shouldn't have been there.

Rachel looks back at him. Don't talk shit, Anton. She had as much right to be there as you and Lewin. You should be grateful she didn't go to the cops.

Anton moves his head from side to side, derisive, mocking, but Rachel doesn't rise to the bait.

Your counsellor called. He says you didn't turn up again.

So?

I thought we'd sorted this out, she says wearily. If you don't turn up they'll put you inside, you know that.

He stares back sullenly.

We'll have to get you into court Monday morning, explain why you weren't there.

Why'd you bring her?

We're friends. We were meant to be going out until your counsellor called.

Where were you going?

Rachel kneads the bridge of her nose. I don't have time for this crap, Anton. Just promise me you'll be at the court on Monday.

Anton stares at her, defiant. And just for a moment there is something else in his face; a vulnerability too obviously tangled up in his anger.

Promise me.

I promise.

Good. Now why the fuck weren't you there this week?

I dunno.

Did Lewin tell you not to go?

No! he says, defensive. Why would he do that?

You spend a lot of time with him.

I watch him work is all.

If you say so. But he's a dangerous man, be careful of him.

He's not, Anton declares, eyes flashing.

Listen, Anton, Rachel says, her voice firm, I know stuff about him from before you were around, bad stuff. A kid like you got killed. So all I'm saying is be careful.

Anton stares at her without replying.

So, Monday morning.

Yeah, whatever.

As they turn to go Anna hesitates, turns back to him.

I liked the song as well. Where'd you learn to sing?

At school, he says. And in church.

Anna smiles. I'd like to hear you again some time, she tells him, and once again the grin is there, disconcertingly puppyish.

Outside, Anna comes close to Rachel.

What did you mean back there, about Lewin?

He's not a nice man.

You said a kid died.

Two, actually.

He killed them?

Rachel shrugs. Blaze thinks he killed one of them. He's known Lewin since he turned up about three years ago. Back then Blaze was working at a refuge in the inner west and Lewin was squatting with a bunch of others in a place in Erskineville. He wasn't painting then, and he was a whole lot scarier than he is now; bigger, meaner, bad rep on the streets. Anyway, one night a kid got killed in the squat, someone beat him to death with a piece of pipe. Apparently there was blood everywhere, the kid was pretty much paste, like the killer had been in a total frenzy. Everyone assumed the kid's boyfriend had done it, he was a nasty little piece of work by all reports, and the cops picked him up within an hour, covered in blood and just a few blocks away.

I thought you said Lewin did it.

Rachel pauses. No, I said Blaze thinks Lewin did it. Anyway, the cops get the kid's boyfriend into remand, but because it's late and this is street business the cops don't really care about, they leave questioning him for a few hours, and in that time he manages to hang himself.

Jesus.

Anyway, that was good enough for the cops, so they just dropped it. Probably thought it was a waste of time anyway, one streetie killing another. But a couple of months later Blaze was interviewing one of his clients and this guy spills a story about how it was Lewin who killed this kid. This guy said the kid owed him money, and Lewin, who hated the kid anyway, started hassling him about it. This client of Blaze's sort of went along with it for a while, but then Lewin went completely psycho, killed the kid. The boyfriend came in at the end, saw what was happening, but once he saw the kid was dead he shot through.

Did Blaze tell the cops?

Rachel shakes her head. This client of Blaze's was on a suspended sentence, so chances are he would have ended up back inside for having been involved. He wasn't a well man and that would have been the end of him.

Do you think Lewin did it?

Rachel shrugs. God knows.

T he studio is in an old print factory in Redfern. Looking at the traffic banked up along Elizabeth Street they decide to walk, so it is growing dark by the time they arrive. Finding the street is easy, but once they are on it they struggle to make sense of the numbers, which jump seemingly at random from one building to the next. Eventually Anna's codex guides them to a heavy door and, watched by a security camera, no doubt transmitting their images to some central registry for storage and retrieval if necessary, they buzz the intercom and are admitted.

Several floors up they come to the right door. A young man, his face angelic beneath blond curls, holds it open.

Andrew? Anna asks and he nods, extending a hand for her to shake.

It's good to meet you. Sorry we're so late.

He looks down at his watch. That's fine, but I'm going to have to run. Come in and I'll show you how to lock up.

Once they have been led through the security procedures and Rachel has been shown the way to the toilet, Andrew hurries off. Anna sets up her equipment, taking stock of the space, while Rachel paces from side to side, inspecting the framed images hung on the walls.

I won't be long, Anna says, running through a systems check on her camera. You might as well get undressed. Surreptitiously she watches Rachel to gauge her reaction, knowing this will be a good indicator of how relaxed her subject will be during the session to come. To her relief Rachel only hesitates for a second before beginning to unbutton her shirt.

Once she is ready, Rachel steps out into the circle of the lights, and as she turns to face the camera, Anna sees the bony lines of Seth's face in hers, but writ softer. Rachel is thinner than Anna had expected, her body long like Seth's, but lither, more muscled. It is the belly and the breasts that draw the attention, the small, high breasts, their dark, helmeted nipples swollen; beneath them the flat of her sternum before the hard protrusion of her stomach, its stretched roundness somehow emphasising the narrowness of her frame. Beneath her stomach her pubic hair runs in a narrow thatch. Her olive skin marked with old freckles across her shoulders and décolletage. Catching Anna watching her, she stares back with a mixture of uncertainty and challenge, a look, Anna supposes, that passes for trust.

Where should I stand?

There is fine. I need to adjust the lights.

This done, Anna turns back to Rachel, who is standing with one arm across her body.

Can you stay like that?

Rachel looks up. Like this? she asks, managing to preserve the attitude Anna had glimpsed.

That's right.

After several shots Anna remarks upon Rachel's capacity to follow directions, and Rachel laughs.

I was a life model for a while.

Anna looks over the top of her camera. Really? Where?

In London. I was there for two years after I finished school.

Did you enjoy it? Anna asks, and Rachel laughs again, a deep, throaty laugh.

God no, it was boring beyond belief. Day after day sitting still in drafty studios. I actually got a chilblain once.

Anna chuckles, snapping her while she is talking and relaxed.

It all seems so long ago.

This wasn't when you were at Cambridge?

No, that was when I did my masters, much later. This was before I even began university, when Seth was over there doing his doctorate at Oxford.

You went with him?

Not really. But I had no reason to stay here once he'd left. He'd only held off going that long because I was at school.

This was after your parents died?

Long after. They died when I was ten.

Lowering the camera Anna stares at her. You never told me what happened to them.

Car crash. Dad had taken a redundancy and they'd decided to spend a few months travelling. They were somewhere between Perth and Broome and they hit a truck.

That's awful. How old was Seth?

Eighteen, just. Child Welfare wanted to separate us, put me into care, because they thought it was unwise to leave a girl my age in the charge of someone they saw as severely disabled. Seth refused to let them.

That can't have been easy.

Rachel shrugs. We had money from the insurance. We managed.

Something about Rachel's tone seems to close this avenue of enquiry, so for a minute or two their conversation reverts to the business of the shoot. Eventually it is Rachel who resumes the conversation.

Why did you give it up?

I'm sorry?

Photography, what made you stop?

I'm taking photos now, Anna says, her voice hard and tight.

I didn't mean to pry.

Through the viewfinder Anna sees Rachel's eyes still on her, unwavering.

It's alright, she says, it was a perfectly reasonable question. I shouldn't have snapped.

You were successful, weren't you?

Sort of.

And then you just vanished.

Have you been checking up on me?

No. I have a friend who has one of your portraits. I've always loved it.

I met someone. He lived in Hong Kong.

There is a moment's silence while Rachel digests the absences in this sentence.

Is he still there?

Lowering the camera, Anna forces herself to look at Rachel. I don't know. Probably.

When Rachel speaks again her voice is tentative. The portrait that my friend has, I saw it again last week. It's of a man. He looks like you.

Daniel.

Who?

My twin brother.

The other night you said he was missing.

He was an academic at Hong Kong University, Anna says, her voice flat and expressionless. He disappeared during the PLA action in August last year.

You mean you don't know what happened to him?

No, she says, raising the camera once more.

The night has grown warmer since dusk, a grimy, fetid heat. In Seth's street it is dark, a dog barking murderously somewhere nearby, whipped into a frenzy by something unseen.

From inside there is the sound of movement, then his voice on the intercom.

Who is it? he asks.

It's Anna, she says.

It's late.

I know. I need to speak to you.

There is a moment of silence then the click of the door.

Stepping into the security space she sees him standing behind the inner door, its weight like a shield between them. Wanting to touch him, she raises a hand to his cheek, but he pulls away, almost imperceptibly, and angrily she withdraws it.

Were you sleeping? she asks, seeing he is barefoot in loose trousers and a T-shirt.

No, he replies, his face looking over her, past her, as he closes the door. Just working.

So late?

I often work late at night. It's quieter, fewer distractions.

Inside, music is playing, cello, the sonorous gravity of its wooden chamber echoing through the airy space. Turning, Anna sees he is still standing by the door, his face empty of feeling, masklike.

My sister, Sophie, plays the cello, did I tell you?

I don't think so.

She lives in New York, plays in a quartet with her husband.

It's a beautiful instrument.

Yes, it is.

Have you been out?

I've been with Rachel, taking photos for her.

She did ask you to in the end?

Yes.

Then there is a long moment when neither speaks. It is Seth who finally breaks the silence.

How is your hand?

Anna smiles, the ordinariness of the question a relief.

A lot better, she says. I had the stitches out last week.

It's Bach, by the way.

What? . . . oh, the music.

As they have been speaking she has moved towards him. Now she extends a hand, takes his. He starts at her touch, but does not resist.

The other morning, I shouldn't have run off like that, she says. It was childish, and cowardly.

I understood.

No, she says, I don't think you did. You asked me what I was afraid of, and I said it wasn't you.

But it is?

She shakes her head. No, or not exactly. I'm afraid of how I am around you, of how vulnerable I am. As she speaks she begins to pull away, but he closes his hand over hers, restraining her.

Can I tell you something? he asks.

Of course.

Normally when women are attracted to me it's about my blindness. They want to care for me, to save me. But with you it's different.

You mean I'm the cripple? she snorts bitterly.

No. But so much of you is hidden, so much is kept in.

It frightens me.

Not just this.

No, she agrees, tears filling her eyes. Oh God, why is this so complicated?

He places a hand on her cheek, his thumb against her cheekbone, one finger beneath the line of her jaw. Do you want this? he asks.

At first she does not, cannot answer. Then, in one abrupt movement she pulls herself up towards him, her arm dragging his mouth to hers.

APOCRYPHA

· 6 ·

It is illuminating to read these later images in the light of Frasier's 'Extinction' sequence of 2012. In the earlier sequence fossilised ammonites were photographed to suggest life in death or, more precisely, a continuity not just between what is ordinarily perceived as living and what is ordinarily perceived as dead, but between the organic and the inorganic. Of course these were issues of some controversy in those years, which saw revolutions not just in biology, but in artificial intelligence and cybernetics, beginning the first substantive blurrings of these boundaries, previously regarded as sacrosanct. In the later photographs the seashells are at once harder and softer than the ammonites of the 'Extinction' sequence, their smooth, almost ceramic surfaces seeming to declare their imperviousness, even as the delicate colours and flanges of their openings suggest something far softer, even fleshy. This suggestion becomes stronger when one considers Frasier's ongoing interest in the continuity of form in the natural world. Over many years she photographed objects and phenomena that demand explanation simply by their existence, whether they were the sculpted lines of sand blown before the wind, the delicate architecture of the primitive ferns of Tasmania, or the geometric curves of seashells. In every case the object or phenomenon in question commands our attention for the way it stands out, yet simultaneously, prompts our wonder at its regularity and clarity. For Frasier this appreciation was the same whether the object was organic, inorganic or, in the case of the ammonites and the shells, some mixture of the two.

Therefore it seems no great leap to see in these pinkly toothed cowries and rosily smooth conch vents not just an eroticisation of the inanimate, but conversely a constitutive understanding of the human body, through which the salt blood of the sea flows.

MICHAELA RUTHVEN, *Anna Frasier: A Retrospective*

Fever

Fever *n., & v.t.* (Path) A morbid condition of the system, characterised by undue elevation of the temperature, and excessive change and destruction of the tissues.

From his window in the Brewery, Anton watches the men move around the truck in the alley below, their shouts rising to him on the humid air. Every morning it comes, four, five o'clock, the whine of the hydraulics piercing his sleep. Sometimes he will lie still, one arm pulled over his head, trying to block out the shriek of the lifter as it raises the skips to its waiting maw, the intermittent thud of the rubbish as it falls; other times he climbs to his window and watches it go about its work. The black drool of the bins leaks from the truck's belly to stain the broken street, as it empties skip after skip, clearing the refuse of the restaurants in the street beyond. Every night more, always more. Sometimes he stops in the street, stands looking at the green bins loaded to overflowing, the blue skips so full they cannot be closed, and wonders where it all goes, these mountains of garbage, day after day after day. Across the rooftops, across the yellow-lit streets, the dark-topped trees and banks of seeping stone, the burning fronts of the fires are red upon the horizon. Overhead a satellite moves silently against a sodium sky. Too hot to sleep, Anton sits watching the truck, waiting for the dawn.

Like the pale line of a finger drawn across sunburnt skin, the liquid crystals blur and reform behind her thumb as she traces Rachel's outline on the slate's screen. Of the photos she took the four nights before, this one is her favourite. Not black and white, although the subterranean cast of the light almost fools one into believing it might be, it shows Rachel standing, facing the camera, her gaze direct and unashamed. One arm crossed over her breasts, the fingers splayed across her shoulder, the other looped beneath the rounded swelling of her belly. Her breasts pressing heavily against the crossed arm. The image's seeming lack of artifice capturing a moment of unexpected candour, not defiance, like a wild thing seen for an instant, then gone.

Last night, in the back of a taxi, her earpiece had chimed, the network identifying the callsign as Rachel's. Looking through the smoked glass at the passing buildings, Anna answered. Outside it was hot, but in the climate-controlled cabin of the taxi, a world apart, it was cool. All day she had been feeling jittery, as if something were crawling beneath her skin, as if her blood were flowing hotter, faster than it should. Colour more intense, sudden conjunctions of words and objects uncanny, irresistible as premonition. Nothing quite real.

Anna? Rachel's voice, as close as if the other woman were there with her, mouth pressed to her ear, whispering silkily.

I'm in a taxi, she said, as if this were explanation enough. Rachel laughed.

I hope it's air-conditioned. They turned ours off again last week.

You're still in the office?

Hopefully, I'll get out of here soon. It's been a madhouse. It's the same every year: Christmas, the heat, they drive everyone crazy.

Anna did not answer, just closed her hand against the stiffness in it.

That's why I called, I wondered if you had plans.

For Christmas? No. As she spoke the taxi cleared Taylor Square, the sky huge above its open space, dwarfing the buildings jutting against it, bats dark against the starless night as they streamed eastward.

I've just been talking with Oliver Bloom—

The chef?

From Twenty-Nine. He's agreed to cook Christmas dinner for one of the missions, it's part charity, part publicity stunt, but Blaze and I have been invited. I thought, if you didn't have plans . . .

And Seth? she asked abruptly, biting back on the words as soon as they were uttered.

There was a moment's silence, then Rachel said, I thought I'd ask him too.

In Seth's bed, two hours later, she rolled away from him, her eyes fixing on the ceiling.

Rachel called, she said. She asked me to lunch on Christmas Day.

He kissed her fingertips, but she drew her hand away.

Did you say you'd go?

I said I'd think about it, she said. Do you want me there?

He hesitated. Yes, he said, I do. Through the open window came the sound of traffic, the klaxon call of a siren. Then the sharp retort of a gun. Then silence.

Lowering the slate to the table, she taps it once to close the images, the whirr of its circuitry barely audible as the slate beams the data to her waiting codex, then onwards to Rachel. There is something wrong with her, she can feel it, an elation in her flesh. It frightens her, excites her, her tumid lips swollen, throbbing like bruises, her body's motions fervid. Her muscles delirious, aching. The clammy fetor of her skin.

The first time the fever took her was three years before, in a hotel on the cliffs of Luang Prabang, high above the muddy waters of the Mekong. The evening air thick with the smell of kerosene smoke and decay as they wandered the crowded markets, the grey mornings soft with incense and the sound of prayer.

She and Jared had been travelling from Vietnam to Myanmar along the river. At first she thought it was her stomach, which cramped and spasmed, leaving her huddled over the cold porcelain of the hotel toilet, but when pills failed to work and she grew weaker, delirious with fever, Jared became concerned and sought the hotel doctor. Swaddled in the stinking sheets of the bed, the smell of her bowels fouling the air, she barely noticed him, only whimpering as he inserted the needle, drew her blood for testing. His diagnosis back within the hour. Malaria.

Not trusting the river transport or the local hospital, Jared organised a medivac to Vientiane, and from there a shuttle flight to Hong Kong. The whole way he stayed beside her, careful lest he touch the sores that had started to flower across her mouth and nose, his concern overcoming his revulsion at the leaking viscera of her body, the uncontrollable violence of the fever. Once, in the helicopter, she woke and looked around, briefly lucid, confused by the heavy beat of the rotor. She saw him seated opposite, attention concentrated on the mountains beneath, the heavy greenery that blanketed their slopes. She wanted to sit, but when she tried she could not, the tight straps of the stretcher holding her in place. Fear welling up in her, she twisted, called his name, but her words would not form, and what issued from her mouth was barely more than a croak.

It was enough though, for he turned, and, seeing she was awake, undid his seat belt and knelt beside her, one hand stroking her forehead. You're going to be fine, he murmured. But it was too late, for as he turned she had seen the quickly suppressed flicker of distaste that had passed behind his eyes, and now she saw the reluctance in his touch, the way her flesh repulsed him, however hard he tried to hide it.

Later she was to tell herself she had imagined it, but its memory would not fade, his every gesture suddenly suspect.

B y Friday she has subsided into the sickness, murmuring in her sleep, calling names Seth does not recognise. Her shallow breath, the heat of her body waking him before dawn. Frightened, he covers her shaking form, trying vainly to rouse her from her delirium. And when he cannot he calls Rachel.

She arrives quickly. Standing by the door in the grey light, she does not quiz him about Anna's presence. But Seth knows her well enough to understand this briskness in her manner; her focus on the matter at hand is likely to be a mask for other, angrier feelings. For the moment though he is unconcerned with Rachel's opinions, interested only in Anna and her condition.

Upstairs, Rachel kneels beside the bed, touching Anna's cheek with the back of her hand.

She's burning up, she says, looking round at Seth, who stands behind her.

I think it's malaria, he says.

Did she tell you that?

Last night.

Rachel shakes her head, glancing at her watch. I'm going to call Vinh, get him over here. It'll be quicker than the hospital. She probably hasn't got insurance anyway.

Vinh arrives before an hour is gone, Rachel answering the door and leading him to the bed where Anna lies. While Seth and Rachel watch he examines her, asking them questions about her medical history neither are able to answer. At one point he asks about HIV and hepatitis and, turning, sees the set look on Rachel's face, Seth beside her, his folded arms and drawn face betraying his anxiety. When neither answers he turns back to his patient, saying he will take blood for tests and give her something for her fever.

Once Vinh has gone, Rachel brews coffee, leaning by the sink and watching Seth's hands cradle the cup. His nostrils flaring as he sips at it.

Why didn't you tell me? she asks at last, her voice level, but angry. Glancing at the sleeping area above them she adds, almost as an afterthought, Why didn't she?

He does not answer immediately, his silence designed to remind her that he is not obliged to, that this matter is his concern.

I would have, he says, in time.

I see, she says frostily. And how long has this been going on?

Several weeks.

The concert?

No. After that.

They are interrupted by Anna's voice, croaky and weak, calling Seth's name.

I'll go, Rachel says, putting her cup down, but Seth is already on his feet.

Upstairs Anna has pulled herself upright, her legs hanging loosely, her body swaying from side to side. She looks up at Rachel's approach, the other woman's identity not seeming to register until Rachel kneels beside her.

Did Seth call you? she asks, and Rachel nods, placing one hand on Anna's brow.

Yes.

Where is he?

I'm here, says Seth, and Anna extends her hand.

I'm so sorry.

There's nothing to be sorry about, Rachel says. You're sick, that's not your fault. She looks up at Seth, who stands above them both, awkward and unsure.

I think her temperature's a bit better.

Is it? Anna asks. I feel awful.

Rachel pushes a strand of hair back from Anna's face, lingering upon the arc of her cheekbone. Even like this she is beautiful. Feeling the heat of her skin she cannot help but imagine the blood moving beneath her hand, the tiny corpuscles changing, bursting, as they carry the malady around her body.

Vinh's doing some blood tests.

She shakes her head. No need. It's malaria. I've had it for . . . she struggles to think . . . three years. You said Vinh was here?

About half an hour ago.

I don't remember. With some effort she extends her left arm, looks at the point where the needle introduced the fever suppressant. A deep bruise has formed already, spreading outwards from the line of entry, the blood pooling beneath the skin's soft barrier. Rachel looks at it, grimacing sympathetically.

I have to go to the toilet, Anna says. But I don't know if I can get there on my own.

I'll help you, Rachel says. Can you stand?

I'm not sure.

Here . . . Rachel turns, getting ready to lift her. As she does she sees Seth's face, the quick flare of resentment. This is an old argument, but none the less painful.

Once she is upright Anna sways uncertainly, but she manages to walk as far as the toilet, Rachel closing the door behind her. Leaning by the door Rachel hears the quick stream of the other woman's urine, watches Seth turn away, as if by so doing he could block it out.

Anna slips back into sleep almost immediately, but Seth stays beside her, stroking her back, Rachel watching. Eventually she reaches out, touches his arm, and after a moment's hesitation he stands, following her back down the stairs.

I have to go, she says. I've got court at ten, and I need to get home and change first. Will you be able to cope on your own?

I can cope, Seth says.

Are you sure? There's a friend, a gallery owner she mentioned.

I don't know anything about a gallery owner. And don't treat me as if I'm a child. For several seconds Rachel does not answer, but then she sighs, massaging her forehead with her fingers.

I don't have time for this, she says, her voice tight, I've got to be in court.

But Seth does not reply, just folds his arms.

Right, she says, whatever.

From somewhere far away she hears their voices rise and fall, slippery and confusing as the back-mind burble of acid come-down. Her body hot and trembling. Much later she is awake again, her mouth dry, still caught in the grip of her illness, but lucid. It is hot in the loft: through the blind she sees the sun—late afternoon? Or another day? Pushing the sheet away, she lies miserably on her side, staring across the room. On a table by the bed there is a jug, a glass of water beside it, and lifting herself on one elbow she reaches for it, gulping greedily at its warm wetness. She calls Seth's name, but there is no answer, the apartment silent. After a while she finds herself wondering where he might be, but she feels too weak to get up and look for him, instead remaining where she is, not moving, tired, but not quite ready to sleep again. Some time later she hears the click of the door, Seth's feet across the hard wood of the boards. The sound of his keys on the table. The room's dim light pierces deep into her head, stabbing a pain behind one eye. Then he is on the stairs, his thin form rising through the shadows as he climbs to the loft. At the top of the stairs he pauses, listening. She knows she should speak, alert him to the fact she is awake, but something holds her back, just as it did that day in the Museum. There is a pleasure in this invisibility, and not just that, the unshared knowledge of his visibility frightening her, exciting her, the combination intoxicating. For almost a minute she lies silently, unable to break the spell of what she feels. Then he steps back, turning away. Not wanting him to go she extends a hand, mumbling his name.

You're awake, he says, seating himself beside her on the bed.

Is Rachel . . . ?

She's gone.

Before, I thought I heard you arguing . . .

He places the back of his hand on her brow, a chill passing through her as his skin brushes hers.

It doesn't matter.

I'm sorry.

He lets his hand trail downwards, across her cheek, picking strands of her hair from her face.

Don't be. Rachel needs to be reminded I can look after myself from time to time.

She takes his hand in hers, drawing it to her mouth to kiss it lightly, her lips hot.

Not just about that; about this, about being sick, imposing on you.

Don't be stupid. After a moment he pulls his hand free and lifts it to her brow once more.

You're hot again.

It must be the fever, she says, turning inwards towards him, closing over into the darkness of his body, the fetid sheets.

It must be the fever.

It should have come as no surprise. For more than a decade, as the planet warmed, this most ancient of travellers had been spreading north and south, recolonising territories lost over the century before. The patterns of contagion moving faster as the disease mutated, the new strains more virulent, drug-resistant. But even as it filtered into areas once considered safe, it remained a disease of the poor, the host mosquitoes breeding in the standing water of the shanty towns and slums, in the abandoned developments and rusting industrial areas, only rarely affecting people like Jared and Anna, safe in their climate-controlled eyries amongst the glass and nanosteel mountains of the cities.

The strain Anna had contracted was one of the more serious, with a high mortality rate, but once hospitalised her condition stabilised quickly and she was soon released into private care. Jared organised a nurse, a Malay girl with bad skin who spent the days watching Singaporean game shows on the feeds and shrieking with laughter. She seemed to have a particular fascination with one of the hosts, Harry Chan, a man whose permahold hair and evangelist smile Anna found particularly repulsive. In the commercial breaks the Taliban ran scripture lessons, piped in from Afghanistan, dour recitations of prohibited acts and proscribed books and films, strangely at odds with the glitz of the game shows. Sometimes, woken by the sound of the feeds or her nurse's high-pitched laughter, Anna would stand at the door to the kitchen, where the girl sat on a stool watching her shows, peeling nuts and eating them open-mouthed. Around Jared the girl was obse-quiously polite, but in his absence she treated Anna with barely dis-guised contempt, an attitude Anna, angry and resentful, had little difficulty reciprocating. She wanted the apartment to herself, and as soon as she could convince Jared to let her she ended her nurse's contract.

Once the nurse was disposed of, Anna was free to spend the long days alone. Jared usually left before dawn, needing to review the overnight trading on Wall Street. Sometimes, when she woke, she would find the sheets still imprinted with his shape, his scent, the warmth of his body, and dozily she would crawl into the rumpled space he had occupied and slip back into sleep. When she woke again, mid-morning or later, she would watch the news channels on the feeds, allowing the endlessly scrolling streams of data to wash over her, hypnotic. Jared had bought one of the new consoles, a state-of-the-art set of goggles and gloves, but Anna found the experience of mersing too demanding, and they lay on the desk in his study, unused.

No-one ever visited, not even Daniel. And it had been so long since they had spoken she could not call him, not now. One evening as he undressed for bed Jared snapped at her, suggesting she should get out, spend some time with other people. His anger frightening her. She asked him who, and for a long moment he stood, hands raised to the tie that hung loosened around his neck, staring coldly into the mirror at her reflection.

Try Frey, he said, or Roger or Tim. They're your friends too for God's sake. Call them. Just don't lie there moping all the time.

But they weren't her friends, they were his. She couldn't call them.

And then one morning she didn't get up, just lay in bed all day, waiting for Jared. The next day the same, and so on for a week, then a month. It was easy for Jared not to notice that the middles had fallen out of her days; the markets had begun the largest, most sustained bull run in history, and with no end in sight, Jared and others like him were working days that stretched from before dawn until late in the evening, constantly immersed in the oceans of data that pumped through the fibre-optic arteries of the nets as they chased the moving line of daylight around the globe. Everywhere: America, Europe, China, Japan, it was the same, a frenzy of speculation on a scale never before imagined, a kind of madness, addictive and intoxicating. The banquet he and his colleagues used to enjoy once a week had become a nightly ritual, an immense, gluttonous consummation of the lunatic euphoria of money, course after course, as, like gamblers, they rode this tide of fortune, not quite believing their luck, their disbelief making their celebrations all the more frantic, all the wilder.

Alone in their apartment, high above the teeming streets, suckled on the endless whispering of the feeds, Anna felt the world outside grow strange and frightening, the faces on the screens ugly, their voices barking and harsh. Sometimes, amidst the news channels she would stumble upon evangelists, plastic faces that preached a gospel of fear and hatred, that talked of revelations and portents, their voices silky and sickening. In Argentina frogs fell from the sky, in Egypt locusts devastated the land, in Idaho mice spread by their millions, consuming everything in their path, the ground moving as their seething bodies poured across it. And with each day it grew harder to hide from the voices that whispered in her own head.

Until one day, outwardly no different from so many that had gone before, she caught sight of herself in the mirror. The lank hair and staring eyes of her reflected image appalling her, transfixing her. Her numbness pierced suddenly by shame, and disgust, and without warning, hot tears, her body subsiding to the cold floor, sobs welling up like water from within.

She did not know how long she sat huddled beside the toilet. It might have been an hour or half a day, but eventually the keenness of her grief passed, burnt away, and she wiped her face, seized with the knowledge that she had to do something, anything, rather than remain here, alone in the apartment. Choking back on the fear that demanded she give this away and crawl back into the waiting bed, she washed herself, scrubbing her body and teeth until her skin was raw and her gums bled. She could not remember the last time she had brushed her teeth, but her mouth felt thick and foul, her breath clotting. In the bedroom she dressed, watching the way her clothes hung loose on her frame, the violence of her hips and ribs beneath her skin frightening her. When was the last time she had eaten a proper meal? she found herself wondering, but could not remember. Eating was something she did with Jared, and he was never there anymore.

In the lobby she found herself hesitating, the movement and light that lay beyond the glass walls seeming uncontrollable and terrible. But by the doors she saw the security guards watching her, their faces contemptuous, and so she swallowed her fear, stepped out into the roar that broke around her as the soundproof doors slid open.

The heat outside was stifling, a wall of humid air and the too-fast, too-loud movement of the street, but she walked on, one step at a time, jostled and pushed by the hurrying crowds, the turbulence of the footpaths pulling her along, people pushing past her as she clung to the escalator rail. She moved amongst this streaming, roaring tide of humanity like an alien, feeling separate, not quite real. Although she had not intended it, eventually she found herself on the pavement outside the Millennium Tower, where she knew Jared would be seated in his office, high above the noise and heat that surrounded her. Oblivious to the angry stares of the passers-by whose passage she thwarted, she looked up, her eyes following the dizzying rise of the black-panelled curves into the glare of the sun. She could go in, she knew that, walk to the reception, ask the cool-voiced receptionist to find him for her, demand they pull him from whatever videoconferences or phone calls absorbed him, but she could not, unwilling to let him or anyone else see her as yet another needy wife or partner, struggling to fend off emptiness with endless rounds of lunch and tennis, shopping trips to Bangkok and Shanghai and Sydney.

The journey back was slower, her body exhausted by the unaccustomed activity, the vividness of light, and by the time she reached the apartment building she had to fight the urge to weep with tiredness. But then she heard a voice calling her name and, turning, saw Daniel waving as he crossed the street towards her, his face so familiar it seemed only hours since they had spoken, not months.

Hey, he said, drawing level with her, I was waiting for you. I wasn't sure when you'd be back. Extending his arms he drew her to him, seeking her embrace, but Anna, suddenly afraid, pushed him away, her movements stiff, not quite natural.

I went for a walk, she said, one hand indicating the way she had come, as if this were no great achievement, but she saw the way he watched her, the concern behind his eyes.

Sophie called. She said you'd been sick.

Anna stared blankly, trying to remember calling Sophie.

Malaria, she said, I had malaria.

Jesus. When? Why didn't you tell me?

She shrugged. I don't know.

Reaching out he gripped her shoulder, steadying her. You look tired.

I am.

Can I come up with you?

Yes, she said. Please.

Upstairs he guided her through the door, seating her on the couch.

Let me get you a drink, he said, pulling a bottle from the fridge.

Inca Cola? he asked, inspecting the label.

Yes, please, she said, as he poured two glasses. One glass in each hand, he flopped on the couch beside her, stretching his legs insouciantly on the table in front of them.

Where's Jared?

At work, she said, and he looked at her in surprise over his glass.

On a Saturday?

Caught unawares, she struggled to keep her ignorance hidden. The American markets will only just have closed for the weekend, she said, dissembling.

He must have been busy.

She nodded. He has. How's Briar?

Great.

As he sipped the green cola his smile grew wicked. His hair was longer than it had been, almost to his shoulders, its fall making him more androgynous, more like her. Dear old Jared, he said, mockreflective. How's his heart?

Anna laughed, despite herself. Still ticking. You really pissed him off that night, you know.

He shrugged. I'm sorry.

It's no use apologising to me, Anna said, her eyes glittering, the recklessness Daniel always seemed to engender in her beginning to return.

I'll make it up to him, Daniel said, really I will, managing to look serious until she elbowed him in the ribs.

Liar.

For a moment he bit his lip, then unable to help himself he began to laugh.

Nabbed, he said, but then she was laughing too, her head on his shoulder, the smell of him immediately, uncannily familiar.

B uoyed by this strange elation, the two of them spent the afternoon laughing and talking, their mood growing steadily wilder, more rau-cous. It was a long time since Anna had felt this feverish, lunatic excitement, an excitement she only ever knew with Daniel. And while she enjoyed it, its madness, its exhilaration irresistible, it also frightened her, for she knew even as it possessed her that it would end, and on the other side lay a melancholy that might last for days.

When they were younger this mood came often, the two of them babbling at each other in the nonsense tongue they used to shut out the world, to close the circle of themselves against others, whipping each other into ever-escalating flights of giggles with sing-song incantations, running and dancing, faster and faster, until their mother or Sophie would scream at them to stop, dragging them apart, both of them in gales of laughter, still chanting, their thin limbs kicking and twirling to their maddening dance. And later, alone in her bedroom or, when they were being particularly difficult, in the front seat of her father's car, Anna would hum their song quietly to herself, chanting steadily beneath her breath, willing Daniel to hear it, to feel the con-nection she felt despite their separation.

As they grew older these moods took on different guises. As adolescent schoolchildren the two of them would lie on their beds, legs thrust upwards against the wall in spite of their parents' exhortations to mind the paintwork, laughing and teasing one another. Their hands wrapping, cutting, blunting. Scissors, paper, stone. Scissors, paper, stone. Her pinafore rucked up to her waist as they hummed and swung their legs to and fro in an upside-down scarecrow parody of dancing. Daniel's girlfriends, of whom there were many, would sometimes be treated to this spectacle, Anna and Daniel's physical sameness and intense intimacy excluding the outsider as surely as their cackling laughter at a thousand unspoken private jokes, their coded language of slang and metaphor even their family could not penetrate. There was one girl, Siri Anderson, her teenage passion for Daniel so consuming that even then it caused Anna pain to watch it, who was reduced to tears one afternoon by Daniel's continued, studied inattention. The two of them laughing until tears ran down their cheeks as Siri fled the house.

Maybe that day was the first time Anna felt the pricks of conscience that were to gradually poison the aftermath of these moods. She had never forgotten the pain in Siri's face, nor the way they continued to torment her even as Siri wept in front of them, this heedlessness, this wild recklessness shaming her.

This was the mood that Jared interrupted when he arrived home, late in the evening, walking in to the sound of thumping music, the stink of dope and pizza, to find the two of them dancing, crazy, grotesque routines of rolling hips and jutting groins and breasts, faces aping the words, mouths stretched wide as tongues flicked in and out. At first they did not notice his presence and he silently watched them dance, his face stony, but eventually Daniel saw him, poking Anna to alert her, the two of them collapsing in half-smothered giggles. A chill stealing across his face as he waited for their laughter to subside, obvious enough to make Anna ask him how his day had been, a question he barely dignified with a response before retreating to the study, closing the door behind himself.

But Jared's arrival had broken their mood and, its hilarity sub-siding, Anna looked at the debris strewn around them, suddenly guilty.

I think you'd better go, she said, and Daniel, perhaps chastened by Jared's brief appearance, acceded. At the door he squeezed her to him.

Be careful, he said, I couldn't bear to see you hurt.

Slipping free she looked up at him, but his face was calm.

You don't need to worry about me, she said. I'm a big girl now.

I do though. I hope you know that.

In the study Jared was working, his codex open in front of him. Anna stood in the doorway.

He's gone? he asked, without turning round.

Yes, she said, suddenly afraid of him. I didn't ask him, he just turned up. He said Sophie called him, told him I'd been sick.

Not really, Jared said, his back still to her.

What do you mean?

He turned, his face cold. I rang Sophie, asked her to call him for me. I thought he might be able to help you. I know I can't, not any-more.

He didn't say.

No? Maybe he didn't want to.

In the darkened space of Seth's apartment the heat lingers, the air sitting heavily beneath the tin roof, but Anna barely notices. Vinh visits daily, checking her fluids, giving her painkillers, but there is little he can do until the acute phase takes its course. At some point he carries a screen to the loft, Seth hovering behind him, and when she is awake she tries to watch it; movies at first, but the plots confuse her, so she watches the newsfeeds instead, the images washing together in the confusion of the fever, overlapping, blurring. Her eyes and head aching from the effort. Twice she wakes to the same item about Murakami, who has developed an infection in his right lung. His body, weakened by the constant radiation and his depression, seemingly unable or unwilling to respond to treatment. Always now with *Prometheus* the talk is the same; of discord in the capsule, of anger and resentment, and although the rumours are denied by mission control, they breed unchecked through the feeds and newsgroups.

And whenever she is awake it seems that he is there too, his hands cool against her skin, reading the lines of heat knotted through her body, releasing them in gentle motions. Once a day he changes the sheets while she slumps, naked and trembling, on a chair, then bathes her, the process of wiping her skin with the flannel making her feel so weak and desperate that twice she weeps as he does it, sobbing quietly against him before sleep reclaims her.

Mid-afternoon on Saturday she wakes, her fever having subsided in the night. Her head spinning as she sits up, she presses a hand to her face, trying to damp down the headache that has already begun. Then, bracing a foot experimentally against the boards, she stands, the ground seeming unnaturally far away as she walks towards the bathroom. Pausing in front of the mirror, she examines her body, the ribs jutting through skin made pale by illness, her face thinner than it has been in a year, her dark hair lank. She touches her nape, her stomach, her breast, as if needing to reassure herself of her physical presence. Twisting the shower taps she feels the water against her skin, its touch normal, no longer jumpy and feverish. As she dries herself, she wonders for the first time about the presence of the mirror. For an apartment designed for a blind man, Seth's home seems uncommonly well equipped with the amenities demanded by the sighted: vidscreens for the feeds, mirrors, lights.

When she emerges from the bathroom he is seated on the bed, his face in shadow. The round lenses of his glasses glinting in the low light of the room. So still and silent that she does not see him immediately. His mouth tightening at the sound of her startled intake of breath when she does.

Did I frighten you?

A bit, she concedes, knowing she should cross to where he sits, but hanging back nonetheless.

How are you feeling?

Okay, she says. Weak, but okay.

When he does not answer she draws her towel tighter around her body.

The air smells of smoke.

It's the fires. Everything smells of it.

She does not answer, just stands staring at him.

The creak of the bed loud in the silence, he stands and walks towards the table.

I've washed your clothes, he says, lifting them and offering them to her.

Thank you, she says, not approaching to take them, so he is left standing, arms outstretched. When it is clear she will not approach he lowers his arms, places the bundle back on the table. She watches the stiff dignity of his stance, the way he holds himself as if ready to flinch at the slightest touch. This is not how they should part, she knows that, knows he too is afraid. In two steps she crosses the space between them, takes his hand in hers.

I have to go, she says.

For a moment he does not respond, his body resisting her touch.

You could stay.

She draws him close so her head rests against his chest.

No, I need to be alone. I think you understand why.

The sound of his breath moving through his chest, loud in her ear.

Yes.

By the door of the taxi he kisses her gently on the forehead, but she reaches up, drawing his lips onto hers, letting the motion linger. Then the seals of the taxi's door hissing, the noise and the clamour and the brightness of the street drops away. Outside he stands immobile, too close to the gutter, making her want to open the window, tell him to step back. His shirt damp where her head rested upon it.

Alone in the back of the taxi she opens her codex, accessing her messages for the first time in a week. There is a vidmail from her father explaining her parents' plans for the Christmas break and detailing where she can reach them, another from Sophie asking her to call. Another from her Hong Kong agent which she cuts off before it has finished. Then a short message from Dylan, saying Seth had told him she was sick, to call if she needs anything. And finally one from Jadwiga, wondering how she is. And in addition to the vids there is a riot of voice and text, advertising mainly, but amongst it she finds a Christmas card from Sophie, her greeting warm and forgiving. Attached to it is a picture Gwynny has drawn for her, a skinny Anna, her hair in pigtails, a wash of blue sea, the arc of the Bridge and a Picassoesque Opera House behind her. Two birds in a white sky. Her feet not quite touching the ground beneath them. Lowering the codex to her knees she stares at the picture, remembering the feel of Gwynny's tiny head beneath her hands five years before; her eggshell skull. Almost six now, in the last vid Sophie sent her Gwynny was fast and lean, her hair black and wiry like her father's, her eyes as green as Sophie's or Anna's. Or Daniel's.

The air in the apartment is hot and close. One by one she opens the windows and doors, careless of the heat from outside. In the kitchen a vile reek rises from the bin. Her hand covering her face against it, she pulls the bag loose and hurries it down to the communal waste area, holding it in front of her, away from her body. The climb back up the stairs is slow and hard and, exhausted, she makes her way to the unmade bed, falls upon it. Eyes fixed on the featureless ceiling, she finds herself wishing it were dark so she could see the spray of luminous stars the room's owners have stuck across it as some kind of joke, lonely for their green glow.

Then suddenly she is awake, the phone ringing beside her. Startled she gropes towards it, but it is audio-only and at the sound of her voice whoever it is calls off. No callsign. Slumping back on the bed she tries to recover herself. Outside the late afternoon sky is dirty orange, a pall of smoke hanging over the ocean. From the beach she can hear the sound of the waves, the occasional shrieks of children. Caught in this glassy wakefulness, her body leaden, mind alert, she watches the last light fail over the ocean, the sky fading first to a red deep as blood, then to the sickly pallor of bushfire night. It is dark when she finally summons the will to pull herself from the grip of this lassitude and, pacing through the unlit rooms, she feels alien, her skin jumpy. Out in the living area her camera bag lies where she dropped it six hours before. Opening it she removes her slate, calling up the image she was working on the night she fell sick. She is pleased to see its effect has not diminished, a stillness captured in its patterns of light and colour that is oddly, inexplicably articulate. She had not intended to work, but now it is in front of her there are things she wants, things she needs, to change. But once she has completed the cosmetic changes she first intended, she finds herself making more corrections, sharpening the resolution on the screen, moving into the grain of the image, isolating flaws and removing them.

Only a decade before, when she was at art school, this was the work of designers and technicians, the tools of the photographer still the antiques of another age: cameras and film and chemicals, but Anna had loved them, loved the fussiness and intricacy of their parts and processes.

Only a few months out of high school she had taken a room in a terrace in Redfern, a winding warren of narrow stairs and tiny rooms, enjoying the floating population of artists and designers and students, the impromptu parties, the dogs, the fridgeless kitchen. Most of all she enjoyed the luxury of privacy, the small room over the kitchen that was hers alone, the peeling walls and unsealed wood of its floor. She decorated it in the manner that was to persist through every place she lived: clean walls, a bed, low shelves for her books, everything spare, almost ascetic, except the flowers—tiger lilies, fleshy orchids, sometimes the deep colours of poppies drooping atop their twisted, hairy stems—which she bought twice weekly from a delivery truck, cheaply, probably illegally, their petals incongruously, voluptuously colourful in the bareness of the room. On one wall she hung a photo she had taken of Daniel one afternoon while he slept stoned and dishevelled on her bed, his face peaceful, lips half-parted as if for kissing. The image's evocation of childhood undercut by the sensuality of his mouth, the bruised skin around his eyes. A silver medal on a thong around his neck falling sideways into the cleft of his throat. The peeling paint of the wall above him caught in the slanting gold of the late summer light. Enjoying the sense of spaces within spaces she had enlarged the photo, hung it opposite the bed like a mirror of another time, a possible future. When Daniel saw it he laughed, not entirely kindly, demanding to know when she had taken it, then moved closer, adding after a moment that it was really quite good, turning as if to look for something he had not seen until now. Later she was to catch him in front of it once more, shifting almost imperceptibly from foot to foot, a habit she recognised as a sign of discomfort. Something about this image, its innocence, or perhaps, in the light of hindsight, the impermanence of the beauty it evoked, unsettling him. And although the image was to go with her from place to place for the next five years, until Hong Kong, until Jared, Daniel never took to it, always claiming it made him feel jumpy.

That first year at art school she almost lived in the darkroom. Every morning she would rise at dawn to wash in the ramshackle bathroom across the backyard, cool sandy soil clinging to her as she picked her way between the scrubby pools of couch grass. The house silent around her as she dressed. On the roads traffic would already be gathering, and she would guide her bike through it, feeling the heat of the sun's first rays as she paced along Crown Street towards the tree-lined tracks that ran through the parks towards the school. She loved the first few hours in the darkroom, before the other students and staff began to arrive, coming to treasure the concentration and discipline they offered. Often it was late before she was finished, and she would wind her way home through the hot dark, the smell of rain and asphalt and rot in her nose, the knobbled tyres of her bike whirring on the broken surface of the road. And then, her bike locked in the hall outside, she would lie on her bed, the chemical stink of the darkroom clinging to her fingers and hair. Her nails brittle from immersion.

She lived six months in that house, until finally the squalls of anger and recrimination over bills and rent and lovers that so possessed her housemates became too much, and she moved on to a tiny studio in Surry Hills. When it came time for her to go, one of her housemates, a woman Anna had come to regard as a friend, who had slept with Daniel and once, half serious, had tried it on with Anna herself, turned to her and spat out a tirade about Anna's secretive ways, her constant snobbery and lack of compassion. Little princess, the woman had jeered, her face livid with her anger, then looking around at the assembled members of the household she had included them in her criticism, declaring that they all thought so too, they were just too gutless to say it. The attack so sudden, so unexpected, that Anna had stood mute, not knowing what to say. Later, as she packed her books into boxes, several of the others had skulked around her doorway, as if wanting to separate themselves from the words that had been said in the kitchen. But unable to find their way into the topic they had drifted off, one by one, leaving her to finish on her own, letting her leave without saying goodbye.

At the time she tried to disregard her housemate's words as jealousy and although there might have been an element of this in the attack she has latterly come to suspect the woman was right; she was a princess, too beautiful, too clever, too used to success, shielded from the blows and setbacks that demand a person grow and change. But there was something else there too, something she did not perceive at the time, an edge to her passionate involvement in her course, its solitariness. Now, when it seems remote and almost alien, she suspects it was a retreat from the pressure of her former life, the burden of being the most beautiful girl at her school, of academic success. Of being Daniel's sister.

A decade later, she is battered beyond recognition, that former incarnation unknowably strange, incandescent in its youth, its arrogance and ignorance. Sitting at this table in the home of people she has never met, she gazes once more at the images on the slate before her, wondering at their relevance to this very feeling of loss, and more strangely, she suddenly realises, of gain, and change.

The call came just after 3:30, jarring her from a deep, dreaming sleep. Next to her Jared groaned, but it was Anna who groped for the phone.

Wen, one of Jared's assistants, appeared on the bedside screen, his voice low and urgent.

Anna, get Jared.

He's asleep, she mumbled.

I don't care, wake him.

But by then Jared had found the light. I'll take it in my study, he said.

Moments later he returned. His face pale.

What is it? Anna asked, as he grabbed for the clothes he had been wearing when he arrived home only three hours before.

It's Tokyo, he said, there's been an earthquake.

Almost immediately the phone rang again, then Jared's earpiece, and soon he was handling three calls at once, barking instructions as he pulled at his shoes. As he dressed he flicked on the feeds, where commentators were trying to assemble the bare bones of the situation, the only images shaking uplinks from a helicopter, some high-res photos from a Chinese weather satellite in synchronous orbit above the Sea of Japan. The very lack of information ominous.

Jared left as soon as he was dressed, leaving Anna alone, trawling the feeds for more news. By dawn, images of the destruction had begun to proliferate as news teams arrived in the ruins of the city: endless vistas of twisted metal and glass, a pall of oily smoke. Fires were burning in the older districts, whole suburbs engulfed in flame. Estimates of the death toll were already in the hundreds of thousands, maybe higher.

By 9:00 A.M. things were clearer. The earthquake had struck at 4:02 A.M., Tokyo time, measuring 8.4 on the Richter scale. A serious aftershock, around 7.1 on the same scale, followed at 7:19, interrupting transmission for fifteen minutes or so. The damage was immense, not just in Tokyo, but in the adjacent city of Yokohama, many 'earthquake-proof' buildings having collapsed, much of Tokyo's financial district subsiding into the harbour. Already there was talk of corruption amongst government inspectors. The UN, United States and China had offered disaster relief and troops, although damage to vital infrastructure and airports was likely to make their deployment problematic. Tsunamis had devastated many coastal settlements in both Japan and Korea, and were now believed to be threatening the eastern coast of Taiwan and the northern Philippines. Fuelled by the first images from the Chinese weather satellite, newsfeed data from seismic research centres in Australia, California and China, and intelligence leaked by US military bases in Taiwan, a mass sell-off of the yen had begun within minutes of the quake, initiating a terrifying plunge in its value. The close of trading on Wall Street at 7:00 A.M. Tokyo time arrested its collapse, but only momentarily, beginning again when Sydney opened an hour later. The yen's precipitous descent dragging the American dollar, the euro and the New Yuan after it. The US Federal Reserve and other central banks were already frantically trying to stem the damage, but the newsfeed commentators seemed dubious their efforts would succeed.

Just after nine the phone rang. Answering, Anna was surprised to see Roland's face on the screen.

Jesus, Anna, are you watching this?

Since it started.

I guess Jared's long gone.

Straight after he heard.

Roland shook his head, disbelieving. I just woke up and there it was. Do you know anything more than what's on the feeds?

I tried calling Jared about half an hour ago, but I couldn't get on to anyone, not even the receptionist.

Fuck. Look, don't go anywhere, I'm coming over. Okay?

Roland was there within the hour, hurrying in with rumours and bites his codex had located on the newsgroups. Opening the fridge he cracked a bottle of beer, seating himself next to her on the couch, eyes glued to the screen in front of them. Without looking sideways he offered her a swig of the bottle, and she took it, the neck still wet with the taste of his mouth. His clothes and skin tinged with the smell of his thick, cloying cigarillos. She took a long mouthful of the beer, then passed the bottle back to him. As he lifted it to his lips once more she found herself watching him, wondering why he had called her rather than someone else. She had never really understood Jared's relationship with Roland. If asked, Jared used to say Roland was his oldest friend, and strictly speaking, it was true, the two of them having met at school, taking their A levels in the same year and—at least until Roland vanished to India—studying at Oxford together. But their relationship had always seemed more complex than this might suggest, for over time Anna had come to notice an ambivalence, sometimes even downright hostility in Jared's attitude towards Roland. But then there were the long hours they spent together, cruising the markets, playing soccer and basketball, drinking. Months would pass without her seeing him, then suddenly he would reappear for a week, a fortnight, sometimes longer, before dropping out of sight once more.

Nor had she ever quite known what to make of Roland himself. Darkly handsome, with full lips and heavily lidded eyes that seem to shine with a constant, private amusement, he had always seemed to her an odd conjunction of qualities—perpetually late, unreliable, raffish, unpredictably generous, sympathetic, charming and vaguely untrustworthy—the last a perception he never seemed in any hurry to dispel. For the past year he had been working for a production house in Bangkok producing a series of cooking shows for the BBC, an activity that seemed to have mainly necessitated spending a great deal of time with the show's host and Roland's partner in the scheme, a Thai prince of questionable financial standing, almost no knowledge of cooking and a positive genius for expensive hookers and cocaine. But this job was little different from many other schemes Roland had been involved in over the years.

Six months before, at a beach house in the south of Vietnam, Roland had kissed her in the kitchen while the others sat drinking on the verandah. His mouth had tasted of nicotine and alcohol, sweet, heady. His tongue had moved in her mouth, his hand around the curve of her arse and lower, lifting her against him. His cock hard against the flat of her belly. Half drunk herself, she did not resist, letting his hand grip her cheek, feeding her into him, until a raised voice from the balcony brought her to her senses, and she had pushed herself free of his grasp, convulsively wiping at her mouth, her lipstick smeared. Roland stayed where he was, smiling at her as she leant back on the sink. She glared at him, almost as angry at herself for having let it happen as she was at Roland for his part, but excited by him, the foreignness of his taste, the forgotten thrill of illicitness.

Fuck! she had exclaimed, only half in anger, but Roland said nothing, smiling his crooked, secret smile while she stared back, lips parted, breath coming heavy and wet. After what seemed minutes but might have been mere seconds, he picked up the bottle he had come for and walked back out to the verandah as if nothing had happened. In the morning he was gone, unexpectedly called back to Bangkok. Or so Jared said.

She had never told Jared about what happened that night. In the gloomy doldrums of her hangover the next day she had wondered whether Roland might have told Jared himself, but Jared never mentioned it, and two weeks later in Luang Prabang she took ill. When she was sick she sometimes hoped he would call, drop in on one of his occasional visits to Hong Kong, but he never did, and Jared never spoke of him.

All of which made it strange that he was here with her now. While the screen flickered in front of them she reached out, taking the beer from him and sipping it once more.

I didn't know you were back, she said, and he grinned.

Last week, he said.

Is the show finished?

For now.

Have you spoken to Jared?

He shook his head, turning to fix her with his dark eyes. I saw Frey. She said you'd been sick.

Anna nodded slowly. Malaria.

Jesus. No-one told me . . .

With sudden certainty, Anna knew he would have come without her asking if he had known. Reaching out she patted the back of his hand.

Don't worry, I'm better now.

As the day progressed the coverage increased, bringing images like scenes from one of Bosch's triptychs: the skeletal forms of towers gaping like broken teeth against a sky turned black by smoke. Streets buckled and torn, buried metres deep in the glinting murderous rain of glass. The quake's timing ensured many died in their beds, killed instantly by the falling masonry, and indeed it seemed the dead were everywhere, their mangled limbs and lolling heads jutting grotesquely from the rubble; bagged and piled like garbage for collection by the roadside. But amongst the dead the living lay buried too, rescuers working frantically to reach them, crawling through the shifting car-casses of the apartment blocks, hands torn and bloodied from digging, faces grimed with fear, exhaustion, loss, heedless of the risk to them-selves. And around them, sometimes beside them, others fought fran-tically to subdue the flames, the water making the rubble slick and slippery beneath them. But amidst the sweeping panoramas of destruction there were smaller moments of loss. The still face of a young man, skin pale beneath the caking dust, the black plastic of the body bag open around his neck. A tiny girl, hair tied in a topknot, naked but for underpants shocking in their pinkness, watching impas-sively as black crows pecked at a corpse. The twisted girders of an office building reflected in the still, dark water that leaked from a pipe. A soldier weeping, slumped beside the protruding corpse of an old woman, nightgown demurely buttoned to her neck.

Everywhere, on every point of the globe, every node in the networks of data that encircled it, from Patagonia to Alaska, from Sierra Leone to Taiwan, even high on the Space Platform, these images spread through the feeds. Watched by billions, they are repeated over and over again, the nets clogging with speculation and figures, messages of condolence and frantic inquiries from friends, relatives, loved ones; money and shares and futures shifting every which way as whole economies slipped and slid. And for a day, maybe two, the world was united, breath caught before this live uplink vision of its own mortality. Sometime during the afternoon Anna and Roland ordered in food, eating chilli pork and noodles from cartons as they watched, mesmerised.

Like a shark slipping through the ocean's depths, the helicopter's baffled engines bear it soundlessly across the darkened rooftops and lanes, the questing finger of its searchlight weaving back and forth, illuminating the beating limbs and leaves of the gardens caught in the downdraft. From a kilometre away it is barely visible, a shadow against the blue of the sky, only the motion of the beam anchoring it to the earth below, but as he watches the twisting haze of marijuana smoke rise against the sky Anton sees it for a moment caught in the glow of floodlights somewhere beneath, its shape briefly distinct, then gone again. Beneath him the couch smells of mildew, but he does not care as he lies back upon it, letting the haze of the dope reveal the design within the twisting coils, each curl a microcosm of some larger pattern, some half-sensed order hidden deep within the rising motion of the smoke.

Tonight was a good night for Anton, tonight he got lucky. A first-timer, nervous and frightened, too green to know the going rate. Not that the man told him, but as Anton crouched by the open door of the car, the silky length of the other man's cock hot in his hand, he saw the fear in his eyes, and later, the taste of the man's semen still strong in his mouth, Anton leant close enough to be threatening as the man fumbled with his wallet, his efforts rewarded with a wad of notes thrust hastily into his hand, a slammed door.

Patting his pocket, Anton is pleased to feel the money is still there. Through the door of the prefab Lewin is working, the yellow light of

the globe flickering as insects suicide against it. Anton cannot see
him, but he can hear his cough, almost constant now. Ordinarily
Anton would go inside and watch him, watch the curving shapes take
form on the canvases, but tonight it is too hot, even out here. It fasci-
nates him, the way Lewin seems to see his pictures before he begins
painting, as if he were not inventing them, but uncovering something
that was always there, just waiting to be found. Music is like that for
Anton, the way the notes form without effort in his head and throat,
harmony coming by instinct, but it still amazes him to see Lewin do it
with colour and shape.

He likes it here at night, the smell of Lewin's paints mingling with
the smell of the grass and the fruit, he even likes the mildew pong of
the couch. Nearby he can hear someone clattering plates, a voice
raised over the burble of the feeds; if he turned he might see the
speaker framed in one of the windows, like an actor on a screen.
Drawing back on his joint again he stretches, his body delicious. With
one hand he strokes the flat of his stomach, his head turning to the
sharp stink of his armpit, his hand rolling the thickening heat of his
cock in his hand, kneading it slowly. Last night he dreamt of his
mother, of her face, but now he cannot remember it, all he remembers
is the fear, the sudden storms of his father's rage.

This is the third time the baby has kicked in fewer minutes, and
Rachel is having trouble concentrating. Raising her hand, she begins
to massage her forehead.

You want a second? the officer in the chair next to her asks. She
looks up sharply, a rebuttal on her lips, but the look on the woman's
face is one of sympathy.

It's been a long day, she says. And I need to go to the toilet.
Looking round she sees the other officer watching her, arms folded.
Between them her client taps the table with an irritating arrhythmia,
his eyes darting from side to side.

You know where it is, the other officer says, his tone notably less
friendly.

In the cubicle she pulls her knickers down and hitches her skirt for the fourth time in an hour. The baby pressing hard on her bladder, a thin trickle of urine falling into the water. In her belly the baby turns once more, punching her hard, and she winces. All week it has been like this, one arrest after another. The government has been promising a crime-free Christmas, which has meant an endless cycle of low-level zero-tolerance bullshit, but nothing seems to be prepared to stay small, the heat fraying tempers so even the most minor situations seem to routinely blow up into major confrontations. Fifteen-hour days, made worse by her swelling ankles, the pain in her back, the constant trips to and from the toilets. Eleven o'clock already, and there's another minor who needs a solicitor waiting to be dealt with after this. And all this mess with Anna and Seth.

Perhaps if she were not so tired it would not look so hard, she tells herself, but when is she not tired, when is there not more to be done than she can ever hope to do? Recently she has begun to hear herself snarl and spit, angry and sick of it, angry and sick of herself, and she wonders where the person she used to be has gone, the one who could laugh, who danced all night and kissed and drank and fucked. The one who climbed to the top of the Harbour Bridge on the night of her twenty-fifth birthday, tripping out of her mind, and lifted her arms wide to feel the wind buoy her upwards, the distant breathing earth seeming to turn beneath her. Two more blows inside her, her headache sharper. At least tomorrow is Christmas, she thinks, at least tomorrow I'll get to sleep in past dawn, and there'll be no arrests, none of this shit, even if it's only a day, even if it's only a day.

Alone in the apartment, Anna feels exhaustion begin to claim her, her teeth chattering despite the heat of the night. Laying her slate to one side, she flicks on the feeds, looking for the weather.

It is going to be hot the next day, creeping past forty, hotter still the next, with no end in sight. A link to related news items informs her there have already been twelve deaths from the heat, the highest toll since '08. Not even the end of December either, the heat of the real summer, which grows later each year, still to come. In the mountains and to the south, fires are raging and the hospitals are choked with the heat-affected, mostly old people, the poor. In New York and Paris it is snowing, coloured lights dancing through clear, icy air, children skating on frozen rinks against pale northern skies. In Moscow there are street marches, violent clashes with police, while fur-hatted bourgeois shop in the boutiques. In Finland radioactive rain has fallen. In New Delhi and Islamabad the sick lie in UN hangars, row after row of beds filled with the shrunken bodies of the dying. On the Scottish moors environmentalists are celebrating the birth of a single egret chick, the first issue of the sole remaining breeding pair. Anna watches each item pass across her screen, patterns of colour and sound that seem so complete, but which fade too quickly. How does the world endure this? she wonders, How do we go on? This ceaseless static of lives, their too-brief traceries of light against dark, this constant promise of completion, of connection, running through our fingers like water; like dreams, their meaning illusory.

Christmas day dawns hot, the streets quiet, the sky murderous with smoke. Some time in the night Seth opened the windows that give onto the street, hoping the air outside might be cooler, but by seven the atmosphere in the loft is stultifying. In the distance a jet rumbles, almost drowned out by the metallic whirr of the cicadas. Rising quietly, Anna crosses to the window, draws it closed.

He was sleeping when she arrived at 3 A.M., buzzing his door until she heard his voice on the intercom, suspicious. It's Anna, she said, and if he was unhappy about being woken he did not show it, guiding her exhausted form towards the bed, undressing her by touch. I wanted to be with you, she had told him, just to sleep.

Downstairs she surfs the feeds, knees drawn up to her chest as she huddles on the couch before the screen. When she hears the phone she starts, unsure whether she should take it, but before she can decide it cuts off, Seth's voice murmuring upstairs.

That was Rachel, he tells her when he comes down, and she takes his hand as he leans over her, places it against the bare skin of her stomach. She said she'd come past on her way.

Rachel arrives just after eleven, Seth answers the door. Anna watches them embrace, noting the wariness in the gesture, a wariness that was not there the first time she saw them together. Releasing Seth, Rachel steps back, turning to Anna, one hand pressed in the small of her back. Beneath her loose dress she has grown markedly in the last two weeks, her belly swelling and tightening, so she moves less easily, burdened by its weight.

Are you sure you're up to this? she asks, leaning to kiss Anna on the cheek.

Anna nods.

I told Bloom I'd be there before the media turned up.

Media? Seth asks.

Rachel snorts in derision. Didn't you know? Homelessness is news when the rich give money.

Outside the streets are hot and quiet. As they walk Anna lets Rachel guide Seth, keeping her distance as they wind their way down into Central. The closer they get the more crowded the streets become, cars growling in the heat which shimmers and dances on their bonnets. The air blue with exhaust, the sweet heatwave cloy of petrol fumes. Even the asphalt has grown soft and sticky, yielding fleshily beneath their feet. Although she tries to hide it, Rachel is sweating, struggling with the weight within her. In a laneway two dogs are fighting, spurred on by a pair of men in sweaty singlets, the dogs' black lips pulled back to reveal gnashing lines of teeth, muscles rippling beneath their fur. Boys and women lounge in doorways, sores like cankers around their eyes and mouths, ulcers scabbing along their arms. On the corner of Albion Street a woman with a mewling baby under one arm moves through the passers-by, entreating one after another after another for change. As the three of them pass her she turns to Anna, the baby slung loosely in her arm, like a kitten in the careless grip of a child, its head lolling heavily on its skinny body. Please, she says, her pupils needle-points, her outstretched hand, her body too close to Anna's, it's for a train fare to my mother's. But Anna recoils, pressing closer to Seth, ashamed and angry but unable to take her eyes from the woman.

Halfway along Elizabeth Street Rachel taps at her earpiece, her pace slowing as she tries to concentrate on the incoming call. A troop carrier bedecked with tinsel rumbles by beside them, and as its noise drops away Anna sees Rachel's face has changed.

We're just around the corner, she says, I'll be there in a moment.

Ending the call with a touch of her finger, she purses her lips.

That was Blaze, she says, Anton's been attacked.

Is he okay? Anna asks.

I'm not sure. Blaze said they're down at the Centre; Lewin brought him in. Shit! I can't be late for this thing with Bloom.

Can't Blaze handle it?

He thinks Anton responds better to me.

Anna is about to answer, but before she can Seth breaks in. Bloom can wait.

Rachel looks at her brother in surprise. Yes, she says, I suppose he can.

Paul is waiting at the Centre door. Grabbing him by the arm, Rachel asks what happened, keeping her voice low.

I'm not sure, Paul says, but I think his dad did it.

Oh Christ, Rachel spits as she opens the security door. Turning to Anna, she whispers, That's all he needs. He grew up in some weird Christian community up north. Prayer eight times a day, the last days are upon us, all that crap. Fucking nutters, the lot of them. But these guys aren't content to proselytise, they like to drop in to Babylon and rough up a few sinners from time to time, show them the one true path.

You think that's what his dad was doing?

Perhaps. But the less Anton has to do with his father the better.

Inside, Blaze is seated on a desk, Anton slumped against the wall with Lewin crouching beside him. The two older men look up as they enter. Hurrying over, Rachel kneels beside him, but Anton does not look up.

Anton? she says, but he does not reply. Blaze and Lewin said your dad beat you up.

Anton shrugs, a sudden, convulsive movement of the shoulders. What do you care? he asks, looking up and away, exposing the livid bruises that mark his face.

Enough to be here on Christmas Day, Rachel says. Do you need a doctor?

Anton shrugs again, less violently this time.

Reaching out, Rachel grabs his chin, turning his face to examine the bruises.

Did he do this?

Yeah, Anton says.

Jesus, Anton, how many of them did he bring with him? she asks, pulling at his collar to expose the marks that extend down his neck, the booted prints on his arm.

Four.

Fuckers, Rachel hisses. We could get them charged.

Anton shakes his head.

Are you sure?

Yeah.

For several seconds the two of them stay like this, not moving, not speaking. Eventually it is Rachel who breaks the silence.

You going to come to this Christmas lunch then?

Anton shrugs. Yeah, maybe, he says. Glancing down he smiles brokenly. How's the baby?

Slipping her arm around his shoulder, Rachel squeezes his thin frame.

Heavy.

While Rachel and Blaze help Anton clean himself up in Vinh's office, Anna is left alone with Lewin and Paul. Paul shakes his head.

It's appalling, isn't it? he asks, his tone inviting Anna and Lewin to share in his outrage. Lewin turns to him with barely disguised contempt.

Fuck off.

Paul, taken aback, says nothing, his mouth opening and closing like a fish.

You heard me, Lewin says.

Paul turns to Anna, as if looking for support, but Anna, remembering his tone at dinner several weeks before, says nothing. In Vinh's office Anton yelps, and Blaze's voice can be heard telling him to stay still, of course it stings. Shooting Lewin a look of pure venom, Paul stalks away towards Vinh's office.

Sanctimonious prick, Lewin says to Paul's retreating back, chuckling to see the way he tenses. All those muscles and he's still piss-weak. Turning back to Anna he grins, exposing his blackened teeth. You don't like me, do you?

Anna shrugs her shoulders non-committally. I don't know you.

He laughs. I'm sure you've heard what your friends Rachel and Blaze think of me.

Yes, she says simply.

He grunts. They're good for Anton, he says, nodding towards Vinh's office. He's not as hard as he makes out. Not as hard as he needs to be.

He seemed pretty hard that afternoon at your place.

Lewin clucks his tongue, considering. You shouldn't have been there, he says. People like you don't belong near us. Besides, he wouldn't have hurt you.

How do you know that?

Lewin shakes his head. I don't, he admits.

Watching the way Lewin stares towards Vinh's office, Anna cannot help but remember the story Rachel told her about the boy in the squat. It is easy to believe; however frail he looks, there is a sense of barely contained threat about Lewin, as if at any moment he might lash out, not in anger, but coldly, calculatedly.

He should go to the police, Anna says. Report his father.

The cops wouldn't care.

They'd have to do something.

Do you honestly believe the cops give a shit what happens to people like us? We're not even people to them, we're just a nuisance, like rats or cockroaches, but harder to deal with. That's what these new laws are for, so they can round us up and put us in camps out west where all the nice people don't have to look at us.

That's crazy, Anna says.

He looks at her, his eyes glittering, and for a moment Anna can see the magnetism Jadwiga spoke about.

You think so?

• • •

Outside the Mission Hall the media teams crowd around the unlikely pairing of the pregnant Rachel and the battered Anton, but as they jostle for a shot Rachel moves almost imperceptibly closer to her young charge, shepherding him past them. Inside the hall long trestle tables are covered with white cloths, waiting staff standing motionless here and there, the minimal black and white of their uniforms in stark contrast to the ragged, grimy figures that sit along the tables. All eyes are on a screen in one corner, on which the *Prometheus* commander, Svenson, is talking. Behind her the other crew members bob and float. As they enter she smiles, wishing everyone a Merry Christmas, and around the room several of the assembled group clap and whistle.

What's happened? Anna asks a waiter.

Christmas message from the astronauts, he says. Apparently Murakami's getting better at last.

Lewin leans towards her. It's all a fucking film set anyway, he says.

Anna shrinks away from him, uncomfortable with the way he seems to have fixated on her. But before she can reply, Rachel returns, a cheerfully shabby man beside her, his plump cheeks pocked and gin-blossomed.

This is Oliver Bloom, she says, introducing him to Anna. Behind her Lewin shrinks away.

We've kept a place for you, Bloom tells Anna, pumping her hand, and I'll get another two set straightaway.

At the table Anna touches Seth's shoulder, leaning into his neck. Now she is seated she feels tired, her weakness returning. Beside her she hears a chair being pulled out and, looking up, sees Lewin standing back as a waiter sets a place beside her with quiet, silver-service efficiency. From across the table Rachel is watching. When the waiter is done Lewin sits beside her.

He loves this kind of thing, Lewin says.

Who? Anna asks acidly.

Bloom. It's absolution for him, and all on the feeds.

A pretty expensive way of getting absolution, says Anna. And anyway, how would you know?

Lewin reaches out and grabs a roll from the basket at the centre of the table, the bread white against the paint-smeared grime of his hands. Stuffing it into his mouth, he growls, He was a friend of mine.

From the kitchen waiters have begun to emerge with silver tureens of chilled orange soup.

He wouldn't remember me now though, Lewin says. Nobody does.

The room seems to have receded, as if she were slipping out of sync with her surroundings. All around her the others are talking and eating, the air filled with the clatter of cutlery and the sound of laughter and voices. Looking down at the heaped plate in front of her, the carefully sliced turkey and ham and stuffing arranged artfully upon it, Anna prods it uncomprehendingly, as if there were some secret to it she has not quite grasped. Next to her Seth is explaining something to Blaze and Rachel. His mouth moving as if he were speaking underwater, or through glass. Opposite she sees Anton listening too. Seeming to sense her attention, he looks slowly from her to Rachel and back again. Unsteadily she rises, Seth turning as she does.

Are you alright? Blaze asks, looking up at her pale, staring face.

I've just overdone it a bit, she says. I need some fresh air.

Next to her Seth begins to stand, but Rachel touches his arm.

I'll go with her, she says. For a moment Anna thinks Seth will object, but then he relaxes.

In the street outside the heat sings with the sound of cicadas, the air totally still. Anna and Rachel walk slowly along the footpath, the asphalt beneath their feet broken by the roots of the plane trees that tower overhead.

How do you do it? she asks Rachel as they walk, their bodies close.

Do what?

This, these people.

We're all they have. Us and a few others. You just learn not to let it affect you. There's no other way.

You stop feeling?

Rachel shakes her head. You just learn to feel differently. Learn to control your reactions.

Lewin said they're building containment camps out west.

Rachel shakes her head. Lewin's paranoid.

In a doorway across the street a bearded man lies on his side, asleep in the heat, his possessions in plastic bags around his head. Anna stares across at him. Can't people see what's going on? she asks. Don't they understand?

See no evil, hear no evil, speak no evil, Rachel says grimly.

Later, her limbs leaden with tiredness, Anna leans against Seth. She feels bloated and gorged, vile in the buzzing haze of heat and flies, but looking up she sees clouds to the east, a long break of grey across the smoke-stained bowl of sky.

There's cloud, she says to Seth. Maybe it's going to rain.

But it does not rain that night, the clouds moving onwards, inland, leaving the sky behind them open once more to space. Somewhere in the small hours she wakes, her body cold despite the heat, Seth's body close to hers. In the moonlight his eyes glisten, his face in chiaroscuro. She moves closer, their faces almost touching.

What's this? she asks, her voice little more than a whisper, her fingertip tracing the line of the scar across his nose, onto his lip.

I fell through a glass window when I was ten.

As he speaks he can still hear it. The cleaving air, solidity giving way to slicing pain. A noise like bells, like ice. The warmth of his blood as it sopped onto the icy tiles, so much of it he wailed in fear, wrung out like a rag, pain coming redly, obliterating everything.

Is that what this is too? she asks, touching the white line that runs across his shoulder at the base of his neck.

Yes. There are more on my hands, along my forearm—he lifts his left arm, exposing another scar that runs from just beneath his wrist upwards, coiling around his elbow—and on my scalp. She watches him, struck that he does not think she might already know them, that she could not trace them herself in darkness.

And here? she touches the wall of his abdomen, where a semi-circular furrow creases the muscles.

Appendix.

Like the astronauts.

I don't understand.

On *Prometheus*; they all had to have them removed in case they got sick on the trip. I think Gromeko had already had his out.

But Seth does not answer. He is thinking of that capsule, its frail skin, the fragile warmth of the bodies within, the ancient cold of the void without. Finding Anna's lips he presses her close, his mouth seeking the warmth of her, letting her breath enter him, willing his into her. The hot motion of her blood beneath the inviolate skin, his fingers' pressure across her back like a scalpel, the deformation before it enters, swift, surgical.

In the weeks after the earthquake she barely saw Jared. He worked from before dawn until late in the evening, only coming back to the apartment to sleep. After the currency crisis came new problems. First the hedge funds went, then the banks. Hundreds of thousands of people were laid off in Hong Kong alone, and soon the numbers of the homeless began to grow. The constant roar of machinery died away, the earth movers and pile drivers falling silent as reclamation projects stalled, and towers froze, half built, plastic flapping forlornly around rusting frames.

Then the protests began. At first it was just the students, but soon that began to change as the unemployed joined ranks, followed by workers' organisations, and finally, the democracy movement.

Every night Anna would watch the feeds, see the protests, and search the scrolling lists of the detained and injured for Daniel's name. She called him, often, but he was seldom there. Once they spoke, and he reassured her that things were fine, the government would bend. She told him it wasn't his fight, he was an Australian, and he laughed, said he couldn't stand by while his friends put themselves at risk.

But then the purges began, the trucks sweeping the streets for the homeless, for illegals, rounding them up and shipping them off to the detainment camps on the islands, and as they did, the protests grew more violent, more frequent. Once she saw him on the feeds, Briar beside him, marching behind a banner, and then a week later, after a protest that ended in looting and violence, she saw his long body crash sideways through three policemen, batons raised, beating a man. Appearing as if from nowhere, he landed across their shields, sending two of them sprawling, throwing the third back like a man possessed, and dragged the victim to his feet, pulling him away into the sheeting gas and gouting water of the cannons.

But Anna saw little of this. All she saw were the road closures and police, the shops shut due to bomb threats. She and Jared and the others still went out, still drank and ate and laughed and shopped, while all around them the city was under siege.

How do you do that? she asks, seated on the stairs to his loft. How do you know which notes to play without sheets?

Memory, he says, I do it by memory.

It is Boxing Day, and Anna has woken to the sound of the piano. Coming downstairs she found Seth, dressed only in ragged combat shorts, seated before it, his fingers moving slowly across the keys.

What is it? I've never heard anything like it.

Seth smiles, his fingers continuing to pick out the notes, in ones and twos, each separated by a gap, this space between them seeming as important as the notes themselves, the way they fade into it, leaving the memory of their resonance hanging. She shivers.

It doesn't have a name, Seth says. An artificial intelligence composed it.

From where she stands she can see the muscles in his back shift beneath his skin, the articulated cage of his ribs beneath them.

I have a recording of it, but I prefer to play it myself. There's an alien quality to it, a sense of another way of being I can get closer to.

It sounds . . . sad. No, she corrects herself, listening to the strange, ghostly sound of the piano, the dying notes, not sad, something else I can't quite describe. Like the sound of wind in grass or moving water, that quietness, that colourless feeling. She hesitates. Maybe I can't find the words because there are no words.

It's like trying to describe the sound of geometry, isn't it? Can you imagine what it must be like to be conscious, aware, but without matter, without form? Without place. A ghost in a machine.

Anna shakes her head. No, she says. But listening to the slow patterns of this music she can hear the loneliness of this thing of bits and light, this artificial mind shifting like the aurora through the circuits of some optical computer, like the siren call of a whale in the oceanic night, the long, clicking song that goes unanswered.

The pesticide fell in a silent rain from the helicopters, drifting sheets that hung shimmering like the rising breath of a waterfall, the beating rotors hollowing licking whirlpools into its mass. Through the tinted glass Anna watched it fall through the space outside. The bellies of the copters hanging overhead like boats viewed from beneath.

Without thinking she raised a hand to the glass, although she knew the pesticide could not touch her where she stood. Like clouds to a child, it seemed almost thick enough to walk upon.

Then, from behind, a discreet cough startled her. Turning, she found Clara, Jared's assistant, at her shoulder.

He won't be long, Clara reassured her, and Anna nodded distractedly.

Clara hesitated. Is there anything— she began, but Anna cut her off.

I'm fine, she said. I'll just wait here. As she spoke she turned back to the windows, the falling clouds.

By the time Jared emerged from his conference the copters had moved on, following the line of the coast eastwards across Wan Chai. Without speaking he stood next to her, but she did not turn to greet him, just stood, arms folded, staring out at the retreating forms of the copters.

Jesus, he said softly, there must be kilolitres of the stuff.

She nodded. Do you think it helps?

Who knows. It certainly didn't help you.

We don't know where I got it.

It's the camps that really worry them, he said after a moment. Apparently it's out of control out there. And nothing else seems to kill the mosquitoes fast enough.

They say it's dangerous.

Jared glanced across at her. With the window's light on his face she could see the dark rings under his eyes, the legacy of weeks with little sleep as the economic situation had slid gradually from bad to worse.

What do you mean?

You've heard the stories, she said, more sharply than she intended. But Jared did not reply, just stared back, her regret made keener by this reminder of his increasing remoteness.

I saw a piece on the feeds. They had pictures of these children who've been getting this disorder. I forget its name, but it's like the thing the Gulf War babies had, some kind of symmetrical distortion.

Bilateral, said Jared. I don't remember its name either, but it was a bilateral distortion.

She paused before continuing. Anyway, normally it's incredibly rare, but over in the camps and in the New Territories it's happening in almost three per cent of the births. Even as she spoke she could see the images from the feeds dance before her eyes, the ceaseless crying of the children, their distorted faces and flippered limbs. The blunt weight of a fingerless hand or handless arm, the pink-plum roundness of a nub where a foot should have been. Organs grown inside out. Faces without eyes, without lips, without noses. And beside it all the heavy, saturnine face of the German correspondent, the English translation scrolling beneath.

And they're sure it's the pesticide that's causing it?

She shook her head. There's so much other shit out there they can never be sure about anything, you know that. Like this leukemia people are beginning to get. But these deformities are genetic, and the pesticide is designed to make the mosquitoes sterile by bonding to their DNA.

Jared nodded, digesting this piece of information. Are you pregnant? he asked suddenly, not turning to face her as he spoke.

What? she stammered. No, I mean . . . no.

Turning, he looked at her, as if not sure whether to believe her or not, and for a moment she was sure he knew she was lying. But then he turned away from the window.

We're late, he said.

In the taxi they sat against either door, not touching, each watching the passing traffic, lost in their private thoughts. The hum of the taxi's electric engine rising through their legs and bodies. As the taxi wound its way up the hillside, Anna felt a cold anger begin to brew within her, a desire to lash out at Jared, to scratch him, to mar the flawlessness of his countenance. But then, as they stood at the security gates outside their destination, he leaned across and kissed her, turning her body to his. The familiarity of his body, the starch-sweat-soap smell of him dissolving her, she gently thumped her head against his chest, once, twice, three times, not wanting to forgive him, unable not to.

Out on the balcony the others were waiting. As they appeared, Roger, one of their hosts, turned, raising a glass in greeting. Across the water on Kowloon the neon lights were coming on, bright against the deep fire of the tropical sunset.

Our man from the front line, he declared, and his wild colonial girl.

Jared took his proffered hand, shaking it and passing on to Tim, their other host, who stood against the balcony wall with Bernard and Frey. Left alone with Anna, Roger raised a hand to her cheek in false solicitude.

And how are you? he asked. We've missed you, you know.

Anna stared back at him. She did not much like his hand on her face, nor, if the truth be told, had she ever much liked Roger. A trader on the futures floor, every dealing with him was a move in some endless Machiavellian web of gameplaying and intrigue.

Better, she said, much better.

That's good, Roger said, then, gesturing towards the vanishing forms of the helicopters, he looked around at the others.

Gin and tonics all round? For the quinine. After all, Contagion Control can't be expected to do it all on their own.

Amidst dutiful laughter Roger leant over to Jared. Roland's late of course, he intoned.

No surprise there, Jared said, an edge in his voice that made Anna look over in surprise. But he and Roger were smiling, eyes fixed on the view over the harbour.

Next to her, Tim offered her a drink. With a surreptitious glance at Jared, she waved it away. Just mineral water.

With a sudden spark of interest Tim raised his eyebrows. Oh? Something we should know about?

At Tim's question Roger and Frey turned in unison, but Anna shook her head. No, just the malaria still, she lied.

At the mention of her illness Tim smiled understandingly and, just for a moment, Anna remembered why she liked him. For while he could be ferociously dull, he was also, in contrast to Roger's malice and scheming, kind and straightforward.

Who else is coming? she asked, the table's set for—

Eight, Tim began, but before he could finish the doorbell chimed. Roger interposed himself between them, a hand in the small of Tim's back.

That'll be Roland, he declared, propelling Tim out of the room, towards the door.

Tim returned with Roland and a woman Anna did not recognise. Tall, taller even than she was; icy blonde with hard blue eyes that could not be natural. Her thin body and high breasts moving free beneath a long dress cut from a clinging fabric as polar blue as her eyes. Next to her she felt Jared stiffen, realised he was watching the woman. Idly she wondered if he knew her. Grinning roguishly, Roland shook Jared's hand, hugging Bernard and then kissing Frey before turning to Anna. There was a moment when he hesitated, then extended his hand to her. Taking it, she shook it firmly, noticing with a start his hair had begun to grey, silver flecking the black curls.

You've been in Bangkok again? Jared asked, and Roland nodded.

Caught the shuttle this afternoon, he said, his eyes still on Anna, questioning.

Then Roger was in front of them, the blonde woman beside him.

This is Tara, he was saying, introducing each of them in turn; Bernard, Frey, Anna. And I think you know Jared.

Beside her Jared extended a hand. Yes, he said, his voice taking on the neutral tone he usually reserved for those he disliked. Surprised, Anna looked over, saw him shoot Roger a look of exquisite venom. But Roger smiled, clearly deeply satisfied by something. Beside her, she saw Roland watching inquisitively and was reminded that for all his affected roguishness he was a keen observer of people. His eyes flicked back, met hers, something like pain in them. Unsettled, she turned her attention to the conversation.

For another twenty minutes the eight of them stood on the balcony, watching the light fade. When they eventually filed inside, Anna came up behind Jared, slipping her arm through his. He jumped like a cat at her touch, and when he turned to face her she saw his eyes were dark with fury. Shocked, she dropped his arm, and he stalked away, settling himself at the far end of the table. As she watched, uncertain how to respond, Roland took the place next to hers, cutting off Tim, who had been about to take it.

Hey, Roland said, leaning over to whisper in her ear. Saved you.

I don't recall asking to be saved, she whispered back, but she grinned as she said it.

He raised an eyebrow. But before he could speak Bernard was interrupting, asking her something about Sydney, where Tara had just been. Turning to them, Anna answered as best she could, finishing by reminding them that she hadn't been home in four years, hoping this caveat would make up for her lack of precision. Tara regarding her with an expression not entirely to Anna's taste.

Why were you there? she asked, hoping a display of friendliness might cut through the other woman's hostility.

Work, Tara replied, with a chilly shrug.

Tara works for Crédit Suisse, said Roger from the end of the table.

Beside Anna, Roland was leaning back in his chair, watching. Idly she wondered why he had not sat closer to Tara, who, she noticed with an uncharitable satisfaction, was moving her food around on the plate in the overly fastidious way associated with eating disorders. At the other end of the table Tim had begun a long diatribe about the rising price of imported goods. As he lumbered inexorably towards no readily discernible end Roland nudged her surreptitiously, raising his eyebrows theatrically, and Anna sipped greedily at her water to stifle her laughter.

Tim's anecdote was the beginning of a steady drift in the conversation towards the Autonomous Zone's worsening political situation, in particular the ongoing currency crisis and the increasingly vocal democracy movement. Roger and Bernard seemed to agree that the situation was worrying, but that over-reacting would only make things worse, an opinion Frey, with qualifications, shared. Tara was silent, as was Jared. All the while Tim tried to offer his views, only to be cut off by Roger, patrolling the flow of talk with ruthless efficiency. Eventually Bernard repeated the conventional wisdom that the government would eventually be forced to give in to some of the democracy movement's demands, if only to settle things down. Having learnt from bitter experience that her own views on any of these matters were likely to be treated as risible, Anna listened in silence. But when half an hour passed and they were still arguing about politics, she excused herself and walked quietly out onto the balcony. A cool wind was blowing and for ten, maybe fifteen, minutes she stood there, watching the sprawling lights of the city and the harbour. Overhead blimps and a skyboard flashed, the names of Sony and Coke and Motorola dancing where once the Milky Way would have been, while northwards the sinister forms of a squadron of half a dozen stealth copters swung over Wan Chai, moving fast towards the mainland. Eventually, her skin pimpling in the cool wind, she stepped back through another door, wandering through a living room towards the kitchen, where Minh, the Vietnamese man Roger and Tim employed as a cook, butler and manservant, was emptying plates into a bin as he stacked the dishwasher. As she entered he straightened, asking her if she wanted anything.

No, she said apologetically, I just wanted a moment away from . . . she hesitated . . . in there.

Minh smiled complicitously, although he remained standing at attention. Then after a moment, he said, You don't mind if I—

No, Anna said, please do. I'll just stand here.

Minh nodded, then went on with his task. His hands quick and efficient as he worked. Roger and Tim called him their maid, an affectation that rankled every time she heard it. As he worked she wondered if he found the term demeaning, or whether he just regarded it as part of his lot. Minh was only one of tens of thousands of Vietnamese and mainlander men and women in Hong Kong, many of them illegal, and therefore without rights, bound to their employers for good or ill by the fear of the street or deportation, most of them maintaining whole families on the one income, families they saw rarely or not at all. Stories of their maltreatment and abuse abounded and, watching Minh, Anna wondered whether Roger and Tim used him as more than just a servant. As if feeling her watching him, Minh looked up.

You're sure you don't want anything?

No, really, I'm fine, she said. As she spoke Roland appeared behind her.

Here you are, he said.

Here I am.

I was worried about you.

She shrugged. The politics all got a bit much.

It was getting pretty heated so I think we're probably well out of it, he said. Although they had never spoken about it directly, Anna always suspected Roland's politics were closer to hers than Jared's, who she had gradually come to understand was essentially a New Tory, disdainful of the rusting state industries and of attempts to fetter the financial sector, but admiring of the government's commitment to fostering enterprise, to its faith in business. Admiring too of the sheer scale of the Chinese economy, its seemingly endless potential for growth. This sort of sympathy between businesspeople like Jared and the communist authorities seemed peculiar to Anna.

Is Tara new? she asked. Or have I just not met her before? He looked at her with sudden, uncharacteristic alarm. But he did not reply. Something like fear began to creep along her spine.

What is it? she asked.

Anna, he said at last, I don't know her. We only arrived together by chance.

She stared at him, feeling something beneath her feet begin to move.

What do you mean? she said, confused, aware she was sounding ridiculous. I don't understand, I thought . . . Connections forming vertiginously in her head, a violent uprising within her.

Anna, Roland said, placing a hand on her shoulder, it may not be—

May not be what? she snapped at him. I'm not a child, Roland, or a fool, don't treat me as if I am. Her eyes shining.

Nodding, Roland withdrew his hand, folding it across his chest nervously. She stepped past him, back towards the dining room. I have to go, she said, holding her voice level, unshaking. Then she was gone. Looking up, Roland saw Minh watching him from the far side of the room, a dirty plate still in one hand. The younger man's sympathetic eyes so steady that Roland looked away in shame.

Jared was standing when she entered the dining room, his finger jabbing at Roger in an uncharacteristic fury. His face, normally so placidly beautiful, red and distorted with anger. Roger reclining in his chair, an infuriating smile on his face, refusing to rise to Jared's challenge. Tim was standing too, saying over and over again to Jared that this just wasn't right, he shouldn't act like this, and it would be better for everyone if he just calmed down. Beside Tim, Bernard and Frey were deep in some private dispute, Frey's head in her hands, Bernard shouting at the side of her face. Red wine spilling out in front of Frey like blood, her overturned glass still on its side. Only Tara was calm, her composure unbroken as she sat watching Jared and Tim with an almost clinical expression. As Anna entered Jared shouted that it was this sort of pissweak liberal shilly-shallying that had got them into trouble in the first place. After all, he said, his voice dropping low, trembling with the urgency of his anger, if the democrats hadn't been allowed to make all this noise the currency crisis would never have reached this point. And anyone who thought the government was going to accede to their demands was dreaming, because if it gave in here, held free elections, let them have the degree of legal and judicial autonomy the idiots were demanding, then the whole fucking show, the whole damn People's Republic would begin to unravel, which Beijing knew damn well. Read your history, he said, remember Tiananmen, the dumbfuck things people said back then about the Chinese government acceding to demands from democrats and reformers? And what actually happened? The fucking tanks happened, and the same was going to happen here, maybe sooner, maybe later, but nothing surer; the PLA would come in and put an end to all this crap, and when that happened people were going to die, and lots of them. And when that happened the markets would go to shit, and if that happened everybody was fucked. And the thing that really galled him was that if they'd acted decisively at the outset, if the democrats had been slapped down before they got too uppity, then it would never have come to this.

Standing in the doorway Anna listened in silence, then, as Jared ended, throwing his hands up in exasperation and stepping away from the table, she said quietly, I'm leaving.

Jared turned to her, wild-eyed.

I'm leaving, she said again. Now.

Jared stared at her for a moment, then glanced towards Tara, who looked up at him with her jaw set, her unnaturally blue eyes opened wide. Anna thought of startled animals, horses, nostrils flaring, and then of lovers, caught in flagrante. Looking back at Jared she saw he was panting, and she thought, his heart, he should be careful, and then remembered why she was leaving and said again, Now.

This seemed to steady Jared, and he turned back to Roger with a calm that belied his anger of a moment before. Anna has the good taste to want to leave, he said, so thanks for a lovely meal. The sentence dripping with chill sarcasm.

Roger smiled. Are you sure she wants to leave with you?

Jared stopped dead. Then, quick as a snake, picked up the glass of wine that stood in front of him and flung it into Roger's face. The liquid exploding purple-grey over the whiteness of his shirt. Roger's mouth opening and closing, the room suddenly silent.

Fuck you, Jared said, enunciating the words slowly and clearly, then stalking towards Anna he grabbed her by the arm and began dragging her towards the door. Frightened by his fury she did not resist as he dragged her out into the street, waving angrily to a passing taxi and, not waiting for it to pull in, lunged out into the traffic. Horns blaring, shouted cries echoing around them, he half pushed, half threw her into the seat ahead of him, slamming the door with a powerful crack. His face set like a mask, he barked their address at the driver, then thumped his fist into the cracked vinyl of the seat. Fucking Roger, he spat. When Anna said nothing, he swivelled to look at her.

Well? he demanded. What are you staring at?

Nothing, she said truthfully. You shouldn't have thrown the wine on him.

Yes I should, he said after a moment, his voice thin, although it was clear his fury was settling, becoming colder.

For several minutes there was silence between them. Eventually it was Anna who spoke, saying simply, How long have you been seeing her? Her coolness surprising her. The question sounding so worn, so ordinary.

It's not what you think, Jared said.

In the mirror she could see the watchful eyes of the driver, enjoying the theatre of the *gwailos*. Suddenly she was tired of Hong Kong, of the Chinese, of Jared, of everything. Tears welled up in her eyes, streaming down her cheeks. Still Jared did not turn around. Finally she sniffed, then sobbed, and Jared turned back to her, the sight of her tears making him perversely solicitous. He extended a hand, but she shrugged it away. Don't, she said softly, unsure what frightened her more, the fact of what she had learnt, or the sudden, uncontrollable movement of feeling it had generated inside her.

What do you want to do?

She shook her head. I don't know. You don't love me, do you? Not anymore.

Jared did not answer, his mouth crumpled and tight.

Did you ever?

He shrugged. When I met you, you were amazing: beautiful, smart, like no-one I'd ever known.

She watched the passing buildings, the neon lights. I gave up everything for you, you know that. My work, my friends, my family.

I know. I never asked you to.

No, but you let me.

Maybe. There's such a thing as wanting something too much.

She shook her head. You mean someone, wanting someone.

Whatever, he said. I'm too tired for this. Can't we talk about it later?

Suddenly Anna was groping for the door handle, pulling on it. In front of her she was dimly aware of the driver noticing, hitting the brakes so the taxi slid along the road's oily surface, the movement throwing her forward, out into the traffic. And then she was moving through the crowded streets, not looking back, desperate to get away.

The rain comes at nightfall on New Year's Eve, moving in waves across the city, spilling over the rooftops and eaves, filling the gutters until they flood. In Seth's apartment Anna opens the windows and doors to it, letting its dampness fill the space, letting the cool of it settle on her skin. Outside the frogs begin to dup-dup, woken from their slumber, crickets shriek. On the roads the cars sled and slide, while revellers dance in the streets, letting it plaster their clothes to their skin, their hair to their heads and necks.

But in her apartment Rachel dreams of the child that turns within her, flesh of her flesh, mind of her mind. One body enfolded, enfolding within the other. Blood pulsing along the umbilicus with the rhythm of her heart. Every night she dreams of the child and maybe, by some osmotic motion, it dreams through her as it waits for its slipping birth, the backwards pull of her lipped vagina, the flanged opening sucking tight to the crown of its tiny head.

Two suburbs away, Anton stares out at the rain, fingering the tenderness that still lingers where his father's boot struck his face. Wordlessly he hums a tune, his voice moving slowly, beautifully, through the lyrics as he watches the rain flood the alley below, plastic bags bloated with refuse bobbing and shifting in the tropical excess of it, the skips awash, the falling water striking the metal lids with a noise like a drum. Down below, the Brewery is asleep, and here, in his roost, he can pretend that he is alone. He has to sing, because when he sings it seems there is a meaning to things, a sense to all this noise and emptiness, as if his songs let him glimpse something better. The preacher in his father's church used to say that it was God's presence he felt, and maybe it is. All Anton knows is that as long as he sings he can sense it, know that it is there.

Anna lifts his left hand in her right, cat's-cradling it, sees the way he pulls against its capture. Even now.

I read a book once, she says, about twins. It said most identical twins are symmetrical, like mirror images, one right-handed, one left, fingerprints, hair whorls, the lot, all reflected.

I have no twin. Only Rachel. I was born alone.

She shakes her head. No, listen. Most twins are not carried to term, most die in the first few months. Sometimes their matter is reabsorbed into the mother's womb, other times it becomes part of the one who's left, a kernel of bone and meat hidden somewhere in the body. That's where left-handers are supposed to come from, they're the twins who are left behind.

You mean I may have had a brother?

More than that, you may have had another you, a reflection, she says, but as she speaks she falters, realising what she is saying. His hand closing on hers, reassuring. After a moment, she continues.

Some people say they feel that loss all their lives, like a ghost, an absence in their being.

And you?

It was hard, the two of us so much the same.

Were you?

On the outside we may have seemed different, on the inside . . . she shakes her head . . . we were like one person.

That must have been frightening.

Without speaking she lowers herself into the length of his chest, curling against it. His hand still in hers, the other one on her hair, her neck. The muffled beat of his heart.

It was, she says, then corrects herself.

It is.

On the intercom Daniel's voice was wary.

It's me, she said, pressing her face to the grille.

Anna? he asked incredulously, the lock on the door activating as he spoke.

Upstairs Chiu sat at the table, a console in front of him. She looked from one to the other, then crumpled, tears streaming down her face. Shepherding her onto the couch, Daniel motioned to Chiu to bring water, which he did, Anna wiping at her face and snuffling as she drank it.

What's happened? Daniel asked, although she could see from his face he already knew.

It's Jared.

From the next room Briar entered, her face wearing the distracted look of someone talking on an earpiece. Seeing Anna, she retreated the way she had come. As if Briar's interruption had reminded him of something, Chiu picked up the console.

I can finish this in the other room, he said, following Briar.

Anna looked after him. You're really deep in this thing, aren't you?

Daniel nodded slowly. Pretty deep. There are things foreigners like me can do for the students, things they couldn't do themselves.

It's going to be okay though, she said, the Chinese government is going to give in, isn't it?

Of course, Daniel said. What else can they do? It's not just malcontents who want reform, it's everybody. The government can't stand in the way of that. Then he hesitated. That doesn't matter though, what matters is you. Have you had a fight with him? Or . . .

More than a fight, she said.

If you want to stay here, you can.

Anna smiled, rueful. I don't think Briar would like that.

Daniel stroked her hair. She'd cope. As he spoke he studied her face. You look pale.

She sniffed. I feel sick. I've been feeling sick a lot lately. Letting the sentence hang between them.

The malaria?

Without turning she waited, willing him to understand, willing the telepathy she once believed they shared to work again.

A moment later Daniel murmured. Oh no.

Against her scalp she felt his hand stop.

Yes, she said in a tiny voice.

But how? Weren't you using anything?

Of course I was. But the malaria must have affected it.

What are you going to do?

Feeling the tears welling up in her again she didn't answer, just shrugged.

Does he know?

She shook her head. No. And there was this thing I saw, on the feeds this afternoon, about the pesticide deformities. What if . . . ? She broke off, not able to finish.

There are tests for all that stuff.

Are you sure?

He pulled her to him. Of course I'm sure, he said, and although she knew he was lying it made her feel safer.

The stupid thing is we've hardly done it in months, she said, laughing bitterly through her tears.

Above her, Daniel laughed too, but as he did she felt him stiffen. Pulling away she saw Briar in the doorway again, her face tight with annoyance. Daniel looked from Briar to Anna and back again.

Without speaking he opened his hands, and Briar, shaking her head, vanished again.

If you have to go . . . Anna offered, but Daniel shook his head.

No, it can wait.

I've ruined everything, she said, staring after Briar. Haven't I?

Daniel extended a hand, but, as if thinking better of it, withdrew it.

No.

She looked at him, sniffing. No?

Not everything.

Just before dawn she came back. Inside it was dark, their bed not slept in. Accessing the apartment's systems, she saw he had left at 12:23 A.M. and not returned.

Silently she moved from room to room, gathering the few things she needed. Only what she could carry, a few clothes, her camera. And then, shouldering her bag, she walked out the door, closed it behind herself one last time.

As she walked through the streets Anna was surprised by their emptiness. Occasionally people ran by, but whether they were hurrying towards something or away from it she could not tell. Somewhere far off there was the chatter of gunfire, then again, but closer this time. Turning, she heard a faint roar and then, in the distance she saw them, the tanks, moving two abreast up the road towards her, the flag of the People's Republic flying above them.

The rain has stopped when the chime of her codex wakes her. Outside it is quiet, the water on the roads deadening the sound of the traffic. Somewhere a bat chirrups and squeaks, noisy in the foliage. Slipping from the bed she crosses the room in the dark, digging through her satchel in search of her codex. In the bed behind her Seth moves, his chest expanding and contracting like the motion of a wave. Tidal sleep. Opening her codex she sees the reason it has woken her. The scanner agent has found Daniel.

APOCRYPHA
· 7 ·

Over many years I have taught myself to play the piano by ear. Being blind, this process has not been easy, and without the luxury of sheet music I am forced to remember every piece in its totality. Of necessity I have developed certain mnemonic tricks that allow me to remember longer pieces, tricks that concentrate my memory upon the inner structure of the music, the internal relationships, harmonic and temporal, which give it shape and meaning. In so doing I come to understand each piece as a whole, rather than a sequence of discrete notes.

Sight imposes a set of epistemic restraints upon the seeing. They tend to regard living organisms as individual things: animals, plants, insects. But to me life is found not just in the sculpted curves and warm bodies I encounter with my hands, but also in larger systems. A termite colony, for instance, functions as one organism, the skills and capacity of the colony as a whole far greater than those of any individual termite. The knowledge of how to build air-conditioning systems to regulate the temperature of the colony or how to design the networks of tunnels so they are easily defensible in case of attack is not written into the genes of the individual termites. Instead it emerges from the collective behaviour of millions of termites, through simple and staggeringly beautiful mathematical processes. Just as the termites themselves are self-regulating organisms, so too is the colony. And if we are prepared to regard the individual termites as living organisms, why not the colony as a whole?

A person used to the visible world is likely to reply that the colony is not a single organism because it is not one thing, it is many, even if they do work in concert. But the emphasis upon individuality is a misplaced one: even individual creatures are in many ways collective organisms, made up not just of many different kinds of cell, interacting to keep the larger organism alive and functioning, but even existing in harmony with other, alien organisms, as humans do with the bacteria responsible for our digestive processes.

I however am not subject to these restrictive habits of thought. It is easy for me to reconceive of the biosphere in the same terms as the arrangement of notes in a piece of music; as a system that exists by virtue of the interaction of its many parts, and from which patterns emerge, just as melody does from an arrangement of notes. And if these patterns—be they the creeping motion of the continents across the planet, the migration of birds and animals with the passage of the seasons or just the ever-changing weather—are organised by the same principles that organise the other, smaller organisms with which we are more familiar, is it so ridiculous to regard this growing, changing, self-regulating entity we call the Earth as an organism in its own right?

Thus understood, life is all around us and exists on every scale, from the cellular to the planetary. It is a part of the very fabric of the universe. Indeed the universe itself is, in some very real sense, alive.

SETH LaMARQUE, *The Language of Shells*

The City of Tongues

And the whole earth was of one language, and of one speech. And it came to pass, as they journeyed from the east, that they found a plain in the land of Shinar; and they dwelt there. And they said one to another, 'Go to, let us make brick, and burn them thoroughly.' And they had brick for stone, and slime had they for mortar. And they said, 'Go to, let us build us a city and a tower, whose top may reach unto Heaven; and let us make us a name, lest we be scattered abroad upon the face of the whole earth.'

And the Lord came down to see the city and the tower, which the children of men builded. And the Lord said, 'Behold, the people is one, and they have all one language; and this they begin to do: and now nothing will be restrained from them, which they have imagined to do. Go to, let us go down, and there confound their language, that they may not understand one another's speech.'

So the Lord scattered them abroad from thence upon the face of all the earth: and they left off to build the city. Therefore is the name of it called Babel; because the Lord did there confound the language of all the earth: and from thence did the Lord scatter them abroad upon the face of all the earth.

Genesis 11

She is at the airport by seven, walking restlessly through the departure lounge, the sleek anonymity of its galleries reminding her of a mall or an office building. She has been awake since three, and in the glare of morning she feels light-headed, slightly drunk with lack of sleep. As she moves through the shifting groups of passers-by, figures glide surreally past upon the moving walkways, stationary, yet in motion. The floor beneath her feet cold and shiny as marble, but with a lacquered sheen that can only be artificial.

She is moving because she cannot stay still.

Pausing by a datanode, she sees there is still another hour until her flight boards, and, agitated and restless, she looks about, realising she is allowing her anxiety to get the better of her. On one side business-people waiting for shuttle flights to Taipei or Seoul or Shanghai stand in public access booths, their faces anonymous behind goggles. The smoked glass tubes that enclose the top halves of their bodies unable to disguise the strange motions of their gloved hands, which hang and weave as they negotiate unseen worlds, accessing and sorting informa-tion. Their voices rising and falling in a gentle susurration. Shifting her bag on her shoulder, she walks on, past a line of billscreens adver-tising dutyfree electronics and perfume, a wallscreen on which newsvid of a stormfront is playing, a vast bank of cloud that rises like a wave above the landscape beneath it, America or China or Russia. Lightning dances within it, while in the foreground sun shines and trees stand, preternaturally still. Pausing before it she shudders, its unintentional symbolism unsettling her.

In a café past the screens she orders coffee. As soon as she is seated she feels exhaustion rise to overwhelm her. Opening her codex on the counter in front of her, she accesses the scanner agent once more. There have been no more traces since the ones that registered last night, but this does not surprise her. After all it is barely dawn here and earlier in Hong Kong. In the light of day the oddness of the first few traces seems more pronounced. Two taxi fares, a series of pur-chases at electronics vendors in Yaumatei and a session in a merse tank at a place called Miss Tong's Virtual Penthouse in Mong Kok. No hotels, no airfares, no new accounts which might yield addresses, none of the things one might expect if Daniel has been in hiding for the last year.

There are so many questions she needs answers to. First there is the mystery of why he has reappeared. If he had engineered the disap-pearance, why reappear at all? What is the point of vanishing if it is not total, a kind of suicide that eradicates a life as surely as a bullet or the runaway bulk of a careering vehicle? When witnesses vanish, trucks arrive in the small hours of the morning, floodlights illuminating the rapid, carefully rehearsed severing of a life's connections, an excision as irrevocable as it is complete. Daniel's disappearance had been as brutal as that, as appalling in its totality. And even if he had managed to slip free of whatever entanglements he was enmeshed within, somehow explaining his sudden reappearance, then why now, why back in Hong Kong? Surely he would have been safer somewhere, anywhere else?

But there is something else that she cannot understand. He must know that she has been looking for him, must know how much pain his disappearance has caused her and their family, so why has he not contacted them? Could it be them he is hiding from? And why?

Seated in the café she turns these questions over in her mind. She knows that in the end they are irrelevant. All that matters is that he is alive. She does not care where he has been or why, as long as he is back. It is all she wants.

The shuttle touches down in the late afternoon. Anna opens her codex as soon as she is away from the plane, but still there are no new traces, the quick flickers of the last twenty-four hours subsiding again, like the fading trails of luminescence behind a swimmer. For several minutes she wills the searchware to strike again, but it does not.

By the time she reaches her hotel it is after five. At reception she produces her credit card and passport, watches the clerk book her in without speaking. The hotel is more than she can afford, and as she signs the documents she experiences a moment of doubt about the expense. But once she is up there with the door closed behind her she knows her decision was right, the expensive anonymity of the room's silence enfolding her, protecting her. From the windows that make up one wall she can see the harbour, the piled neon and concrete of the buildings reddening in the dusk.

Throwing her bags on the bed, she opens her codex once more, but again there is nothing. Frustrated, she bangs her fist softly against it. For several seconds she assesses her options, determined to track down the first of the traces tonight. The obvious place to start is with the electronics vendors. Although no addresses are given, the stalls are registered with the business police as part of a market in Kowloon. Anna does not know the market itself, but the terms of the licence ('not to trade before 1800 or after 0600') suggest they are part of the seemingly endless night markets that sprawl through Yaumatei's narrow lanes.

Packing her codex back in her bag, she heads out into the street. It is almost dark, and a cool wind is blowing, the warmth of the day already gone. This time last year there was snow on the Peak, freezing rain and icy hail, while the year before winter brought heat, temperatures in the high thirties for weeks on end, a ceaseless hot, dry wind. From the streets, escalators bear her downwards, deep into the bowels of the island, the crowds drawing her on as they surge towards the MTR. Down here the world moves with a strange, almost surreal speed, the train sliding in noiselessly, heralded by a rushing wind, the crowd surging forward to claim the limited space, cramming themselves in, body against body against body. The boundaries of vision made soft by the floor to ceiling LCD billscreens, their advertisements repeating in ten-second cycles, soundtracks booming. Anna has never liked the passage under the harbour, brief as it is, the sensation of millions of tonnes of earth and water over her head making her skin crawl, but the MTR is faster than the ferry. In two stops it is over and she is out, moving upwards with the tide to the street. She has not forgotten the trick to foot traffic in the narrow streets, the light sidestepping gait that carries one around the eddies and whorls of the streaming humanity that moves everywhere constantly, restlessly, and she quickly makes it into the nest of streets she is looking for. It is after six now and the smaller artisan shops are closing, while in front of them, on their doorsteps, the night stalls are going up. Cars and taxis wind their way down the narrow lanes, nudging and bumping through the milling crowds, which part reluctantly as they approach, only to close after them like water. And between them scooters and motorcycles stop and start, beeping their horns and pushing their way through.

And everywhere, people. Men and women in suits and shirtsleeves returning from work pushing past the hurrying figures of shopkeepers and stall owners and tourists; the giraffelike figures of stiltshoed teenagers giggling and clinging to each other in twos and threes and fours, their gleaming hair piled high in Marie Antoinette curls; Chinese yips and ferals on skateboards and blades weaving their way past soldiers smoking on a corner, the sinister forms of AK-47s leaning against the wall beside them. Down one street, North Korean punks, their jackets sprayed with holographic images of the Supreme Leader in a touching, contradictory show of neo-Confucian conformity, shout and gesticulate over a dog held by a tiny woman, which strains at its leash, barking behind a steel muzzle. As Anna passes she sees the image on their jackets has been designed to wink and leer as the wearers move within the garment, an effect which in combination with the Leader's pompadour hairstyle is strangely disconcerting.

Eventually she finds the part of the market she is seeking, a rag-tag collection of stalls selling pirated ractives and illegal feed jacks, cut-price Chinese consoles and stereos and screens, codexes, new and second-hand, low-quality gloves and goggles churned out in the Philippines and Myanmar, even second-hand skingear. Her heart beating faster she picks her way from stall to stall looking for documents, hoping they will be displayed somewhere like a licence or a degree in a doctor's office, but by the time she reaches the far end of the street she has not located any. Turning, she starts again, stopping at each stall and listing off the names she has, but the stall owners wave her away, uninterested, barking incomprehensibly time and again, or worse, ignoring her outright. As she nears the point where she began she feels despair rising in her, born of tiredness and fear and the sense of something she needs too much slipping away from her, its sucking pull only made stronger by the roaring noise and the massing weight of people on every side. Finally, the boy behind the second to last stall stands as she approaches and looks at the names listed on the screen of her proffered codex, his wide face friendly. Pointing to the first three he waves back the way she has come, opening his hands in a gesture of resignation. But when he reaches the fourth he taps the screen, his face opening in a grin, and points over her shoulder at a crowded shopfront on the other idea of the street.

There? Anna asks, that's this one, that's . . . she twists to look at the screen of her codex . . . Good Fortune Music? But the boy only nods again, still grinning. Clutching her codex Anna turns, shoving her way in a half run towards the shop. Inside, the narrow space is crowded with ractive cases and peeling posters, minidiscs glinting in plastic slips on racks behind the counter. Cantopop blares. In front of her a middle-aged man is busily overcharging two Germans, but Anna, unable to contain herself, pushes past them, slapping her codex down on the counter.

Here, she says, pointing to the trace, this man, and as she speaks she calls up a photo of Daniel, he was in here last night. He bought something. Do you remember?

The shopkeeper glances at the codex in front of him, then back at Anna. Why?

He's my brother. I need to find him.

The man looks at her disparagingly.

Lots of people come here.

I know, Anna says, but here, look again, do you remember him, remember anything?

You *gwailo* all look the same to me, he says, laughing rudely.

Aware now that she has made a mistake, Anna looks at the two Germans who are regarding her with the uncertainty reserved for people who might at any moment behave irrationally.

Please, Anna pleads, but the man cuts her off.

I'm busy, can't you see that?

Can't you just look?

But this time the man does not even answer, just waves his hand contemptuously, turning back to the Germans.

Ashamed and angry, Anna backs away towards the street. Outside a car alarm shrieks in Cantonese at two kids who bounce on the car roof, its voice like cutting metal. Looking down Anna sees an armless child huddled by the steps in a nest of soiled newspaper, the lipless hole of its mouth crawling with blisters as it waves a plastic cup in its flippered feet. Nausea rising in her she steps sideways, away from the child, almost falling, groping for the wall and lowering herself to the ground.

How long she sits there she does not know, the noise of the street moving around her, indistinct through tears and loss. The lights spinning. But eventually she feels a hand on her shoulder, a voice saying her name. Gasping, she looks up, realising she recognises the face that swims before her. Not knowing what else to say she says the first thing that comes into her head. His name.

Roland?

Anna? he is saying. What are you doing here? What's wrong?

Blinking, she stares at him, dumbfounded. Anna, he says again. Did you fall?

She nods stupidly, then catches herself. No, I . . .

Have you taken something? Roland asks, turning her face so he can look at it more closely.

No, she says, no drugs.

Then—

It's complicated.

Can you stand?

I think so, she says, letting him help her to her feet, but as she stands she feels herself begin to shake, the ground moving sickeningly beneath her. Beside her Roland supports her as she sways.

Whoa, he says, are you alright?

I'm okay, she says, holding a hand to her forehead, trying to concentrate. Just . . . just hungry, I think.

When did you eat last?

I don't remember, she says. Yesterday. I was on a plane all day.

Maybe we should get something inside you.

Looking around at the stalls she shakes her head. No, I have to find someone.

Roland grips her arm. You can barely stand up. You can find them later.

She is about to contradict him, but the steadiness of his gaze stops her. Yes, she says, you're right.

Are you up to walking? he asks. The Dragon's just around the corner.

I'll make it, she says.

As they walk she surreptitiously examines him. He looks just as he did when she last saw him, more than a year before, except for the goatee, a sprinkling more grey around his temples. She remembers Frey, who, despite her oft-professed dislike for him, Anna had always suspected of having been involved with him at some point, remarking that he looked rather like one of Ali Baba's thieves. Frey did not mean it kindly, but the description has stuck in Anna's head because of its aptness. Catching her watching him, he smiles.

You've lost weight.

Thanks, she says.

It wasn't a compliment.

I was sick again, she says, laughing at his bluntness.

A look of concern passes over his face.

I'm fine now, she reassures him, and he nods, not looking entirely convinced.

The Dragon is crowded, but after complicated negotiations and a hefty tip, Roland manages to get them a seat near the window. In the street below a troupe of acrobats and fire-dancers are twisting and leaping, the tribal flare of their flame incongruous beneath the neon lights. Once they are seated, a silence falls, both of them watching the performance outside.

Where did you go, Anna? Roland asks at last, his face un-characteristically serious. I looked for you, I was worried. I left mes-sages on your vidmail but you never returned them.

She looks down. I'm sorry, she says, and in that moment she means it. I didn't want to worry anyone, I just needed to get away. The truth is she is more than a little ashamed.

Roland watches her, not speaking. His expression is not angry, or unkind, just a little perplexed.

Have you seen any of them? she begins, a little too quickly, Bernard or Roger or . . . and here she hesitates.

Jared?

She looks at him suddenly, her eyes wide, afraid.

Roland shrugs, looking down at the fire-dancers. I see him occasionally. He's okay.

Is he, I mean has he—

Mitsuko, she's Japanese.

Anna looks at the tablecloth.

Roger and Tim I haven't seen, but I guess they're no different. Bernard, he's not so good.

Anna looks up. Oh?

Ever since Frey died, he's been hitting the mnemonics real hard. He's dosed most days now. The bank fired him—oh, it must be six months ago—and he was supposed to be going solo, but it never seems to have happened. I think Jared's been lending him money. Roland hesitates. You did know about Frey, didn't you?

I read about it. I don't know the details.

The whole thing was terrible. She got caught in a firefight over in Western on Red Friday. One bullet, a stray, but it took her hours to die. Bernard didn't find out for almost a week. You know how it was.

Anna does not reply.

You understand why I was worried now?

Anna nods. Poor Bernard.

The moment is interrupted by the arrival of their meal, Roland chatting and laughing in Cantonese with the waiter, whom he seems to know. Anna watches, smiling quietly. She had forgotten that Roland spoke Cantonese well and Mandarin at least passably, far more than most expats managed, herself included. As soon as the waiter has gone, Roland starts serving the salty fish, heaping it into her bowl and then his own.

Eat up, girl, he says, you look half starved.

Yes sir, she says, blushing and laughing all at once.

That's what I like, he says, through a mouthful. A bit of respect. But as he speaks he winces, raising a hand to prod tenderly at his cheek.

Is there something wrong? she asks.

Dentist, he says, grimacing. That's where I was coming from when I found you.

Pretty late for a dentist.

He grins. Old friend, does it for free out of working hours.

You had a filling?

He shakes his head. That's next time. I've got a broken one that's bothering me, but today it was new enamel around the bases where the roots are getting exposed. It's not my teeth that are the problem. It's my mouth, gums and shit. It's like the Somme in there.

Ouch.

And nothing I do seems to be helping. I've even given up the cigars.

Thank God for that.

Catching her eye, Roland chuckles, ladling more fish and rice into her bowl without asking whether she wants it. She watches him, indulgent, happy.

You never answered my question, he says. What happened to you? Where have you been since that night at Roger's?

Anna looks down at her food. I had a flat in Western for a while, although I wasn't there much. Some work, a bit of travel. And then about three months ago I went back to Sydney.

Why didn't you leave after the PLA came? So many people did.

When she does not answer, he looks up. Don't, it's okay, he says, but she lifts a hand to silence him.

Daniel vanished, on the day the tanks came. I've been trying to find him ever since.

Oh Jesus.

She nods.

Have you, I mean—

I hired a scanner agent.

And?

Until the other day, nothing, but in the last twenty-four hours it's been picking up traces here in Hong Kong. That's why I was at the market, some of them were there.

The shop?

Yes, and some of the stalls. But no-one would talk to me.

Pricks, Roland says. Although I suppose they've got reason to be careful. What about the others?

Some kind of porn palace, some taxis.

Porn? Doesn't sound like Daniel's scene.

Anna shakes her head. It doesn't, does it?

Have you got an address or phone? Feed subscription, vidmail?

She shakes her head. No. Nothing like that. It's so frustrating.

He leans back in his chair. It must be. Have you talked to the people at the porn place?

No, I was going to go there next.

Roland glances around, looking for a waiter.

I'll come with you.

Madam Tong's is north of Mong Kok Road, almost in Sham Shui Po. The two of them zigzag through the markets, north, then west, then north again. As they walk Roland asks her questions, about Daniel, about Sydney, about her work, and Anna answers them carefully, if not entirely honestly. When he asks her about Sydney she tells him she has tried to avoid people she used to know, but that she has been spending time with some people she met through work, suddenly reluctant to tell him about Seth, but the evasiveness of her answers makes her squirm. While they have been eating a light rain has begun to fall, misting dankly across the rooftops, and now water trickles across the garbage-stained asphalt. Along Tung Choi the rain beads on the glass walls of the aquariums that are racked three metres high along the footpath, the darting colours of the fish illuminated like magic lantern shows, fantastic and bizarre. Lion fish, guppies, carp, scorpion fish, the impossible blue of reef fish and the mad striping of the coral eaters that dart around them. Further north they cut through the Bird Market, the air filled with the trilling, squawking, shrieking clamour from the cages which hang from every conceivable point. Jared always hated birds, a terror she never understood, but he would cite their scaly feet, the vicious jab of their beaks, the too-quick blink of their reptilian eyes as evidence of their relationship to snakes, which he also disliked. Never trust anything less evolved than a mammal, he occasionally said, only half in jest, as if there were some antediluvian envy that drove non-mammalians to lurk, hungry and dreadful, in the darkness around the feet of the placental orders. He was prepared to walk several blocks to avoid this place, Anna remembered, far enough to ensure the birds' songs would be left unheard, nightmare fuel that they were to him. But it was never the birds that frightened her, it was the dark enclosures of the cages with their elaborate teak bars and engraved bases. As they pass a rack of them she sees one bird, its bright yellow and black plumage sleek, watching her, head on one side, and looks away.

They follow Mong Kok Road as far as Canton Road, turn north once more, then Roland, checking the address she has in her codex, leads her sideways, into a maze of alleys and concrete buildings, grim, charmless and vaguely ominous. Anna has never been in this part of Kowloon before, and certainly not after dark, and even with Roland beside her she feels a creeping unease. The lights atop the buildings catch in the puddles beneath their feet, so the reflections ripple and tear as they walk, breaking outwards like phosphor. Air-conditioners and satellite dishes block the sky, while beneath them cloth banners jostle with flashing signs for the attention of passers-by, ad hoc strands of cable and wire piping power and bits through the mass of the buildings strung between them. In the doorways men and women watch them pass.

As they pass a group dressed in expensive suits, their narrow-collared shirts white against the dark material of their jackets, Roland glances over. This is Triad territory around here, he says. Not many westerners.

The men study them from behind red-tinted glasses. One of them is cleaning his teeth with a pick that glints silver in the light, his fish-sharp fangs startlingly, artificially white.

They won't bother us if we don't bother them, Roland says, placing a hand behind her to guide her past a pair of motorcycles that block the way. See the glasses? They're to hide modifications, most likely, wet-ware, smart stuff. And if you got their shirts off they're probably armoured under the skin too, carapace work from Manila.

Anna quickens her pace. Jesus, how do you know this stuff?

Roland shrugs. I hear things.

By the time they reach the address Anna has in her codex she is well and truly lost. Roland walks along a particularly unsavoury alley, counting with one finger until he comes to an open door. A sign over it in Chinese characters is placed next to a billscreen on which a porn video is playing, a heavily made-up Chinese woman methodically working her mouth around a man's swollen penis, one hand at the base, her lips distorted by the effort as she tries to smile for the camera. The image flicks to his face occasionally, then into long view, then back to the close-up. Anna watches in distaste.

You're sure this is the place? Roland asks.

If this is Madam Tong's he was here, Anna says.

Okay, Roland says, stepping into the doorway. If you say so. At the end of a passage a lift door gapes into darkness, the shaft empty. Someone has strung a rope across the opening on which a sign inscribed with Chinese characters hangs. Anna leans past the rope and looks down the shaft, but it is too dark to make out the bottom.

I presume the sign says 'Out of Order' she says, stepping back again.

Something like that, Roland says.

They walk side by side up the stairs, of which there seem to be a great many. Water is leaking from above, and a rusty trail of liquid stains the treads beneath their feet, the smell of mildew pervading the chilly space. Somewhere ahead an air-conditioner rumbles. Finally, five floors up, they reach a heavy door. A camera points down at them. Nodding at it, Roland presses a button by the door.

After a moment a woman's voice says something Anna does not understand, and Roland answers too quickly for Anna to make out.

There is a pause, then the woman's voice is there again. A brief conversation, then the door in front of them swings inwards.

They thought we were warepolice, Roland murmurs as they enter.

In the dimly lit room two heavy-set men lounge on couches, smoking and examining Anna and Roland with interest. As the woman closes the door behind them Anna moves closer to Roland, the click of the latch making her jump.

You want tank? the woman asks. She is middle-aged, or at least seems to be, her bony form wrapped in some smart fabric that flows as she moves.

No, no tank, says Roland.

Anna steps forward. We're looking for my brother.

Why look here?

He was here, we think he booked a tank.

She watches him, still wary but softening. How do you know this?

Roland smiles blandly. We had a trace on him.

Lots of people come here.

Maybe we could give you his details.

The woman hesitates, considering.

And maybe, Roland produces his wallet, pulls out a dog-eared 5,000 New Yuan note, you could look him up, see if there's anything on your systems.

The woman glances to the men on the couch, who shrug. Extending a hand she takes the money, walking over to a console in the corner. Opening her codex, Anna shows her the information the scanner agent turned up and the woman enters it into her own system. Over the woman's shoulder Anna can see down a narrow corridor. To one side a door is open, and the bulk of an immersion tank is visible, a pair of skinsuits hanging behind it like the discarded shells of some bipedal insect, the webbing of fluid pressure pipes clear against the black polymer fabric. Headpieces, appropriately reminiscent of the helmet of Morpheus in the old comics, are lined on a shelf. In one corner a clear-cased quantum machine hums, its innards restless, prismatic arrangements of light, thick coils of optic cords twisting out from behind it towards the tank. Anna has only experienced total immersion once, and found the experience both unsatisfactory and unsettling. Eighteen months later she still remembers the tactile nano-web of the skinsuit like a living thing around her, crawling across her as it invaded the wet spaces of her body with an unpleasant, unwanted intimacy, clammily, crawlingly eager. The program was an erotic one, and almost seamless, but she found the sensation of simulated hands and bodies and tongues somehow dirty, its intrusion into her cunt and mouth, the pressure of it encircling her nipples, sliding between the cheeks of her arse invasive, although she gritted her teeth and tried to enjoy the process. Later, someone told her this response was not uncommon, it just took time to get used to the interface. But Anna knew that what she hated was the sense that she was a toy in someone else's fantasy, floating in a tank, blind, mute, deaf to the world outside, the vulnerability of letting someone else's dreams loose upon herself.

Locating the reference in the files, the woman flicks through several screens too quickly for Anna to take in what is on them.

There is nothing here, she announces almost immediately. He came, took a tank, paid, left.

What program? Anna asks.

The woman looks up, suspicious again, then jabs the keyboard another time.

Sorge, she says.

Roland and Anna look at each other in bewilderment.

Nipponese program, the woman says. Very sexy, very violent. She smiles cruelly, revealing jewel-encrusted teeth and a pierced tongue. You want?

Anna shakes her head. Calling it up on her codex once again, she shows the woman her photo of Daniel.

This is him, she says. Are you sure you don't remember him?

The woman regards it blandly. Lots of people come here, she says again.

Anna swivels to the men on the couch.

What about you? she demands, brandishing her codex in front of them. Do you remember him?

The men glance at it, shake their heads and return to their conversation. Anna bites her lip, willing herself to be calm. Beside her Roland's heavily lidded eyes steadying.

Here, he says, to the woman, producing another 5,000 New Yuan note. Call us if he comes back. Here is my number.

In the street outside Anna walks quickly away, leaving Roland to hurry after her.

Well that was useless, she spits.

Not entirely, Roland says, placating, we know he was there.

So? Where he's been isn't any use to me. I need to know where he is.

It's a start.

She looks at him, allowing the crest of her anger and frustration to bear her up.

You don't have to do this, she says. You don't have to help me.

I know— Roland begins, but she cuts him off.

And you shouldn't waste your money on me. Here, she says, groping in her pocket.

Roland places his hand on her.

Don't. I'm doing this because I want to. Let me.

Anna hesitates, relenting. Are you sure?

Yes.

I'm sorry, she says, her anger abating. I shouldn't have snapped at you. I'm tired, it's been a long day, and—

You don't need to apologise. It's okay, I understand. He pauses, considering. Look, he says, I've got space in my apartment. Why don't you come back there, get some sleep, and in the morning we can start again.

At the hotel the clerk at the reception desk, seeing Anna has only just checked in, asks her worriedly whether there is some problem. She tells him not to worry. And then, as she and Roland are leaving, a woman steps aside to let her pass. Anna is already past her when she realises the woman is staring at her, and, without thinking, turns back.

Yes?

The woman shakes her head. I'm sorry, she says, I thought for a moment we'd met.

. . .

It is after midnight by the time they reach Roland's apartment in Stanley. It is quieter away from the hubbub of the city, the roar of the traffic and the crowds replaced by the sound of the feeds drifting between the balconies.

I've never been here, she says, as Roland opens the door to the entry arbour.

Don't get too excited then, it's pretty small.

It is small, but comfortable, two rooms with a narrow balcony and a view across the bay. A rumpled couch is pushed against one wall, more books than she would have expected piled on shelves against another. On the balcony there is a bench, a rack of weights. Roland throws her bag on the couch.

I'll make up the bed for you. Do you want tea?

If you're having some, she says, opening the door to the balcony and stepping out into the cool air. From behind her the apartment's security system suggests the external temperature is too low, and that she should close the door to avoid possible discomfort. Appearing beside her with a cup of green tea in each hand, Roland shrugs.

Stupid thing, he says, but the owners won't disarm it. Say they can't get insurance without it.

Anna takes the cup from him and turns back to the view. The steam flutters like the beat of a tiny heart in the wind from the bay. Far below, across the rooftops, boats move against their moorings, the soft clinking of metal on metal carried on the wind to where they stand.

It's so peaceful.

Roland is standing so close she can hear his breath, feel the warmth of him through the cool air.

I like it, he says, the north side gets me down after a while.

We didn't find anything.

He shakes his head. No, but it was a start. We know he was there. And anyway, he may contact you.

Perhaps. I should check the scanner agent again, see if there are more traces.

The tea still cupped in her hands, she walks back inside, leaving Roland still staring out over the water. Opening her codex she sees it has registered more traces. Her hands shaking, she accesses each in turn, the agent presenting them along both temporal and spatial axes, and with the aid of a cartographical assistant she follows him along a trail from a cash vendor in Mong Kok to a merse gallery, then to a supermarket and another sex shop. As she flicks through them, Roland appears behind her.

More traces? he asks.

A lot of them, she says, and in Mong Kok. Pointing at the supermarket she says, Look! We walked past that. Picking up the codex, she gets to her feet.

I've got to get back there.

Roland leans across to see the trace she indicated. Those traces were before eleven, Anna. It's almost one now. Even at this time of the night it'd take you half an hour to get back there. He'll be long gone.

No, Anna says, he might not be—

He will, and even if he's not, how will you find him? Get some rest tonight. He was in Mong Kok last night and again tonight. Chances are he'll be there again tomorrow, and if he is we'll be there too. And I've got some friends who may be able to get some more detailed information on him for you. Maybe even an address.

We could go there now.

Roland shakes his head. They live out in the Territories, and anyway, it's the middle of the night. We'll go tomorrow.

Anna slumps back against the table, raising her hands in despair.

I was so close to him. I might even have walked past him in the street.

I know, Roland says, and I understand how frustrating this must be. But if you wait until tomorrow I promise these friends of mine can help.

Anna is awake at dawn. Grey winter light spilling through the curtains. From behind the bedroom door she can hear Roland's breathing, slow and heavy. In the narrow galley of the kitchen she brews coffee, the espresso maker gurgling loudly in the quiet of the apartment. The wind buffets the window above the sink so it rattles in its frame. Raising her hand to silence it, she feels the chill of the air beyond. Daniel feels very far away this morning, his absence less keen. For the first time she feels she could turn, walk away from this thing, but she knows she will not. Having come this far she will see it through, she will find him.

In the next room she hears the rhythm of Roland's breathing break. With sudden urgency she realises she does not want him to come out, does not want this day to begin. But even as she thinks it she hears the bed beneath him creak, the sound of his feet on the parquet floor.

The Mass Transit takes them as far as Tsuen Wan, where they change onto the LRT, the endless dormitory suburbs and hydroponic gardens whipping by outside. Here and there the windowless bulk of prefabricated infotech installations rise above the monotonous ranks of townhouses and apartment blocks, razor-wired security fences surrounding them. Somewhere between Sham Tseng and Tuen Mun a pair of PLA soldiers enter the carriage, checking identity cards as they work their way along it. They're looking for illegals, Roland tells her, they're not interested in us, and indeed, when the soldiers reach them, they take Anna's passport seemingly without interest, swiping it against their dataport and handing it back without a word. Up close Anna sees they are barely more than children, probably only eighteen or nineteen, and, struck by their youth, she smiles at the one who took her passport.

Thank you, she says quietly. As if noticing her for the first time the soldier focuses his eyes on her, saying something she does not understand. Anna stares back helplessly, but he does not wait for a reply, just walks on and away down the carriage.

What did he say? she asks Roland, who sits stiffly beside her.

You don't want to know, he says, his eyes following the retreating forms of the soldiers.

At Tuen Mun Station, Roland ushers her out through the arcades to a taxi. In the street outside someone has sprayed 'Free Tibet' on a wall in English, the letters two metres high, but spidery, as if painted hurriedly. Anna watches the two overalled maintenance men who are scrubbing at it with something out of a pressure tank, the 'F' already faded almost to nothing beneath their rags. The smell of acetate strong in the air.

The taxi takes them out of town along a main road, then down a series of side roads along which the apartment blocks are slowly replaced by warehouses and abandoned industrial estates. On a corner where a monstrous totem pole rises, the faces of the Ruling Council carved in leering, mock tribal caricature upon it, the palsied side of the Supreme Leader's face drooping like wax at the top, they turn again, finally drawing up at Roland's direction outside what looks like an abandoned warehouse. After the noise of Tuen Mun it is unsettlingly quiet.

A lot of artists and writers live out here these days, he says. People who don't want too much to do with the government.

Is it a writer or an artist we're here to see? she asks sarcastically, but Roland does not reply, leading her through the gate and across the car park towards the warehouse.

Inside, he leads her up a stairway towards a door. This is the place, he says, pressing a buzzer. The camera over their heads swivels towards them, then a moment later the door opens to reveal a thin figure in black army cast-offs, his tattoo of a coiling dragon running down the side of his shaven scalp from his ear to his shoulder.

Roland, he says, stepping forward to shake Roland's hand.

Tung, this is Anna, the friend I told you about. Tung steps forward and takes Anna's hand. His dark eyes are intelligent.

Roland told me you wanted to find someone.

My brother, she says, and Tung steps back to let them pass.

Then come in and we'll see what we can do.

Inside is a long room, sparsely furnished and divided here and there by huge thinscreens, on which Warholesque images are displayed. Along one wall a line of smaller screens is connected to a pair of consoles, the wires from them wound together into a skein running away towards a power jack. On them different images play: MSNBC outside the provisional capital in Bombay; Scooby Doo; the Stock Exchange feed; images from *Prometheus*. A woman is seated before them, her feet up on a table, talking animatedly on an earpiece. As they enter she looks up, but does not wave. Like Tung she is dressed in old combat gear, her head shaven and tattooed. As they move towards her the woman ends her conversation and advances on Anna, Roland and Tung. Anna cannot understand what she is saying, but it is clear she is upset, her finger jabbing angrily. Roland stays calm, answering her in single words, short sentences, until finally the woman throws up one hand in a gesture of contempt and stalks back towards the screen and console. Tung follows her, and while the two of them continue the argument, Anna looks at Roland, who smiles not altogether convincingly.

She said I shouldn't have brought you here.

I guessed, Anna tells him, looking around nervously. Who are these people?

Friends. Of a sort.

Eventually the woman comes back, arms folded. A keloid pink brand marks her right arm just beneath the shoulder. Involuntarily Anna tenses, the woman's anger seeming to radiate from her. Extending one hand, without the trace of a smile, she speaks. I am Wei.

Taking it, Anna sees the nails have been bitten to the quick.

Show me what you have.

There were some traces last night and the night before, Roland says. Anna's got the details here, in her codex.

Wei stares at her for what seems a long time, before finally nodding.

Give it to me.

Wei and Tung download the information from her codex into their consoles, arguing animatedly in Cantonese as they work.

What now? Anna asks.

They'll work through the data, try to get some more information. It might take a while.

Anna watches the two of them slipping into goggles and gloves. She has never enjoyed looking at people who are mersed, and now, when so much depends on it, she likes it even less. On the screen behind them MSNBC is running an item about a rat plague in Shanghai, a stream of dark fur crawling and biting and clambering one over the other in a bid to escape the men and women who strike wildly at their hurrying bodies with spades and sticks. Shuddering, she turns aside.

Can I go for a walk? she asks. I'd like to be alone.

Roland nods. Sure, but don't go far.

Leaving him to watch over Wei and Tung, Anna wanders past the thinscreens towards the door, winding slowly down the stairs into the abandoned car park. Outside it has grown colder, as if rain is close, and Anna watches the clouds move low overhead, blue-black and threatening. Not knowing where to go she walks slowly around the car park, amongst the rotting paper and discarded plastic. She feels the weight of the clouds upon her, the loneliness of the place seeping into her. Once again it is there, this sense that now she is so close perhaps she does not want it. The sadness. Arms folded she leans against the creaking cyclone wire, bouncing slowly in its grip. But then Roland appears at the door, waving at her.

Wei has something she needs you to see, he says, as he hurries her up the stairs. It might be Daniel.

Upstairs the six competing images have been replaced by a set of six identical frames. Grainy and pixellated, they appear to be security footage of a shop's interior. In the bottom corner a time code is caught, waiting. At the consoles in front of the screens Wei is still goggled in, but Tung stands beside her, his dark eyes visible through the smoky lenses.

We cross-referenced the time he made the purchase at the sex shop with the security systems, Tung says. As Anna watches, the screens jerk into life, shadowy figures moving around the dimly lit space.

That's him, I think, Tung says, pointing. Anna makes out a figure taking magazines from a rack, flicking through them one by one.

He's got his back to us, she complains.

I know, Tung says. Suddenly the footage speeds up, and the figure by the magazines comes towards the camera.

You see, Roland says, beside her, I told you they'd find him.

He's limping, Anna says.

I see.

I wish I could see his face.

But at least we know he's alive.

But we still don't know where he is. I might as well go back to Mong Kok, chase the traces as they appear. I just wish I knew what he was doing.

Wei swings her chair to face them, pulling off her goggles. He's your brother. Don't you know how he thinks? She taps the side of her head as she speaks, a gesture that is somehow deeply dismissive. Without looking at Anna she turns to the frozen image of Daniel on the screen, his face obscured by a beanie.

This is not all we got, she says. We also accessed his security file. She lights a cigarette.

What was in the file?

That was strange. Nothing. It was as if someone had been in there deleting things.

Why would someone do that? Anna asks.

You tell me, Wei replies.

Taking a breath, Anna tries to ignore Wei's calculated bait. You can't find a contact for him, an address, some way of finding him?

He's been very careful not to be found for more than a year, those habits don't die quickly. No address, no vid- or e-mail, no phone, not in his name at least.

Anna feels something beginning to tear loose inside her. No, she says, the note of desperation in her voice frightening her, there's got to be something.

Has it ever occurred to you that it might be you he's hiding from? Wei asks, a nasty glint in her eye.

Anna shakes her head, refusing to countenance Wei's suggestion. He wouldn't; he's in some kind of trouble.

And you're going to save him?

Anna stares at Wei, her smirking face and tattooed scalp. Don't patronise me, she says, her voice cold with fury. You know nothing about me or Daniel. She feels Roland's hand on her shoulder, but shakes it loose.

For several heartbeats Wei stares back, challenging. Then, shrugging, she returns to her console. Here's what we can do. We'll put a series of traces on him, so that next time he merses he'll be notified that you're trying to find him. That's a good start. There are other things we can try if that doesn't work.

There is a long silence, Anna still staring angrily. Eventually Roland steps forward.

Give him my address.

They're criminals, aren't they? Anna asks. That woman.

Next to her Roland hesitates. They're non-persons.

This new information making her anger seem childish.

What did she do?

Said the wrong thing at the wrong time. At least she's alive.

Did she inform?

He shrugs. I don't know. Probably. She was very different when I first met her, Roland says, looking past Anna at the endless sprawl of the city rushing by outside.

An hour later, deep in the MTR, Anna's codex chimes, registering another trace. Struggling for space amidst the press of bodies, Anna opens it to see that Daniel has accessed the merse at a public terminal near the Chungking Mansions. Frantically she searches for a link to it, stabbing violently at the codex's interface, its slowness and inadequacies making her shake with rage and frustration. Finally she accesses a channel, but as soon as she does Daniel's trace drops out.

Damn! He disconnected.

That doesn't make sense, Roland says. He must have got the message Wei posted.

The same thing happens twice more that evening. Brief access followed by a rapid disconnection immediately Anna tries to open a channel. She paces around the apartment, trying to find an explanation, waiting for him to call or make contact. Roland waiting with her, his calm presence steadying, but nothing fits. Nothing fits.

Like a child she lies before the screen, letting the images wash over her. It is late, after two in the morning, but she is wide awake. On the screen *Prometheus* turns against the darkness, the face of a woman newsreader moving soundlessly beneath it. The ballet of the craft's movement, its precision, calming her. Opening her codex she scans through the traces once more, looking for a clue, some pattern, but none reveals itself. Noticing she has mail she flicks over, and, seeing it is something from Seth, she opens it. Inside is a datapacket, and, curious, she pulls her console from her bag, transferring the packet. In the darkness of the room the tiny sound of the two machines, the hum of the drives, the data streaming between them along a beam of unseen light. Unclipping her gloves from inside the case she pulls them on, feels the familiar strangeness of the pressure systems crawl across her skin, the silkiness of the nanofibre, then slips her goggles on, the world falling away.

Inside it is dark, and with a sudden pang of disappointment she thinks the data must be corrupted. But then her left hand strikes something hard and ungiving. Lifting her other hand towards it she feels the surface of a stone, soft and flaky like shale. And then, rising from it, a millimetre or two, something smoother, something that slips beneath her hand like the mother-of-pearl scalloping of a razor shell. As she slides her hands across it she realises it is an eidetic, but with no visuals, just the spatial grid, the textures; a smile tugging at her at the conceit of it. Gradually she explores the shape of it with her palm and fingertips, feeling the way the shell has been flattened, probably by pressure from above, so now it sits flat within the stone, its surface slippery like the gloss of glaze on baked pottery. Feels too the close-bunched ribs, the turning whorl of its spiral running inwards, outwards. The system of cracks and fissures that crisscross its coils, marring its perfection, but also, somehow, increasing its beauty.

Is this all there is, she whispers to the system, is there any message? And as she speaks soft light rises from nowhere, from everywhere, revealing the fossil, grey-white against dark shale. Touching it again she tries to reconcile her tactile impressions with this visual one, finding, not for the first time, each is both more and less than the other. Words appearing across the stone as she touches it.

Dear Anna

I have handled specimens like this more times than I can count, but today, with this one, I was struck by its fragility, by the sheer unlikeliness of its preservation. When one handles the remnants of the past every day, when they are things to be bartered and classified, labelled and stored, there is a tendency to become inured to them, not just to the way their preservation is itself a testament to the loss of so much, but also to the accident of their survival. Today though, as I felt this one beneath my hand, I was reminded of both. Reminded of you.

I suppose it was epiphany, a moment of clarity, but what I felt—indeed, more than felt, in that moment what I was—was the want of you. I wanted you there, with me, our skins touching, wanted to feel the soft warmth of your breast beneath my cheek, to hear the motion of your breath within you. The smell of your skin and hair almost there, on the edge of my consciousness, its memory almost tangible. This was not a mere sexual desire, although it was that too, it was a desire for the very being of you, for the warm, flowing aliveness of you.

Was this love? This desire for you so powerful it seems to remake me. This sense of the infinite preciousness of each moment I spend with you, of each detail of your being I have committed to my memory. This sense that in the space between a heartbeat a whole world might be suspended, a world defined by the closeness of our bodies, of your breath against mine.

Eons from now, what trace might remain of something so extraordinary, so perfect and eternal? Might it leave a mark on the stone, in the stone? Might there be something to be dug forth and remembered? For it seems impossible that it could just vanish, that it might just leak away into nothingness. Astronomers can read the memory of the Universe's birth from the hissing of the radiation that surrounds us, that permeates us, but would this thing be remembered like that?

Or in the immensity of time are these moments so few that we must cast away these questions and just trust them, just live them?

There is nothing more, just his name, the shell's eidetic. But outside, her body painted with the play of light from the screen, the white form of *Prometheus* turning against her breast and shoulder, gloved hands outstretched before her. And in the doorway to his bedroom, Roland standing, silently watching.

They are woken at seven by the peal of the phone. Anna hears Roland answer it from the bedroom. There is a brief conversation in Cantonese and then he appears at the door.

It's Wei, he says. They've got an address.

Where? she asks, clutching her shirt closed as she stands.

Mong Kok somewhere.

They are there in forty minutes. Seated beside the driver, Roland guides the taxi through the streets. Eventually they find the address Wei has given them, a narrow building sandwiched between crumbling apartment blocks. The lobby is dark, lit only by a fluorescent globe that strobes irregularly on and off. They almost run the five flights of stairs, ignoring the way the fourth creaks ominously beneath them. At the door Anna raises her hand to knock, sees it is shaking. The rap of her knuckles echoing along the empty corridor. For a long time there is no answer, and she lifts her hand to knock again, but as she does the door opens a sliver. Inside it is dark. A shadowed form regards them in silence.

Anna tries to speak but cannot, and so it is Roland who steps forward.

We're looking for Daniel, he says, his voice soft.

The figure behind the door does not reply.

Please, Anna says, we know he's here.

I do not think so, the man says, slowly, and with effort. His voice heavily accented, Russian or Polish.

You don't understand, Anna says. I'm his sister, I've been looking for him. We're not police.

The door closes, too quickly for them to stop it, although Anna leaps forward, her hand and shoulder striking it dully.

Please, she calls. Tell him it's Anna. Anna!

From behind the door comes the sound of a whispered conversation, two men, their voices rising and falling urgently. Then, as abruptly as it closed, the door opens again, all the way this time. A dark-haired man, not much older than Anna, is standing there.

You should come in please, he says.

The room is tiny, barely big enough for the two sleeping mats that are spread on the floor, a cheap console and screen in the corner. The curtains are drawn, and the room smells of sweat and sleep. As they step inside the dark-haired man closes the door behind them. The man who answered the door first, his face weather-beaten and unshaven, regards them from in front of the window.

Where is he? Anna asks, looking from one to the other. What have you done to him?

The man who invited them in shuffles nervously, while by the window the other says something in what sounds like Russian, his voice angry. But the dark-haired man raises a hand to him, his tone dismissive, and the man by the window turns aside, making a show of concentrating his attention on the cigarette he is smoking.

I am thinking you do not understand, the dark-haired man says at last. I am Daniel.

Anna stares at him in bewilderment.

Is this some kind of joke? she demands, glancing wildly from the younger man to Roland and back. Do you think this is funny?

But Roland's face is as startled as her own, and in front of her the dark-haired man is waving a hand placatingly. No, he is saying, please. It is not joke. I will try to explain. But first you must make promise to me and to Mikhail—with his hand he indicates the man by the window—you promise us no police. Yes?

Of course, she says. No police.

The dark-haired man relaxes visibly at this. Thank you, he says. My English is . . . he gestures helplessly . . . not so good, so you forgive me perhaps? I am sailor, from Russia, so is Mikhail. He extends a hand to Anna, who stares at it numbly. My name is Alexander.

Realising the hand is for her, Anna takes it. At her touch Alexander smiles nervously.

You are the one who sent me the messages?

Yes, she says, I mean no, I sent them to Daniel. What have you done with him?

I have done nothing to him, Alexander says, but—

But what? Anna demands, stepping towards him. Sensing her anger, he takes a step back. By the window Mikhail straightens, tensing for some kind of confrontation. Roland places a steadying hand on her shoulder, pulling her back towards him.

Please, Alexander says, I promise you, I had nothing to do with it.

To do with what? Anna almost screams. Where is he, where's Daniel?

He is dead.

What? Anna asks, her voice suddenly quiet. How could you know that?

I do not, not for sure, but I buy his identity from a fence. The fence say he is dead almost a year.

Beside her she hears Roland release a long, slow breath.

I don't understand, what do you mean, you bought his identity? What fence? This is insane!

Alexander looks at Roland. I am thinking your friend here, he understand. Maybe . . . He gestures with one hand, as if imploring Roland to help him.

Anna, he might be telling the truth—

No! she says. None of this makes any sense. Feeling Roland's hand upon her once more she twists away, but Roland is too quick for her, catching her wrists in his hands. I should have thought of it myself, it explains everything, he says, trying to hold her, calm her.

He's lying, she says, struggling against his grip. Daniel's alive; we saw him!

Roland shakes his head, his eyes full of pain as he holds her there, forcing her to listen to him. It happens all the time. You buy a complete credit profile, established existence in all kinds of places, access to a birth certificate, driver's licence, passport, the works. Hackers break the databases and alter the information they need to, rewrite DNA and retinal tags, substitute photos. It's not foolproof, but it doesn't need to be if no-one is suspicious. After the PLA came the cops were selling the identities of the disappeared to illegals and mainlanders out in the camps. Because they were the records of activists, they came with baggage, but they still must have been better than the camps for the people who bought them. At least they let them move around freely, get a place to live. Work. But Daniel was white, his must have been hard to get rid of.

Anna has gone limp while he has been speaking, but still he does not release her. No, she is saying, no.

Looking past her at Alexander, Roland asks softly, Two nights ago, were you in Mong Kok?

Alexander nods slowly. Yes.

And did you buy anything?

Uncomfortable now, Alexander clears his throat nervously.

Yes.

What? Roland demands.

We buy . . . we buy magazines, and ractives.

Those ones? Roland asks, looking at a pile of pornographic magazines by one of the sleeping mats. Behind them ractive disks lie scattered by a cheap console.

Yes, Alexander says softly. You must understand, I only buy the identity so I can get away, have new life in Australia.

Roland nods. And the night before. What did you do?

A skinsuit program.

Turning back to Anna, who stares blankly at Alexander, Roland shakes her wrists. You see, he says. It was him we saw on the video. It was him at Madam Tong's.

It can't be, she whispers. It can't be.

Yes, says Roland. It can.

As they walk from the building Anna does not speak, her eyes staring forward, unfocused. Ushering her towards a taxi, Roland folds her into its back seat, her limbs rubbery, but unyielding. He wants to hold her, but he is frightened by this stiffness, frightened the touch of a hand might destroy her. And then, quite suddenly, as they clear the tunnel and the taxi swings out over the flyover, her lip begins to quiver, and sobs break forth, choking her. Only then does he reach across, try to draw her to him. But she resists his touch, shaking him off with a convulsive movement of her shoulders. Undeterred, Roland pulls her close again, and this time she subsides into thick, gurgling sobs in his arms.

The police killed him, didn't they? Anna asks through her tears.

Maybe. Or the PLA. Or maybe he was shot. Who knows.

What happened to his body?

Anna . . .

Tell me.

Some people say there are mass graves out in the reclamation projects, but there are towers on top of them now. Others washed up on the beaches. Others were buried in the graveyards they keep for the unidentified dead.

Like Potter's Field?

Yes.

Against his shirt she has begun to weep again.

She is like this all afternoon and into the night. Sometimes calmer, sometimes not, her bouts of weeping slowly giving way to an agonised yowling so primal it is painful to be near. And although every fibre of her being seeks to deny it, like an amputee confronted with the brute absence of their loss, somewhere within she feels the chill of a growing certainty that Roland is right, and Daniel is gone, his body cast into the ocean or swung limply into some pit of anonymous dead. Roland does not leave her side, stroking her back and hair as she weeps against his body, until his shirt is sodden, until her throat and her eyes are swollen, until finally, after midnight, there are no more tears and she sleeps.

He is still beside her when she wakes the next morning, his shirt and trousers unchanged from the day before.

Have you been there all night?

He smiles. Pretty much. How're you feeling?

She thinks about this for a moment. Tired, she says, very tired.

Can I get you tea?

She nods. A glass of water would be good too.

I'll get them, he says. You stay here and rest.

I have to piss, she says.

He laughs. Okay, but if you want to get back in once you're done, do.

She places a hand on the stain on the front of his shirt. I ruined your shirt.

Pulling on the fabric, he inspects it gravely. It'll wash out, don't worry.

Three minutes later, a towel wrapped around her, she wanders into the kitchen where Roland is fussing with the teapot. He looks up at her and smiles, before returning to what he is doing. Anna does not speak, just watches him. Eventually he turns back to her.

What is it? he asks.

She hesitates before answering, and in that space she sees his expression begin to change, as if he knows what is coming.

Why did you do this for me? she asks. Help me like this?

He shrugs. No reason. You needed help and I'm your friend.

Yes, she says. But it's more than that, isn't it?

He looks down a long time before answering.

Yes, he says at last.

You know I have someone else, don't you?

He nods.

And there's Jared.

Roland looks at her sharply. Fuck Jared, he says. Look how he treated you.

I thought he was your friend.

He was, he is, but it doesn't change how he acted towards you or—

How you feel about me?

I love you.

She shakes her head. No you don't.

I don't think it's fair of you to say that.

Maybe not. But I think I should go.

Where?

Home. There'll be a flight some time this morning.

Two hours later, she stands by the window in the departure lounge, gazing out across the runway. It is raining again, a heavy, dismal rain, puddles lying like oil across the runway, the water blurring the horizon across the slate grey sea beyond. Her face and sinuses ache from weeping, but she has no more tears today. Just a weariness that seems to permeate everything. Roland did not protest when she announced her intention of returning to the airport alone, and at the door he shivered beneath the brush of her lips upon his cheek, against his own, but he did not try to prolong the moment, letting her leave. As she watches the rain grows heavier, sweeping sheets of it, the departure lounge reflected in the window against it. Then someone behind her is saying her name, the intrusion so unexpected that she hears it three times before she realises she is the one being addressed.

She turns to find a European woman dressed in an expensive suit. Supposing the woman is from the airline, she straightens to face her.

You're Anna Frasier, the woman is saying, aren't you? Her accent flat and Australian.

Yes, Anna says. Do I know you?

The woman shakes her head. No, but as she says it Anna feels sure she has seen her before somewhere.

Are you sure?

Yes, the woman says. But I was at the Empire Hotel three nights ago when you were leaving.

Anna looks at the woman, puzzled.

Perhaps we could go somewhere more private, the woman says.

Anna walks with the woman to a nearby row of seats, obscured from the surrounding seats by a pillar.

I'm Victoria, the woman says, once they are seated, handing her a business card. Paper, almost a novelty these days, she says apologetically as Anna takes it.

I needed to talk to you, because . . . Victoria hesitates, looking down at her hands as if uncertain how to continue. No, perhaps I should start from the beginning. When I saw you at the hotel the other night I recognised you, but it took me a few seconds to work out where from. By the time I did you were gone.

Are you saying you know me? Anna asks.

No, the woman says, and that was why I didn't recognise you straightaway. The reception clerk told me your name, and I had a trace put on you by my employer. It alerted me when you bought the plane ticket.

Increasingly unsettled by the woman's conversation, Anna begins to stand. I'm sorry, she says, whatever it is you want—

I don't want anything, Victoria says, I just—

Just what? Anna demands, beginning to grow annoyed.

You have a brother, a twin?

Anna swallows. I did. He's dead though, she says. It is the first time she has used the words, and they sound hard and cold in her mouth. Her voice does not shake.

So you know?

Know what?

What happened to him?

Anna shakes her head, and Victoria clears her throat. I was afraid of that, she says.

Did you know him?

No. I only met him once, the morning the PLA came. She hesitates, as if hoping Anna will ask her not to go on. But when Anna does not speak she continues, slowly.

I was on a flight back to Sydney that morning, one of the last before they closed the airport. It was insane here, there were people everywhere, all desperate to get out. A guard opened fire on some tourists. I was terrified.

We all were, Anna says, gritting her teeth at the memory of that day, against what is coming.

I was here on my own, so you can imagine how frightened I was. I . . . I must have been crying, which might have been why he came up to me. Maybe he heard my accent though, or maybe he was just being kind, I don't know. But he knelt down beside me to see if I was alright. He said his name was Daniel.

Anna feels a lump swelling in her throat, but she swallows hard against it.

That's right, she says.

He looked so much like you, Victoria says, staring at her, eyes bright with tears. That's why I thought I knew you.

We were twins.

Anyway, he sat there with me. He was on a different flight to me, and he seemed jumpy, but he stayed there with me, just sitting, talking. He said he was waiting for his girlfriend, but she kept not arriving and not arriving, and he was clearly getting worried something had happened.

And then?

And then there were police, lots of them. They were looking for people, that was obvious, and there was nowhere he could hide, and . . . well, they just came and took him.

He didn't struggle?

Victoria shakes her head. No, it was almost as if he was expecting it.

When Anna does not reply, Victoria goes on. They killed him, didn't they?

I think so.

I'm so sorry, Victoria says. He was a good person, I could tell.

When Anna still does not answer she clears her throat nervously. I thought you should know.

Yes, Anna says, distractedly. Thank you.

APOCRYPHA

· 8 ·

It is no more than vanity to suppose that a world, even a universe conceived as one interconnected, living thing would have any regard for the creations of so small a part of itself, any more than we have regard for the bacteria that dwell upon our skin and in our gut. Life and death are inextricably connected within larger cycles of change. And continuance.

SETH LAMARQUE, *The Language of Shells*

Fracture

Do we, holding that the gods exist, deceive ourselves with insubstantial dreams and lies, while random careless chance and change alone control the world?

EURIPIDES, *Hecuba*

I can hear the nesting gulls again, their cries carrying across the rooftops to the open window above my desk. Closer, on the cliffs above the rookeries, their sound is louder, almost deafening. I have heard others, mid-lifers mostly, claiming their clamour destroys the serenity of the ocean view, that their shrieking cries wake them in the mornings and prevent sleep until long after dark, that the beach below is filthy with their guano, but I find their exuberance, their noisy, dirty, violent testament to the presence of life and its continuance exhilarating. The birds were here before we came, and most likely shall remain once we are gone, like the cliffs, like the land itself.

In the next room my new carer is tidying my books. I like this one, Rebecca she said she was called. She is not as pretty as Denzel, but she knows how to lie to an old woman, how to make me believe she is interested in my books and photos. And the first day she came she opened the windows, saying it was spring, we should let the breeze in, not like Denzel, constantly checking the house systems and fussing about opportunistic infections.

Later I will make her walk me along the cliffs, near the birds. From the point you can see the coast as far south as Malabar. Once the cliffs were a dirty brown, but as the nanites eat the accumulated waste of centuries of industry they are turning golden once more, stained here and there with the ochre taint of the oxidated water that wells up from within the earth, the darker shadows of grass and creepers where they have taken root in the crooks and crannies of the broken stone. I will tell Rebecca what it was like three hundred years ago, when the sea was poisoned, before the seals and the humpback whales returned, before the sea swarmed once more with shoaling fish. And she will nod and smile, too polite to say that she does not care, that this is how her world has always been and my memories have no meaning for her. Too young to know that one day she will be old and boring as well.

You cannot step into the same river twice, said Heraclitus, but the river will endure, regardless. Even these cliffs, the crumbling, fractured sheets of sandstone upon which this city is built, were once mountains, their matter borne across the plains of Gondwana and deposited here, grain by grain. The river that bore them, once larger than the mighty Amazon, is gone, the plains it bore them across vanished too, cracked and torn by the motion of the continents, leaving only the cliffs, the broken sandstone. Perhaps one day the sand will once more be the stuff of mountains, butting skywards from a continent new torn from the planet's crust, or perhaps they will pass outwards, into the ocean that breaks against them. The only certainty is that they will not stay the same, change will come, no matter what.

At Sydney airport Seth is waiting, Rachel beside him. His tall body inclined slightly inwards, towards her smaller form. She stands awkwardly, back swayed with the protuberant weight of her belly, feet angled outwards. Her hand grazing the back of Seth's as she sees Anna emerge, careless in the gesture Anna remembers from that first afternoon at the café. They do not approach her as she crosses the short space towards them. In front of them she stops, reaches out a hand to Seth, who takes it wordlessly, wrapping it in his and drawing her close. There is a sureness in his embrace, as if something has changed between them, and as she smells the rough skin of his neck she feels herself subside into it, her hands gripping the material of his jacket tightly, not wanting to let go. Finally she releases her grip, stepping back, sniffing and wiping at her face. She is aware of Rachel watching her, the solicitous touch of her hand.

Outside in the car park the marshy air is warm and still. The sodium lights around Botany Bay diffuse in the salt mist of the water, a blanket of luminescence against the darkness beyond. Seth and Rachel walk slowly beside her, not speaking, for which she is grateful. Neither of them knows what she has found out, why she has returned, but nor do either of them ask. She'd called Seth from Hong Kong airport to tell him she was coming home, and had thought to tell him what had happened when she arrived, but that was before Victoria. Before the story that came, finally, as a relief.

On the freeway the car seems to float, the noise outside the cocooning space of the cabin a distant hum. Turning to the passing shadows of the trees, Anna reflects she will have to call her parents in London, call Sophie, tell them at least the substance of it. All day she has been wrestling with the implications of Victoria's story. Around the certainty of Daniel's loss hover other, less easily resolved mysteries: Briar's lateness that morning at the airport; her survival. The way she knew without needing to be told he had missed his flight.

Back in Seth's apartment she climbs to the loft, peeling her clothes from her body. Beneath the shower she surrenders herself to the water, its pressure against her face and eyelids massaging away her tiredness, unknotting her face and shoulders, running across her scalp and chest, washing her clean. She dries herself slowly and dresses, enjoying the cool weight of her hair where it lies wetly against her neck, the press of her skin against the fabric of her singlet.

Downstairs Seth and Rachel are seated at the table.

Have you eaten? Rachel asks. We haven't had a chance to.

And so, forty-five minutes later, they eat pizza out of boxes, Seth opens a bottle of red he has in his kitchen. As they eat, Anna stays close to him, their bodies touching, sipping at the wine, enjoying the scent of its alcohol, the smoky breath of the oak, the blackberry warmth of its taste. Rachel's eyes following her movements, watchful for signs of distress. Their conversation muted, neither Seth nor Rachel wanting to pry, but her silence leaving little room for other words. Once they have eaten, Anna puts her glass down, leans forward, and slowly, but without tears or hesitation, begins to tell them what she has found.

It does not take long, the facts are simple, and neither Rachel nor Seth interrupts. Once she is finished there is silence, until Rachel leans over, places a hand on hers.

I'm sorry, she says. I truly am.

Later, at the door, Anna and Rachel stand before each other, uncertain of how they should part. Eventually they embrace, but the ungainliness Rachel's swollen belly forces upon the gesture makes Anna chuckle, and Rachel, catching her eye, begins to laugh as well, and suddenly the two of them descend into helpless giggles. Beside them Seth tenses, and Anna, sensing his concern, extends a hand to him, reassuring.

It must only be a few weeks now, Anna says, and Rachel groans.

Three, but first ones are always late.

What are you going to call it?

Wiping a tear from her eye, Rachel shakes her head.

I don't know, she says, I've been hoping something will come to me when I see her. Or him.

Back inside, Anna draws Seth to herself, kissing him slow and long, then cradling the weight of his head against her hand. Come to bed, she says, and with his hand in hers, leads him towards the loft.

He is dressed when she wakes, seated beside her on the bed.

I've got a meeting, he says. Will you be alright on your own?

Rolling into him she kisses his hand.

I'll be fine, she says, surprised to realise that she means it.

Once he has gone she rises, brews jasmine tea. The channels are clogged with news from *Prometheus*, the preparations for the landing tomorrow. The weather feed says it will be hot today, but on the satellite image cloud can be seen approaching from the west.

Opening her codex she accesses the searchware for the last time, closing her account. As she authorises the deletion she pauses for a moment, aware that this is part of her life that is ending, then makes the transaction. Once that is done she leans back in her chair, aware she should call her parents and Sophie, but in London it is after midnight, and although it is only evening in New York, she decides to wait until she can deal with both at once, not wanting her parents to be the last to know.

Closing her codex she wanders slowly through the apartment. It is strange, she thinks; so much ending, yet she feels somehow freer than she has in longer than she can remember. Not happy, but not quite sad either, yet the feelings, whatever they are, seem genuine, lived. Last night, after Rachel had gone, and she and Seth lay together, bodies warm, she had turned to him, her face against his neck. Through the windows the sky was visible, cloud moving fast in some unfelt wind, its breaking patterns grey-white against the deeper blue of the firmament. No stars, just the moon, its eggshell surface.

Sometimes, when I look at Rachel . . . she began.

Next to her she felt Seth stir, one finger rising to touch the soft skin of her hip and waist.

What?

She shook her head, drinking in the smell of him, the texture of his skin against her cheek, their reassuring reminder of his presence.

After Daniel . . . she said, her voice petering out once again, the words catching in her throat. This second hesitation making Seth roll towards her, one hand brushing the hair from her face.

Anna— he began, but she put a hand on his mouth, silencing him.

No, she said. I need you to hear this.

He did not answer, just took the hand she had placed upon his mouth in his, waiting. When she spoke again her voice was level, her words careful.

I was pregnant, she said, by Jared. After I left him, it was too much. The world seemed to be falling apart. There were troops on the street corners, tanks everywhere. I couldn't find Daniel . . .

Yes, he said, patiently, gently.

I decided to have a termination. It seemed like the best thing. I'd never had one before, I thought it would be easy, but . . . she broke off, sniffing.

You don't need to feel guilty, he said. It was the right thing to do.

I know, she said, but afterwards . . . She shrugged, not able to finish.

Did you ever tell anyone? Did Jared know?

No, I never even told anyone I was pregnant. Except Daniel. I felt so stupid, so ashamed.

When she did not continue, Seth drew her close without speaking, pressed his lips to her brow.

She can still remember the feeling of his lips on her skin as she stands before the display case in his study, watching the misting imprint of her skin fade and die as she trails her fingers along the glass of its lid. At the end of the case lies a slab of stone, the scaled form of a fish compressed within it. Its blunt head shovel-like. One night, weeks before, she had asked Seth about it, and he opened the case, his hands exploring the flattened scales of the fish.

It was blind, he said, adapted to life far below the light's reach. You see here, the carapace that covers the head? No eyesockets. It must have lived near an underwater volcano, because when it died its body sank into volcanic mud, then later, much later, the ocean floor was forced upwards, into the air. Its body is radioactive, the radium in the mud permeated its flesh as it lay there.

Radium? she queried.

From the volcano's vents, he said. Even now the ocean floor is radioactive, the earth seeping poison through the welts in its crust.

Why doesn't it kill the fish?

Life adapts. Anyway, it's not a lot worse than the air we breathe. Maybe better since Delhi.

Opening the case she runs a finger across the fish, wondering at the invisible radiation that is ticking through her matter, even now. Seth said they could date the fish's death from the decay of the radium, and something about this remark nags at her. Eventually she closes the cabinet, her fingers on the glass. Noticing again the fade of moisture around them she taps suddenly at the surface, grasping what it is she needs to do, her intuition coming suddenly, powerfully into focus.

From Seth's desk she calls Dylan, drumming her fingers on the table as she waits for him to pick up.

He answers in his usual harried way, but when he sees it is her his expression softens.

Anna, he says, you're back. Then, as if frightened he has intruded, he clears his throat nervously.

Do you need to come in again?

She shakes her head. No. But I need to know if you have eidetics of ammonites.

I think we do. Why?

I want to use one in a photograph. Do you think the Museum would give me permission?

Sure, he says. Do you know which one?

No, but if you can send them over I'll look at what you've got from here.

I'm doing it even as we speak, Dylan says, accessing his console. Yes, here they are. I'm forwarding them now. Looking up, he smiles. It's good to see you, Anna, he says. I've missed having you round.

Thank you, she says, although I'm sure your life will be easier without me.

Slipping on her goggles and gloves, she accesses the eidetics Dylan has sent her, sorting through the shells. Finally she finds one, almost perfectly preserved, its ribs elegant and widely spaced, the coil of its spiral smooth and continual. Slowly, carefully, she begins to explore it, teaching the eidetic to remember the passage of her hands, to mark them out in trails of light. And once she has done it, she deletes the eidetic's visual, just as Seth did in his message to her three nights before, then freezes the remaining image.

That done, she downloads the data into her slate, calling up the other images she captured in the weeks before she grew ill, cleaning and smoothing them, pleased by the way the work comes quickly and fluidly.

It is almost six when she finishes. Leaving a message for Seth with the apartment's systems, she takes the finished images and hurries out into the crowded streets, the Friday night traffic banked up, heat shimmering on bonnets, engines humming. Now the sun has dropped away, the trees release their dusty scent into the warm air where it mingles with the scent of exhaust, the feculent waft of the drains. On Bourke Street she turns towards Taylor Square, relieved to discover the lab she used to use is still there and open. Inside it is cool, the hum of the printers lost beneath the beat of music, a dance beat, diva vocals. Behind the counter several technicians are working, and when she approaches, one stands to greet her.

I've images I need printed, she tells him. Can you fit me in this evening?

To her relief he nods. Not a problem. You know what stock and dimensions you want?

185 x 127. Semi-gloss, acid free. Double-weight.

The clerk raises an eyebrow. You want a cost on them?

She shakes her head. No, I know they'll be expensive. I'll need some test prints first on something smaller.

Shouldn't be too complicated, he tells her, opening the counter so she can join him.

So for three hours, maybe four, they work, the printer humming and purring as they print the twenty images she has chosen onto the stock, their colours deep and sombre, the edges of the printing left rough to give an impression of texture, of the overlay of the ink onto the paper. As they are finished, one by one, the other technicians gather round, silently at first, just watching, arrested by the beauty of the photos, then with more excitement, talking amongst themselves, to her. One woman remembers Anna from before she went away, and strikes up a conversation, time passing, until finally the last image is printed.

When she emerges, the street is crowded with people moving towards the restaurants and clubs. Anna manoeuvres the prints into a taxi, gives directions for Jadwiga's apartment in Elizabeth Bay. She makes the taxi wait in case Jadwiga is not home, but she answers quickly.

I need to come up, Anna tells her. I've got something I need to show you.

Jadwiga suppresses the twitch of a smile. I'll buzz you in, she says.

In the apartment Anna clears the table of the remnants of Jadwiga's solitary meal. Here, she says, slipping the protective cardboard from the prints. The first is the image of the shell she made that morning, huge and wondrous on the paper.

How did you do this? Jadwiga asks, leaning over it.

With an eidetic, Anna says.

It's magnificent.

Anna does not reply, just slipping the print aside to reveal the next, the image of the broken-chambered mica shell.

Jadwiga tilts her head, examining it from different angles. This is also very impressive.

And so, one by one, Anna shows her the others, coming to rest at last on the image of the counterpart, its ghostly intricacy made all the more powerful on the print, more like the signature of some vanished god than the impression of a simple shell. The tight-coiled centre drawing the eye irresistibly. On this last one Jadwiga stops.

Dylan said you went back to Hong Kong, she says, not looking up.

Yes, Anna says quietly.

Did you find him?

She shakes her head. No. But I think I know what happened to him.

When she does not continue Jadwiga nods. If these images are his memorial then he would be happy, I think.

Yes, Anna says, blinking back tears. I hope so.

At the door Anna embraces her, but Jadwiga pushes her away. Enough sentimentality, she says. You will embarrass me. Anna sniffs, wiping at her face with the back of her hand.

Dylan's mother tells me you have a man at the Museum.

Anna smiles. Yes.

But not Dylan? That surprises me: he is a handsome boy.

He is, Anna says, laughing now.

Will I meet him?

Soon, she promises. Soon.

In the taxi on the way back to Seth's she begins to laugh, exhilarated by its motion along the broken surface of the road, the swooping speed of its turn. With one hand she flicks the button in the door, lowering the window to admit the rushing air, which strikes her face like a slap, the air washing over her like a wave, knocking her hair loose so it whips and pulls. In front of her the driver, a tiny Sikh, his thin face surmounted by a green turban, turns to her worriedly, but seeing her face he cannot help but grin as well. Closing her eyes she releases herself to the booming sound of the wind, the pressure of it against her face and body. Then the sound of it changes, its pitch shifting, and opening her eyes she sees the driver has opened his window as well, his laughter rising over the rush of noise.

Seth is working when she arrives, the apartment sombre with the sound of chanting voices. They embrace without speaking.

Rachel called, Seth says. She's going to come round in the morning to watch the landing.

Good, Anna says. How are you?

Hot, he says, stroking her hair, but okay. More importantly, how are you?

She presses her head to his chest. Fine, I think. After a moment she pulls away from him. Will you let me do something?

What? he asks, smiling warily.

Can I take your photograph?

For a long time he does not answer, just stands, head resting on hers, considering the question.

Yes, he says at last, if you want to.

Rachel calls at dawn, the phone pealing through the apartment. Anna grabs for it, trying to stifle the sound.

I'm sorry to wake you, Rachel says, but I need you to get down here.

Where? Anna asks, confusedly. Get down where?

I'm at Lewin's squat, the cops have trashed it. I need you to bring your camera.

Alright, Anna says, I'll be there as soon as I can.

What's happening? Seth asks, climbing out of bed.

I don't know, Anna says, as she pulls on the clothes she wore the day before. Something's happened at Lewin's squat.

You'll be careful? he asks, and she leans over him and kisses his lips.

Of course. And I'll make sure Rachel's back here in time for the landing.

She dials a taxi as she hurries down the stairs, grabbing her camera case from the table where she left it the night before. This early the streets are quiet, the sky grey with low-hanging cloud.

Rachel is waiting by the prefab, seated on the arm of the sagging couch. All around debris is scattered: old clothes and blankets, paints, the broken frames of canvases. A smell of turpentine strong in the air.

Oh Jesus, Anna says, looking at the mangled paintings and strewn possessions. What happened? Where's Lewin?

He's inside. He heard them in the warehouse and hid around the back.

Why did they do this?

Rachel shakes her head. I don't know.

But his paintings . . .

Not able to finish, she crosses to the door, and, looking in, sees Lewin crouching by one of the broken canvases, trying to flatten it. The fabric has torn, the painting severed a third of the way up.

Lewin? she says softly. It's me, Anna. When he does not reply she crosses to him, kneels behind him, but at the touch of her hand he starts, spinning away from her.

Don't worry, it's just me, she declares, raising her hands. I'm not going to hurt you.

They've ruined everything, he says, everything, and as he speaks Anna is still not sure he has recognised her. He looks sicker than the last time she saw him, his face paler and more anaemic. Lesions creep down his neck from his scalp, leaking darkly.

Anna does not reply, just nods.

They had a van to put me in. I saw it.

What?

It was black.

You mean they were going to take you away? Anna asks, incredulous.

My paintings, he moans.

Then Rachel is at the door. Anna? I've got Blaze on the line. He says this isn't the only place the cops have been, they've been sweeping squats in Redfern and Erskineville since before dawn.

But why?

Rachel shakes her head. I don't know. But it's a major operation. I need you to get shots of this.

Anna fumbles with her camera, beginning with the blankly staring Lewin. As she works her way around the debris of the room, he speaks to her for the first time. Anton, he says, what about Anton?

He'll be at the Brewery, Rachel says. We need to get over there. Are you almost done? she asks Anna, who lowers her camera.

As good as.

With Lewin beside them they flag down a taxi, the driver gawping at the three of them: Anna with a camera bag, the heavily pregnant Rachel, the grimy, reeking shadow of Lewin. Rachel opens her codex, frantically searching for information.

Is there anything there? Anna asks, and Rachel shakes her head. Just endless *Prometheus* stuff. In the front the taxi driver swivels in his seat.

They're doing the approach, he says. I have a feed here. With one hand he points to a screen set into the dash of the taxi. On it the Martian landscape rolls by, deep, desert red, its ochre surface criss-crossed by the scars of ancient geological activity: the wandering lines of dried rivers, the broken backs of mountains, the pocked violence of a meteor scar or a volcano's cone. And even as they watch, it begins to change, growing smoother, flatter, as the landing craft passes over one of the vanished seas, its surface blurred by some disturbance in the atmosphere.

It's a sandstorm, the driver says excitedly. Next to him, Lewin stares as if he is looking at something incomprehensible.

Here, Rachel says, reading headlines from her codex. Government Gets Tough on Inner City Crime. About Time! New Detention Laws Face Test.

But Anna does not answer. Outside her window a line of troop carriers rumbles by, their black bulk blotting out the light, towering over the taxi. Behind them comes a line of black trucks, their sides broken here and there by grilles. Lifting her camera she shoots, not interested in composition, just in making sure this is documented.

That's them, they're the trucks that came for me, Lewin says. Looking up, Rachel turns pale. Oh Jesus, what the fuck are they planning?

The camps, they're taking us to the camps. I told you they were planning this.

But Rachel does not reply, just stares after the retreating bulk of the trucks.

Outside the Brewery it is quiet. The driver drops them by the gates, Rachel leaving Anna to pay while she finds Blaze. He is inside, talking with a group of older men, their grimy feet bare.

What's going on? Rachel demands.

You know as much as I do, Blaze says. Is Lewin alright?

Rachel nods. He'll live for now. We saw a line of troop carriers back on Regent Street. And trucks.

I've seen them too, Blaze tells her. They've been loading everyone they can into the trucks. and they're not being gentle either.

If they've been everywhere else they won't leave this place alone.

But if they try to clear it forcibly there'll be a riot. They must know that.

Rachel looks past him at the watching faces that are gathering around them. I'm not sure they care, she says.

As she speaks a wind begins to blow, and, looking up, they see the black form of a police copter, its baffled engine barely audible as it hovers overhead. Two more can be seen across the rooftops, hanging like stinging insects, poisonous and bloated.

They escorted a media copter away from here about ten minutes ago, Blaze says. Rachel looks at him and then Anna, her eyes afraid. We need to get them out of here, she says. All of them. Now.

But as she speaks the copter above them lifts itself, darting silently away across the broken shell of the Brewery. From outside comes the rumble of engines. Blaze begins towards the gate, Rachel and Anna just behind him. Two troop carriers have taken up position at either end of the street, and on each side of them stand black-suited police, their bodies dark behind the smoked Plexiglas of their shields, heads blunt in their visored helmets. Behind them loom trucks like the ones that passed them in the street only minutes before, rear ends towards the gates, doors open and waiting. With one hand Anna gropes for her camera, lifting it to her face and quickly, convulsively, begins to shoot, image after image freezing in its memory. All around them the people of the Brewery are gathering, as in ones and twos they find their way to the gate, only to be confronted by the sight of the police. No-one speaks. And then, slowly, deliberately, the troops begin to move towards them, their batons striking their shields in an ominous tattoo.

We're too late, Rachel whispers, but Blaze does not answer. Even Anna has fallen still, her camera held before her. The beat of the batons hypnotic, terrible, like the dance of a cobra before its prey. For what seems like a lifetime the dreadful heartbeat of the batons continues, the troops growing closer, until finally it ends, the air suddenly still in its absence, the silence as awful as the tattoo. The morning air hot.

And then, as if from nowhere, comes the sound of a single voice, breaking the silence and rising, clear and glassy, carrying the words of 'Jerusalem' across the street, slow and pure and pulsing with all the power and anger of Blake's poetry. Anna and Blaze and Rachel all turn, trying to locate its source, but before they can a voice comes from behind them calling, There he is! A pointed arm directing them to where Anton sits, perched in a broken window.

Looking round, Anna sees tears welling in Blaze's eyes, and, reaching out, takes his hand and squeezes it. And as Anton's voice rises through the last verse, there is a glorious moment when none of this seems so awful, when it seems possible that this may not end in disaster, that everything will be alright.

And then everything turns to shit.

Afterwards it is Lewin who will be blamed. For it is he who turns back to the troops in the strange, almost surreal silence that comes after the song has ended, he who picks up a broken brick, and in a shambling, hobbling joke of a charge shuffles out into the street towards the serried ranks of troops. It is he who sends his arm swinging over, hurtling the brick's weight into one of the Plexiglas shields, so it strikes with a brutal thud, knocking the shield's bearer back before it bounces to the asphalt. It is Lewin who turns back to the gate where the others stand watching, and raises one skinny arm in an angry salute, his voice rising in a war whoop of defiance.

But the inquest that blames Lewin will ignore the fact that even as he looses that first, improvised missile, the order to fire is being given to officers armed with gas grenades, that fingers are tightening on triggers, bodies bracing for the backward thump of their release.

One of the canisters lands near Anna and Blaze, striking the ground and rolling with an ominous hiss towards them. The sight of the gas that sprays from it sending them stumbling backwards, into the melee of the panicking crowd. The rising clouds of gas blocking their view so they do not see the advancing ranks of the first squads, their shields locked in lines like legionnaires, their batons clattering against their shields.

Rachel sees them though, as she is carried sideways by the surging retreat from the gas. She sees the way the crowd parts before them, sees the batons begin to rise and fall, hears the thump of titanium into flesh, the sickening crack of bone. The blood. Panic rising in her as she sees the blank-visored figures drag a woman, barely more than a child, back towards the waiting trucks, her thin body thrashing and screaming against their grip. With one arm folded in front of her as if hoping to shield the child within her body from the chaos, Rachel turns frantically from side to side, not knowing where to go, only knowing she needs to keep moving, needs to get away from the troops. The sudden thump of a canister beside her, the cloud of gas enveloping her, her face and ears and eyes and nose and mouth suddenly on fire, so she screams and gags, stumbling forward, her foot slipping, the gravel slicing her hands and knees as she strikes the ground.

As Rachel falls, the first of the snub-nosed riot vehicles collides with the cyclone wire fence beyond the tents, its front end rising against it, until the metal bends, then breaks, dropping the eight-wheeled nightmare with a heavy, hydraulic whump, the tents and shanties collapsing before it as it growls forward. The impact of the first blast from the water cannon on its roof slicing through the crowd, passing close enough to Anna to leave her sodden from the sidespray. Turning, she sees Blaze struck in the chest, his massive figure lifted like a doll's and flung backwards, a look of ludicrous surprise on his face. The gas closing behind him. Bulldozers are following the riot vehicle, the tents rising in a tide of wreckage before them. The first screams of the people trapped in their meagre homes. Then, with sudden dread, Anna realises she can no longer see Rachel. Behind her she can hear screams, see the gas billowing outwards, but she turns nonetheless, screaming Rachel's name, the threat of the gas driving her back, around, bodies everywhere, running and crawling, knocking her as she tries to skirt the vapour. And then she sees her, huddled beside the bleeding figure of a woman, coughing and gagging. Shouting her name, Anna stumbles towards her, and Rachel, perhaps hearing, struggles to her feet, her eyes screwed shut against the gas, face red and streaked with tears and dust. But as she stands a baton strikes her in the crook of the neck, and she crumples, the officer who struck her rolling her falling figure forward with his boot as two more appear out of the gas beside him, batons raised to strike. No! Anna screams, no! as she rushes forward heedless of the gas that sears into her eyes, needing only to stop the batons that rise and fall, Rachel's pregnant figure writhing beneath them. But Anton is there before her, his body striking the first officer from behind with such force he knocks him sideways and down, the length of pipe in his hand coming down on the smoked perspex of the helmet once, twice, three times, until it cracks, and there is a terrible, sickeningly wet crunch.

Years later Anna will remember the numbness of that moment, remember the blood on the pipe as he lifts it to strike again, his wall eye turned crazily sideways, not even able to look straight at the man whose life he was taking. The flecks of blood and something thicker, bone or brain or snot, that comes with it as it rises.

But then she is on them too, her arm under the throat of one of the police, pulling at the helmet, yanking it backwards, her fingers scratching beneath the chinstrap so it comes loose in one movement, revealing a face barely older than Anton's. A girl's face, Anna realises as she is thrown sideways, its shoulder-length hair tied back. As she hits the ground she sees the baton that has fallen from the hand of Anton's victim, and, her fingers closing around it, she swings it out in a wide arc towards the figure looming above her. The weight connecting with its jaw, knocking it out of its socket with a pop, throwing the girl down screaming on the ground. Struggling to her feet she hefts the baton, her streaming eyes fixed on the helmeted figure who stands over Rachel, her lolling head hanging by its hair from his hand.

Maybe he sees the fury in Anna's eye, or maybe it is the blood that covers Anton's face and shirt and arms, the dripping pipe in his hand, but whichever it is, he seems to hesitate, then straightens, dropping her head so it strikes the ground with a dull thud, and backs away. Careless of his retreating figure Anna slides to the ground beside Rachel. Her eyes open slightly, her lips mumble something Anna cannot make out, a thin dribble of blood and saliva trickles from her mouth.

You're going to be fine, Rachel, she says, you're going to be fine, cradling Rachel's head to her chest as she says it, trying not to hear the crunch of bones in her neck as she moves her. Knowing she needs to find an ambulance or a hospital, she tries to get underneath her, to lift her, but Rachel is too heavy, her body swollen with the life within her, so instead she half carries, half drags her past the bulldozers, towards the ruined fence. Staring back she sees Lewin swing a length of wood, nails jutting rustily from it, into the back of a policeman, who crumples to the ground. Sees Anton staring after her, his arms bloody to the elbow, the pipe still in his hand. Their eyes meeting for a moment in which the look of anguish on his face washes away, replaced with a fury she could not have imagined this boy with an angel's voice ever knowing, but then a canister of gas falls between them and he is gone.

She drags Rachel to an alley half a block away, stroking her hair and begging her to speak. Please, she keeps saying. Please. She looks around wildly for help, but there is nothing. And then, at the far end of the alley, the red lights of an ambulance, and releasing Rachel she stands, waving and screaming until someone appears, shouting to her to wait, figures in light blue uniforms running towards her. Kneeling again she sees Rachel has opened her eyes, red and puffy and weeping from the gas.

Anna? she is asking. Is that you? I think I'm hurt.

Stroking her hair Anna feels the thickness of the blood that clogs in it.

You are, she says. But you're going to be fine, I promise. But even as she says it Rachel's eyes close and her head falls sideways.

She does not speak again, not in the ambulance on the way to the hospital, not while she lies on the cot as it is raced towards surgery, not in the prep room before the anaesthetic. At the door a nurse asks Anna if she is family, and when Anna shakes her head, marks something into her system, and vanishes after the cot.

Once she has gone, once the nightmare charge through the corridors is over and Anna is left alone by the swinging doors, she remembers Seth and, heart heavy, taps her earpiece and calls him. And then she is on her own, the adrenaline draining from her, leaving her weak and shaky so she sways, bracing herself against a wall to keep from falling.

On a screen in one corner the feed from *Prometheus* shows the red surface of Mars still turning beneath it, but in here no-one cares, the audio drowned out by the whimpers and moans of the injured, the clattering movement of beds and equipment.

Seth is there within minutes, helped into the room by a girl dressed in combat boots and a silver dress, her eyes spookily large with last night's amphetamines or ecstasy. Anna hurries towards him, and the girl starts to explain she found him outside, as if Anna were Seth's keeper, but Seth ignores her, demanding to know what has happened. Nothing, Anna tells him, she's still in surgery.

Beside them the girl has noticed the screen in the corner, and with a cry she points at it. The landing, she exclaims, and, weaving her way through the chaos of the room, she clambers, monkeylike, onto a chair and then onto a vending machine in search of the manual, cranking the volume up so it roars over the clamour.

Anna stares blankly at the screen. The graphic in the corner shows the descent path, already more than half over. Satisfied, the girl swings herself down with a thump, seating herself on a chair to wait for the landing. For the first time Anna wonders what she is doing here.

An hour passes before Anna sees the doctor who was tending to Rachel appear through the swing doors. Her body tensing so that Seth grips her arm.

It's the doctor, she tells him, pulling him to his feet and moving towards the door.

What's happened? she demands as soon as the doctor enters. Is she—

The doctor lifts a hand to silence her. I think you should come with me, she says, her face tired.

They let the doctor lead them through the swing doors into an alcove, drawing a curtain to shut out the tumult beyond.

It's bad news, isn't it? Anna asks, and the doctor nods.

Yes, I'm afraid it is. Allowing a moment for her words to sink in, she continues.

Rachel suffered a severe head trauma. There was extensive haemorrhaging which we were unable to staunch. A brain stem test conducted fifteen minutes ago showed a total cessation of brain activity.

Beside her Seth is completely still.

I don't understand, Anna says.

In lay terms it's usually described as brain death.

But she was talking, I talked to her. Before the ambulance arrived.

That's not uncommon, the doctor says. But the subsequent haemorrhaging caused too much damage.

Beside her Seth speaks at last, his voice shaking. The baby? he asks.

The doctor smiles thinly. The baby was delivered by caesarean section. She's alive and well.

Can we see her? Anna asks.

Of course, the doctor says. We're arranging a transfer to a neo-natal unit, but that may take a while. In the meantime I'll get one of the nurses to take you through.

As she turns to go the doctor hesitates. There's one other thing, she says. This is never a pleasant thing to have to ask, but Rachel's records show she elected to allow her organs to be harvested in the event of her death. It will help others, stop them suffering the same—

Take them, Seth says, his voice brittle. She would have wanted that.

The nurse brings the child swaddled in a white hospital blanket, handing her tiny form to Anna. Her head crowned with dark hair, like Rachel's, her face puckered and red. In Anna's arms she feels so light. Without speaking she turns to Seth, his arms closing uncertainly around the bundled body. His stiffness relaxing at the warmth of her, the soft pant and gurgle of her breath. Looking past him Anna sees a screen, mute behind glass, the suited form of Commander Svenson standing by a ladder, a jumbled plain of boulders beneath a pale sky. Beyond the glass she sees figures clapping, shaking hands, but she does neither, just turns back to Seth, to the orphaned child he holds.

APOCRYPHA

· 9 ·

But perhaps it is in the shell that we find the most eloquent expression of this. For in its wholeness unto itself, the perfection of its curved shape and the accretive spiral of its growth, it is an expression of the simplicity of the constitutive principles that underpin life, of the unity of nature, and an expression of an order so perfect, so complete, that it offers no response beyond awe. And silence.

SETH LAMARQUE, *The Language of Shells*

Epilogue

Of the state of mind which, in that far-off year, had been tantamount to a long-drawn-out torture for me, nothing survived. For in this world where everything withers, everything perishes, there is a thing that decays, that crumbles into dust even more completely, leaving behind fewer traces of itself, than beauty: namely grief.

MARCEL PROUST, *À la Recherche du temps perdu*

They call them the Deep Field.

Those scattered pinholes in the sky through which we see beyond the stars that surround us, and out, out into the far reaches of space, where galaxies teem, like jewels against the velvet dark, as countless and varied as the grains of sand upon a beach. Their ancient light a memory of a time when the universe was young, testament to an immensity our minds can barely encompass.

Against this vastness of time and space, these lives of ours seem no more than flickers, firefly traces in the night of forever. Tiny motions of light and sound that pass too quickly, too brightly. Even mine.

Maybe it is fitting that my memories begin with the First Relic, that ancient shell from a vanished sea Leonid Gromeko prised from the cold Martian stone. For on that barren ghost of a world we found proof not just that life is everywhere, but that where it flickers, something always remains.

Ten thousand years ago the people of Europe revered the shell as holy. Those who dwelt by the cold northern seas buried them with their dead, hoping that, like the snail, which each winter seems to shrink and die, only to wake with the spring, these totems might promise resurrection for the body. And maybe too they saw our lives are like the shell, its eternal spiral of enfolding, our future covering the past as we grow, an endless curve back towards the point where we began, a circle that never closes.

I never knew my father; Rachel took his name with her to the grave, and if he knew that it was his seed within her he never told. Anna and Seth raised me as their own. She was my mother, as surely as anyone, and he, my father. I loved them, and I grieved as a child grieves their parents when influenza took them in the winter of my eighteenth year, one only days after the other.

Perhaps I have become a shell myself, the vessel of their hopes and lives and dreams. Perhaps through me they will yet be reborn, coalescing from the raw matter of dreams, incubated in the heat of my body as I was born from hers. I still have the shell that Lo gave Anna that morning, long ago, I still have the photos she took. And I have my memories of them both, however they might fade and fracture.

And I have my mother's name.

Rachel.

ACKNOWLEDGMENTS

For those interested in blindness and its implications for the formation of the individual consciousness, a good starting point is Oliver Sacks' lucid and thought-provoking study of recovery from blindness, 'To See and Not See', in *An Anthropologist on Mars*. Diderot's iconoclastic, gossipy and unreliable 'Letter on the Blind' is also recommended, as is John M. Hull's remarkable description of his descent into blindness in *Touching the Rock*. More technical but rewarding is von Senden's *Space and Sight: The Perception of Space and Shape in the Congenitally Blind Before and After Operation*.

My thinking about life, autopoiesis and complex systems draws upon the work of a number of scientists, biologists and mathematicians, most notably Stuart Kauffman, James Lovelock, Steven Rose, Edward O. Wilson, Niles Eldredge, Lyn Margulis, D'Arcy Thompson and Brian Goodwin. For anyone interested in these issues one starting point is Stuart Kauffman's *At Home in the Universe*. Ian Stewart's *Life's Other Secret* and Peter Coveney and Roger Highfield's *Frontiers of Complexity* are also good general introductions to the issues underpinning the study of natural order and complex systems.

The material in *apocrypha (2)* about birds' footprints and cuneiform is closely based on a section in Alberto Manguel's *A History of Reading*, while the image of life as a complex metabolic whirlpool used in *apocrypha (4)* is drawn from Stuart Kauffman's *At Home in the Universe*. The definition of fever given in the text is adapted from *The Oxford English Dictionary* (2nd edition).

A great many people have helped me with the research necessary for this novel and I am indebted to them. They include Dr Craig Hargreaves and Dr Melanie George, my brother Patrick Bradley and my father, Michael Bradley, Linda Jaivin, Jonathan Delacour, Mac Walker, Ky McManus, Jonathan Cohen, Richard Fidler and Danni Townsend. I also want to thank Belinda Morrissey and Ian Parsons for their hospitality in Hong Kong; Peter Goldsworthy, McKenzie Wark and Tim Storer for reading various drafts of this novel and giving their invaluable advice; and Rob Jones from the Australian Museum for taking the time to talk to me, although I must emphasise that the Museum and staff depicted in this novel are entirely fictional and any resemblance to persons living or dead is entirely coincidental.

Dr Shane Richards may be pleased to see that the ammonoid cannibalism scene he requested has survived into the final draft, although perhaps not in the form he envisaged. If this can be some kind of thanks for his generous help over many years with my questions about mathematics, modelling and research problems I would be very happy.

At my various publishers I wish to thank Lisa Highton, Karen Deighton-Smith, Amanda O'Connell and Bernadette Foley, Tracy Brown and Geraldine Cooke. I owe too many debts already to my agent Fiona Inglis at Curtis Brown Australia, but her support during the writing of this book was greatly appreciated, and I thank her again. My thanks also to Jill Grinberg of Scovil, Chichak and Galen.

The writing of this novel was made considerably easier by a Developing Writers Grant from the Literature Fund of the Australia Council and I am grateful to them for their assistance.

And finally I want to thank my partner, Mardi McConnochie, for her love and patience.